This book belongs to:

Winner
Takes All

Winner Takes All

Vanessa Drucker

Crown Publishers, Inc., New York

Published by Crown Publishers, Inc., 201 East 50th Street,
New York, New York 10022

CROWN is a trademark of Crown Publishers, Inc.

Manufactured in the United States of America

Library of Congress Cataloging-in-Publication Data
Drucker, Vanessa.
Winner takes all. / by Vanessa Drucker.
p.   cm.
I. Title.   II. Title: Winner Takes All.
PS3554.R74A614   1990
813'.54—dc20
89-7896
ISBN 0-517-57469-1

10   9   8   7   6   5   4   3   2   1

First Edition

For Marcel

Winner Takes All

I've gotta go," said Peter Courage. "I've got a call coming in from Tokyo."

"From Tokyo!" said Peter's cousin Ellis, who made his living teaching early-twentieth-century history at Hunter College. His voice expressed mild awe. Courage lived by alien dimensions of geography and time.

Several lights on Peter's telephone started flashing simultaneously, accompanied by the energetic buzz of the incoming calls. Courage pushed the button to connect with the Hotel Okura. The connection was razor clear, as usual, and the Japanese operator spoke better English than his own secretary.

"Is that Mr. Courage speaking? One moment, please. I will connect you with Mr. Kahn."

What time would it be in Japan now? Thursday, 5 A.M.? Kahn was a financial genius who did not know the meaning of jet lag, dawn or dusk.

"Peter?"

"Good morning, sir. I hope you've recovered from your flight."

"I've been up since three. I've been rereading article eleven, paragraph B. I'm concerned about the time frame for the buyout."

Peter sighed and rifled through the stack of pending files that

1

strewed his desk. It was a strain dividing oneself among several deals, particularly when one was for the tyrannical Kahn.

"I've got it in front of me." Courage tried to sound alert. He had slept only four hours the previous night. "Do you feel three years is too long?"

"Too short. The research is just getting off the ground."

Kahn was hell-bent on acquiring Misuki, a Japanese company that owned an invention for the removal of notoriously difficult stains: egg yolk, catsup, and semen.

"The time period is a crucial issue, Mr. Kahn. Misuki may even make it a deal point."

"It's up to you to convince them," snapped Kahn impatiently. "That's what I want."

Courage could pass that buck to Tristan Barrett, the partner on the case. It was up to Tristan to figure out what to do with Kahn, his short-tempered client. It was up to Courage, as a fifth-year associate attorney, to persuade Kahn that he had Kahn's interests on his mind twenty-three hours a day, and Kahn's files at his fingertips, even when he slept.

"You can call me back in two hours. I'll be back here after my breakfast meeting." Kahn hung up.

Peter's telephone still danced with the flashing lights of incoming calls. Priorities first, he told himself, passing a grimy hand through his chestnut hair and sipping the dregs of cold coffee from the nearest of the army of Styrofoam cups across his desk.

"Mr. Barrett's office."

"Is he there, Gloria? It's Peter Courage."

"Mr. Barrett went to a meeting at Citicorp."

"I must speak with him as soon as he gets in. It's urgent."

"I'll leave him a note." It was five twenty-nine. No more than sixty seconds remained in Gloria's workday. A crisis in Toyko, the salvaging of Courage's career, meant nothing to her. She was young, blond, and her manicures always gleamed like the jewels in a fourteenth-century reliquary. She had a bus to catch to Staten Island.

When Courage had first come to Cheltenham, Arbuthnot &

Crewe, seven years ago, as a summer associate after his second year of Columbia Law School, he had assumed the firm would be populated by partners with names and manners like Tristan Barrett. Cheltenham, after all, was not just any old Wall Street law firm, cranking out documents in a global machine age. Cheltenham was a tradition, a distinguished name, a venerable practice. The firm had a reputation for hiring character, even before brains, and cultivating a fraternal, Vatican-like clubbiness.

It had all been a lie, or times had drastically changed, or perhaps a combination of the two. Somehow Cheltenham still managed to preserve its formidable veneer in the eyes of the outside world, but once Courage had been initiated that first summer into the order, he discovered that the image was a myth. Except for Tristan Barrett.

Tristan belonged to the twilight of a century-old tradition of law practice. These days, except in the movies, there were no attorneys left like Tristan. Most of the other partners formed a lean, mean, impersonal breed, which had no time for mistakes. The young associates hired from the law schools no longer brought social clout. Peter Courage, who had been educated at Choate and Princeton, and whose family had settled in Litchfield, Connecticut, before 1800, now found himself an exception in the Jewish, Irish, and Italian melting pot that seemed to have taken over from the patricians.

During his first couple of years, Courage had been flattered to sense Tristan taking an interest in him, although he suspected that the senior partner was responding to his WASPiness and ease of manner rather than any legal virtuosity. Tristan's work, which involved private placements of money, was more interesting than the standard Cheltenham corporate megadeals. Tristan was fairly easy to work for, at least as easy as they got. He never made his associates look like fools in front of other people. When his work was laid, proofread, on his desk after eight excruciating hours, Tristan would puff on his pipe benignly and make sure at least to say thank you.

So at the beginning Courage was grateful to have found a

seemingly safe harbor. But since he had been sucked into the mainstream of so-called corporate finance, and routinely worked a ninety-hour week, he had less time and energy for the luxury of Tristan Barrett's old-style law. It was a nuisance to be swept off into these side deals, like Kahn's Japanese takeover, although somehow Tristan, and everyone else, insisted on viewing it as a privilege.

Lorraine, Courage's secretary, buzzed him on the intercom. "Mind if I leave now?"

"Do you want to do overtime?"

"Not tonight, mister. I been here past nine every night this week. I'll be getting myself a new man if I keep this up."

Lorraine, a black woman in her late forties, was a cheery soul who wasted a lot of time, made maddening mistakes, and survived everyone.

"Don't you be forgetting to get yourself some hot dinner tonight, Peter," her milky voice admonished. "If you're going to be up all night again, you've got to eat."

The previous night Courage had ordered a hamburger just before midnight, got caught up on a conference call, and by the time he turned back to his food, the fries and meat had congealed in grease. So he ate a bag of potato chips instead, which he had found tucked away in a drawer under some old law-school notes.

"Okay, I promise. Appreciate your concern."

"You'll end up on the scrap heap, the way you look after yourself. Burnout, that's what they call it. I been here twelve years, and I seen plenty of associates burn right up."

Lorraine's associates had burned themselves up for over a decade, while she sailed on stubborn and faintly amused, floating across a sea of lost files, late bills, and careless typos.

Courage hung up and turned toward the window, stealing a quiet moment to gear up for the evening's battle. Outside, the early December sky had already turned pitch black. Forty-eight floors below him, the lights of windows and bridges glittered like Christmas ornaments. After dark, Courage cherished his expensive view. During daylight hours, however, the great height discomfitted him. He would have preferred to be closer to the tawdry streets of downtown, the sounds and smells of what the lawyers contemptuously called "the real world." It was unnatural to spend all one's waking life wrestling with financial jargon at such a rarefied distance from the earth. After twilight though, when Cheltenham, Arbuthnot & Crewe came suddenly alive, everything was suddenly inverted. Then it was a joy to rest one's eyes on the tree of light balanced between the black hole of the East River and the sky.

It usually seemed to be at about five-thirty, when most of the secretarial staff went home, that the law firm, like a sleeping giant, grunted and turned over and sprang to life. In the cells of their offices, hundreds of attorneys concentrated, pumping out brainpower, filling reams of paper, much of which would be rewritten and shredded before the following morning. We live in an upside-down world, thought Courage. Lorraine and her friends go home now to TV sitcoms, while my day is only beginning. Kahn, on the other side of the world, has already been pacing the thick Hotel Okura rugs for two hours. All day the clatter in the corridors and secretarial chatter has linked us unceremoniously to "the real world." Now that that is over, the brethren, the great fraternity, draw close together again.

"Peter."

"David."

"What's up?"

"Shearson wants a new draft of their indenture by midday, so I guess it's an all-nighter at the printer. What's more, I've got this lunatic in Tokyo calling in every two hours and trying to get me to change nonnegotiable terms."

"I'm really losing it this time," groaned David Gleiner, a tax associate at Courage's level, with whom he had, somewhat surprisingly, struck up a friendship over the years. "I've got that rash again."

"It's gotta be an allergy. Something you're eating."

"I saw another dermatologist on Monday. They all say the same thing. Nerves. I look like a mottled lobster. Last time it only got as far as my elbows. This time it's down to my wrists."

Gleiner, even without his rash, was not a handsome man. He had loose, plump, pale skin and kinky, thinning hair. He walked lopsided, a human question mark, as if to ask continually why his life was beset by accidents and neurosis, panic and humiliation. It was something of a wonder he had lasted five years at Cheltenham. But he was an incisive tax attorney as long as he did not get riled, with flashes of creative brilliance. He could analyze a client's fiscal situation, digesting all the facts, and produce a seemingly obvious solution that had foxed several senior partners for weeks.

Courage, on the other hand, was tall, athletic, gifted with a confident smile and candid eyes. Grown women whispered and giggled over him, while other men were drawn helplessly into his easy authority. He was extremely well liked. He was appealingly unconscious of his powerful looks and charm. To the extent that Peter had realized their effect, he would have said that deep inside he did not feel at all the way he looked. Inside he was strangely troubled. It was growing worse. The malaise was an itch, a trickle and drip at the back of his conscience.

"I just don't get it." Gleiner sweated out his existence in paranoia, opiated only by the exhaustion brought on from overwork. "For three weeks I've been researching the tax liabilities of these annuity funds. I've been in the library till two in the morning, seven days a week. I was so sure I'd got it nailed. I'd got everything outlined, footnoted. Last night I go into Hopper to discuss my research. He was kind of cold—well, he always is. Kept me sitting there for forty minutes while he dithered around on some conference call. Have you ever noticed the weird pictures in his office? Dripping Dali watches and that Buñuel poster of the eyeball. And those Tiffany lamps. Anyhow, he gets off the phone and he looks at me curtly, like he's just noticed me."

"He does that with everyone. He's only thinking of SEC rulings."

"He says, kind of sharply, 'Yes?' My palms are sweating and I've got this knot in my stomach. 'I've read your memo. You missed the crucial decision. Lucky we put a first year on it a couple of weeks ago. He picked up the case right away. I assumed your work would provide thorough backup. I was wrong.'"

"Prick. How much did you bill?"

"About two hundred and fifty hours. I haven't had an evening at home in a month. The only time I've taken off is lunchtimes to go to the doctor. Why did he do that? He deliberately entrapped me, setting up a first year to work in secret competition with me."

"He's cunning like that."

"Does he hate me?"

"Hopper's incapable of hatred. It's a human emotion. He can't feel things. He doesn't care about anyone or anything. Except the SEC."

"You think he's smart?"

"I guess . . . in his field."

"I hate that. Everyone thinks he's smart. He's not. He just talks faster than anyone else. Like a little machine gun. Rat-tat-tat-tata-tat. The only way you can understand what he's saying is to filter out every fifth word."

"Forget the whole thing," Courage advised. "If you brood over it, you'll only get your rash worse. Go home and get some sleep."

Gleiner groaned. "I can't go home. I just get more depressed."

Courage knew it was no use to argue. Gleiner would loiter around the office anyway, no matter what he said. That was the trouble. After being closeted with a project for an entire month, you could not just snap back into normal life again. It happened to Courage often too. You became a mole, fearful of blinking into the sunlight.

Courage extricated a half-eaten stick of Toblerone from a pond of paper clips in his top drawer. He chomped at it absentmindedly. "You're going to end up sick, David. You must calm down."

"If I can just hold it together till the end of the year. After that I can collapse. Did you hear, six associates are getting axed this Christmas?"

Courage had heard some rumors. "For God's sake, no one's firing you. You've got heavy billables. Twenty-six hundred hours already."

"It won't save me. When your number's up, your number's up. They throw you to the wolves and don't think twice."

Courage wondered. He had seen several generations of associates leave, sometimes inexplicably and sometimes in cloudy circumstances. He resisted the conclusion. In a business that demanded intense loyalty and a monastic sacrifice of life's gratifications, there must be some quid for the quo. Maybe all pockets of human activity were the same. Perhaps it was an unfair deal everywhere, perhaps there were no real contracts.

His cousin, steeped in the history of World War I and indoctrinated in the absurdities of Verdun and Sarajevo, certainly thought so. They had discussed it at Thanksgiving dinner. It was clear Ellis regarded Courage, who was supposed to be the worldly Wall Street one, as naïve and tractable. He had even called him "cannon fodder." Courage had laughed and helped himself to more sweet potatoes.

He tried to reassure David. "You're not cannon fodder. You're a tax whiz. You see shortcuts the other lawyers miss. They need you."

Courage, generous of spirit, sincerely liked Gleiner and sympathized with his angst. Gleiner articulated and lamented, while others, choosing the right to remain silent, winced and soldiered on. Tonight, however, Courage already had enough on his plate. He was tired, the long vigil at the printer lay ahead, and anyway, where the hell was Tristan Barrett? On cue, the other line buzzed. But it was not Tristan.

"Peter," thundered Kahn. "Where's Tristan?"

"I've gotta go," Courage told Gleiner. "It's Tokyo again." He returned to Japan.

Kahn rumbled, "I've been trying to get hold of him for thirty minutes. Don't you people do any work?"

"I've been trying too. He's due back at the office soon."

"Soon isn't good enough. I need to talk to him now. And don't just try. Find him."

Courage was only thankful that Tokyo lay twelve thousand miles away.

"I'll call you the moment he gets back," he promised.

"I'm going into a meeting with the research director of Misuki. They claim their people have a way to dissolve the stain of prune juice."

Courage felt suddenly light-headed, rash. "That's a pretty rare stain," he ventured boldly.

His kamikaze shot was countered by a silence that endured many seconds. I've put my career on the line, thought Courage wildly. He's going to explode.

"That's an excellent point, Peter. Excellent. I shall certainly reinforce it. Obviously they're playing for better terms." The despotic voice over the twelve thousands miles became magnanimous. "I will say it, you people are expensive, but you're worth it."

Outside the moon, the same ancient moon which, a few hours ago, had loomed over Tokyo, smiled aloft over the East River. Courage abandoned his desk to pour himself fresh coffee and search for Tristan Barrett.

He walked down the corridor, past the offices, row upon row. Few were empty yet. Their occupants sat, heads bent in concentration, reading weighty agreements, drafting, speaking softly into the microphones of dictating machines.

Cheltenham, Arbuthnot & Crewe enjoyed a physical distinction unrivaled by most of the other Wall Street institutions. The partnership had invested a great deal of money and effort into the layout and décor of their offices. It had been resolved, when the mysterious Management Committee met in conclave, that a clear but subtle message must be conveyed to the clients of the firm. The message was twofold: that Cheltenham, whose origins dated to Colonial days, preserved a historic legacy of excellence, and that, no less important, the firm had whizzed to the forefront of the age of high technology. The practice, inaugurated by Jeremiah Crewe, Esquire, in 1769 from a modest parlor in Philadelphia, had changed location several dozen times during the subsequent centuries. Its members now chose for their home a polished teal-green slab of a skyscraper at 57 Water Street, a beacon among beacons presiding over New York Harbor.

Cheltenham's offices occupied five floors of the slab, from forty-seven to fifty-one. The surrounding views, captured through floor-to-ceiling windows, were of course spectacular, and most visitors experienced the sensation of being in a magic airplane. Yet the cunning advertisement for the firm's blessing of tradition was revealed in the imperious Chippendale mahogany furniture and the red carpeting, with its somber hue of coagulating blood. Fresh flowers were imported twice a week to guard like gladiators conference rooms and reception areas. In all seasons the same waxy gladiolis, flowers of the morgue and mausoleum, whispered a memento mori, reminding that the power and influence of Cheltenham, Arbuthnot & Crewe reached well beyond the grave.

Courage took the elevator up to Tristan's office on the forty-ninth floor. The light in the office had been switched off, and Courage saw no sign that Tristan was planning to return. The whole space lay awash in a sea of documents and redwells—as the lawyers called their russet accordion document pouches—crushing the desk and stacked across the floor in turrets that de-fied gravity. An array of pipe racks peeked out from behind the papers, and the seductive aroma of his tobacco lingered.

Courage considered whether he ought to try to reach Tristan at home. There was no inhibition at Cheltenham about calling attorneys to duty from anywhere. As the small gold firm manual stated, "An attorney is on duty twenty-four hours a day, three hundred and sixty-five days a year, and is expected to act accordingly." Quite the meaning of that cryptic "act accordingly" Courage had never fathomed, but it certainly did away with any semblance of private life.

Should he call for Tristan's help? He simply did not know how he could single-handedly bulldoze the Japanese into accepting a nonnegotiable deal point. To admit defeat would be construed as a sign of weakness. His job, as Tristan's fall guy, was to absorb the flack. The usual impasse whereby every path led to damnation.

"Mr. Peter Courage. Mr. Peter Courage, please!"

Courage was shaken from his dilemma by the boom of Big Brother's voice on the omnipresent paging system. The merciless summons of Big Brother pursued the employees and members of Cheltenham through every nook and cranny of their five floors, with the exception of one certain blind spot in the library, and a couple of the men's rooms.

Courage picked up Tristan's phone and dialed the Cheltenham switchboard. "This is Courage."

"One moment, Mr. Courage. I have a call from Tokyo for you. I'll connect you now."

Kahn no longer troubled to say hello. "Peter, I'm here with Mr. Yakihami Makashuda, who is the senior vice president of Biochemical Research and Development at Misuki Corporation. I have just been discussing with Mr. Makashuda our assessment of the new prune juice technology, and I wondered if you would care to elaborate."

Courage groaned silently. "Good morning, Mr. Mashakudo."

"Makashuda!" bellowed Kahn.

"People in Japan like prune juice very much. Is good for you too," giggled Mr. Makashuda.

"That may well be." Courage took care not to concur prematurely. "But I believe Mr. Kahn's concern is that prune juice removal does not command a substantial market in the United States."

Kahn's voice trumpeted in the background. "I've been telling them, Peter, that we wish they'd just stick with the egg yolks and semen. That's a valuable consumer item."

"Semen very bad stains," trilled Mr. Makashuda.

The negotiation ebbed and flowed. Courage glanced at his watch. Ten o'clock. He was due to leave for the printer now, where the other lawyers from Milbank and Cleary Gottlieb and the investment bankers from Morgan Stanley and Caroline

Brothers would all be waiting for him. During the conference call with Tokyo he had already heard his name paged several times, which indicated that his clients from Caroline Brothers were probably looking for him. But he had not dared interrupt the surreal argument over the stains caused by food and other agents. Which client would be most dangerous to offend? Kahn was mercurial, prone to temper tantrums, and likely to be vindictive. On the other hand, Courage himself carried the responsibility for the Caroline Brothers deal, only reporting occasionally to the partner in charge.

"May I put you on hold for a moment, Mr. Makashuda?" He took the other line.

"This is Michelle Peterson from Caroline."

"Hi, Michelle." He had spent hours on marathon conference calls to which she was one of several parties. They had never yet met.

"Will you be at the printer soon? The proofs are beginning to come out now and the whole gang's assembled here."

"I'll make it as soon as I can. I got tied up on another matter this evening. Are you planning to be there for a while?" He hoped he was not going to lose his chance to meet her, if only briefly. There was something about her voice, or her manner, that had caught his attention during the interminable conference calls.

She had a thin, crisp voice, like a flute, which made him think of the snap of icicles falling from a window. Many of the women investment bankers Courage was used to dealing with came across either as prickly or defensive. Michelle Peterson was thankfully neither. She was civil and precise, and when she gave instructions or asked for explanations, she asked in a voice that carried a musical ting.

For several years women had played a small part in his life, least of all those he worked with. The attorneys and bankers, even those with whom he sometimes had to spend eighteen hours at a stretch, projected an aura of untouchability on the job, in their little navy suits and silk cravats. As for after hours, the establishment of any intimacy more complicated than a drunken one-night stand after a party took more energy than Courage ever had these days. Sometimes, especially on Sunday afternoons, he felt a twinge of loneliness. Sometimes he dreamed of finding someone glamorous and presentable who would make no demands, would just be there waiting, to soothe him when he was ready.

So while it was unusual for Courage even to notice the femininity of the other members of a deal, he was intrigued by Michelle's silvery voice, and the promise of meeting her added a dash of spice to the prospect of a long night at the printer.

"Yes," she said. "I'll be there all night. Or at least as long as it takes."

"Good. We can get to know one another." He knew he was flouting the code of professional etiquette, but his weariness made him careless.

"We're all going to be busy."

He enjoyed the rebuke. At least she had registered his interest.

He plugged back into Tokyo and apologized for the interruption.

"We've got Tristan on the line now," said Kahn. "Tristan, can you hear us?"

"Where are you, Peter?" asked Tristan.

"In your office. Are you at home?"

"No, I'm still over at the Citicorp offices. We're winding up."

Some of Courage's resentment dissipated. At least the boss was sweating too. These days even the partners had to put in some grueling hours if they planned to maintain their positions.

Now Courage listened to Tristan taking the brunt of Kahn's temperament. Although Kahn, having no choice, would ultimately defer to Tristan, he was determined to put him through the hoops first, as some justification for the extravagant legal fees he would later be expected to fork out. That he was paying, in ten-minute increments, for the pleasure of domination did not seem to matter. Domination is a fat chunk of the pie we're all fighting for, thought Courage. That elusive prize.

The negotiation looped in circles, returning intermittently to the theme of the merits of prune juice removal. Kahn took the position that the refinement of such technology was a waste of Misuki's resources. Tristan maintained that the R & D was immaterial to the purchase price of the acquisition. Makashuda, sidestepping the argument, insisted that prunes were both nutritious and beneficial to digestion.

When Courage sensed that Tristan was being worn down, he chose that moment for his exit, suspecting that the partner was relieved to be spared further humiliation in front of his associate.

Courage still needed the caffeine he had been craving for two hours, and the muscles ached along his lower back. He had eaten nothing yet except the Toblerone, but most of all a warm shower would have been heaven. At least the limousine rush hour, between eight and ten at night, was well over. Love, the cab company, sent a car right away.

When he arrived at Pandick, the printer on Varick Street, a discreet client servicer ushered him down the corridors to the room where the Caroline Brothers 9¼ percent $400 million bonds were stationed.

Although no one seemed to be watching it, the television was on, showing an ice hockey game. The long table was strewn with a litter of Coke and Seven-Up cans, nuts and pretzels, and the cartons from the remains of the lobster and filet mignon that the others had already ordered in.

Brad Carpenter, Michelle's superior from Caroline, rose from the table where he had been reading proofs, to greet Courage. They had met a couple of times already, once at another printer on a previous deal and once at a closing dinner. Over the past four weeks they had spoken on the telephone sometimes nine or ten times a day. Despite all that contact, Carpenter remained a cardboard-cutout figure, a tall, gaunt thirty-seven-year-old workaholic, with tortoiseshell glasses hiding steely eyes and a prematurely wrinkled forehead hiding a brain where billions of deal dollars had danced.

"You know everyone?" Brad Carpenter introduced Courage to the cast of characters. The attorney from Milbank, counsel to the underwriter, a shrimp of a man whose luxuriant black mustache overwhelmed his scrawny features, raised his head from his notes and nodded. The attorney from Cleary Gottlieb, trustee's counsel, sprawled engrossed in the *Wall Street Journal.* He, too, was short, but square and pudgy, with an unhealthy ruddy skin. He rustled his newspaper by way of greeting. The woman from Morgan Stanley, the underwriter, jabbered on the telephone, ignoring Courage.

"Where's Michelle?"

"I sent her back to Caroline Brothers, to pick up the latest draft of the underwriting agreement. Do you want to go over the indenture?"

Courage nodded and reached wearily for one of the menus scattered on the table. He cast his eye down the veal medallions, lobster thermidor, and chicken primavera, and ordered a rare cheeseburger with a double portion of french fries. He was too tired to struggle with knives and forks.

He and Brad settled down to work through the revisions to the indenture. The portly woman from Morgan Stanley continued her stream of telephone calls. The red-faced attorney from Cleary Gottlieb dropped his *Journal,* kicked it aside, and leeched onto a bowl of pretzels, munching morosely. Finally the client servicer delivered Courage's cheeseburger. She asked if there was anything else anyone needed.

"Yeah," growled the ruddy attorney from Cleary. "When's the next set of revisions on the guarantee coming?"

"It won't be long now," promised the client servicer.

"You said that an hour ago," grunted Cleary. "Will you fucking people get your act together? This fucking printer's the worst in New York. I never want to use them again."

"Just a few more minutes."

"I don't want to hear that crap. Just get them in here if you want to keep your job." Cleary violently ripped open a Coke can and slurped down a noisy draft.

Courage had heard of him by reputation. While it was conceded he had the manners of a pig, he was considered a brilliant virtuoso, headed shortly for a young partnership.

Morgan Stanley at last put down the telephone and turned to Courage. "We want to strike the paragraph about the riskiness of the collateral."

Courage blinked. "The SEC will never let us get away with that. It's damned risky collateral."

"I don't care. I guarantee you, if my investors read that this whole deal is backed up by toilet paper, I won't sell a single bond."

The shrimp from Millbank supported her. "Take out the language. Let the SEC come back and argue. We can wear them out."

"They're a bunch of assholes at the SEC," said Morgan Stanley. "They won't know the difference."

"We're supposed to be smarter than they are," said Brad. "That's why we make a lot more money."

"Yeah, and sneak through deals that should never go public," muttered Courage.

"Till one day a big one just goes pop," chortled the virtuoso pig.

One day he'll just go pop himself, thought Courage.

The pall fell over the room again. The shrimp lit a cigar, forcing the acrid fumes into an overheated atmosphere already reeking with tired bodies and the leftover grease of the food. Morgan Stanley stood up with resolution, yawned, and juggled the television stations, replacing the ice hockey with Betty Grable. Courage had not been able to face the second order of french fries. Without asking permission, the Cleary virtuoso reached across the table for the carton and helped himself, stuffing handfuls into his mouth at a time.

Then Michelle Peterson walked in.

Courage thought he would always remember the image of how she stood in the doorway, clutching an Hermès attaché case that held the revised underwriting agreement. Her lunar beauty glowed all the more unreal in the stuffy dungeon of exhaustion and ragged nerves and cigar smoke. Despite the bundle of gray mink that wrapped her, he could tell she was slender and delicate from the way the pale skin stretched over her cheekbones. She was all moonshine, there was no other word, with her silvery blond hair falling straight to her shoulders and the stare of her blue, blue eyes. The eyes were slightly round and gave her the questioning look of a china doll. Courage wondered how something so fragile could survive down in these ruthless trenches, and how the vinyl complexion could still gleam like a ripening summer fruit.

"You got the agreement?" asked Brad Carpenter.

"It's here." She opened the attaché case on the table and passed it to him. All eyes were on Brad as he ruffled through the text. The other men hardly seemed to acknowledge her presence, except as the bearer of the document.

"Good," said Brad thoughtfully. "I think we can all live with this."

She slipped off the bundle of fur and draped it over a chair. Thank God, Courage noted, she was not wearing the obligatory navy-blue suit. She had on something clearly expensive, in soft peach and apricot suede, and a string of pearls around her neck, just large enough to be real.

"Hi. I'm Peter Courage."

She turned the unnaturally bright eyes on him and extended a slender hand.

"How're ya doin'? Michelle Peterson." The voice was now professional, masculine, but the cool of the fingers in his was not.

Then she turned abruptly back to Brad. "How's it going?"

"We're waiting for one more revision on the guarantee. If it's okay, we may all be out of here by five."

She nodded. "Great. There'll be time to cadge a couple of hours' sleep before tomorrow."

"We can all sleep tomorrow morning," said Courage. "There's nothing we can do on the deal until noon."

She looked at him superciliously. "I have several other matters to work on." He felt squashed and inadequate.

Who has a chance, thought Courage, with a creature so lovely and expensive and cool? Many a heart had doubtless been wrecked on that mountain of glass. Why should she look at me, a fifth-year corporate associate, like a million other beetles on Wall Street? I have no special talent to distinguish myself, and nothing to show for my life but a *Law Review* article I wrote at Columbia on "Current Regulation in Toxic Waste and River Pollution Control," and a dozen Lucite paperweights, the souvenirs of completed bond deals. But there was no wedding ring and the worst she could do was to wound his pride and subject him to public humiliation. Oh well, go for it.

He poured himself a Seven-Up and sat down next to her on the couch, where she leaned over a chart speckled with numbers and equations.

"You look great. Not at all tired."

The blue eyes flickered. "I'm tired. I flew in on the red-eye from California this morning."

"You mean you haven't slept for two days?"

"I caught a couple of hours on the plane. I don't need much sleep."

"That means you'll be a great investment banker."

"I'll be a great investment banker because I'm smart and tough and I work damn hard."

"Are you that tough?"

"Darlin', I'm as tough as any man at Caroline. My bosses know that. That's how I got to be a vice president."

"You're already a VP? You look so . . . young."

"So I had to work twice as hard as all of you guys to make up for having the wrong genes."

"Don't say that," said Courage softly. "Your genes are great."

"Please. Spare me the sexism. It's been a long day."

He caught a glance of male complicity from the shrimp and a dart of ugly resentment from Morgan Stanley. He had not given her any attention.

"Excuse me, but I've got a lot of work to do," said Michelle. She opened her spread sheets.

For a while he contented himself with watching the way she

flicked the pencil between her long fingers, and absently fingered the diamond stud in her ear. She made him think of crême brulée, crusty on its surface, but, as he hoped, sweet and fondant underneath. He wondered what she did in the evenings. He wondered what she would look like in tight bluejeans. He wondered whether she played tennis, whether she skied. He wondered whether she had orgasms.

"Yes," said Michelle suddenly, breaking into his fantasy, and he looked up sharply to realize she was talking to Brad Carpenter. "If we display the receivable pool chart by year and not by quarter, the trend looks more positive."

Brad turned to Courage. "I've gotta be in Oklahoma City on Tuesday. It looks like I won't make it for the closing. Michelle's standing in for me. I'd appreciate it if you'd bring her up to scratch, Peter, on anything we haven't covered."

"Sure. My home number's on the distribution list. Just call me any time, Michelle, about anything you need."

"Will you be in your office on Saturday?" she asked.

"I guess so."

"We should touch base then. To make sure we've got everything for the preclosing on Monday."

He would have her all to himself, on a deserted Saturday on Wall Street. They could romp through the awesome corridors of her offices or his, and perhaps she would even be wearing the tight jeans. Then he reflected dismally that it would hardly help, that he still did not know how to talk to her about anything except letters of credit and distribution dates and overcollateralization.

A Yank in the RAF was over now. Morgan Stanley took the initiative to switch off the television at which no one had glanced all evening. The hour was taking its toll. The shrimp's dusky complexion had gone a sickly shade of olive green. The virtuoso pig lay back in a chair, his face to the ceiling, and snoozed, emitting little snores. Morgan Stanley sat very still, sipping coffee. Her eyes, under the smear of peacock shadow, were bloodshot. Only Michelle seemed more or less in one piece, although even she was yawning delicately. Courage stole a look at her Cartier watch, strapped on a tiny wrist streaked with pale blue veins. Four thirty-nine. Would the night never end?

He tried once more. "How long have you been at Caroline Brothers?"

"Four years."

"Straight from business school?"

"I worked a couple of years at Merrill Lynch first."

"You like Caroline?"

"I love it. We're first rate among the smaller investment banks. We've got some brilliant, creative people. We're on the cutting edge of the most exciting deals."

"Hard work."

"So, everyone in Wall Street works hard. I love what I do. I wouldn't want to be doing anything else. I'm lucky."

"Did you always want to do finance?"

"No. I was real good at math. I wanted to be a rocket scientist. But that was in the early seventies. This is much better."

"It pays better."

"I like the pay. How about you?"

"Sure, the money's good. Though not compared to what you all make."

"I meant, did you always want to do this?"

"Me? No way. Before I went to law school, I worked a couple of years in Rhode Island, building boats. And sailing them. When I went to Columbia, I never thought it would end up like this."

"What did you expect? You'd be defending rapists and arsonists?"

"Not quite. But I thought it would have something to do with people."

"Numbers are much more interesting."

People. Crushed and pulped by this inexorable life of numbers on the march.

He felt a pressure on his arm and, turning his head very carefully, realized that Michelle had finally collapsed, a dainty heap of peach and apricot, deep into the couch against his shoulder. She was sleeping. Courage looked around the room. They were all half comatose.

He felt her breath fanning his shirt. He would have been glad to let her lean there all night, and tomorrow too, with the strands of blond hair tickling his neck.

The client servicer reappeared with the long awaited revisions of the guarantee.

"I'm calling a limo," Morgan Stanley announced like a car backfiring.

Michelle twitched and sat up straight. She was still drowsy. "I'm sorry."

"We might as well go too," said Courage. "Which way are you headed?"

Her head rocked wearily. "Seventy-ninth..."

"We could share a ride. It'll be quicker than waiting."

She did not object. Courage felt a last flicker of energy. She would curl beside him in the limousine as they glided though the empty street, and then onto the Drive along the river. Soon, it would be Thursday's dawn behind the twisting skyline. Would she kick off her pumps in the car? Would her calf brush his leg as they drove through the deserted city?

The phone rang.

"That must be our car," said Michelle, reaching for her fur.

The shrimp answered it. "This is the Caroline Brothers group. Who? Yes, he's here. Peter, it's for you. I think they said Tokyo."

Courage groaned and picked up the extension. Wouldn't it soon be time for bed, even in Japan?

"Peter," rumbled Kahn, "we've come up with a new method of structuring the stock acquisition. Suppose we were to buy the whole company outright, according to a price formula pegged to future earnings..."

Michelle was already standing at the door. Courage waved at her despairingly and cupped his hand over the mouthpiece. "You'd better go ahead of me. This'll take a while. It's Tokyo calling."

TWO

*T*he partners of Cheltenham, Arbuthnot & Crewe convened for a general partnership meeting every other Thursday at twelve-thirty. They met in the large Horatio Arbuthnot Conference Room, helped themselves to an excellent buffet lunch laid out on the side table, and proceeded with loaded plates to one of the three long trestle tables that stretched down the room. The eleven members of the Management Committee of the firm presided from a kind of raised dais at their head.

The layout of the conference room had been designed by the famous Horatio Arbuthnot himself, who in the early part of the century had spent several months at Oxford, where he had learned to drink port and shoot grouse and recite obscene lampoons in Latin. There he had been so impressed by the architecture of the Gothic dining halls, he had returned to his native New York to become a legendary trial lawyer, then a name partner in the firm, and finally, in a testamentary bequest, to provide that the conference room named after him should be modeled on a medieval great hall. The walls were paneled in oak, and the ceiling hatched with beams. The oil portraits of those partners who had in ages past left some dent in the chronicles of advocacy, frowned and glared and scowled down on the diners.

It was on the first Thursday in December that Hopper, the

young securities partner, arrived early in the conference room and found Cyrus Sweet there, flipping through the obituaries in the *Times*. Cyrus Sweet, who was twenty years Hopper's senior, specialized in trusts and estates and Southern-style flirting with young female associates, and did his best to steer clear of firm politics. He was still a handsome man in his mid-fifties, with distinguished salt-and-pepper hair and elegant suits. His eyes had a come-hither look that had kept him young looking. The practice of trusts and estates no longer thrived, now that so many of the aged and dying had retired to Florida and California, where they made their wills, and Cyrus Sweet's department had shrunk over the years. Fortunately he had preserved a sizable roster of personal clients, many due to his family connections in Lexington, Kentucky. He was thereby able to bring in enough business to keep the Corporate Group vultures off his back. He also provided an important public-relations function. Like Tristan Barrett, he belonged to that dying breed of the old-school elite. He lunched with other people's clients, interviewed and recruited young lawyers, was active in Episcopalian community affairs, and altogether helped propagate for Cheltenham its "white shoe" image of traditions long extinct.

Red-headed young Hopper nodded briskly at Cyrus Sweet. As Courage had pointed out to Gleiner, Hopper was a man incapable of human rapport or relationship, with one all-consuming exception. He served with a blind devotion his boss, Ariel Lamb, chief titan of the Corporate Finance Department.

The only language in which it was possible to communicate with Hopper was that of securities law. Cyrus Sweet, who had been trained in the near-defunct art of social conversation, was most at his ease when he and his wife entertained for eighteen in their Second Empire dining room, which overlooked Park Avenue.

Cyrus Sweet looked up and cleared his throat. His manners impelled him to make conversation. "So I hear last month the firm did record billings."

"We did a lot of deals. Two billion with First Boston, one-point-five billion with Salomon, a couple of nine-hundred-million with Prudential and Goldman, eight hundred million with Caroline Brothers."

"Litigation picked up some big oil and pharmaceutical cases too."

"Litigation," snorted Hopper. "It's time they started pulling their weight. Do you realize the Corporate Finance Group now brings in one half of the firm's total income? That's as much as all the rest of you people put together."

"Business runs in cycles," responded Cyrus placidly. "Always has." Long before Corporate Finance reigned, the departments of Tax, Real Estate, Trusts, Admiralty, Labor, and Litigation had propelled the firm through two centuries. Their day would come again.

Hopper helped himself to a slice of pimiento, which garnished the cauliflower salad on the buffet table. His teeth snapped like a busy little guillotine.

Cyrus Sweet tried again. "Is it true Ariel's about to unleash a new bombshell on the securities industry?"

Hopper's eyes glistened. Ariel Lamb's creative talents in structuring new varieties of asset-backed bonds were the only expression of genius Hopper was able to appreciate.

"It's the most exciting concept anyone's had on the Street in years, maybe ever. It'll put us right back at the forefront of the firms that do asset-backed work. Cadwalader, Skadden, Cleary—they have nothing to compare to this. We could be the richest firm in America."

"How does the gizmo work?"

"It's really quite simple. It's based on the same principles as a mortgage-backed security, only this time the issuer makes a deal with the government to buy up pools of taxes."

Cyrus Sweet sighed. "I wish I understood mortgage-backed securities." He was mature enough to admit to areas of ignorance. Everyone at Cheltenham was a specialist these days anyway, an expert in a limited field. The times of so-called general practice were long gone. Litigators today knew nothing about trusts. Tax attorneys were a mad breed unto themselves. And none of these highly paid princes of the profession could handle something simple, like fixing a parking ticket.

Hopper, lured into his subject of passion, looked benign. "A mortgage-backed security is just another way of selling each flow. The issuer, which is often an investment bank, buys up a pool of mortgages. What do those mortgages represent? A future stream of payments, over the years, which produce a flow of money as the homeowners pay off their homes. So the issuer takes his pool, divides it up into new chunks, and sells those chunks afresh to investors, right? In return the investors get paid regular interest, from the same money that is coming in from the homeowners."

"That's all perfectly sensible, Hopper. I understand that the issuer is happy to sell loans off at a slight discount. He gets the benefit of the use of the money today, instead of having to wait many years, until the loans mature. Money in hand is worth more than money later. But how do you make the jump from mortgages to taxes?"

"It's brilliant, it's dynamite. The secret is that you can use any kind of income-producing collateral. We'd all been doing the mortgage-backed deals for a few years, when we began to realize that you could collateralize other kinds of obligations. Automobile installment payments, for instance. It's the same theory, with somewhat smaller payments. Leases on equipment, like telephones and computers, which also involve a stream of regular payments. Credit card interest payments. You see, it's endless. But you're sticking to the same rule. You're buying up somebody's debt, their obligation, and reselling it to the public at a slight discount."

"Okay, okay, but how in hell do you squeeze it out of taxes?"

"Simple. Taxes represent the ultimate form of a continuing obligation. Nothing else is certain but death. It's true that the level of taxes of any individual will fluctuate from year to year, depending on his income, but in the same way the mortgage payments are also uncertain. You bundle together a huge pool of individuals' tax obligations, and you can come up with a pretty good estimate of what you're going to get over a five- or ten-year period."

"I'd have thought it would be damned difficult to make such a projection."

"The investment banks are wizards at working out those formulas," answered Hopper airily. "They've got a guy at Caroline Brothers who's plotted out projections down to the last cent."

"If you say so. But how the devil do you buy up the right to collect tax revenues?"

"You buy it from the government, of course, just like you buy up the pools of mortgages."

"Wait a minute. Mortgages are one thing. The government's been issuing Freddies and Fannies and all those other mortgage instruments for years. But taxes? There's something special about taxes."

"Not necessarily."

"Are you telling me the U.S. government is willing to sell off pools of taxes to an investment bank?"

"Who said anything about the U.S. government?"

"You mean...other governments?"

"Look south, Cyrus. Look at Central America. Look at South America. They want money now, not next year. They're delighted to assign their future tax receivables over to us."

"Isn't it a bit risky, relying on the political stability of banana republics?"

"The risk's built in. Everyone takes risks these days. They buy junk bonds. Caroline Brothers are convinced they'll be able to sell our new baby."

Cyrus frowned. The idea was brilliant, as Hopper said, but there was something about trading in future taxes of South American peasants that struck him as less than kosher.

"South America," he repeated.

"That's only the beginning. Caroline's sent out a team of V.P.'s down to Bolivia and Colombia to start negotiations. Ariel spoke with them yesterday; apparently they're hot to trot. When they see how smoothly it works, some of the Western European countries will soon be taking an interest too. And what do you know, with a few of the right strings pulled in Congress, in the end even Uncle Sam will be raring to get in on the act."

The other partners, also known as the "members" of the firm, were beginning to filter through the vaulted oak doors. They milled between the trestle tables, sizing up the seats of political vantage.

"If Ariel can pull it off," said Cyrus Sweet reflectively, "I guess it's good for the firm. There's no way we can lose."

"Ariel can do it, if anyone can. He believes in the concept. When Ariel makes up his mind...you'd better have faith in him, Cyrus."

The older man looked at Hopper thoughtfully. "When it comes to securitization, I've no doubt Ariel's the best. Oh, hello, Mick. How are you?"

Mick Finnegan, his hair sticking up on end and his shirttails untucked over his ripening paunch, belted toward them. Finnegan still exuded the irrepressible energy that Cyrus Sweet remembered had distinguished him even twenty-two years ago, when he had first come to Cheltenham as a young associate. Finnegan had been better kempt in those days, almost an orderly young man, although he already showed signs of the eccentricity that amused some and rankled others.

"Brother Hopper, Brother Cyrus," said Finnegan, bowing toward them.

"How are your vaginal exercises?" asked Cyrus Sweet.

"Not good, not good. Plaintiff's produced fresh evidence that the cervices of certain users have been permanently dilated."

"The servicees?" said Hopper idly, his mind on servicing payments of interest.

"Cervix, cervices," boomed Finnegan. "Does no one learn Latin anymore?"

Mick Finnegan, a temperamental and one-time brilliant litigator, had spent the past two years embroiled in a class action brought by the users of Vaginex, a product designed for mild exercises intended to strengthen the muscles of the vaginal walls and which had allegedly resulted in the distortion of the users' inner contours. It had been a nightmare of a case from the beginning. Although Finnegan struggled valiantly for his client Vaginex, sympathy was on the side of the mutilated women. So the matter dragged on, and the legal bills mounted, while scores of gynecological experts contradicted one another's testimony as to the degrees of elasticity of the female interior.

"Any chance of a settlement?"

"Would that there were. Five years ago I was litigating real issues: nuclear power explosions, oil slick contamination, aviation disasters. Now what have I been reduced to? Ladies' genitalia! I mean," he added hastily, as Hopper sidled away to less frivolous company, "I've nothing against the object in its proper time and place. But I never expected my career would culminate in its pursuit."

"We live in treacherous times." Cyrus Sweet arched his bushy eyebrows.

Finnegan held up a warning hand. "Careful. Here comes Fishman. He's joined the ranks of Ariel's minions. Don't let him hear you."

Cyrus Sweet looked away. He detested firm politics, which had never been so perilous as now. "Shall we get some lunch, Mick?"

Finnegan helped himself to cold poached salmon, asparagus, and potato salad. Sizing up the distribution of friends and foes already seated along the length of the trestle tables, he avoided eye contact with some of the more deadly piranhas and chose a seat next to Tristan Barrett, who had remained his friend.

"I see that Der Fuhrer and Il Duce are both fashionably late today," he murmured softly to Tristan.

"Working to line our pockets," grunted Tristan. Most of the time he tried to discourage Finnegan's excesses, particularly the public displays. He still had some affection for the tempestuous litigator, who had worn out the patience of all his other friends. He also felt an inkling of responsibility for him, since it was he, Tristan, who had energetically promoted Finnegan's partnership over a decade ago. At that time it had been easier. Finnegan had been a slavish worker, had a reputation for lopsided genius, disgorging a tidal wave of rhetoric and articulation. He had been a respectable protégé. Now he was often out of hand, a "loose cannon," as Ariel Lamb once sharply put it, antagonizing clients, and too often seen lurching back to work after a lengthy, boozy lunch.

Today Tristan was out of sorts. Kahn had kept him talking late on the telephone last night. When he had not slept enough his sciatica bothered him. He was bitter, too, about Ariel Lamb and his Corporate Finance troops. They believed they ran the firm, that brigade, down to the most junior first-year associates. They already stole the best secretaries, booked priority time in Word Processing, thereby preventing other departments from getting work typed on time, and even refused to return his telephone calls. Tristan Barrett had been a partner at Cheltenham for twenty-one years; the first-year pipsqueaks implied that their time was more valuable than his.

"At least our pockets will be full this month," said Finnegan.

"It's the best Cheltenham's ever had."

"Lord knows I needed it, and a few more like it. I nearly missed my mortgage payment on the house in Nantucket."

"You've got to stop living like a millionaire playboy, Mick. Whoever buys a ten-room house in Nantucket? And when you've already got that enormous spread in Greenwich."

"It made sense when I had eight points," said Finnegan bitterly.

"Now you've got four. It's time to stop living like a lord." Tristan knew too well that it was when the partnership had finally cut back Finnegan's partnership points that they had broken his spirit. Finnegan had always enjoyed his wealth and spent it freely both on himself and his friends. While Finnegan regretted its passing, that regret was secondary. What had whipped and enraged him was the insult to his career, the professionalism to which he had dedicated his lifework. They had all dedicated themselves, taking an unspoken vow, every man now sitting here in this room, under the rebukes of old Percy Cheltenham, Horatio Arbuthnot, and Jeremiah Crewe, whose portraits presided behind the dais.

There had been several recent rumors that, with the dawning of the new era of Corporate Finance, a redistribution of points was inevitable. Each point represented about a hundred thousand dollars a year in pretax income. Ariel Lamb, "Der Fuhrer" and Mel Samson, "Il Duce," enjoyed twenty points, which yielded them over two million dollars apiece a year. Would they never be satisfied, Tristan mused. Gary Fishman, the senior tax partner, already had twelve, which was a lot considering he was only forty-three. Tristan himself and Cyrus Sweet, in part as a token to their longevity, each had ten. Although the youngest partners usually started with only two, Hopper, under the patronage of Ariel Lamb, had already vaulted to seven.

Ariel Lamb's dominant position derived not merely from industry or legal skills, but from his "rainmaking," that is, the seduction and continued cosseting of major clients. The rainmakers were those partners directly responsible for bringing clients and new business into the firm. Mel Samson, head of General Corporate, made rain too, although it was the entrepreneurs he wooed. Ariel, darling of the banks and financial institutions, made love to the commercial instincts of the money managers.

Finnegan groaned. "What happens if they cut me back again in March? I can't live on any less."

Other people, reflected Tristan, managed to scrape by on four hundred thousand a year. The standards by which the brethren of Cheltenham lived bore no relationship to the world outside 57 Water Street.

"Don't worry about March. A lot can happen in three months. All you need is one big case."

"It wouldn't fix things. Ariel wants my ass."

"Maybe Samson'll win."

"Mel Samson's getting old and tired. I don't know if he's up to fighting this duel. Tristan, I think we may have hitched our wagons to the wrong star."

"Mel's a wily old bird. He always keeps a card up his sleeve. I'd never be surprised to see him pull some punch and topple Ariel for good."

"Ariel's fifteen years younger than Mel. He looks good, like a wind-up doll looks good. He's slick. The investment bankers like him. They see him as the future of the firm."

"He's tied to a limited practice. When the wind blows, Ariel Lamb'll be history. He might not even get his portrait up there on the wall."

Finnegan shook his head anxiously. "And what if that wind keeps right on blowing?"

"There's still Mel. He made this firm the giant it is today by building a practice in general corporate law, old-fashioned mergers, divestitures, and partnerships. It's much broader-based than Ariel's securities gimmicks. Mel's not going to give up the fight easily. He loves power, Mick, more than any other man I've ever known."

"Sometimes I wonder what they're fighting over. They're both rich men. They've both got massive influence. In a firm of four hundred attorneys, isn't there room for two chiefs?"

"They're not like other men."

"I think it's primitive, Tristan. Barbaric. Oedipal. Lamb's gotta kill Samson. The new order replaces the old. It's all pagan."

"Maybe it'll go the other way. Like Abraham and Isaac."

"That's appropriate. They're both Jew boys after all."

Tristan lowered his voice. "Never let Ariel hear you say that."

"Oh, I forgot. He converted, didn't he? What is he now, Episcopalian?"

"Presbyterian."

"Maybe the old God of vengeance will give Mel a few extra points for sticking with the faith."

"Speaking of points, can they really give Hopper more again? It's an outrage."

"He's loyal to his Fuhrer," Finnegan answered wryly. "That's what counts these days."

"He's a fanatic. If Ariel told him to jump out of the window, he'd go without a murmur."

The noise level in the room suddenly subsided. Tristan looked up from his plate of duckling mousse. Mel Samson had arrived at last. He strode down the length of the center trestle table, turning his head in neither direction. He did not need to. The eyes, under the heavily hooded lids, took in everything he needed to know. When he reached the dais he nodded curtly with his gleaming bald head at the nine already seated members of the Management Committee. He took his seat, stretching out his long, bony legs. Only Ariel's chair was still empty.

Business always commenced at one o'clock sharp. Would Lamb arrive in time or would they begin without him? Clancy Maxwell, an admiralty partner and member of the Management Committee, was due to chair the proceedings. Tristan watched him with interest, where he sat in the center of the dais, clearly reluctant to open the meeting without Lamb. Maxwell's power base depended on his rainmaking rather than his slightly outmoded specialty in shipping. He had a roster of fertile social connections. He owed that network to his wife, Eleanor, whose Bostonian family dated back to the Pilgrims. During the past year Maxwell had hugged neutrality in the struggle between the two senior partners. Tristan now suspected that Maxwell had finally decided to cast his vote with Lamb. A discouraging sign. Maxwell must realize that keeping pace in an area of law no longer fashionable demanded a keen political nose. If he had concluded that Lamb was to be the winner...

Maxwell could not hold out any longer. The meeting began. "The first item on our agenda today, one in which I know we all take an interest, is the matter of whether the forty-seventh-floor reception area should be repainted in mauve as a more suitable background for the new paintings painted by and donated to our firm by Margaret Lamb."

"It'll look like a hairdresser's!"

"It'll clash with the rug."

"Burgundy is the traditional Cheltenham color."

"Hell, what's wrong with pink?"

"Mauve would be elegant."

"Classy."

The din mounted. Once the majority of the room had grasped

the significance of the decision, the meeting was soon divided between the Lamb and Samson supporters. The Fuhrer fans expressed an exhuberant enthusiasm for mauve. After all, if their general's wife had indicated a preference for the color, what did it matter what happened to reception anyway? The Samson tribe leaped at the opportunity to remind the group that in former days Cheltenham had been proud to coordinate its décor around its theme color of blood.

When Maxwell finally contained the uproar, and the proposal had been voted and counted, it was decided that the reception-area walls would remain off-white as they always had. Finnegan exchanged a triumphant look with Tristan. A small round lost by Lamb.

The next item concerned the escalation of starting associate salaries. These had risen each year by five- and ten-thousand-dollar increments, in a competitive bidding auction by the major firms to attract the young legal brains of the generation. Somebody had to put a lid on the increments, but which firm would be brave enough to buck the trend?

"We have it on good authority," Maxwell announced, "that Cravath and Skadden intend to raise the ante yet again next month. Should Cheltenham follow suit?"

Mel Samson spoke out sharply against the raise, his measured, glacial voice reminding the brethren that another such salary hike would hack a substantial dent in the partners' personal incomes. A murmur of approval followed his argument. A consensus was developing that the associates should be overpaid no further, when Ariel Lamb made his entrance.

Every head was turned toward him as he glided up the aisle to the dais, smiling discreetly at his partisans. The rhythm of the meeting skipped a beat while he took his place.

"We must all think of the good of Cheltenham in the long term," he pronounced. "The lifeblood of a great institution like ours derives from the continuing levels of excellence among both its members and its younger employees. As you all know, we've become one of the richest firms in Wall Street. We are in a position to buy the best brains to match our dynamic practice. I warn you all not to let short-term personal interest stand in the way of Cheltenham's development at the pinnacle of the profession."

Cyrus Sweet, who loathed politics, but also hated Ariel Lamb, spoke up. "Surely the leading Wall Street firms have a responsibility to one another to put the brakes on the bidding war. Someone has to take a stand. Otherwise we'll destroy each other."

"This Corporate Finance," said Mel Samson. "Any idiot can do it. We don't need the best brains in the land to churn out the documents. They're cookie-cutter similar. You could practically teach a gorilla to draft them."

The gauntlet was cast, the declaration of war. No one else would have dared to trample so flagrantly on Lamb's terrain.

Lamb's riposte hurtled back. "We must move with the times, Mel. Law's more than just a game of wits these days. We're a big business. And when you run a business, you hire the fellow you need to do the job, and you pay the market price for him."

"I agree with you, Ariel. But the fellow we need to do your Corporate Finance work doesn't have to come out of Harvard cum laude. We can afford to scrape the barrel. We can pick up the bottom twenty-five percentile of the lowest-ranking law schools. In fact we may do better with those people. They work harder. They're grateful. They need the job. Best of all are the women starting careers late in life. They're fanatics. They'll sweat blood for us."

Several years earlier the firm had already begun to open its doors to associates of mediocre education and scant intellect. The net still scooped up some Ivy League applicants, seduced by the prestigious old name, but every year their numbers thinned.

"Don't forget, Mel, that my Corporate Finance lawyers and I bring in one-half of Cheltenham's income. If you all value your partnership draws, you'd better allow me to hire the best team."

"They'll soon be throwing food at each other," whispered Finnegan.

Tristan frowned. "Il Duce's right. This assinine salary bidding's got to stop somewhere. I can't give up any more income, with my divorce."

"When's that coming through?"

"God knows. It's costing the earth, even though my children are grown up and I've given her all the money she's asked for. The lawyers are still squeezing me...."

Gary Fishman, the wunderkind of tax, spoke next. "I propose that we postpone further discussion over the salary hike until we've had more feedback from the other law firms. First let's see what steps they take."

Fishman's suggestion was popular. Everyone in the room dreaded the vile dilemma that threatened to affect their personal incomes.

"Gary has an idea he would like to share with you." With some relief Maxwell handed the floor over to Fishman.

Fishman cleared his throat. He never liked speaking in public. He was comfortable lecturing to one client at a time, armed with his photographic recall of the Internal Revenue Code. "Now that it's become standard for our associates, and often our members too, to put in regular sixteen- or seventeen-hour days, we all need exercise and relaxation more than ever. Under our kind of pressure it's increasingly hard to find the time to work out."

"He's an exercise freak," Tristan murmured. "He goes to his gym every morning at six."

Finnegan nodded. "Every time he gains half a pound he goes on a diet for three days of nothing but boiled cabbage and dry bagels."

"Have you met his wife, Suzy? She's like an emaciated Ethiopian."

"You're all familiar with some of our sadder incidents of associate burn-out," Fishman continued. "Pneumonia, suicides, coronaries; unfortunately we've seen them all in the past few years. I mean, what major law firm hasn't? It's time we did something to improve health and morale. We can't cut down their hours. We need the money. So I suggest we build a fully equipped gymnasium next door to the cafeteria."

"There's no room," interrupted a litigation partner. "Except in the Crewe Library."

"We don't need the Crewe Library. It's nothing but a bunch of our old eighteenth-century law reports, all falling apart and full of Scotch tape. The mold's got into them. I suggest we auction them at Sotheby's."

Ariel Lamb warmed to any proposal that undermined the history of Cheltenham or replaced it with modern efficiency. "I second the idea," he said. "An auction would get us good publicity. We could even give a big party afterward and ask our friends from First Boston and Goldman."

"You can't do that," objected Cyrus Sweet. "Those antique books are our legacy."

"Screw the books," said Fishman. "What's important is to get a gym set up where our lawyers can work out any time of the day or night to improve their cardiovascular fitness."

"Would we have to allow women associates to use the facilities?" asked Mel Samson.

"What about secretaries and paralegals?" asked Tristan Barrett.

"Maybe we could let paralegals in at off-peak hours," suggested Hopper. "Like between four and six A.M.."

"I don't see why paralegals should be allowed," said Lamb. "We aren't all that concerned about their state of health."

"Exactly." Fishman warmed up. "Whereas our attorneys are an investment for us. We can't afford to go on losing our best people to burn-out. It gets us a bad reputation and makes our hiring more difficult."

"How much will all this cost?" asked a real-estate partner.

"We could probably do it for half a million."

The usual rumble of indignation, which always followed the mention of expenditure, swept the room.

"What's half a million anyway?" asked Hopper.

"It's a lot when you've only got four points," grunted Finnegan.

Over the babble of excited voices, Ariel Lamb was seen to lean toward and confer with Clancy Maxwell, who then brought the meeting to order.

"Ariel has an important announcement. As we are running out of time, I propose we postpone any vote on the gymnasium until the next general meeting. Ariel?" He turned over the floor.

Lamb waited a moment until the hall was so silent you could almost hear the heartbeats. He calmly took off his tortoiseshell-rimmed glasses, drew out his handkerchief with long fingers, and polished them. "I have both good news and bad news to report to you today. As you all probably know by now, we've enjoyed a record month of profits, and judging from our bills submitted this autumn, January may be even more fruitful. My Corporate Finance department is of course largely responsible for our unprecedented earnings, and we see every likelihood that we will continue to generate such vigorous business well into the future.

"Some of you are already familiar with the novel variety of collateralized obligation recently developed by our longstanding clients, Caroline Brothers. We have named this new debt security a TBO, or tax-backed obligation, as it is collateralized by a future stream of tax revenues purchased from Third World countries. This cutting-edge innovation, if successful, promises to open up a mine of business to bring us deal opportunities into the next decade.

"Delighted as we are with our ingenious new vehicle, I must report to you an alarming development. While Caroline Brothers and I have taken every precaution to move discreetly, someone from Cheltenham has been selling or passing information to a competitor, Samurai Robinson."

Samurai Robinson was an investment bank with which Cheltenham had had little association. As a result of the merger between two major U.S. and Japanese firms, Samurai had become one of the largest and most dominant players in the industry.

Thanks to its $3.6 billion capital base, its resources were phenomenal. Caroline Brothers, while a well-regarded institution, was by comparison little more than a boutique.

"A week ago the following distressing facts emerged. A small team of vice presidents from Caroline has recently been in Bolivia and Colombia, negotiating with the governments of those countries for the purchase of their future taxes. Last Friday one of their people spotted Joe Tikawa, international managing director of Samurai Robinson, playing gin rummy with the chief economist in Bogota. Tikawa was also sighted drinking a Coca-Cola with the minister of finance in La Paz, and a couple of days later, coming out of a movie theater in Asunción, Paraguay. Although unconfirmed, there is evidence that a Japanese man of Tikawa's description purchased a duty-free carton of Marlboro Light One Hundreds at the airport of Montevideo.

"I need hardly remind you of the significance of these ugly reports. A race between Caroline and Samurai is comparable to a match between David and Goliath.

"I know that it is profoundly disturbing for all of us to harbor suspicions about our Cheltenham employees. The fact remains that someone has alerted Samurai Robinson as to the structure of our TBO. It's unthinkable that such a mole could exist within the partnership itself. Therefore I must ask all of you to scrutinize the associates working under you and report to me any incidents of suspicious behavior or other indicia."

Lamb paused for breath and took a swig of Diet Coke. A stunned silence followed his explosion of rhetoric.

Mel Samson, narrowing his hooded eyes, broke the tension. "Which partners and associates have been involved in the TBO deal to date?" he inquired.

"Hopper and I have been working together closely," answered Lamb. "And we've consulted Gary Fishman on various international tax issues."

"I had one associate do some research for me," said Fishman.

"Who?"

"David Gleiner. He's a quiet, hard-working type. Thin on personality, but bills a lot of hours."

"Partnership track?"

"Definitely not. More of a workhorse."

"Keep an eye on him," said Lamb.

"He's always been conscientious," said Fishman. "He wrote an incisive memorandum on state taxation of multistate commerce."

"If no one else has worked on the TBO..." began Clancy Maxwell.

Lamb raised an admonishing hand. "A few weeks ago, I noticed that my desk had been rifled. It didn't concern me much at the time. I encourage my Corporate Finance team to make free use of my books and resources for their work. Now that I've reflected on it, it looks like the thief, who could be any associate, might have picked up the idea from my personal notes."

"I'm afraid we've run out of time for today," Maxwell broke in apologetically. "We have one additional proposal here, that hot pizza and guacamole be available in the cafeteria at two A.M., on an experimental basis. I think we can assume that no one would be opposed."

"Why guacamole?" objected Finnegan loudly. "Why not Cajun refried beans?"

"Shut up, Finnegan," shouted an impatient litigator.

Samson stood abruptly, glancing at his watch. His movement provided a cue. With a scraping of chairs and renewed babble of conversation, the sixty-eight partners present prepared to return to work. The meeting was over.

THREE

A couple of hours later, Clancy Maxwell took the elevator down to the forty-seventh floor, sauntered along the corridor hung with reproductions of Constables and Gainsboroughs, and knocked briskly on the door of Gina di Angelo's office.

"Come in," she called softly. When she saw who it was, she sprang up from her desk, where a stack of admiralty reports stood piled. He closed the door firmly behind him.

"Clancy!" she said, gliding toward him.

He put his hands on the supple hips, cinched at the waist with a Gucci belt. "How's it going, gorgeous? You look great."

She fingered the expensive belt. "You like it?"

"Did I buy you that?"

She smiled at him docilely under her feathery lashes and laid her cheek against his shoulder. In heels she stood a couple of inches taller than he.

"How was the meeting?"

"Ariel and Mel got into a skirmish. All to do with those vile paintings by Ariel's wife."

"Have you seen them?"

"They're all over the walls in their house in Montclair. Collages made of ice-cream wrappers and loops of toilet paper and subway tokens."

"They're going to put those in reception?"

"It's Ariel's wife."

She caressed the hair behind his ear, avoiding his temples where it was beginning to thin. "How about the salary hike? Will we be getting a raise?"

"It's still undecided. But you needn't worry. I'll take care of you."

"I know, sweetheart." She moved back to her desk and reached automatically for the pack of Virginia Slims in the top drawer. She drew back her hand in midair. Although he never criticized, she sensed that he did not like it when she smoked. Most of her wanted to be perfect, for him.

"How's work?" He glanced over the array of cases spread out on the desk. *"Ploof* v. *Putnam.* I remember that. Didn't Plaintiff moor his boat to Defendant's dock, and Defendant untied it during a storm, causing Plaintiff to fall into the water?"

She stared at him in amazement. He had the most prodigious memory for the details of obscure cases, which he had not looked at for twenty years, since he was at Harvard Law School.

"That's exactly right. I'm researching the defense of necessity. Defendant moored his barge to my client's wharf."

He nodded. "Check out *Vincent* v. *Lake Erie Transportation Company.* Big storm—vessel moored to dock—dock sustains damage—court holds vessel owner liable—reasoning: inequity to dock owner when vessel has trespassed on dock."

Gina ripped a sheet from her memo pad and scribbled down the case name with the gold Cartier pen he had given her as a Thanksgiving present.

He fingered a china ashtray molded in the shape of a butterfly. Gina reminded him of a butterfly, with her dark, curling hair, her pale skin, her long body.

"Who gave you this?"

She did not look up. "We bought it. At the street fair."

He remembered the street fair along Columbus Avenue they had strolled through together in September. The weather had been perfect. She had frisked beside him. She had tried on a pair of turquoise earrings, held up a mirror, wrapped herself in a rose-embroidered shawl, munched on a skewer of yakitori. He had caught her mood, feeling a sudden rush of enjoyment, and that golden sun on his back. It had been ages since he had been happy like that. He wanted to feel it again, often. He had bought her the shawl and the earrings.

She had not been his first affair in all the years at the firm, although sometimes it occurred to him that she might be his last. She was different from the others. While her friskiness bewitched him, even more than that he was intrigued by her dark side, the poignant, serious Gina. He had seen it cloud her face that afternoon when he had interviewed her three years before, on August 19, a sweltering day. Her shoulders had been decorously covered with a jacket and only her long neck exposed. He had looked away quickly from that mysterious pain to the résumé in his hand.

Education
St. John's University of Law, J.D.
Temple University, summa cum laude
(English and Renaissance History Major)
St. Francis Xavier High School

"Renaissance history. Interesting. Borgias and Michelangelo. You speak Italian?"

"A little. I used to speak it better."

"*Lasciate ogni speranza voi ch'entrate.*" His reading glasses slid down his nose as he proclaimed Dante's famous warning in an Italian overwhelmed by his WASPy New York intonation. Gina stared at him in astonishment. He wondered if perhaps he had inverted a word or two. "That's about all I know. The first partner I ever worked for here—he's retired now—had a sign on his desk that said that. Abandon hope." He chuckled. "He was a nice fellow. We're still a pretty nice bunch at Cheltenham. We care about getting along with one another." She was still staring. He wondered if she saw through the standard interview patter. He glanced hastily back to the résumé. "So I see you made *Law Review*. Good. We need hard workers."

Later he learned that Gina came from a poor Italo-American family, who eked out a shabby existence in Allentown. Perhaps that was why he found himself showering her with presents, at the least excuse. She seemed to prize every little thing he gave her, from a chocolate Venus de Milo to a pair of sapphire ear studs.

Then, on that fateful August interview, he had looked back from the résumé into her wide eyes, and paused too long. He knew; she knew. With an effort, he picked up the conversation again, and asked her about her *Law Review* article on capital punishment.

She had been an easy hire. It had been clear to the Hiring Committee that she was dedicated, motivated, even a little desperate to work hard. During her first two years she had been absorbed into the Litigation Group, so Maxwell, who was immersed in his admiralty practice, had no official reason to run into her. From time to time they would cross paths in the library. Maxwell remembered watching her one evening, half hidden behind a stack of shelves. She sat in a circle of light, very straight and very still, her long neck arched in concentration over her case research.

He had stood, for no reason, for a long time, fascinated while she slowly turned the pages. Inexplicably sensing his attention behind her, she turned her head and met his stare.

He was obligated to speak. "How do you like being a lawyer?"

"It's hard. But I'm learning."

"You've got interesting work?"

"I'm working for Mick Finnegan. We're preparing an order to show cause."

"For Vaginex?"

She nodded. Printed diagrams of distorted vulvas lay strewn among her cases and notes.

"You work a lot in the evenings?"

"Most evenings till ten or eleven. Weekends too."

"You ought to take some time off. You're getting thinner."

She felt his eyes traverse her shoulders and ribs. "I'm always thin. I love doing this. I like spending evenings here."

"You get out at all? You go to movies? Plays?" Maxwell himself had not seen a play in many years. He was curious about how she lived.

"I go to the ballet once in a while. That's all."

"You must take care of yourself. Some of our young women attorneys, in a year they look gray and sunken. I don't want that happening to you."

"Do I look sunken, then?"

He paused. "God, no."

Their conspiracy excited him. They read each other's thoughts. When they ran into each other in the elevator or the corridor, they both always stopped, no matter their hurry. He tried to turn those snatches of conversation around to some personal comment. He would remark on her hair, her clothing, the bracelet she always wore. She would gaze at him levelly, but her lashes fluttered, and he knew that she was keyed into the game. He knew she wanted him. He could tell by the helpless flutter.

They were riding the elevator down to the street one frigid January night. Although her face was muffled in a wool hat and scarf, her wide eyes leaped out at him.

"Were you skiing in Colorado this Christmas?" he asked.

"No. I was at home in Allentown."

"Amazing. I saw a woman on the ski slope. I could have sworn it was you. She was all wrapped up, and it was at a distance, but she moved just like you."

The elevator stopped and he held the door for her. He knew she read his code. Even in the faraway mountains in Aspen, he was still thinking of her. Wherever he went, the image of the lithe body taunted him.

Their encounters remained a game until the firm's July outing. Cheltenham, like many of the major firms, traditionally organized a day at the Duchess County Country Club, to which all the attorneys were invited. There was golf and tennis and softball, which gave the junior grunts the chance to take revenge on the partners who slave-drove them all the rest of the year. For many years Maxwell had played in the tennis doubles with Tristan Barrett. Both played well, even the middle-aged Tristan, and they felt particularly smug whenever they trounced some twenty-six-year-old duo. Heading toward the showers after the match with Tristan, Maxwell caught a glimpse of Gina's bare legs by the swimming pool. She lay on her stomach sunbathing, encircled by a group of enthusiastic first years. Suddenly, the pleasure of their tennis victory was wiped out. Maxwell felt old and exiled.

At six-thirty, after the day of sun and sports, the attorneys gathered on the terrace for cocktails and hors d'oeuvres. It was amusing to see the women in summer dresses, with uncovered arms and legs, the only day of the year when etiquette permitted the grim suits to be left behind. The drinking was well under way. Maxwell saw Mick Finnegan sway against the railings of the porch, heckling Ariel Lamb.

"Remember when you used to come to me to pick my brains on bankruptcy and UCC issues?" he slurred. "You knew I was the expert. Now you send some first year to me when you have a question."

"You were good then, Mick. You knew your stuff. You're still knowledgeable, but you're losing your edge. Don't screw up."

Maxwell thought Finnegan was about to punch Ariel out. "Are you threatening me?" He lurched a step closer.

Lamb, who never drank, stood his ground. "I'm warning you." He turned his back on Finnegan and fell into conversation with Gary Fishman.

At dinner there was no prearranged seating. Maxwell stood aside, nibbling at a plate of stuffed mushrooms, until he saw where Gina had sat down, next to her friend Cheryl. At the identical moment, Maxwell and Gary Fishman lunged for the empty chair. The two partners eyed each other stubbornly. Maxwell felt the draft of Cheryl's scorn. She was a senior associate, sharp and solitary and jaded in the ways of men.

She pointed at an empty place opposite at the same table. "There's more room, Gary."

So Maxwell managed to sit next to Gina, who looked demure in her baby-blue dress with its starched white collar, except for the knowing smile she slipped him.

"Do you play tennis?" he asked her.

"I never learned. And there's no time. I'm always working."

Maxwell refilled both their glasses with white wine. He was beginning to feel its effects, coupled with the sun and exercise and two strong scotches before dinner.

"Ah, but you speak the language of Dante," he said. "And you have the passion of the Borgias in your blood."

"I'm a second-generation immigrant. I was the only person in my family ever to go to college."

"You're brave." He raised his glass tipsily. *"Corragio!"*

"I wanted to use my brain."

"I'm glad you didn't waste it. You've certainly got a good one."

She gave him the poignant look, over the rim of her wineglass. "I sometimes wonder. I'm so slow. It takes me twice as long to do the work as everyone else, which is why I spend so much time at Cheltenham."

"You've been doing some fine research. Finnegan told me. Very thorough."

She looked pleased. "I am careful."

Across the table, Cheryl turned her lipsticked smile on Fishman. She was rapidly becoming a woman of a certain age, thought Maxwell. She even lied about her age to the other associates. Maxwell knew she was thirty-seven, because he had once, out of boredom, checked her file.

"Are you coming dancing with us afterward, Gary?" she asked.

Maxwell wondered why Cheryl had never remarried. She had been divorced shortly after she had joined Cheltenham, and had two young children. She was attractive, in an overgroomed fashion. There was something untouchable and forbidden about her shell of sleek hair. Yet Maxwell knew a lot of attorneys who might like to muss it, once or twice.

He poured himself and Gina more wine. "Are you going dancing later, Gina?"

She fluttered her lashes. "Are you?"

"Sure. Where's everyone going?"

"The Palladium," Cheryl told him.

After dinner, some speeches, and another hour of serious drinking, the country club was ready to close its doors. The attorneys streamed out into the summer night toward the waiting row of small buses.

Fishman took Cheryl's hand. "Get in that one," he ordered. Gina and Maxwell, clutching three wine bottles, followed behind them.

"There's no room."

"Yes, there is. The two front seats."

Cheryl arranged herself next to the window, smoothing her Louis Feraud skirt over her knees, took out a compact mirror and rewaxed her lips. Fishman sat beside her and pulled Gina onto his lap.

"Do you mind? You're the lightest."

She shrugged and still managed to look graceful perched on his knee. Maxwell hung in the open door, drinking wine from the lip of a bottle.

"What's the delay?" called Fishman, curling his hand around Gina's thigh.

Maxwell stuck his head back through the door. "It's the driver. He says he won't leave with so many people on the bus."

"Why not?"

"He says it's illegal," answered Maxwell, the luminary of the Admiralty Bar.

"Illegal!" echoed Fishman, the senior tax partner.

"He refuses to discuss it. He says he knows."

"Tell him to shut up and drive the bus."

"It's no use. He says he won't break the law."

Fishman sighed. "I guess I'll have to pay him off. Excuse me, Gina." He lifted her by the waist from his lap and scrambled out of the bus.

A few minutes later, the driver got in and started up the engine. Fishman took his seat again under Gina. Maxwell hoisted himself onto the floorspace next to the driver, where he crouched in front of Fishman and Gina and continued to guzzle.

The radio played loudly as they all bumped toward Manhattan.

Maxwell reached for the arch of Gina's naked foot in her skimpy sandals. The skin, all along the instep, was baby smooth, just as he had imagined. He ran his thumb around her ankle. She did not move. The bus lurched at a traffic light. Maxwell took another swig and returned to explore the crevices between her toes.

Maxwell knew he was too drunk for a firm party. It was a lush, easy, thrilling intoxication. As long as Gina did not move her foot away...

Cheryl and Fishman were occupied talking together. Boldly Maxwell reached higher, up her calf, where he felt the cloth of the baby-blue skirt, and beneath it the firm leg muscles, warm with racing blood. Still she did not draw back.

They crossed the Henry Hudson Bridge into Manhattan and roared down the West Side Highway. For Maxwell it was all too soon. He would have liked the bus ride to last for hours, while all the time he caressed the baby-blue gingham. The bus jolted and heaved him toward the driver. His head swam. Maybe he should have resisted those final bottles.

Fishman murmured in Gina's ear, "I have a dilemma. What shall I do? Do I pay for all these associates to get into the Palladium?"

"How much does it cost?"

"Ten dollars a head."

"Why should you pay?"

"Because I am the richest person on the bus."

"Shouldn't Cheltenham pay for them?"

"You see, I am Cheltenham."

"I guess you should pay."

While he was standing in line to check Gina's tote bag, which held her towel and bathing suit, the nausea hit Maxwell. The floor rocked beneath him, reminding him of his wife Eleanor's scorn, which would greet him later when he dragged himself through the door. He hoped she had gone to bed already. But he knew she always stayed up late on the evenings of firm parties, waiting, like a jackal, to trap him at whatever hour he returned.

He found Fishman dancing with Cheryl, and he pressed Gina's coat check into his hand. "Take care of this," he grunted. "It's too noisy for me here. I have to go."

Drunk as he was, he could not cope with Gina tonight. Anyway, more pressing was the cross of Eleanor he would have to bear in the next hour, and then tomorrow, and years into the future. Maxwell had long since resigned himself to the disappointment of his decaying marriage. Yet he had considered divorce only fleetingly. It would involve the reorganization of so much money, not to mention the four children. He had never met another woman who tempted him sufficiently to explode his well-ordered life.

Almost a year later, as they lay on her lumpy mattress, sipping Courvoisier and half following *Camille* on her VCR, Gina had recounted to him the scene he had left behind at the Palladium.

"Where's Maxwell gone?" she had asked Fishman, whom she finally located drinking at the bar.

"He went home. He left your coat check."

"He left? Why?" Gina felt crushed.

"He's totally shit-faced. I haven't seen him in such bad shape in years." Gina had realized Maxwell was drunk, of course. Actually it made him approachable, stripped him of several layers of the superiority he commanded by his confidence and articulation and partnership.

Fishman ordered her another drink. "That was quite a bus ride!" he shouted. "That's the closest I've ever got to knowing what faggots feel."

"What?"

"I had Clancy Maxwell feeling up my legs all the way from the Henry Hudson Bridge. I think the pass was intended for you, Gina. At least I certainly hope so."

"Maxwell was stroking your legs all the way to New York? And you didn't say anything?"

When Gina had finally recounted to him the horrible tale, Maxwell had pretended to laugh, while inside he groaned with mortification. Did the members and associates of Cheltenham smirk at him, remembering that he was the man who had caressed Gary Fishman's legs all the way back to Manhattan?

"Oh, that bus ride," sighed Maxwell, closing his eyes and withdrawing his hand from Gina's thigh.

The day following the July outing she had met him carrying a tray of lasagna out of the cafeteria at lunch. Their eyes exchanged the usual glance of complicity.

"I looked for you," said Gina. "I'm sorry you left so early."

"It was so darned noisy there. I think I'm getting too old for these wild nights of disco parties after firm functions." Did she notice, he wondered, the chalky hue of his hangover and the deepened furrows around his mouth and forehead? "You looked beautiful yesterday. That blue dress suits your coloring."

Summer yielded to fall. Clancy and Eleanor Maxwell took a two-week trip down the Rhine and on to Vienna, which they had planned for a long time. Afterward, Maxwell was glad to get back to his work. At Christmas Eleanor's mother died, and his eldest son turned down an acceptance at Harvard in favor of a career as a rock musician. In the early spring, he and Eleanor spent a long weekend with old friends in St. Croix. They quarreled on the airplane. Then she withdrew sullenly into herself.

Eleanor had preserved her talent for cool withdrawal. Despite her fine bones and once ash-blond hair, she had never been a pretty woman; distinguished, at best, in her tartan kilts and cameo brooches. Now she had withered, as if her inner frigidity had finally taken hold in her face. Over the years she had lost her husband's attention and the proximity of her powerful family, along with her youth. But she had hung on to her capacity for disdain.

Eleanor's Bostonian family had been a valuable asset to Maxwell during his early years at Cheltenham. Even before he had become a partner, he found himself able to introduce prestigious old-time clients of the musty variety Cheltenham so cherished in those days.

That had only been a part of Eleanor's appeal for him. It was just as important to Maxwell that her ancestors lay buried in the King's Chapel burying ground, alongside John Winthrop and the Reverend Joseph Cotton, who had led the powerful Congregationalist church with seventeenth-century zeal. When Maxwell watched her measuring out the cat food, or labeling her homemade boysenberry preserves, or picking at her needlepoint, he sometimes fancied he could see in her sober gestures the ghosts of her Puritan family who had settled in Salem in 1628. He also sometimes caught a glimpse of the mercilessness of her ancestor Thomas Prescott, who had burned witches, and the stubbornness of Otis Cobb, who, disguised as an Indian, had hurled the bales of tea into Boston Harbor.

When he first knew her, Eleanor's background had fascinated him. Their bickering, however, had dulled the sheen of her one trump card, the thrilling history she carried in her blood. These days, as Maxwell glanced at her pruning the window boxes in her rumpled gardening gloves, it seemed less compelling that Otis Cobb had fought at the bridge at Concord, the first encounter of the American Revolution.

Meanwhile Maxwell continued to come across Gina, sometimes after long intervals. Her lashes still fluttered when they spoke. It was astonishing how, in a large firm, between the five floors one might not see people for weeks at a time. They were all closeted in their office cells, tangled in their telephones. Maxwell noticed that Gina rarely ate lunch in the cafeteria.

One June day, eleven months after the infamous bus ride, he resolved to visit Gina's office.

When he opened her door, she sat smoking idly, staring at the wall, a blank legal pad in front of her.

"Are your busy?"

"No, no. Come in."

"Still working on Vaginex?"

"It never ends. The plaintiffs keep coming up with new expert testimony."

"Still enjoying the life of law?"

She exhaled and stubbed out her cigarette. "I get frustrated and depressed at how little I know. People here are so brilliant. I'll never be able to remember and explain things and argue the way Mick Finnegan does."

"You mustn't let Finnegan get you down. He's an interesting guy, but he's always been a showoff."

"The way he can take an issue and turn it inside out. The way he uses language."

"It comes with practice."

"I'll never get it. Sometimes I work here all night, till three or four A.M., to prepare a draft for him. He'll look at it for five minutes the next morning and tell me I've missed the whole argument."

"Maybe you need a change of pace. Wider experience. Are you interested in shipping?"

"I don't know anything about it."

"I'm working on a time charter for the *Shanghai Emerald*. You want to help?"

"What's a time charter?"

"The contract between the owner and operator of a vessel."

"Okay." She crossed and recrossed her legs. She was wearing gray patterned tights and a plum-colored skirt.

"Why not stop by my office then, say around nine-thirty, after dinner. I'll give you the preliminary documents and explain the procedures to you."

Maxwell returned to the forty-ninth floor, sat down on his low-slung leatherette couch, and stared gloomily at the rug. Normally he avoided looking at the carpet, which gave him a blinding headache. Eleanor had picked it out, an electric blue criss-crossed with black-diamond hatching. He grudgingly admired the subtle sadism of the choice. She had decorated his entire office, choosing the colors that most disgusted him, pictures that depressed him, furniture too uncomfortable to sit in for long. Beginning to feel dizzy, he looked away from the carpet and reached for the private line of his telephone.

"Hello, dear."

"Yes, dear."

"I'm really sorry. Something's come up. Ariel wants me to come to dinner with a new client at the Harvard Club. I won't be able to make it back till late."

"Clancy! We're supposed to have dinner with the Madisons. We haven't seen them in months."

"Sorry, dear. I can't do it. You'll have to go without me or make an excuse."

"Really, Clancy, you're infuriating. Can't you stand up to Ariel and tell him you've got an engagement? You're a powerful partner. How can you let him push you around? What are you, a spineless wimp?"

"I guess I am," said Maxwell. "Sorry." He hung up.

Gina came to his office at nine twenty-eight. He motioned her to the couch.

"Have you eaten?" he asked.

"I sent out for Chinese."

Without asking her, he took a bottle of Four Star Napoleon from a lacquered side cabinet he particularly loathed, with a couple of brandy snifters. Maxwell was one of the few partners who, flouting protocol, dared to keep a small supply of alcohol in his office. He put the bottle on the coffee table, scooped up an armload of files, and settled himself next to her. He thanked Eleanor for finding him a couch so low to the floor.

They raised their glasses to drink. Gina's lashes fluttered.

Maxwell spread the papers and explained the components of the agreement. Price, duration of voyage, permitted ports. He brought out samples of some earlier contracts as models. She studied the terms with concentration.

She looked up suddenly. "Is that your wife?" she asked sharply, pointing to the silver-framed photograph of Eleanor leaning against the porch of their Massachusetts summer house.

He looked at her intensely. "I'm married. I'm sorry. Do you mind?"

She put down the brandy snifter and leaned back against the Navaho embroidered cushion. "Of course I know you're married. Eleanor Charlotte, age forty-four. Children: Michael eighteen, Julia sixteen, Louise twelve, Oliver nine."

He was taken aback. "How do you know?"

"It's all listed in the Cheltenham Professional Directory."

He stared at her hesitantly, first at the bracelet she always wore, then into her glinting eyes. "Gina, I don't have to tell you, do I? You know how I feel."

"Of course I know."

He picked up her wrist and fingered her palm lightly. "You don't have to do this."

"I know."

"I can't give you much time. It's complicated, with my family."

"It's all right."

"You are discreet, aren't you? If Lamb or Samson found out..."

"I'd lose my job. Not you."

"Gina," he said. "You're so beautiful." And he kissed her.

She let her sandals slither from her feet to the floor. He reached around her back, slid his hand between her skirt waist and her back, then on under her pantyhose, to explore her nymphette hips and behind. Her ass was taut and lean, like a boy's. Feeling the warmth and pulse against his little finger, he squeezed her body to him and kissed her again, more deeply. She breathed heavily and reached for the zipper on her plum skirt.

"No. Wait. Let me do it."

He wrestled with the clasp, and as it finally released, slid the skirt down her hips and over her long legs. The silk cravat knotted around her neck dissolved with one tug. Deftly he undid the blouse and drew it from her shoulders. Her breasts were small, and that excited him more. She stretched her body the length of the couch, so he could more easily roll down the pantyhose to her ankles, past her feet.

This was a million times more real than he had imagined. She lay obediently on Eleanor's wretched sofa, her straight-hipped body as fresh as a Botticelli goddess in spring. She was his.

She watched tranquilly while he caressed the delicate breasts and the inside of her thighs. Then, swiveling her whole body, she pulled him onto the couch and, reaching for his fly, kneeled on the floor with bowed head. When she took his cock in her mouth his blood raced and he felt his whole body heave. It was delicious, irresistible, beyond negotiation. He came in a torrential rush, over her mouth and chin and chest, over the criss-crossed hatching of Eleanor's electric-blue rug.

"I'm sorry. I couldn't wait."

"It's all right."

He reached for her hand for a second when they heard the brisk knock at the door.

"Just a minute! Who is it?"

"Tristan."

Maxwell, glancing at Gina, who crouched like a Venus de Milo against the couch, put a finger to his lips and sprang up to meet Tristan at the door.

"Are you feeling well, Clancy? You look a little . . . er, flushed."

"I'm fine. Could we talk tomorrow, Tristan?" He edged through the door and closed it behind him.

"I've just got a quick question for you. Trading with the Enemy Act."

"Can't it wait until the morning?"

"Not really. I have to advise at a breakfast meeting. Which are the prohibited countries for commercial transactions these days? North Korea, Vietnam, Cuba . . ."

"Iran and Libya. I really can't go into the details now."

"How about South Africa? Surely there are some restrictions?"

"No overall prohibition. Certain forbidden goods, like weapons. I'll be glad to give you a full explanation tomorrow."

"Okay. Thanks, Clancy. You sure about South Africa now?"

"Good-night, Tristan."

She was already dressed again when he returned. She stooped, patting at the white smear on the carpet with a Kleenex. "I'm afraid this won't come out."

He examined the trophy of his victory with a touch of complacency. "Tristan's got a client with a Japanese product that removes all kinds of stains. I'll ask him for a sample."

During the following forty-eight hours Maxwell wallowed in a morass of indecision. He sat at his detested ebony desk, his gaze drifting from the damaged rug to the silver-framed photograph of Eleanor and back to the couch where Gina had lain like a nubile Greek statue. The memory of Gina's white shoulders and adolescent hips made him dislike Eleanor more than ever, so he bought Eleanor a bunch of peonies on his way home, and did not telephone Gina.

Two evenings later, he telephoned Gina at her home number.

"It's Clancy. What are you doing?"

"Reading an article on vaginal contractions."

"Is it entertaining?"

"I'd rather be reading Tolstoy."

"Or how about seeing me?"

"That would be better than Tolstoy."

"I'm on my way home. May I stop by your apartment?"

"It's Four D. My name's not on the door."

He stopped by the florist en route, where he had bought Eleanor's peonies, and picked out the same for Gina, a double quantity.

She greeted him at the door of her apartment, wearing only an oversize man's shirt. Tossing the peonies into the kitchen sink, he scooped up her weightless body and carried her through the living room, into the bedroom at the back. The parquet floor, which needed polish, was strewn with files and papers. None of the colors of the upholstery matched. The furniture and slipcovers all looked as if they had been snatched up in a single afternoon, from a bazaar or street fair. Lamps and ashtrays and crazy bric-a-brac crowded on one another.

Maxwell did not notice the mess until later. He hoisted the fragile body onto the bed and fell on top of her. The affair was well and truly launched.

W hat is it, Clancy?"

He looked away from the butterfly ashtray and smiled creamily. "I love you, Gina."

"How much?"

"More than I ever thought possible."

"Enough to take me to the movies?"

"Not tonight. I must get home. I have to see Eleanor."

Gina turned her head to the window so he should not see how the jealousy still stabbed. It was only a matter of time, they had agreed, until he made a clean break. He wanted to marry her, Gina. She would become his wife. The assurance of it taught her patience, strengthened her resources so that she felt she could deal with anything—her work, her solitude, her isolation.

The isolation was almost bearable. She and Clancy shared the exile of a truly illicit relationship. It was bad enough, Gina knew, to get involved with married men in any event. This liaison, which had imperiled her career, had also ostracized her from her friends, her family, even the support of her Cheltenham peers. She had confided in no one at the firm except, in an unguarded moment, Cheryl Litvak.

"Sorry about tonight," said Maxwell. "I'll make it up to you."

"Will you take me to *Swan Lake*?"

"Gina, don't do this to me. You know I can't. It's too public. Someone might see us. Someone from here."

"I guess." She checked herself from reminding him of the early days of the affair when he had run around like an intoxicated addict, incapable of refusing her anything. A year later he had become more circumspect. "You got any friends in the Tax Department, precious?"

Except for Cheryl, Gina had few friends at all. One after another she had abandoned those she had made during her first year. She ignored the invitations to the associates' parties, the after-work get-togethers at Flutie's Restaurant, and the noisy, sweaty Saturday night crushes of fifty people in someone's one-bedroom apartment.

"I know a few people."

"You know David Gleiner?"

"I know who he is."

"What's he like?"

"Kind of a nerd. Works twenty-three hours a day. He's always got a panicked look like a frightened rabbit. People say he's a sweet guy, though."

"You ever really talk to him?"

"He once lent me twenty bucks for a taxi. Oh, and he gave me a long explanation of the tax treatment of foreign holders of mortgage-backed securities. He was very patient. He's nice like that. Why, Clancy?"

Maxwell hesitated. He shared most of his partnership gossip with Gina. He had told her about Tristan Barrett's divorce, and how Mick Finnegan had been seriously reprimanded for his drinking, about the warfare between Der Fuhrer and Il Duce, how Gary Fishman padded his billing and cheated his clients, how he himself had taken a private trip to buy upholstery in Hong Kong and written it off against a client. He had already mentioned to her the excitement over the new TBO instrument, and the partnership's hopes that it would yield a windfall.

Yet he shrank from discussing the mole. Something about the crime, which threatened the fortunes of the whole partnership, tangled with the deepest roots of Maxwell's loyalty. Flip though he might be about his work, his marriage, and even his brethren, the mole story smacked of a treason at which he drew the line.

He glanced at his watch. "I must run. I've got a conference call at four with Aegean Lines. You heard any news about the TBO?"

"Nothing major. Someone mentioned that Caroline Brothers has a team down in—where was it—Ecuador."

"Ecuador!"

"Or maybe it was Paraguay. Why would they be there?"

"Who told you that?"

"I forget. It sounded screwy anyway."

She looked at him questioningly as he stood in her doorway. Why should he ask her, of all people, about the TBO? Now that they had formed a working coalition, he had Ariel Lamb's own ear. He could go straight to Der Fuhrer himself for information.

"Will you be on the deal, Clancy?"

"Who knows? Maybe. Everyone's got to be prepared to do some corporate finance these days if they want to stay alive here."

He turned to leave. They both twitched at the sound of the knock at her door, as they always did when they were together in the office. Maxwell stepped aside to let Cheryl enter.

"Am I interrupting?"

"I was just going." Maxwell hurried out.

"He really was," said Gina. "He's got a conference call. You must be busy, getting ready to leave for your spa in Arizona."

"I had to cancel. Fishman needed a stockholders' agreement drafted at the eleventh hour."

"Did you reschedule?"

"Not yet. But I will. I haven't managed to get away in eighteen months."

"You must take some time."

She shrugged. "It's that final year before partnership."

"You'll make it. You've put in nine solid years."

"None of it counts if you screw up in the final one."

Cheryl sat down in the chair by the desk and examined a loose thread in her jacket. There was a strictly observed rule among associates at Cheltenham of "one office, one chair." It was part of the unwritten constitution that, in a gathering of three or more associates, the most senior-ranking lawyer was entitled to the single extra chair. As attorneys stuck their heads in and out of one another's offices, the chair was deftly surrendered and acknowledged according to the prevailing seniority. The rule, in addition to containing costs on associate furniture, tended to discourage prolonged and time-wasting group gatherings. On the other hand it encouraged tête-à-têtes and conspiracy.

"Nice belt, Gina."

"He bought it for me. He's promised to take me to Saint Martin."

"It's about time. He's never taken you farther than the Bronx Zoo till now. You have to start training him. This is no fun. It's no way for you to live."

"He's doing his best."

"Men! He's got a terrific deal."

"Don't be like that. He really loves me."

"Clancy's always been a player."

"He's told me about the other affairs. He's been honest. They were different."

Cheryl looked pitying. "There are no secrets at Cheltenham. Not for long, anyway. You'd be amazed how walls have ears. Plus they bug the telephones."

"Not Clancy."

"I've known him for nine years. We've always been friendly. We used to have dinner together in the cafeteria from time to time. I remember once he danced with me a whole evening at the Christmas party, and it was," she said, smiling, "nice."

What Gina did not know was the small story Cheryl had neglected to report. She had never described how Maxwell, after some pleasurable dancing at the Christmas party at the Waldorf, had nimbly organized a room for the two of them in the hotel upstairs. They had spent an hour or so frolicking in a double king-size bed together. Cheryl remembered the Christmas party better than she remembered the sex, which had not been sufficiently compelling to leave her with a lingering nostalgia for him. In fact, before the drama of Gina's affair, Cheryl had almost excised the brief physical memory. Unless Clancy Maxwell had managed to obliterate it altogether—unlikely—he, too, had "forgotten" to mention that encounter to Gina.

"How was your date on Monday, Cheryl?"

"After a thousand and one dates, Gina, you learn the knack of weeding them out early. I don't need this guy. I'm smarter than he is, I've got a bigger career, I'm going to make more money. What's he got to offer except stepfathership?"

"Does he like kids?"

"When I told him about Peggy Ann's dyslexia he didn't exactly jump for joy. They're problem children. Face it. Bobby's only ten and he's already had three and a half years of therapy. Peggy Ann's gifted, that's what all the teachers say. So how come she's eight and she can't learn to read?"

"It can't be easy growing up with a working mother."

"It's true I don't get much time with them. But God knows I bought them the best. There was the English nanny when they were babies, and then Claudine, the French governess. I wanted them to grow up bilingual." She sighed. "Well, I tried."

"I'm sure it would be good for them if you got married again."

"Yeah, all the psychiatrists and teachers say so too. But I can't give up my life and interfere with my career just to provide an atmosphere for my children. Now that I'm older and much more successful, my standards are higher than ever. I'm not going to settle down with anyone who isn't very prosperous and very high-powered and very savvy."

Gina nodded. Cheryl's worldliness still intimidated her. When it came to experience in restaurants or clothes or men, she did not question Cheryl's sophistication. She had traveled all over Europe, to Paris and Vienna and Rome. She knew the paintings of the Louvre and the Uffizi and even went to antique jewelry auctions at Sotheby's. She shopped at Hermès, at Cartier, at Christian Dior; she picked up two-thousand-dollar creations at

Martha. Every now and again, when she finally managed a vacation, she would spend a precious week in Palm Air or at the Golden Door or one of the other ultraexpensive spas. To Gina, whose entire notion of materialism and sophistication dated back to the day she had joined Cheltenham, Arbuthnot & Crewe, Cheryl passed through life on a remote, intangible plane. One day perhaps Gina, too, might be able to criticize the quail's egg soufflé at Lutèce or the new autumn colors at Balenciaga. For the present, though, Cheryl's disdains and concerns seemed as remote as those of the Romanov emperors.

"Are you working this weekend, Cheryl?"

"Yes, damn it. Gary Fishman needs a whole group of new companies incorporated in the Bahamas. He wants it first thing Sunday morning. You know it's Bobby's birthday on Saturday, and I'd promised to take him to the circus, so I can guarantee there are going to be tears again. But what can I do?"

"It's his tenth birthday. Surely Gary would understand."

"Try again. Clients before kids."

"Tell him to get fucked."

"I can't. He's putting me up for partner. Without his support, I'll never make it."

"You can't let that spoiled baby of a man ruin your life."

"Partnership's so close. I've put in a lot of years. Now I want the big bucks."

"I want you to make it. I'll be so proud of you. The second woman partner ever out of all those men."

The first woman partner, a specialist in environmental law in Cheltenham's Santa Fe office, had little visibility.

"Clancy thinks you've got a good chance. Cheltenham needs another woman partner at this point. Almost all the other major firms have a tiny handful of them. We have to keep up our reputation."

Cheryl grimaced. "At what price glory?"

"Isn't there any way you could get away on Saturday? Poor Bobby."

"David Gleiner knows a lot about these offshore deals. If he'd help me, I could probably speed it up."

"Ask him."

"The guy's up to his eyeballs already. He bills even more time than I do. He was here ninety-five hours last week."

"Try." Gina dialed Gleiner's internal number and handed the telephone over to Cheryl.

"David? It's Cheryl Litvak. Are you crazy busy? Yeah, I know, I mean, who isn't? I was going to ask you a hell of a favor. Please feel free to refuse. I've got to set up a bunch of offshores in the Bahamas for Fishman. Could I pick your brains on it? Right now? I'm in Gina de Angelo's office. God bless you, David. Fantastic. See you in a minute, then." She hung up and turned back to Gina. "What a real nice fellow. He's on his way up here now."

"He is nice."

"Poor David. It's a pity he's so funny looking. I wish he could find a girlfriend."

"If only he could stand up straight. Who wants to go out with a human question mark?"

"And that weird way he twists his mouth, so he kind of mutters out of the side of it."

"I heard that he was in a terrible car accident and that's how he got that Frankenstein look. Apparently something went wrong with the plastic surgery and they couldn't quite fix it afterward."

"I don't believe it. It's just a myth. He was born that way."

"Shh."

Gleiner limped into Gina's office, holding his neck at the distorted angle. His skin was brilliant pink around the cuffs and collar, where his nervous rash had arrived in its inexorable progression.

"I really appreciate this, David," said Cheryl.

The issue of the single chair had first to be resolved. Cheryl, being two years senior to Gleiner, was privileged to maintain the seat, but as Gleiner was here purely as a courtesy to her, she stood.

"That's okay. You sit."

"No, please. Go ahead."

"No, it does me good to stand. I've been sitting all day. Besides, I seem to have dislocated a muscle in my back. I'm supposed to try to keep moving."

"How awful," said Gina. "Does it hurt badly?"

"It's excruciating. Nothing helps but this morphine compound I've been taking. I've been to two orthopedic surgeons and a chiropractor. None of them can do a damn thing."

"How did you do it?"

"The usual way. I'd been working all night and the next day I had to carry a heavy suitcase of documents down to Atlanta. The exhaustion and the strain."

"What a bummer."

"The drag is, now I'm back in physical therapy again. Two mornings a week. As if I can afford the time."

"How can I ask you for even more time?" said Cheryl guiltily.

"Forget it. What's the problem? Shoot."

"I wouldn't normally do this, but it's my son's birthday on Saturday. I'd promised to take him to the circus—you know I'm divorced—his father's in Michigan—and now Fishman wants me to set up these offshores."

"No problem. I do that stuff all the time. I've got a dozen files of good models in my office. We'll do it together."

"Have you any time this evening?"

"Tonight's no good. I'm having dinner with Courage. Tomorrow night."

"That would be swell. We could order in pizza together."

"I'm not allowed pizza," said Gleiner mournfully.

"You on a diet?"

"Kind of. Nothing spicy or hot or cold or raw vegetables. My ulcer. I eat chicken chow mein mostly. Or mashed potatoes. How old's your son?"

Cheryl thought for a moment. "Ten."

"I like the circus. I'd go with you."

"You're a saint, David. That way I can stay at the office and you can take Bobby for me."

"He wants you, not me."

"I've got a lot of other things here to finish up. That'd be such a help, David. I can't thank you enough."

Gleiner checked his watch, took a capsule out of his pocket, put it in his mouth and swallowed. "I'll call you tomorrow and we'll crack those offshores. I've gotta run now."

*   *   *

"I'm selling the house in Nantucket," grieved Mick Finnegan as they weaved past a television news crew who had set up their vans and cameras on the corner of Water Street. In the heady eighties, it sometimes seemed as though the downtown financial district had become the news center of the earth.

Tristan Barrett shoved his right hand deep in his overcoat pocket. In his left he carried his battered, crammed briefcase. "Maybe it's a good time to sell," he agreed. "If this recession everyone's predicting hits soon, property prices are going to plummet."

"God knows what I'll do."

"Litigation business might pick up."

"Wouldn't make any difference for me. I'm a dead man here. You see how they all looked at me today at the partnership meeting? Even if I doubled my billables, they'd never reinstate my points now."

"You should start looking around, Mick. At least start talking to people about other jobs."

"I've been a partner at Cheltenham for fourteen years. It's not so easy to get started again at my stage in life. I'm too experienced, too expensive for people to hire. Sometimes I think of throwing it all up and going to live on some peat farm in County Clare."

Thus far in his life, Finnegan had never spent more than four

65

consecutive days in Ireland. Tristan knew the proclaimed nostalgia for his grandfather's ancient soil had no foothold in reality.

"Hmm. And what would your wife say to that?"

Finnegan shouted back, over the din of a construction drill, "She'd probably leave me. But she's probably going to leave me anyhow."

"Hang in there. It's been a hell of a month. It's a bad time of year. You'll feel better when we get to the Athletic Club and get a drink or two inside us."

The north wind howled down Wall Street, swirling the garbage and fast-food wrappers like confetti across the sidewalks, and spitting the city's dust and grime into the partners' eyes. The rush-hour crowds still streamed toward the subways, buffeted by the wind like flotsam and jetsam in an angry sea. Despite the tinny festivity of the Christmas decorations, it was that time of day, and that time of year, that could drive even comfortable souls to thoughts of despair.

They passed the hot dog vendor, an old woman in a Ukrainian head scarf, who always stood with her cart at the same corner of William Street. Tristan had noticed her now for a couple of years, although perhaps she had been there long before her presence made any impact on him. He had first caught her eye one summer evening as he hurried past. She had then worn a torn, stained cotton dress, stretched too tightly over her huge hips and stomach. Even at a distance he noticed her black palms and fingernails. Had it not been for the filthy hands he might have bought a hot dog, as a token almsgiving. He could not have eaten it, though; he did not want to carry it with him, and he could not throw it away in her sight. Her fat face, with its slit eyes, was impenetrable. Did she feel anything at all as she watched the surge of office workers in crisp collars flow from their sterile cubbyholes down into the earth to the jammed subway platforms? Then he became doomed to notice her every night, as the evenings grew longer and chillier. She always wore the same floral-patterned rag of a dress, with no sweater or shawl. Only late in the damp of autumn she wrapped her fingers in pieces of cloth, like a tramp. But she was not a tramp. She still had her vending cart. Finally, after the temperatures dipped below freezing, she buried herself in a dirty quilt. She probably still wore the same dress underneath. Just once, the day his wife had announced she was divorcing him, and he knew she meant it too, Tristan had given the old woman a ten-dollar bill. She had taken it in the cloth-bound fingers and looked at it suspiciously, waving the metal tongs confusedly at the row of sizzling frankfurters. "Just keep it," said Tristan uncomfortably. For a moment he thought she was going to give it back. After the hesitation she nodded matter-of-factly, without smiling. He wondered if she ever smiled.

"Sometimes," said Finnegan as they crossed Broad Street, "I almost wish I were a young associate just starting out now. I'd do things differently."

"We had more fun," said Tristan. "These kids nowadays get overpaid a fortune, but they sweat blood for it."

"We worked hard too. Didn't we?"

"It was different. It felt more like a family then. The firm demanded your life, but in return you knew they'd take care of you if you did your job and said your prayers. Nowadays it's anyone's guess who'll be the next victim."

"Probably me," answered Finnegan grimly.

The crowd hummed around the massive Christmas tree outside the Stock Exchange. A persistent Santa Claus clanged his bell loudly in the partners' ears as they braved the mean wind. A couple of secretaries, laden with shopping bags, teetered a few steps ahead.

"Don't be paranoid, Mick. It only makes it worse. But maybe you should think about getting some kind of résumé together. Just in case."

"A résumé! At my age! You know there was a time I was a litigation superstar in one of the top law firms in the country."

"You'll get back again. You've still got the talent. The brilliance."

"Remember my legend? The whiz kid. The irony is they still

say I'm brilliant, an eccentric litigation genius, and yet nobody gives a damn. They don't need genius these days. They still come to pick my brains with their questions on obscure points of law, 'cause they know no one else in the firm can answer them. But they don't need me anymore to perform a day's work."

They reached the Irving Trust Building at the corner of Broadway. A beggar in a sinister dark hood blocked their path, rattling a can of coins practically in Finnegan's face. In his other arm he carried a crudely lettered sign with the legend, I HAVE NO HOME AND NO WORK. PLEASE HELP ME AND MY FAMILY. The partners avoided looking at each other as they brushed past him. Tristan reached into his pocket for a couple of quarters.

One landed and one missed, rolling onto the sidewalk. The beggar stamped down on it expertly to break its spin. "Thank you, gentlemen. Merry Christmas. God bless you," he hissed.

"Sometimes I hate this place," said Tristan.

"It's no better in Midtown these days."

Tristan gritted his teeth. "Poor fellow."

Turning into Rector Street, Finnegan shook his head. "That could be me."

"Not quite yet." They hurried on silently toward the warmth and cheer of the New York Downtown Athletic Club, passing Trinity Church, where the monumental statue of John Watts in his judicial wig kept quiet vigil in the graveyard.

*   *   *

Gleiner went to Courage's office. He found him hunched over his desk, munching reflectively from a carton of Oreo cookies, and glowering at the amplifier of his speaker phone. He appeared to be in an interminable argument with a lawyer from Moody's rating agency. Seeing Gleiner, he whispered with a sigh, "We go round and round in circles. They know I've got to get a triple A rating, that Caroline can't sell the deal with anything less secure. They know they'll give it to me. They just carry on and on, wearing me out with their clueless questions."

"Take your time, Peter." Gleiner picked up a copy of *Sailing World* lying under a stack of registration statements.

Finally Courage finished and asked, "You want to go up to the cafeteria? There's roast loin of pork tonight."

"No. Let's go out to the Seaport."

"You've got time?" The senior associates rarely went out to one of the restaurants at the South Street Seaport mall. It took too long when they knew they must return for many more hours into the night.

"I want to talk to you privately. If we go to the cafeteria, someone'll sit down with us."

Courage was surprised. Gleiner rarely broke away from work for longer than to fetch a tray from the cafeteria and bring it back to his desk. His office, as a result, usually smelled of food, as dirty plates piled up neglected amidst the documents, and the windows took on a sheath of thin grease. Even Courage, who was not particularly fastidious, preferred not to go in there.

The two lawyers strolled along Water Street toward the Seaport. The mall consisted of a cluster of restaurants, and of novelty, souvenir, and scented-candle shops, built up along what had once been a real pier. Although rush hour was over, the sidewalks were still thick with office workers hurrying home through the brisk night, swinging briefcases and swerving past the curb to bellow for taxis. The red and white lights of Christmas decorations shed an artificial cheer, a charmless festivity that never quite convinced the financial district. For the attorneys, the holiday season represented little more than a few extra drinks and, with luck, a couple of extra days to grab some longed-for sleep.

"How's the rash?" asked Courage.

"It's itching like hell around my ankles. The dermatologist wants to put me on fifteen milligrams of Valium a day, but how can I keep up with the work if I'm doped like a zombie?"

"I still say you need that vacation."

"Maybe in January. But I've nowhere to go. I've no one to go with. I usually end up going with my aunt to Miami. I can't face another week at the Fontainebleau, watching stand-up comedians and being fixed up with very kosher dates to go out with and eat ice-cream sundaes. I'm too old."

"Take a cruise by yourself. You can afford it. Go round the islands."

"I'd only get more lonely. I'm better off at Cheltenham."

They ate at the Liberty Café, a glorified sandwich restaurant that served blackened crayfish with avocado and alfalfa shoots on a split croissant. The drinking crowd of brokers had gone home now; only a couple of tables were occupied. A man mopped the aisles around them with a flood of soapy water, while somewhere behind their table a bucket caught a drip from the leaking roof in depressing monotony.

Courage ordered a Budweiser and Gleiner a Coke and fettucini in clam sauce.

"How's your Caroline deal, Peter?"

"I met a goddess at the printer."

"At the printer? What kind of goddess?"

"A Viking goddess, I think. At least she comes from Minnesota. Her name's Michelle Peterson. She's on the team from Caroline Brothers. She's really pretty—gorgeous actually—and she's unbelievably smart. She looks young, but she's already a vice president."

"Is she nice?"

"She's not a human person like us, David. You can't use words like *nice* to talk about superhuman beings. And I get to spend the weekend with her."

"Fast work."

"Not quite the way I'd want. We have to fix up the board resolutions and the officers' certificates for the preclosing on Monday. She's been assigned to work with me over the next couple of days."

"Dirty, maybe, but not my idea of a romantic weekend."

"I've got to start somewhere. This is a quality woman. She wouldn't even look at me if I just asked her out. It's a gift from heaven, getting two days' access to her in a work environment."

"Maybe you'll even find out what she's like."

"Who cares? I mean, I sort of got the picture already. This woman's no bimbo. She's real serious about what she does. Real good at it too. She thinks about her job, and she makes a lot of money, and she looks like a porcelain doll with the body of Brooke Shields."

"She sounds like a boring, tight-assed yuppie pinup to me."

"She's beautiful, David."

"You're thinking with your dick, Peter. Again."

Courage threw up his hands in a gesture of surrender. "I can't argue."

Gleiner plunged his fork into a mound of his pasta, and scratched behind his ear, where the rash had suddenly gained territory. "I was born to be a bachelor."

Courage ordered a second beer from a surly Irish waitress who skulked behind a row of tables already stacked up with their chairs. The Liberty Café reminded Courage of a deserted train station. "Enough about women. Let's get real. What did you want to tell me about?"

"It's about these new TBO's," began Gleiner, chasing a runaway chunk of fettucini with his fork.

"TBO's," echoed Courage with a hint of surprise. Had Gleiner dragged him out to the Seaport just to talk about the technicalities of corporate finance? "I hear it's Ariel Lamb's latest brainchild. Some kind of tax-backed debt obligation. Sounds like a lot of work for us slave labor, if you ask me. They'll tell us soon enough when they need us. What's the big deal?"

"It is a big deal. That's the point. A very big deal. If the concept flies, it'll be the biggest deal Cheltenham's ever done. And then they'll spawn like tadpoles, series and series of them."

"We'll be keeping the printer in business."

"This is major stuff, Peter. I'm not exaggerating. The partnership's staked Cheltenham's financial future on these new deals."

"We're a rich firm. If the TBO's a fuck-up, they'll invent something else."

"We're an expensive firm. We've doubled in size in the past five years. We rent the most costly office space on earth. We're on a roll, but we've got to keep up the velocity. We need those TBO's."

"You want to try some of this chili, David?"

"No, thank you. I'm not allowed chili. Too spicy. You're on partnership track. You should be concerned."

"Partnership's still several years away. A lot can happen."

"Come on. You were on P.T. from your first day. They love you. You work hard, you're handsome, you're obedient. You'll make partner. And you deserve it."

"Only 'cause I'm the last WASP at Cheltenham. But what about the TBO?"

"I've seen the initial drafts, Peter. Gary Fishman sent me a copy, so I could do some research for him on reciprocal tax treaties. Then he took the TBO papers away before I'd even had time to think of making a copy."

"So what?"

"These guys are paranoid about the deal. Someone, maybe Lamb, ordered Fishman to get those drafts back. God knows what they thought I'd do with them."

"Maybe he just needed them in a hurry."

"No. When I asked for another look, he made an excuse. And acted real strange with me. The point is, Peter, the deal is a bag of shit. It doesn't work. The SEC should never let it through."

"So what's all the fuss about, then?"

"I don't know. These guys have lost it, they've got so cocksure they think they can bulldoze the Commission into anything. That deal, as is, should never fly. It's not worth the paper it's written on."

"What's wrong with it?"

"Everything. How the fuck can anyone predict a cash flow of South American taxes five, ten years down the road? With that political instability? There'll have been a dozen revolutions by then. And what about the currency problem? Ultimately that's got to convert to a dollar value. No one'll do a swap. Who can predict the exchange rates six months from today? And what happens as the big debtor nations go into default on their loans? What's the impact? I tell you, my friend, this is the wackiest lunacy any Wall Street law firm ever dreamed up."

"Does that matter to us?"

"Not to me. I've already started talking to headhunters. I'd like to go on practicing in a smaller firm, where I'd have a shot at partnership, and maybe I could build up my own practice. I'm sick of the big time anyhow. I want to sleep at night, I want to be able to eat tamales again, I want to win the war against this rash before it gets to my toes. Maybe to you the TBO's important, though. The partnership's all riled up about the dumbest deal in eighties jazz age history."

Gleiner waved for the waitress, who had now retreated to behind the bar, where she sat huddled impenetrably behind the *National Inquirer.*

"I want the pecan pie with whipped cream," said Gleiner. He turned to Courage. "I'll probably pay for it in pain all weekend, but I can't resist."

"Now let's hear the real gossip."

"It's wild. You probably won't believe me."

"Shoot."

"I think Ariel Lamb's got a girlfriend."

"No!" Courage stared at him, incredulous. "There's no way."

"I even got a glimpse of her. From behind."

"You've been working too hard. Or maybe it's all those medications you take. Lamb would never never jeopardize his position for the sake of fooling around. He's a wind-up soldier anyhow. He doesn't care about sex."

"Maybe he does. Here's how I got suspicious. Last week I had to stop by Lamb's office to borrow his copy of the Louis Loss securities book. I happened to notice an envelope lying in his out tray, addressed to go by messenger to 888 Fifth Avenue. I only noticed it because my gastroenterologist, Doctor Goldfarb, happens to have his office downstairs in that building."

"Lord knows, you've got some doctor in most of the buildings on the Upper East Side."

"I know it's a residential address, so I look at the name of the addressee. Ms. Betty Law. How could she be an attorney with a name like that?"

"Be serious, David. That doesn't prove anything."

"Gimme a chance.

"Last night I get this uncontrollable craving for one of those shish kebabs they sell on the corner of Maiden Lane and Broadway. Of course it's equivalent to a suicide urge for someone with my condition. I just couldn't help myself. What else do I have in my life? I leave the office. I go buy the fucker, it tastes like manna from heaven. Half an hour later I think my guts are going to spill out all over the Cheltenham library. I was literally doubled over with pain. It's almost eight o'clock, but it's so excruciating I have to call Doctor Goldfarb. I get his service, it turns out he's operating, and I arrange to go up to his office and wait for him there. He's really terrific that way. He'll see you at any hour.

"Naturally I was embarrassed, having to explain what I'd eaten, but I figure there's no way around it. I pick up a cab and get to 888 Fifth. The night receptionist lets me in and I sit down in the waiting room for two of the most agonizing hours of my life. I vowed I'd spend the rest of my life on mashed potatoes if I could get through this one.

"It's almost eleven o'clock now, okay? I'm beginning to feel a little better. I flip through a few magazines. I figured maybe I could pretend to the doctor it was only a tuna fish sandwich that had started the whole thing off. I look out the window."

Courage leaned forward on his elbows. Their wobbly table rocked wildly. Coffee sloshed in the saucer and a dollop of cream splattered Gleiner's tie.

"Exactly. You guessed it. Who was at that split second getting out of a limousine outside? Not Doctor Goldfarb, alas."

"Jesus!" breathed Courage, who was paying attention now.

"No, not Him, but the next closest thing. The great Ariel Lamb himself. You get it? Eleven P.M., Ms. Betty Law...

"Well, you'll be relieved to hear that Doctor Goldfarb showed up shortly afterward. I told him I'd forgotten to take my Zantac. Like it was nothing to do with that shish kebab. He believed me."

"Wait. You said you'd actually seen her. Where?"

"I asked the doctor if he knew her. I told him I'd noticed her name 'cause it was funny, and that she was one of our clients. He said he'd talked to her a couple of times since she's got a cute dog—a Great Pyrenees—and she always walks it around eight-thirty in the morning when he's coming to work."

"Lamb's got a mistress with a Great Pyrenees!"

"Maybe he gave it to her for Chanukah. Or I guess he does Christmas these days, since he converted. So this morning on my way over to physical therapy, I hang around Goldfarb's building. It was just like he described. At eight thirty-five a woman in a lynx coat comes out with this big white monster of a dog."

"You didn't see her face?"

"I couldn't get a good look. She said something to the doorman and headed off right past Doctor Goldfarb's window."

"Amazing," said Courage, waving his vinyl menu to attract attention for the check. Their waitress seemed to have disappeared for good. Only the floor washer stood leaning on his mop and eying the Liberty Café's last customers mournfully.

"Hell, why shouldn't Lamb fool around for once?" said Gleiner, dabbing at the cream spot on his tie. "The others do, lots of them. He'll keep it separate from his work, that's for sure. We'd better pay up and get out of here. I've got to get through the First Boston prospectus before I go home. Another late night, I guess."

"Oh, shit," said Courage, glancing at his watch. "Kahn's arriving in Helsinki in a couple of hours."

As a last resort they left forty dollars in cash on the table. Outside the piazza of the Seaport was deserted. The inescapable smell of fish from the market still lingered on the knife-edge chill of the air. Gleiner pulled his coat tighter and hobbled painfully at Courage's side.

"You need a rest, David. You don't look well. You're going to get really sick and end up in the hospital like what's-his-name, that first-year litigator."

"Don't worry about me. I'll be fine. I've developed a range of antibodies for this crazy life. I'll end up outliving all the rest of you."

They turned left at Water Street and hurried toward the teal-green slab at number 57, where fifty stories above, the firm, like a primitive organism, pulsated with a life of its own.

"But I've got a call into Cyrus Sweet," Gleiner added. "He's going to do up a will for me sometime. I'd feel kind of dumb, being an attorney, and dying intestate. You got one, Peter?"

"Hell, no. Wills are for laymen."

*　　*　　*

Zuleika Elizabeth Sweet blew out the eighth of the guttering candles in the massive ebony candelabra ranged down the long dining table. Now that the room was lit only by the dim lamps reflected in the mirrors at either end, the intoxicating beauty of Park Avenue fifteen stories below them came alive. Zuleika cast an eye across the Irish lace tablecloth, where the dessert plates had not yet been cleared away. The peach and rum tart had elicited the usual cries of delight. That recipe, inherited from her great-grandmother Sadie, had stood her in good stead for forty years now.

She had been pleased by the staging of the evening. The pale silk she was wearing flattered her. She had caught Cyrus looking at her a couple of times. In the right light—and the caress of Zuleika's lamps was carefully stage managed—she could at least re-create the impression of her younger prettiness. The light was kind to him too, she had reflected. Both he and Zuleika had aged remarkably well. They had been a wonderful-looking young couple forty years ago in Kentucky, graced with every blessing of youth. She had been one of the loveliest young heiresses in Lexington, flush with old tobacco money, and Cyrus an ideal match, tall and clean cut, recently graduated from Yale Law School, with a seemingly boundless future before him.

Indeed, the promise of his career had been fulfilled, more or less, thought Zuleika, brushing away a few pastry crumbs and flicking at a speck of dripped candle wax. They had moved a couple of years later to New York, where he had family, and he had gone to work for Cheltenham. They had lived elegantly from the start, first on her tobacco money, then later, when Cyrus was crowned with the inevitable partnership, on his income.

She paused at the mirror to readjust the wilting Christmas rose pinned to her shoulder. Her chestnut eyes stared back at her, calm in their knowledge. For Zuleika Sweet, although she disguised it, was a great deal more intelligent than her husband.

She sat on committees for the zoo, the welfare of Native Americans, and the Junior League. She spent most afternoons in her Second Empire living room, surrounded by the gray-striped brocaded cushions on her Duncan Phyfe sofa, reading. She liked ancient history and archaeology.

The intelligence, as well as the tobacco money, had contributed to her happiness. Even at twenty she had guessed it was wiser to marry a man who was good looking and decent and able to converse, without being overly complicated by the drive of ambition or real brilliance. Cyrus's law practice in trusts and estates suited his temperament. It was the most personal area left among the Wall Street specializations, as it involved the old-fashioned nurture of whole families, along with the nurture of their fortunes. Cyrus and Zuleika liked to spend their time with wealthy, educated, privileged people. They were used to them.

They rarely discussed his work or Cheltenham in the evenings, because Cyrus firmly believed it to be a token of bad breeding to talk shop. Zuleika accompanied him to every one of the Cheltenham functions at which wives were allowed. She shook hands, balanced cocktail food, and made sensible conversation with a host of fresh-faced young associates and other partners' wives. As Cyrus eventually noticed, to his astonishment, she never forgot the name of any associate or the salient details of his life. She invited Tristan Barrett and his now-separated wife Pamela to dinner about four times a year, and quite enjoyed the occasion. Once a year, for Cyrus's sake, she gritted her teeth and invited the man she called "that parvenu Mel Samson," and loathed every instant of those annual ordeals.

"That was fun, darling," said Cyrus, coming up from behind

her in the dark, and brushing her bare neck with his lips. Cyrus had a theatrical side. He enjoyed the image of their reflection in the mirror with its ebony-carved cherubs and odalisques cupping candles.

"You looked lovely tonight," he said chivalrously. She wondered if he had ever told another woman just the same words in just the same tone. There would never be real competition, however. Zuleika, in the spirit of her Confederate great-grandmother Sadie, had seen to that.

A grandmaster of organization, she had arranged for Cyrus exactly the life he wanted, planting and reaping and tending his existence like a garden. They would carry on for another ten or fifteen years just this way: Cheltenham at nine each morning, twice a month the theater, once a year Mel Samson, winter weekends in Palm Beach, summer weekends on Martha's Vineyard, the River Club at Thanksgiving, once a year to Europe, Zuleika's hairdresser appointment on Wednesdays, a week in Kentucky in May.

She turned toward him, leaning against his shoulder the way they used to dance forty years ago at the Keenland Country Club in Lexington. "It was a good party. The peach tart turned out well. I'm surprised old Grenville Madison is actually retiring. I thought he'd just go on practicing until he died at his desk."

Grenville, a hoary litigator in a distinguished Midtown law firm, was an uncle of Porter Madison, the Maxwells' longstanding friend.

"Grenville's seventy-two," said Cyrus. "He's had an impeccable career. He's got nothing to be bitter about."

"He seems in perfect health. He could go on working. He'll die of boredom living out in Palm Springs." She unpinned the Christmas rose, which had begun to shed its drooping petals.

Cyrus took the rose gently from between her fingers. "He had no choice. They pushed him out." He plucked out a couple more loose petals.

"I thought old attorneys were like old soldiers, just going on."

He tucked the remains of the skeletal rose in a wave of her pale hair. She smiled up at him with coquettish Southern belle eyes.

"Zuzu, love, it's about time for me to go, too."

"What? Retire? You?"

"I'm not having fun anymore."

"But you're only sixty-one."

"I don't want to end up like Grenville. Getting squeezed out."

"What would you do instead?"

"I think I'd like to breed horses. Or maybe we'll buy a villa on the Riviera or in Tuscany. Would you like that?"

"You won't work at all anymore?"

"What could I do? I'm not fit for anything else. I've spent my whole life practicing old-fashioned law and there's nowhere except Cheltenham in the whole world I'd want to work."

"So why quit?"

"I hate to see what's happening to the place. Every day the rot gets a little worse. Ariel mentioned some shocking goings-on in this afternoon's partnership meeting. I used to care about the spirit of Cheltenham. The institution of Cheltenham. I used to think of us as a kind of beacon in a sleazy city, a real fraternity where a man could find satisfaction."

"Cyrus. That was years ago."

"I was lucky. At least I got to spend my best years building up a career in the finest professional institution in our country. And I had fun. Boy, did we have fun."

Wistfully she stroked the back of his neck. How easy it was to know someone inside out, yet still not know what he was thinking. He must have been brooding this way a long time. "Did you like Sadie's peach tart tonight?" she asked vaguely.

"Shall we have some more?"

He followed her into the kitchen, where the Haitian maid stood over the sink scouring a casserole dish.

"The tart was excellent tonight, Desiree," said Zuleika. "Everyone said so. Is there any left?"

Desiree fetched the remains from the refrigerator. Zuleika cut the wedges and slid them onto the Worcester dessert plates. They sat at the kitchen table, tired but relaxed, oblivious to the noise of running water and the maid behind them cleaning up.

"When they asked me to head up the Ethics Committee ten years ago," said Cyrus, "I thought it was a great idea. I was really interested in the codification of ethics in the Cheltenham manual, and I tried to set up a system to last us."

"Like Hammurabi," said Zuleika tenderly. "You should have been a law giver."

"Too late. Anyhow, all they really wanted was some fall guy to make decisions on matters of client conflict. To push it as far as we could get away with and bill everybody. It was a waste of time. So then I chaired the Hiring Committee instead. I figured it was a privilege to be able to round up the young lawyers who one day would be the life blood of the firm."

"You hired a lot of first-rate people," insisted Zuleika loyally.

"First-rate technicians, sure. But they have no character. Cheltenham doesn't care about character anymore. We don't even encourage it. We used to be famous for our hiring philosophy. If it were a question of law-school grades or personality, we'd take the man with personality."

"Or woman."

"Ah. That's another problem. We've got too many of them. One out of three associates is a girl these days."

"What's wrong with that, darling?"

"Oh, some of them are very dear. I have a couple working for me. They work hard and they're reliable, but they don't belong in a community like Cheltenham. We are soldiers, Zu. There's no room for women."

"Now then," protested Zuleika mildly, piling his plate on hers, "as long as they can do the work, it's not fair to keep them out." She touched the stem of the Christmas rose, where it still hung in the wave of her hair. She carried the plates and forks over to the sink. The final remains of the rose tumbled onto the linoleum. As she moved she accidentally pierced it with her spiked heel. "Though why any girl with brains would want to live a life like that, I can't imagine. No dates, no boyfriends, no fun."

FIVE

*T*his Opinion is solely for your information and is not to be quoted in whole or in part." Cheryl looked up and clicked off the recording lever on her dictating machine.

Her secretary mouthed the dreaded name. "Miss McKenzie."

Cheryl's strawberry-pink lips pouted in a gesture of impotence and she shook her head hopelessly.

Miss McKenzie was the assistant headmistress at Bigelow, where ten-year-old Bobby had now completed four semesters. Cheryl had dared hope, when he began there last year, that Bigelow might prove the long-sought solution. As a "progressive" private day school, which offered imaginative subjects to the fifth graders—Polynesian History and Arctic Environmental Studies— it claimed to encourage the children's creativity and individuality. Although the tuition was slightly higher than the other Manhattan prep schools, the amount seemed a small price to pay for such liberality.

As Bobby had already been removed, on the principals' suggestions, from two other exclusive and more traditional schools, Cheryl looked on Bigelow as a last resort. Both his previous schools agreed he was intelligent, and possibly would turn out to be gifted at math. But he was a troublemaker. First there had been a few high-spirited pranks, but then the incidents became disruptive and eventually, Cheryl swallowed as she remembered, downright nasty. He bullied the other children, he stole their books and baseball cards, he cheated, he blackmailed, he terrorized. Cheryl had tried to defend him to the headmasters; he was precocious and frustrated; perhaps the solution was for him to skip a grade, so as to compete with older children. They politely declined her suggestions. Bobby was bad news. Something was seriously awry and his mother should be seeking professional help for him.

"He already sees Dr. Fingerman twice a week," Cheryl had explained hastily. "He could go three times, I guess."

The teachers were adamant. They did not need to make special allowances for just one more bright child. They had their pick from long waiting lists of children from the most interesting, powerful, and *generous* families of New York.

Cheryl knew that they held her single parenthood against her. Of course they were all sympathy and extra-understanding smiles on the surface. They claimed they admired her for her double commitment to career and children. It was easy to gush admiration when things went well. Cheryl wondered, if Bobby's father had been tough and supportive and living in New York, would they have gone into battle against the teachers together? She put the notion aside. It did no good dwelling on the not-to-be.

So famous, permissive Bigelow had accepted Bobby. They were used to dealing with aggressive children, or as Miss McKenzie cheerfully referred to them, "little monsters."

That had been last year. The months passed. Cheryl had learned to recognize the stirrings of the gathering storm. Every morning now Cheryl glanced at the letter from Miss McKenzie, which lay under the Steuben paperweight. It was typed on the Bigelow School letterhead, an elegant creamy rag paper, headed by the motto of the school, "A man should *be* upright, not be *kept* upright." A quotation from the Roman emperor-philosopher Marcus Aurelius.

It read,

Dear Mrs. Litvak,

I would like to set up an appointment for you to come to the school and discuss some incidents of Bobby's behavior. I appreciate that your schedule is busy—as is my own—but as this is a serious matter, would you please call my office right away.

> Yours sincerely,
> Felicia McKenzie
> Assistant Headmistress, Bigelow School

Cheryl was becoming more afraid of Felicia McKenzie than of anyone else, even Ariel Lamb. Although Cheltenham had schooled her for years in obedience by intimidation, tiny Miss McKenzie, with her bright blue eyes, her badly cut tweed skirts and inexpensive polyester blouses, posed a unique threat.

Cheryl's secretary buzzed her through again.

"Shall I tell her you're busy?"

"No, I'll take it. Miss McKenzie? This is Cheryl Litvak speaking."

"Ah ha. Glad to reach you, at last, Mrs. Litvak." The voice was reproving, ironical, impeccably polite. Cheryl blushed in the privacy of her office.

"I know you are extremely involved with your work, Mrs. Litvak"—she pronounced the word *work* with a trace of disdain—"which I'm afraid may account for some of the difficulties we have been having with your son."

"Difficulties?" Cheryl tried to feign astonishment.

"Do you recall, Mrs. Litvak, receiving your invitation to Bobby's class play?"

Cheryl did not have the faintest idea. She had so many bills and pieces of mail. She would heap them all on one side of her desk and sort through them on a Sunday afternoon every month or so.

Miss McKenzie continued, "*The Mikado*. Your son was playing the Lord High Executioner."

"I remember," lied Cheryl, suddenly remembering she had agreed to call the Federal Home Loan Bank Board this morning.

"I'm truly sorry you couldn't manage to come," said Miss McKenzie. "I believe every other boy had a parent or family friend who was there. We suspect that deep down Bobby was bitterly wounded that he had no one."

"We have a Burmese au pair. She really should have gone."

"In any event, in the middle of the performance Bobby sneaked away and set off one of the school fire alarms."

"How could he get to it?"

"They're located in all the stairwells. Look, the point is, the entire school was disrupted, the play was ruined, the children were extremely upset, and you can imagine our embarrassment at having to explain to the whole audience of parents and alumni."

"So what actually happened?"

"We followed the Bigelow Fire Alarm Procedures, naturally. Everyone in the building was herded out onto the street, where they waited in a freezing snowstorm for fifteen minutes until we could ascertain whether it was a false alarm."

The other line of Cheryl's phone had started beeping. "It's really up to the school to reprimand him," she protested. "May I put you on hold for just one moment?"

It was Gary Fishman with a query on Glass-Seagall Act interpretation. "Gary, can you give me just a moment to get back to you? I'm in the middle of an urgent discussion."

"Make it snappy," growled Fishman. "This can't wait."

Now Cheryl's secretary loomed over the desk, waving a fan of pink message slips.

"God fucking damn it," whispered Cheryl, but absolutely inaudibly, as she made it a firm rule never to swear in front of anyone at Cheltenham. Proving one's eligibility as "partnership material" was an all-round exercise. Cheryl knew she had a particularly tricky image to maintain. She had to appear ladylike and tough at the same time. She sometimes thought of Margaret

Thatcher as her role model. While it was all right for the men to curse and splutter, Cheryl was not allowed to let go for an instant.

"I've got Mr. Wallace from the Bank Board," said her secretary.

"Could you ask him to hold for just a couple of seconds? Miss McKenzie? Sorry again. We're trying to shore up a terminal S and L here."

"Mrs. Litvak, I suggest we make an appointment for you to come to the school next week. I'm extremely busy myself this month with Christmas alumni activities."

"It's impossible next week."

"Maybe I'm not making myself clear. Bobby is having serious problems at Bigelow, and frankly, we are not sure if this is the right school for him."

I've paid their vast fees through June, thought Cheryl. Surely they can't expel him earlier than that.

"Bigelow will not deal with problem students without the parents' full cooperation."

Something in the authority of Miss McKenzie's schoolteacher voice overrode the inhibitions of Cheltenham. Cheryl needed someone to turn to, just briefly. She had no one she could confide in; she could not talk to Fishman or her children or the au pair or even Gina di Angelo. Gina had enough problems of her own, and besides, she was a more junior lawyer. It would be inadvisable to tell her too much too often. Cheryl found herself confessing to her most dangerous foe.

"This is a particularly difficult time for me. I'm up for partner in a couple of months, so it is really the turning point of my career. As I think you know, I have two children to bring up on my own, with very little support, financial or otherwise, from their father, so I hope you'll understand this once."

The answer came back measured and stately. "My job is to look after my students' welfare. Their interests must come first. Nevertheless, I do appreciate your unusually difficult circumstances, so shall we say we'll give it one last chance. Please meet me in my office a week from Tuesday, at five."

As Miss McKenzie rang off, Cheryl determined, come hell or high water, that Friday evening she was going to have a meeting with her son.

She called home to say she would try to be back in time for dinner with the children. Kim Phong, the new Burmese au pair, answered the telephone. "Tonight we are eating coconut shrimp on banana leaves. Shall I make extra for you?"

"What time do the kids normally eat?" Cheryl asked. It had been so long since she had been home early.

"Seven o'clock."

"Oh. Well, I'm not sure I can get back that soon. If I'm a little late, just keep some banana leaves for me."

"Yes, ma'am."

Cheryl was beginning to like Kim Phong, with her scrubbed round face and obsequious English. She exuded cleanliness and honesty. It would be such a relief if she would last, if Bobby would only hit it off with her. They had been going through au pairs recently at an alarming rate. Brit the Norwegian had taken up with a successful arbitrageur, and Cheryl had had to fire that poor Russian when she found out she suffered from epileptic fits. Annette the Swiss had been efficient and intelligent and precise. But Bobby had routed her, by refusing to utter a single word at home during the final five weeks of her employment. Cheryl wondered how the children were getting on with the Burmese. Cheryl herself found it impossible to hold any kind of conversation, outside of one involving household arrangements, with Kim. Not that it mattered; Kim was not paid to be an intellectual companion. It would be nice though if her children had found some key to communication with their inscrutable new nanny.

At nine-eighteen Cheryl's limousine pulled into the underground drive of the Waterside Towers, the expensive complex of fortresses over the East River, where she lived.

"Good evening, ma'am." Kim Phong answered the door. She was wearing baggy cotton pants and a rather stylish brocaded jacket.

"I couldn't make it sooner." Cheryl set down her heavy briefcase next to the Louis Philippe ormolu grandfather clock, which she had bought at an antique store in the rue Jacob near the Sorbonne. "Have you all eaten yet?

"At seven, ma'am." Kim Phong's intonation was as expression-less as a computer-recorded message.

Cheryl stepped out of her Fendi pumps and luxuriated in the thick fleece of the rug between her stockinged toes. Kim Phong stooped and obligingly whisked away the shoes to be polished.

"I'll have some of those banana leaves on the tray in bed. Where are the kids?"

"Peggy Ann went to bed early. She had an earache. I gave her some Tylenol. Bobby's in the den, watching wrestling."

"I told you, Kim. Not so much television. He should be doing his schoolwork."

"He's finished his homework."

Cheryl sighed. She was too tired to argue. Tired and hungry. "Would you bring me the tray, please. I'll see Peggy Ann in the morning. And could you send Bobby into my bedroom to talk to me?"

After Cheryl had snuggled between her crisp Ralph Lauren sheets, she began to feel better. Kim Phong brought her a plate of the Burmese delicacies on the wicker tray off which she seemed to eat so many of her non-Cheltenham meals.

She flicked the remote control of the television. The chant of "The Nightly Business Report" was beginning to blur in her weary brain when he knocked.

"Come in." She pulled the satin bedjacket back over her shoulders and dimmed the audio of the television, keeping a look-out on the screen for the flash of the day's market results.

Bobby was wearing his pajamas and bathrobe, with its alligator hood and train of an alligator tail. He was growing up tall, with a good jaw and clear, cool eyes.

She patted a corner of the bed beside the supper tray. He obeyed slowly, fixing her with his level stare. Cheryl nestled back against her pillows, to make room for him. She knew she ought to hug and kiss him (she had hardly seen him for days) but recently physical contact had become more awkward than ever.

Cheryl had never been quite comfortable about touching her children. It was her secret shame. She lived in dread of the day when one of the child psychiatrists might bring up the subject. Cheryl herself had grown up in an undemonstrative family, with a sickly mother and one much older sister. One of her only physical memories was that of her paper-skinned mother washing the back of her ears for her. It made her doubly guilty for visiting the same inhibition on her own children. She never kissed women, and men she preferred not to touch outside the combat zone of the bed.

Bobby, who was reaching the age anyhow when boys are grateful not to be petted and coddled, sat gingerly where she pointed.

"Ring! Ring!" announced Bobby sternly.

Bobby and his jokes. "Who's there?"

"Hurd my."

She closed her eyes. "Hurd my who?"

"Hurd my hand so I can't knock. We're building a medieval town at school. A whole town, as big as your bed, with horses and armies outside and battering rams. I'm doing the models of the dead people. You want to see one?"

"Maybe tomorrow. Mother's very tired."

"They have arms and heads coming off and one guy has all his brains and stomach spilling out."

She smiled at him and shook her head sleepily. Now she had to choose which tack to take. On the one hand she was supposed to be giving him a grave talking to, trying to explain the rights and wrongs of dealing with other people. She was meant to be strict and implacable. Should she show anger or iron authority? On the other, she saw him so little these days, it seemed sad to cloud their precious few moments with censure. Of course she loved her son and of course she wanted him to love her back. Ideally she preferred that punishment and discipline should appear to flow from other people, the school or the au pairs or even her ex-husband.

She knew proper mothers were supposed to take responsibility, not merely hand out toys and allowance money. Maybe after she became a partner, assuming she became a partner, all that would improve of its own accord. Besides, every week and month that passed, Bobby was getting closer to growing up. Cheryl, for some time now, had been looking forward to having teenage or grown-up children she could really talk to. She was easily bored playing Battleship or Stratego or Miami Vice—The Game. It was tedious reading aloud from *Spooky Tales* or the Hardy Boys books. She had never quite shared the imagination of the children's world.

Ariel Lamb liked to begin his client meetings with a remark unrelated to the business at hand. "How are you getting on with Kim Phong?" she asked guilefully.

"Kim's okay. I like the food she makes. Specially the papaya noodles."

"Are you being nice to her?"

Bobby shrugged and did not deign to answer. After a moment's silence, he announced, "This one's for you, Mother. The lawyer for the defense asks the witness, 'Did you really *see* my client bite off his friend's nose?' You know what the witness says, Mother?"

"No." Cheryl realized she was losing control of the tide of the meeting.

"He says, 'No I didn't see him bite it off, but I saw him spit it out.'"

"Very funny. Ha ha ha. How's geography? You been doing better on the quizzes?"

"Geography's stupid."

Now was the time to strike, before she lost her nerve. But she had lost the battle already, before she had even broached the issue of Bobby's disruptive attitude, and what was worse, her young son guessed it himself. It was all too much to deal with, after a long week at Cheltenham. How could anyone expect her to bill seventy-five hours, including one all-nighter, to come to work each morning fresh and gleaming and manicured, to hang attentively on every sentence uttered by Lamb or Fishman, and then to give her children moral instruction? There were limits.

"We'll talk some more in the morning. Come and give Mother a kiss."

But instead he just shot her an impish smirk of victory and scuttled away.

*   *   *

When Courage woke on Saturday morning, he lurched out of bed to slam the window that was rattling back and forth in a torrent of icy rain. To his surprise he felt reinvigorated.

Friday had slipped by in a haze of fatigue. Fortunately jet lag seemed to have caught up even with the unrelenting Kahn, who was spending a day remarshaling his energies in Finland. He had called Courage only twice, both times briefly. The rating agency and the Securities and Exchange Commission had both okayed the final drafts of the Caroline 9¼ percent $400 million bond deal. Courage was therefore able to spend a few quiet hours during the afternoon catching up on the forms required to qualify a corporation to transact business in the states of Illinois and Pennsylvania.

He had been looking forward to the evening. He had been invited to dinner by his cousin Ellis, the historian. Courage usually enjoyed his cousin's small parties. The curries and spinach fettuccini were soggy enough to put a yuppie to shame, but the conversation was animated, and for Courage's circle, oddly outré. His cousin knew artists and academics and homosexuals and people with whom Courage had no normal contact. He was always the richest guest present, and he tolerated their scathing references to his income, assuming that on some level they were goaded by jealousy. He never came across Ellis's guests twice, had never taken a telephone number or made an effort to establish a lasting rapport. He felt, and believed they also did, that his presence represented a conjunction of two unlikely planets, to be pulled, at evening's end, back into their respective spheres of gravity. Courage would return from Ellis's bohemian apartment to his own and experience a gentle relief at being himself.

The last time he had been over to one of Ellis's gatherings on 4th Street must have been almost a year ago. His cousin lived on the fifth floor of a walk-up, in a small apartment with molded cornices and uneven floorboards, with a view of treetops and other people's backyards out of the bedroom window. At some point in conversation Ellis's friends always referred to the apartment as a "great find." Ellis, too, was proud of his surroundings. The walls of his living room were hung with violent Expressionist oil paintings, purchased at steep discount from his intimate friends. The picture of a naked woman in stiletto heels, gagged and bound with ropes, hung over the sofa, facing a monochrome study of an embryo in a bottle.

"He's become quite famous," the girl had said, misinterpreting Peter's vacant stare for interest in the painting. "One of the Düsseldorf school." They were sitting at opposite ends of the lumpy sofa, scooping slivers of tacos into a dish of lumpy guacamole.

A battery of whirring and thumping from the kitchen next door promised that Ellis was whipping up more last-minute hors d'oeuvres.

Courage snapped to attention. "I'm sorry. I was daydreaming."

"Long day at work?" She took in his neatly creased suit.

"Actually it was a pretty good day. The money supply figures came out. The market closed up twenty-four points." He noticed she was wearing a patchwork jacket. It made her look youthful, or perhaps it was the relaxation of her face. There was hardly a line of tension in it. "I took a sizable profit in a couple of retail stocks I've been trying to unload for a long time," Courage explained.

The girl looked blank. "I don't follow the stock market. All I know is that I've never seen so many beggars on the streets of New York before now."

"They've gotta do something about that," Courage agreed. "It's a real disgrace what's happening in the inner cities, especially when the economy's going gangbusters."

"The economy's screwed. It's all based on deficit financing." It had been one of those months when the networks began their news broadcasts each evening with reports on the budget deficit.

"Deficit financing can work," said Courage. "Up to a point." Who was this girl anyway, in her thrift-store patchwork jacket, and what did she know about economics?

The whirring in the kitchen came to a temporary pause. Ellis poked his head around the partition. "Hey, guys, no one else here yet? Answer the door for me, will you, when they ring. You two met? Helen Farmer. Peter." He turned to Helen with the tiniest trace of something between an apology and an explanation. "Peter's my cousin. He's a big Wall Street hotshot. Pride of the family." Ellis vanished again to a clonking, rattling sound.

"It's all paper," said Helen. "This country isn't producing any goods anymore. We're just bankers, charging excessive interest rates."

"That's not entirely true," Courage said. He knew he must sound patronizing, but how else was he to explain to this woman in scuffed silver cowboy boots? "The nature of our economy has shifted. We've matured from a heavy industrial to a service and communications economy."

"I don't buy it. The poor are getting poorer and the rich are heaping up stacks of paper."

Courage was thankful when the doorbell rang. He stood up hastily to let in a couple of jazz musicians.

Later, as he helped Ellis clear plates away, Courage murmured, "I didn't mean to be rude to your friend, that woman."

"Helen Farmer?" Ellis salvaged the remains of the lumpy guacamole. "Don't worry about Helen. She can look after herself. You can say anything to her."

That Friday, a year later, though he had been looking forward to going to Ellis's, by the time work was over he had found himself too drained to make the effort to go over to 4th Street, to subject himself to the barbs of the intelligentsia. He called his cousin to beg off.

"I'm sorry. I'm dead beat. It's been one of those weeks. I need to go home and sleep."

"Pity. I have an interesting group coming tonight. I've got a film director you'd like, and a friend who's just opened a book store on Tenth Avenue and a woman who's doing a thesis on Mayakovsky."

"Where's that?"

"Who, Peter. The Russian poet. He said a pair of boots is worth more than a madonna."

"A good night's sleep is worth more than a pair of boots."

"Cute. So they're working you to death down there?"

"No more than usual. I'm just getting old."

"You should be writing this dissertation, not me. 'Irrational Optimism of Participants in Trench Warfare in the Great War.' It's your life. Ten million men, buried in mud, living in filth, crippled with dysentery, who went on fighting for a few feet of ground because they believed that God was on the king or the kaiser's side."

"I'm doing a four-hundred-million-dollar offering. It's not a few feet of mud."

"Sure it is. It's a pissing contest."

"You're right," said Courage, remembering Cheryl Litvak's contempt for him last week as she mentioned she had just done one for nine hundred and fifty. "So her dick's longer than yours," Gleiner had commented wryly.

"I'm sorry," Courage apologized to his cousin again. "I've gotta go. I've got a call in from Finland."

He had returned home early, by eight, too tired even to order in Chinese food. He had eaten a couple of bowls of cereal and fallen into bed. Perhaps it was the storm that had broken during the night that had helped him to sleep so soundly. In any event, he awoke eleven hours later, reborn and ready to pitch back into battle.

He showered, shaved, took out an armload of laundry, bought beer and frankfurters and tortilla corn chips, rewired his stereo, mended the vacuum cleaner, and scattered some Ajax around the sink. Two hours later he was back at his office.

There was a horrible hominess about Cheltenham on week-ends. Depending upon which attorneys were at work, certain patches of the interior corridors were lit up, other stretches of hall dimly visible by the phosphorescent glow of the crimson emergency lights. There was no ventilation, so even after one night the atmosphere was heavy, like a house unoccupied for years. The silence brooded, different from that of the night. The footfalls of sneakers, permissible weekend civilian attire, were muffled in the blood-red carpets.

Courage signed in at reception on the forty-sixth floor. Out of habit he ran his eye down the line of signatories already inside, noticing that Gleiner had been there since eight.

The rain outside his office window still lashed at the panes, shrouding the river and bridges below in a haze of lost focus. His telephone flashed with its light from the message center. He dialed the switchboard. He had three messages: from Kahn, from Tristan Barrett, and from Michelle Peterson.

"Michelle? This is Peter Courage at Cheltenham. I'm sorry I couldn't get in sooner. It was an emergency. I had to do my laundry."

"Buy new clothes," she said. "That's what I do when run out of clean ones."

For one pleasant moment Courage envisaged her making lingerie purchases. "It looks like we're in good shape with the SEC and the rating agency," he said. "I'll be drafting up the officers' certificates this afternoon."

"So all that's left," she answered, "is the letter of credit and the guarantee."

"We can work on those together. Would you like to come over here? Is it convenient?"

"I could make it in a couple of hours."

"Call when you're ready to leave. I'll meet you downstairs at the security desk."

Courage set about drafting the standard officers' certificates:

I, the undersigned hereby certify individually and on behalf of Caroline Brothers Debenture Partnership, a partnership organized under the laws of the State of Delaware, that attached hereto as Exhibit A is a true and correct copy of the partnership...

He used a previous deal as his model, and made a photocopy for his alterations. He had hardly begun when the powerful Xerox machine gave out on him, as always seemed to happen when he worked weekends. He spent three quarters of an hour tracking down the errant sheet of paper mislodged in its guts. Wiping his ink-smeared fingers across his sweatshirt, he returned to his office to find Gleiner staring gloomily at the rain.

"So, where's the goddess?"

"She'll be here soon. What's wrong?"

"Hopper wants me to do up a bill for First Reliable."

"Haven't they just gone into bankruptcy?"

"That's the trouble. We're only getting back fifty cents on the dollar in legal fees."

"Don't look so traumatized. It's not your money."

"They owe us fifty thousand."

"We'll get twenty-five."

"No. I just spoke to Hopper. He said, 'Double it. Put in a bill for a hundred thou.'"

"That's fraudulent!"

"So, what do I do? Blow the whistle?" He added sarcastically, "Go to Ariel Lamb or Mel Samson?"

Courage reflected. "Do his cooked bill. What do you care?"

"It's unethical. It's a flagrant abuse of the bankruptcy laws."

"So, what else is new? You think that's the first screwy bill we've ever sent out? Just do what he says."

Gleiner stared at him. "I have a code of professional responsibility. I don't care who I'm working for. I won't lie and I won't cheat."

"David, I know it's sleazy. But don't lose your job over it. This system's way over our heads. And it's corrupt, all up the line."

"You really think I should go along with it?"

"You have no choice. You can't afford a fight with Hopper. He gets more powerful every day. He'll have your hide."

"He probably will anyway. He hates me. I can tell. I keep feeling like he's trying to entrap me."

"Don't do his bill. Get into trouble. Lose your job. Throw away three years of law school and five years of grunt work. What do I care?" His telephone rang. "That must be her. Don't confuse me with morality, David. I need all my wits about me for this woman."

He took the elevator down to the security desk to meet her. She was wearing a different fur coat, this one tawny colored like a lion's mane, and streaked with blue. She was carrying the Hermès attaché case.

"Did you get wet?"

"No. The limo brought me straight down the street."

"Have you been to our offices before?"

"Never."

"I'll show you around. We can leave your things in my office first," said Courage, pressing the elevator button for forty-eight.

She tossed her blue-streaked lion's mane over her arm and Courage's heart leaped up. She was wearing the jeans, tight and tiny, skillfully slashed at the knee and thigh, in the season's fashion, to show slithers of skin. Over them she wore a sculpting cashmere sweater that promised that her breasts were full. She seemed, thought Courage, younger than ever in her civilian clothes. She could have been twenty-five or -six, with her sheaf of moon-spun hair and the faultless body. Yet she was clearly a few years older, an officer of Caroline and in receipt of several hundred thousand dollars a year in salary, as well as a hefty bonus.

He ushered her along the corridor past the alternating pools of fluorescents and the obscure unlit corners. She paused at a reproduction of a George Stubbs racing horse.

"I hate those pictures," said Courage. "They've got horses all up and down this floor. It doesn't make any sense to me. You see, every floor, they've got some theme. Forty-seven—that's a Litigation floor—is all English eighteenth-century portraits, what's his name, Gainsborough and so on. Up here's horses and dogs for Corporate Finance. Don't ask why. Forty-nine's a mixed floor of Admiralty and Trusts and Estates. Fifty's Tax and Labor. They've got a kind of royal portrait gallery of Holbein repros of Henry the Eighth and Queen Elizabeth and stuff. And fifty-one, our top floor, that's the library, the cafeteria, and some conference rooms."

"What's their art?"

"Medieval religious art, you know, saints against gold backgrounds. It's meant to be symbolic of heaven, get it? As you get out of the elevator, you almost expect some celestial choir to burst into a hymn. A mighty fortress is our God, a bulwark never failing. The inner sanctuary."

"Who figures all this out?"

"The Interior Decoration Committee. One of our partnership committees. Only now there's some screw-up 'cause Ariel Lamb's wife—he's head of Corporate Finance—does this avant-garde stuff with loops of toilet paper, and they can't figure out how to blend it with the Gainsboroughs."

"You seem to know a lot about art."

"Not really." Courage knew almost nothing about paintings. In idle moments, as he waited for documents to come out of Word Processing at 3 A.M., he had, pacing the corridors, noticed the names on some of the plaques along the walls. And once a year, when Cheltenham threw its annual party at the Guggenheim, he made the effort to spend a few minutes between drinks surveying the pictures.

"This is my office."

Her eye fell on the stacks of sailing magazines and the models of his former boat, *The Candle in the Wind.* "You like boats?"

"Yeah. When I was twenty-two I once sailed that twenty-eight-foot Hinckley sloop across the Atlantic. It was great."

"All alone?" She looked mildly appalled.

"Sure. It's the only way."

"You didn't get lonely?"

"Occasionally. But you get into a special frame of mind. It's a drug being out there on the water. Like meditation. You don't need other people."

She shuddered. "I like my creature comforts. A week at the Beverly Hills is more my idea of a good time."

"Come on. I'll take you up to the fifty-first floor. Pity there's no view today."

He caught a whiff of her scent as they rode the elevator. It reminded him sweetly of sawdust and spice and matched to perfection this cool, dry person.

The elevator doors peeled open to confront them with a wide fresco, modeled on some anonymous masterpiece of quattrocento Sienese art, which depicted The Last Supper. Christ's haloed apostles surrounded him, listening, gesticulating, and sipping wine at what was clearly a board meeting at the table of a boardroom.

"See what I mean?" asked Courage. "Get this."

He led her beyond the Horatio Arbuthnot Conference Room into the library, where a triptych of a Perugino Angel Gabriel presented a lily to a pregnant madonna.

"Wow," she said. "It feels like being in some kind of temple."

"You should see it when they have their Friday evening cocktail parties up here. They get in a string quartet to play Mozart and Vivaldi. Maybe you'd like to come to one sometime," he suggested as an afterthought.

"Sometime. Evenings are usually pretty busy."

"What do you do?"

"I work hard. And I run."

She turned her head away from him to stare at the shelves of the *United States Code Annotated* as they passed down the aisles. The library was moderately empty for a Saturday afternoon in December. Courage spotted no more than a couple of dozen associates, burrowing through the shelves and reading in the window niches.

"That's pretty," she said, glancing at a particularly baroque arrangement of the all-pervasive gladioli, a fountain of spiky yellows and scarlets and tangerines.

"Do you think so? They get you down after a while, when you have to live with them everywhere. I mean, don't they remind you a little of . . . a funeral parlor?"

"I've never been in a funeral parlor. I think they're handsome."

"The cafeteria's closed Saturday," apologized Courage. "But we can get some Coke from the machine."

She followed him past the rows of tables, draped with red-and-white checkered cloths. The plastic chairs, in matching colors, must have been designed for a children's classroom or a fast-food franchise. At the center of each table stood a lean vase of plastic replica gladioli.

"Not," said Courage, "one of the Interior Decoration Committee's finest hours."

He bought them each a Coke and a package of animal crackers for himself, and they sat down in a forty-eighth-floor conference room, the letter of credit and reimbursement agreement spread out between them.

"It seems to me," said Michelle, "that the problem with this L.C. is the draw-down provision. If the trustee for some reason misses a payment date, then the letter of credit is automatically instated and the bondholders get paid, but the L.C. collapses."

"I see the problem." Courage munched thoughtfully at a tiger's head.

"Let's get the bank on the phone."

"They won't be at the office."

"Call them at home. Call their lawyers too. Call everybody."

Two and a half hours later, after innumerable suggestions and explanation among the six participants to the conference call, one sentence had been struck and two new ones added to reflect a more efficient mechanism for the letter of credit. Courage put down the telephone and ate the last of the giraffes.

"It's stopped raining. I need some fresh air. Do you want to take a walk over to the Seaport?" he suggested.

"I'll get my coat."

The rain had eased off but the sky still threatened. It was a picturesque setting for the silhouettes of the historic clippers and schooners, now permanently moored to the dock as a tourist museum. Courage walked with Michelle along the wooden slats to the extreme point of the pier jutting into the river. She sat, careless of her precious fur, directly on the steps, so Courage did the same.

He was glad at first for their silence as they privately contemplated the angry sky. The silence, coupled with the violent weather, created an intimacy. They sat almost alone on the pier. The thunderstorms had driven away the afternoon tourists, leaving them the perverse, swirling sky that crushed the Brooklyn Bridge.

Courage spoke first. "Doesn't this make you feel small?" he asked, his concentration still fixed on the bridge.

"What do you mean?"

"All that energy out there. It makes what we're doing seem less important somehow."

"You can't think that way. Those thoughts are dangerous. You've got to focus on what's next."

"Don't you like to think sometimes?"

"No. I mean, only about my work. I used to think when I was younger."

"What happened?"

"I decided I wanted to be damned good. The best. A star. It takes every particle of my energy. There's no room left for daydreaming."

"Do you read?"

"Books, you mean? Hardly. I read *Barron's* and the *Journal* and our analysts' reports. Do you?"

"Not as much as I'd like to," he admitted.

He stole a sideways glance at her pale cheeks. A warmer southern wind had whipped up, an absurdly provocative wind for the season. He was overwhelmed by a gust of curiosity, a bewilderment at how this lunar creature could cloister herself with such assurance against the age-old forces of life. He wondered why indeed she should so want to.

"Have you always been ambitious?"

"Yes and no. It was easy growing up in St. Paul. I was pretty and smart and popular and I guess I never had to kill myself to be the best. Even at college I always got the best grades and dated the best guys and it just seemed, well, natural. It wasn't till I got to the B school that I realized what I could be up against. I found myself with a bunch of people who weren't just smart; they were ruthless. It was then I made up my mind that no one was ever going to dismiss me as just a pretty face."

"It must be hard to be a woman."

"You play with the cards you're dealt. That's what I like about the money world. You take good care of other people's money, and they won't worry whether you're black or white or a woman or a chimpanzee. Once you hit a certain level, it's all very fair. There are rules. And once you're out there on the field, everyone plays by them."

"You like games?"

"I'm a gambler. I used to play a lot of backgammon when I had the time. My career is a little like high-stakes backgammon."

"How about the sacrifices?"

"What sacrifices?"

"I don't know. Personal life, families, time..."

She turned the big blue eyes on him. "Everything has its price. Even so-called personal life. Have you ever lived with really rich people?"

Courage thought about Lamb and Samson and Kahn, who was probably being lashed at this moment with birch leaves after a sauna in Helsinki. "We're all pretty rich, comparatively."

"I mean rich rich. Millions. They don't think like us. They buy things...differently. The needle's eye."

"I don't get it."

The doll's eyes seemed to widen, if that were possible. "When you get too rich," she explained, "you get somehow cut off from the mainstream. It's a price you pay. But it's worth the try. I want to do something big. I hate mediocrity. Sure, I mean, I could have studied art or literature or teaching and gone to work in a relaxed job and earned forty thousand a year. Would that be better? Would that have made the world any different?"

"I'm not criticizing you."

"You have a big job too. I can tell you're good. I bet you're on partnership track."

"Maybe. But I don't feel committed like you."

"You're a man. You don't understand the struggle. It's starting to rain again."

"Shit," said Courage as the first drops pattered, brought by the malicious warm wind. "We'd better get back."

The cloudburst really hit them before they had even reached Water Street. He pulled her instinctively under the narrow ledge of the Café Fledermaus as the torrents smacked down the sidewalks. The luxuriant lion's mane of a coat now clung like a soggy sack and even the bright sheaf of hair hung in a twisted clump.

He towered over her, enjoying his height and stature.

Her eyes flashed. "If we do a few hours on the guarantee when we get back, we should be able to finish up tonight."

"Let's hope. You got plans tomorrow?"

She squeezed out the rat tail of hair like a sponge. "I run."

"Where?"

"In the park. Or by the river."

"What time?"

"Early. Seven."

"On Sunday?"

"I like it early. You don't have to come."

"I want to come. I'll be on your doorstep at seven. You'd better be ready. I'll bring the croissants."

"The rain's letting up. Let's make a sprint."

*　　　*　　　*

He set his alarm for six-fifteen. This time he woke up groaning. Still bleary with sleeplessness, he rummaged for his track suit, picked up a taxi at the corner of 72nd and Columbus, and directed the driver to stop at the first open delicatessen. A few minutes later, clutching at a leaking paper bag of coffee, croissants, and bagels, he was borne in a smooth elevator, to the tune of "O Come All Ye Faithful," toward Michelle's apartment on the nineteenth floor.

"I'm here."

"So, you really made it. Come in." She had on a navy track suit and a headband across her forehead. He gave her the leaking bag of breakfast.

"You didn't have to."

"I don't know about you. I'm hungry."

He followed her through the living room toward a glass-encased alcove around the dining table. Everything in the room was white, a polar landscape. A fleecy rug covered the parquet like a plain of windswept Arctic snow, billowing beneath the white leather sofa and the glass coffee table. The only colors that interfered with this white radiance were the green prickles of the human-sized cacti and the earthy brown of two tribal masks on the wall.

Courage examined the collection of prickly pears and organ pipes and other exotic plants. "You like the desert?" he asked, while he remembered the surface of the sea.

"Not particularly. I keep cacti 'cause these guys don't need much water, and I haven't a lot of time to look after houseplants." Or anyone else. "That one's a cholla. It's quite valuable. And that's a saguaro. They're pretty rare."

Courage turned from the menacing greenery to examine the flat-nosed masks with tattoo-striped cheeks, which seemed to mock this high-rise civilization.

"Where do these fellows come from?"

"Papua New Guinea."

"You been there?"

"Sure. I did a tour last year of the South Pacific. TWA-organized. Twelve days, stopping in Fiji, Samoa, couple of other islands, I forget which, Honolulu, and then home."

"Sounds exotic."

"The scenery was exotic. Everything else was a bunch of American tourists eating sweet-and-sour pork and tossing their leis around."

"Did you like that?"

"It was convenient. Expensive, but I didn't have a lot of time to waste. I found some lox in the fridge."

"I'd like to sail my own boat around the South Seas. But only if I had plenty of time."

She brought the plate of lox and cream cheese from the kitchen and set it between them on the glass dining table. "Good croissants. Real flaky pastry. You've got to watch it sailing round there. The water's full of sharks."

"We're used to those on the Street, God knows. Nice view."

The sliding doors of the dining alcove led onto a narrow balcony, which jutted north over the Upper East Side. "You get to see both the park and the Triboro from here."

"It's pretty at night," she answered, discarding a nibbled croissant. "In the good weather I like to come home and drink a glass of Taitinger, while I look at the lights. Of course I hardly ever get a chance to see it during the day."

"How about the mornings?"

"I usually leave for work before dawn. In winter anyhow."

Courage finished the last gulp of coffee. "This is a very neat apartment. You should see the mess in mine."

"You like it? I had it decorated professionally by a woman who specializes in high-rise minimalism."

"It's sure minimal. It's somewhat austere."

"So it should be. It cost me fifty grand just to establish a context. Simple lines and a feeling of infinite space. Like a Buddhist temple."

Courage could not tell her that the only feeling it evoked in him was the memory of a thousand corporate offices, of lawyers and bankers and venture capitalists and all the other soldiers of the financial service industries.

She carried the half-full plates back to the kitchen. "We can finish eating later. You ready to run now?"

"I'm ready."

Yesterday's tempest had swept the city clean of the usual grime. It was still too early for the traffic to have repolluted it. Courage followed Michelle in the direction of the park. She paused at the first traffic light to warm up the tendons with a few lunges, bending supplely toward the sidewalk. They ran a couple more blocks. The fresh air flushed her skin and, as she jogged beside him, to Courage she looked more tiny and fragile than ever.

They turned down Fifth and into the park at 72nd Street. The early-morning Sunday jogging crowd was out in droves already, taking advantage of the clear and unseasonably mild weather. They pounded past the investment bankers and brokers, wearing their Goldman Sachs or Dean Witter or Shearson sweatshirts. The advertising and media caste proudly displayed on chest and back their logos of Ogilvy, Young & Rubicam, Public Broadcasting. A college kid from the University of Texas shimmied by on a skateboard. Michelle waved at a red-haired girl who ran speechlessly past, cocooned by the music of her Walkman; it was like two trains roaring down parallel tracks in opposite directions.

"You know her?"

"She works at Bankers Trust. We did a deal together. Isn't this great? You glad you came out with me?"

"You bet. Who needs sleep, anyway?"

They trundled around the lake, where the skyline of Central Park South beckoned glamorously in the morning sunshine.

"You want to stop a minute?" She threw herself, flushed and slightly panting, like a young animal, on a bench. A thin line of sweat shone at her temples. Courage sat down with her and craved her body.

"You often have dates like this?" he asked.

"It happens. I figured you'd like it. You look strong and healthy."

"I'm strong. You play tennis?"

"Once in a while. I mostly work out at the Vertical Club. How about you?"

"I've never had this kind of date before."

"You've got to watch it. You can't be too careful these days."

"Careful of what?"

"Have you heard of a few diseases around?"

"Oh, that," said Courage.

"I'm really into the New Chastity. Most of my friends are too."

"Oh, sure, me too," agreed Courage without enthusiasm. He had no ideological conviction in the New Chastity.

Her eyes sparkled. "Have you had the test?"

He briefly considered lying. In matters of the heart men and women had lied to one another since the dawn of civilization. "No," he answered truthfully. "Have you?"

"Of course."

A fifty-year-old hippie, sporting a headband and small bells, began strumming at a sitar from the small hillock directly behind their bench. Courage turned his head and caught sight of another nature worshiper at a distance, performing a bizarre ritual dance of Tai Chi. An avalanche of birdshit spattered onto the bench right between them.

"Let's move on," said Michelle.

They circled the pond a couple of times, and ran back east down the 72nd Street Transverse.

"You want to go out for brunch?" suggested Courage as they turned onto Fifth Avenue.

"Why not? You can come back and shower at my apartment if you want."

"Okay." He glanced at the porcelain profile that bounced rhythmically at his side. As he turned his head toward the east side of the street, he saw the Great Pyrenees.

He knew it must be Betty Law's dog, as Gleiner had described, even before he had time to check the numbers of the canopies. They had just passed 888.

The princely animal tugged at its leash, lunging ahead of its owner in her voluminous lynx coat. From the distance Courage could tell she was short and saw that from behind her black hair was cut in a Joan of Arc pageboy. It occurred to him he might jog across the avenue and try to glimpse her face. Yet how would he explain to Michelle? She might suspect he was personally interested in Betty Law. This was no moment to provoke the goddess's impatience.

Back in her apartmenet she offered, "Go ahead. You take the first shower."

"No, please, after you."

"That's okay, really. I'll make some more coffee."

She pointed to her bedroom door, through which route the bathroom lay.

There were no books in the bedroom either, just a formidable array of mechanical equipment. Courage took in the video recorder, the computer printer and monitor, the stereo, the exercise bicycle. It was not a particularly feminine room, but for the Plexiglas designer telephone by the bed, undulating beneath its dial with a rainbow of trapped colored liquids, and a large solitary bottle of Bal à Versailles on the dressing table.

In the bathroom he noted the terrycloth robe hanging on the door, while he wondered what she wore, if anything, while she slept.

He stepped under the blast of the shower. Her soap smelled of the same spice and sawdust that clouded her as she moved. He lathered himself and considered where to take her for brunch: Café des Artistes, Café Luxembourg, Auntie Yuan's, or head over the water to the River Café?

The shower door slammed shut. Before he even had time to open his eyes under the running water he felt her long limbs pressed against him. Locking her hips against the inside of his thighs, she arched back her neck to let the water stream through her hair.

He cupped her backside with one broad hand, while with the other he traced the soft line between her legs. Was she aroused when she had surprised him with her act of erotic daring? With all the soap and water it was hard to tell. Her eyes were closed against the spray.

She pulled him out onto the bathmat, where he reached for a towel.

"Forget it," she ordered and guided him to the bed, where they fell in a wrestled embrace, soaking wet through the eiderdown.

His muscular frame crushed down her body. Finally he felt her moan in response under the pain of the weight.

"Yes," she whispered plaintively. "Hurt me. Hurt me if you want."

"What?!"

"Slap me, bruise me. Make me feel like a whore. Rape me. Hurt me."

"You like that?" Courage liked his sex energetic, hearty and wholesome and gymnastic. He might bring a little aggression to it, but never raw violence.

"I want to feel," she begged. "Make me feel."

Her glorious body under his seemed to retreat and evaporate, enticing him into her masochism. He thrust harder, deeper, deep enough that he could hear the pain mixed in her cries.

He hit her face, not hard enough to disfigure her, but just enough that he would be able to see the mark later. She writhed underneath him, pulled away and turned over.

"You like it there?"

"Do you?"

"I'm not very experienced."

"You can hurt me," she promised. "Quite a lot."

What really excited him was her helpless shriek as he dug into the flesh. He understood, finally, how much she must sacrifice for the fleeting satisfaction of feeling.

He was never sure whether she came or not. Her responses

were so different from those of the other women Courage had known, and her cries were so loud, and unquestionably real.

Afterward he watched her sit in front of her mirror, wearing only her bluejeans, drawing a brush through her silver-gold hair. He got up from the bed, and prying the brush gently away, ran it through the beautiful hair.

"Thanks," she said, staring vacantly with a melancholy into the mirror. A small tear trickled from the corner of her eye.

They brunched at the Manhattan Café. She ate eggs Benedict and drank a Bloody Mary. She seemed relaxed and at ease. He proposed a movie, so they wandered up to the cluster of theaters on Third, but all the show times were out of sync. They gave up the plan and he walked her back to her apartment, where she said she had some reading to do.

*   *   *

Before he went to sleep, Gleiner telephoned.

"Will you do me a favor, Peter? I've agreed to do an associate interview first thing tomorrow morning. Will you take it for me? I need to stop off at Doctor Goldfarb's for a new prescription."

"I'll do it. How was the circus?"

"It was a blast. The kid loved it. I ate some cotton candy though, which was a terrible idea. It's still burning. How was the goddess?"

Courage sighed. "David, that woman experiences levels of loneliness that you and I can hardly begin to imagine."

M onday's preclosing, which
constituted a dress rehearsal
for the closing the following day, ran smoothly. To Courage's
relief, the formalities had been scheduled to take place at
Milbank Tweed Hadley & McCloy, counsel to the underwriter;
the preparations accordingly became the responsibility of the
shrimp from that firm with whom Courage had passed the night
at the printer.

In a conference room at Milbank a massive table had already
been piled with little heaps of the thirty-four documents that
would exchange hands at exactly twelve noon on the following
day, when the deal would officially close, exploding into the miracle of life, like a spermatozoon mixing its unique chromosomes
with the fated egg. As the numerals of their digital watches would
melt from eleven fifty-eight to eleven fifty-nine to noon, all being
well, at the stroke of midday the check for $400 million would be
handed over by the underwriter to the issuer, in payment for a
pile of parchment certificates, which represented the $400 million
debt obligations. Then all the participants in the deal, the issuer,
the underwriter, the trustee, the letter-of-credit bank, and all their
respective attorneys, would move in brisk progression around the
table, like hungry guests at a buffet, each scooping up his copy
from each of the thirty-four little piles. All of them would pack

their sets of documents in their briefcases, shake hands briskly, and by twelve-fifteen have departed for lunch, some of them to do further deals together, others never to meet again.

Preclosings were usually drawn out and tedious. Most of the participants spent the day closeted in the conference room at Milbank Tweed waiting for their various documents to arrive from the printers and duplicating facilities and federal agencies. As each new bundle would appear, its originator would lay it neatly in its allotted space, like his gift under the Christmas tree.

Courage, who had arrived that morning well prepared, marched along Water Street to Milbank, accompanied by a messenger who carried two suitcases of the Cheltenham documents. He enjoyed his first sight of Michelle, resplendent in her Italian serge suit, proofing and checking documents, and relaying messages from Brad Carpenter. She had become a grown-up goddess again, aloof and dispassionate, gracing the room with her scent of sawdust and spice. The doll eyes addressed Courage impartially. He wondered how long she would carry the memory of their morning in her bed. Next week, next month, next year? At least today she must surely still feel the stir, while he could still trace the faint shadow on the cheek where he had struck her.

He managed to draw her alone into a corner to ask if she wanted to have dinner that night.

"I can't. We've got a big dinner meeting up at The Quilted Giraffe with a group from First Royal Bank of Ontario. Maybe tomorrow."

"I can't tomorrow. It's the Cheltenham Christmas party. I might be able to break away early, though."

"You mustn't do that," she objected. "Those parties are important. You want to be seen. You want to talk to the right partners."

"I want to talk to you."

She took out a pocket diary. "Wednesday's possible."

"I can't. I've got an all-day trip up to Buffalo. I won't finish till very late, if at all. But Thursday'd be fine."

"I'm leaving Thursday lunchtime for Seattle. I've got a new deal out there."

"When will you be back?"

"Sunday or Monday."

"Maybe I could fly out there and meet you for the weekend."

"That's nice of you, but it's not worth the trouble. I'll be wrapped up with business. How about Monday night for sure, if I'm back?"

"I promised I'd have dinner with my cousin. What the fuck, I'll cancel him."

"No, don't do that. We'll be seeing each other anyhow on Tuesday night at the closing dinner."

"But that's a business dinner. I want to be with you alone."

"Be patient. We'll have some time to talk after the dinner. In my apartment."

"You sure about that?"

"I've already penciled it in."

The next day they closed. The check passed from hand to hand at noon, the parties dispersed, and Courage returned to his office to find a confetti of telephone messages from Kahn strewn over his desk and chair. Misuki had proved intractable over the development of its prune juice product, which had thrown the deal into a stalemate.

Courage called the volatile entrepreneur, who was now back pacing the luxuriant nap of carpets high above Park Avenue.

"Fuck the lousy yellow bastards," he raged. "Who's to trust those slimy toads? I fly round the world to finalize negotiations and they try to alter the acquisition terms at the last minute. Let some other schmuck go screw himself in their semen stains. From now on we're focusing on Goldilox, Inc. At least there's a company that concentrates on its best product."

"They still haven't got FDA approval," Courage reminded him.

"How long before the Food and Drug people come through? We know anyone down there?"

"I'll ask Tristan. It could take a while. We should get a better picture after we check out their books in Buffalo tomorrow."

"You want me to come up with you?"

Courage shuddered. An entire day with a pent-up Kahn was a more formidable notion than a dip in a swimming pool of sharks. "It's not really necessary at this stage. I'm taking one of our junior associates with me to help out on the due diligence, going through all their records and so on. The preliminary question is whether their cosmetic cream really can make women's hair grow two and a half inches a month."

"You're wrong, kid. The question is, A, whether they can convince the FDA that this laudanum compound's safe and B, whether I can market the crazy elixir to the public. I'll call you back tonight."

"I'll be out of the office from seven till ten."

"You got a date? Cancel it."

"It's the firm Christmas party. I should at least make an appearance."

Kahn had no patience for office protocol. "You can leave the party early. We have to talk before Buffalo."

Courage sighed. "I'll be back in my office by ten. I'll be expecting your call."

He heard Kahn bark instructions over another telephone line. The voice, as friendly as a sharpened machete, snapped back. "Keep it up, kid. Otherwise, I may have to take my business across the street."

Lorraine knocked on the door. "Would it be all right if I leave a couple of minutes early today?"

A couple of minutes meant a couple of hours. It was useless to protest. The afternoon of the Christmas party a wild abandon ripped through the stately corridors of Cheltenham, Arbuthnot & Crewe, and even the most conscientious secretaries turned out pages splattered with typos.

"Are you going to the party tonight?" he asked.

"Am I going to the party, mister! I'm going to be the soul of it."

"What are you wearing?"

"That's the secret. It's a hot little number, that's all I'm saying for now."

"I won't even try to guess," he promised gallantly. "If you promise you'll dance with me."

"I'll have to check my dance card, sir. It's getting filled up pretty quick."

"Save me the waltz. I've been a nice boss, right?"

"Most of the time. When you aren't too crazy on those all-night deals. Who's that coming to bother you now?"

"Come in!" he called, and looked up into the earnest tortoise-shell glasses of Benedict Hamilton, his junior associate.

"I have a message from you," said Benedict crisply.

"Ah, yes. It's about our trip up to Buffalo tomorrow. My secretary checked the flight times. I'm afraid we've got to catch a six-fifteen to get enough time for a whole day's work there."

"Good," said Benedict brightly. "I'd really like to get back to New York in the evening. I've a meeting of the Fin de Siècle Society."

"Meeting of the what?"

"The 1890s. It's my period," said Benedict, as if that explained everything.

"Your what?"

Benedict stared at Courage owlishly with a patient resignation. "I collect lamps and inkwells, principally. Occasionally mirrors too."

Courage had no suitable response. "Well, we probably won't get back until late, but we'll try."

"I've been reading the Goldilox financials you sent me. I spotted a couple of worrying figures you might care to discuss."

"On the plane tomorrow."

"As you prefer," said Benedict with patronizing deference. "Or perhaps we might have a word later at the Waldorf."

"Are you going tonight?"

"I thought I might look in for a while. Though the conversation at these firm functions tends to become rather mundane after they start drinking."

*　　　*　　　*

Cheryl walked up the marble steps of the Waldorf lobby at the same time as Gloria, Tristan Barrett's exquisitely manicured secretary, who teetered in silver lamé stilettos and tossed a white foxtail coquettishly over her shoulder.

The attorneys in office clothes had all come directly from 57 Water Street. The secretaries, who had locked themselves in the ladies' rooms at Cheltenham and all over town, to clip and paint and spray the finishing touches, blazed among them like a sea of fireworks.

"You look dazzling," Cheryl told her. "Your hair's a work of art."

"I left early. I had an appointment at the beauty parlor," Gloria explained, fingering the diamanté clips that held up an elaborate cascade of curls. She flicked at the foxtail with a long orange nail. "I guess you attorneys don't get a lot of time to fix yourselves up nice." She appraised Cheryl's appearance undisguisedly. The Cheltenham party had its roots in the shuffles of traditional carnival, when the servants and tradesmen could for once run riot over the seigneur's domain.

Under the sleek shell of hair and the expensive Marcella Borghese cosmetics, Cheryl's face showed hollows. "I haven't stopped for days. I really shouldn't have broken away tonight."

"Sure you should. You need a little recreation once in a while, even you. I don't mean that, like, disrespectfully, but you do drive yourself. There comes a time," Gloria added boldly, "when all us girls need our beauty sleep."

Cheryl laughed good-naturedly. "'Fraid I passed that point of no return some time back."

"I didn't mean it like that. You look fine. It's just that, well, you should treat yourself a little. Everyone has a good time at the Christmas party."

The ballroom was already thronged with the employees of Cheltenham. The Christmas party was the only social function of the year to which the entire staff was invited, from the messengers and mailboys up to Lamb and Samson themselves. No one, except for the cleaners, was excluded, but in the historical tradition of the firm, spouses and dates did not attend. When the whole firm got together to kick up its heels, for one night all the world was turned away, just as a thousand years ago, during high and holy festivals, the great oak doors of the monastery were firmly bolted.

Courage spotted David Gleiner near one of the bars, trapped in conversation with an already lurching Mick Finnegan. Gleiner gestured frantically and helplessly to Courage.

Cyrus Sweet, martini in hand, watched Finnegan's deterioration with mild interest.

"Hi, Cyrus," said Courage. "Great party."

"How're you doing, Peter?"

"Great, thanks, great. I'm glad I could make it here for a couple of hours."

"You have to get to the Christmas party," replied Cyrus with fervor. "It's an important Cheltenham event. Once a year we just have to put our clients on hold for the evening."

"Once a year, right."

"I've only missed the Christmas party once in twenty-eight years. And that was an unavoidable incident. My client, who was dying of a dislodged thrombosis, wanted to cut his children out of his will and leave the estate to the Planetarium. I had to go up to Mount Sinai Hospital with a new draft of the will. Turned out it was lucky I did, 'cause he passed away in the middle of that night."

"Not so lucky for his children," Courage pointed out.

"Lucky for Cheltenham, Arbuthnot and Crewe. His children contested the will and we raked up legal fees for years. Excuse me, Peter. I have a supper engagement with this charming young lady."

Cheryl Litvak came up to Cyrus, who, catching her hand, kissed the back of it theatrically.

"I hope she'll honor me with her company again." He explained to Courage, "Ever since Cheryl's first year here as an associate, she and I have always dined together at the Cheltenham Christmas party."

"Of course, Cyrus, I'd love to."

He steered her toward the buffet table, laden with lobster tails and gargantuan shrimp.

"Can I help you to a little of this?" He held her plate for her.

"Just a spoonful."

They carried their plates to a quiet corner table away from the roisterous crowd and the music of "Good King Wenceslas."

"Would you mind if I took off my antlers during dinner?" Cyrus asked, raising the papier-mâché crown and laying it on the plush cushions.

Some time about the turn of the century, early in the reign of Horatio Arbuthnot, the famous Cheltenham Santa Claus costume tradition had been inaugurated. The senior partner, dressed in full Santa regalia, handed out the prizes after dinner. In former days, when the firm consisted of only twenty-eight partners, it had seemed fitting that they, too, should dress up as Santa's reindeer, each of them sporting a crown of papier-mâché antlers. Yet the tradition survived, and every member of the partnership was still obliged to play his role as an antlered reindeer—every partner except one, that was. Two decades ago Mel Samson had inherited the honor of wearing the Santa Claus costume. At that time Ariel Lamb, a promising young partner, had put on his antlers for the party like everyone else. No longer. Students of Cheltenham politics had watched in stunned amazement the year Ariel had turned up in his plain dark suit, antlerless. It was clear there could not be two Santas. Equally it was evident that Ariel Lamb, already Samson's rival and possible successor, refused to play reindeer to Samson's Santa. So amongst the nodding heads of the partnership, which bobbed like a sea of plumes, only Lamb's remained bare.

"Of course," said Cheryl, stroking the antler tips longingly.

"I hope one day you may be wearing one of those too."

"Oh, Cyrus, thank you. Thank you very much. I appreciate your support."

"We'll be putting you up for partner this spring, I assume. You can naturally count on my vote."

"Thank you very much. I'm glad you believe in my work."

"Some people don't realize I'm quite a liberal fellow at heart. I believe we should have another woman partner. We must move with the times."

"I hope my work's as good as anyone else's."

"We all put a great deal into Cheltenham. You've certainly done some Trojan service over the past seven years. And, my dear, the truth is, you can't hold back the tides of history. The floodgates of equal opportunity have been opened, and my partners and I would not want to be thought of as—retrogressive."

He leaned closer to her. "Now let's be frivolous. No more business for tonight. What a delicious perfume you're wearing."

While Cheryl was canvassing her vote from Cyrus Sweet, Lorraine and Gloria met in the peachy light of the powder room. As they shared the mirror, Gloria readjusted the diamanté clips in her hair. Lorraine sprayed her endless cleavage with a sultry, musky scent.

"You eaten some shrimps?" asked Gloria.

"I always make a beeline for the shrimp at the Christmas party. That's half why I'm here, honey."

"What's the other half?"

"I gotta keep track of what's doing with them crazy attorneys. You seen Mick Finnegan? Drunk as a monkey. There's a career going nowhere."

"Remember last year, when he passed out in the lobby behind the palm tree? Mr. Barrett had to carry him home."

"How you know that, hon?"

"Mr. Finnegan sent him a thank-you note. I read it in Mr. Barrett's mail." Her voice quavered.

"There's no future in it, princess," said Lorraine sternly. "He ain't going to marry you."

"Yeah, I know. I had my horoscope cast. I'm supposed to marry a tall, dark Sagittarius. Mr. Barrett's a Pisces."

"I been here twelve years, Gloria treasure, and I could tell you a thing or two about them wacko attorneys. They're all just married to their jobs, the whole heap of them. Their marriages ain't worth nothin'. If they got enough energy left to cheat once a year at the Christmas party, they're doin' pretty good. Forget him, princess."

"Mr. Barrett's divorce is almost done."

"How you know that?"

"I heard him telling Mr. Finnegan."

Lorraine tugged at the ruffle across her chest, which lent a last shred of decency to the décolletage. "Mine's chasing some cookie over at Caroline Brothers. Every time he gets off the phone with her, he bums a cigarette off me. He gave up two years ago."

"You seen her?"

"No. I take her phone calls. I reckon it won't last. But at least he's getting it regular for a change."

"How do you know?"

"He jived in all bouncy on Monday, cracking jokes. I always know when my boys' personal lives start steaming."

"He's pretty cute. Probably the cutest associate in the firm. I think maybe you've got a little hots for him, Lorraine."

"Shut your mouth, girl. I'm a respectable married lady. If I wasn't happily married to Joe, plus a grandmother of three, well, there's another story for you." She bent down to straighten the scarlet flounces on her skirt. "You like my dress?"

"It suits you great."

Lorraine pirouetted her hippopotamine figure to examine the scarlet expanse at the back. "You don't think it's too short?"

"Short's in this year. I threw away all my longer hems."

As Gina di Angelo appeared in the mirror behind them, the secretaries exchanged a glance of complicity. "C'mon, honey, let's get back to the shebang."

The band was playing "God Rest Ye Merry Gentlemen." The seemingly inexhaustible shrimp had been replaced by fruitcake and chocolate truffles. Gleiner had finally shaken Finnegan, and made his way through the crowd to Courage's table.

"We've got to talk," he told him urgently.

"What?" yelled Courage above the din.

"Let's go somewhere quiet."

"Is it that important?"

"I think so..."

"Hello," said Benedict Hamilton, emerging with a sprightly step. "Would you mind if I joined you?"

"Sure," groaned Courage. "David, do you know Benedict? He's helping me out on the Goldilox matter for Kahn. We're traveling up to Buffalo in the morning together to do a due diligence."

Gleiner turned to Courage anxiously. "You'll be out of the office tomorrow?"

"Only for the day, I hope. We hope. Benedict has some meeting to do with inkwells in the evening."

Benedict Hamilton explained again, with a patience clearly labored to breaking point, "My engagement tomorrow evening is not connected with inkwells. I was telling you earlier that although I specialize in inkwells, I am a collector of various objects from the 1890s."

Courage shrugged. "It's his period, David."

"His what?"

"You heard. His period. We all ought to have one."

Benedict blinked coldly at the attorneys and took a draft of his Black Label. "I take it you have no interest in art? I happen to have some photographs on me of my personal collection, if you'd care to take a look." He whipped out a Kodak envelope from his breast pocket and leaned across the table. "This tea urn probably dates from the late 1880s. You will see it has the characteristic handle and gold leaf of the Philadelphia School. Yes, that's an interesting set of wall brackets. I actually picked that up at a small auction in New Hampshire for only, let's see, I believe it was seventy-nine dollars. I could probably easily resell for three hundred. Ah, here's one of the inkwells, not my finest, but important to note that molding around the base..."

"Oh, my God," breathed Courage. For Lorraine, resplendent

in her scarlet flamenco skirt, like a full-blown amaryllis, was swooping upon them.

"Your Highness promised to dance with me. Remember?"

A drum roll announced the prize giving as Lorraine was beginning to work up to an orgiastic frenzy on the dance floor. Courage, passing his arm lightly as far behind her wide waist as it would reach, escorted her back to the table.

"Can I get your coat or a taxi?"

"No, sir! I'm not leaving before they give the prizes. I might have won something. One year I won a free breakfast at the Liberty Café."

As the band launched into "Good King Wenceslas" once again, Mel Samson, escorted by the six senior partners who enjoyed the privilege of most-intimate-reindeer status, bounded down the central aisle between the tables toward the bandstand. A pale blue spotlight followed his spindly red-stockinged legs. Conversation petered out and forks were laid down.

Gary Fishman, the youngest of the senior reindeer, stepped into a lilac spotlight of his own.

"Ladies and gentlemen." The lilac beam danced across his bobbing antlers. "I am honored to welcome you to the ninety-second grand prize drawing of the Cheltenham, Arbuthnot and Crewe Christmas party. I am delighted to see that so many of you could attend tonight to celebrate with us the end of what has been a splendid year for the firm. I wish you a very Merry Holiday Season, and as Horatio himself would have said, 'God bless you all.' And now, ladies and gentlemen, I give you Santa Claus himself!"

Mel Samson stepped out in front of Fishman, where his pale blue spotlight melded with Fishman's lilac one, creating a chilling effect of indigo light. Mel's arm reached into the sack. "Our first prize this evening is a glittering night on the town for two, including dinner, with one bottle of wine, at Sardi's restaurant, followed by tickets to *A Chorus Line,* that stirring perennial classic, and has been won by"—a loud drum roll—"Cyrus Sweet!"

The room applauded politely as Cyrus paraded his way down the aisle to collect his tickets.

"Our next prize, a long-established Cheltenham tradition, is the famous fifteen-dollar gift certificate to Brooks Brothers. This year, however, in recognition not only of our growth as a firm, but also of the overall inflationary pressures of the last two and a half decades, the Reindeer Committee has resolved that the amount of such certificate be increased to two hundred and seventy-five dollars. And now, as you all are eager to hear who the winner is ... Miss Gina di Angelo!"

Gina, flushed with embarrassment, headed for the bandstand. Did they know as they applauded, on whose behalf the certificate would be cashed?

"And now, mesdames and messieurs, I am well aware you are all itching to find out who is the lucky winner of a day trip, including a complimentary breakfast at La Guardia, to the Washington, D.C., office of Cheltenham, Arbuthnot and Crewe. The winner of this grand adventure is ... Miss Gloria Ortiz!"

Gloria, with a tug at the spiraled tendrils that nestled around her throat, minced between the tables on her sparkling stilettos.

Gleiner whispered to Courage, "Meet me downstairs for a couple of minutes by the postcard kiosk. I want to talk to you privately, as soon as this idiotic ceremony is over."

"Let's go right now."

"No, you stay put," answered Gleiner as he stood to sneak away. "You've got a big career here ahead of you. Don't screw up by walking out at the wrong moment."

Two tables behind them, in a dangerously loud voice, Mick Finnegan rumbled to Tristan Barrett, "Who gives a fuck about the stupid prizes? It's all rigged anyway. Do you know, in twenty-two years at Cheltenham, I've never won anything at the party, not even the book of vouchers for the Staten Island ferry."

"Shh. Keep your voice down, Mick. I'll buy you a trip on the ferry."

"That's not the goddamned point!" shouted Finnegan, and belched. "I've been passed over and they all know I was the best.

Our friend Der Fuhrer used to ask my advice on UCC matters. Now his lowest minions won't return my phone calls."

"Shut up, Mick. You're out of control."

"I'm a dead man anyhow. And you know something? I don't give a flying fuck. Why is it, Tristan, no one ever asked me to be on the Reindeer Committee? I've been at Cheltenham a long time and I've won some major, major litigation. You know why? 'Cause Ariel Lamb wants my ass, and I'm telling you, it sucks."

"Mick, I'm taking you home. Can you walk?"

"I don't want to go home. Why doesn't Ariel just come and talk to me, man to man? You want to know why? I'll tell you. 'Cause that Fuhrer knows that if he got talking with me, I'd rearrange his face."

Samson's voice reached a final crescendo. "And now for our last prize, but indeed not least, a set of six silver-plated oyster forks from Tiffany's..."

A couple of paralegals at the next table tittered as Finnegan lurched and slumped into a dish of chocolate ice cream.

"Mick," said Tristan in an urgent sotto voce, "remember the Management Committee. You were warned if you were ever again found drunk on the firm premises—"

"I'm not on the firm premises," rebutted Finnegan, with litigious logic. "I'm at the Waldorf Astoria."

The prize giving was over and the party kicked back into full swing. Courage left the table to look for Gleiner at the postcard kiosk. He tried the main lobby without success. On the lower floor he checked the boutiques, where he found a souvenir shop selling cards and New York memorabilia, and T-shirts that read, NICE GUYS FINISH LAST, but Gleiner was nowhere in sight.

Upstairs Ariel Lamb prepared to depart. A number of the partners were already drifting away, and Lamb was not one to straggle. He shunted off the members of his entourage as he made his way out of the ballroom.

"Ariel!"

Lamb turned to an urgent Hopper, the red hair bristling and the schoolboy face ruddy with concern. "Can we talk?"

"Of course." Ariel waved apologetically at Fishman and guided Hopper into an empty alcove alongside a potted palm. "What's up?"

"It's the TBO deal. I just got off the phone with Caroline Brothers. The word's leaked out on the Street. Samurai Robinson has a memorandum of understanding with the government of Costa Rica."

"Are you quite certain?"

"There's no doubt. As you can imagine, the telephone system down there in Costa Rica leaves a lot to be desired. One of the junior Caroline people, who was assigned to keep an eye on Joe Tikawa from Samurai, got on a crossed line and managed to intercept one of Tikawa's phone calls. They were caught on the tail of Hurricane Beatrix, and the phones were going crazy. 'Course he called New York immediately to report."

"What else did he discover?" asked Lamb.

"Far as I can tell, that was the gist of it."

If Lamb was taken aback by the news, his poker face showed nothing. "Would you like another Perrier, Hopper?"

"Sure, Ariel."

They moved over toward the nearest bar to order Perriers with lime twists.

Lamb took a thoughtful sip. "You have a big future with our firm, Hopper. A very big future."

"Thank you, Ariel."

"If the TBO flies there's a major piece of action in it for you. I want that TBO to work."

"We all do, Ariel. It could be the best thing that's ever happened to Cheltenham."

"Not only to Cheltenham. To me. And to you."

"You think Samurai's getting an edge on us?"

Lamb, who stood six inches taller than Hopper, gazed impassively down at him, and took another long draft of Perrier. "Hopper, some mole's selling our secrets. That associate, David Gleiner, was snooping in my papers."

Hopper was shocked. "How do you know?"

"Last night he was seen sneaking into my office at one A.M."

"Who saw him?"

"One of the Albanian cleaners. I pay her a hundred bucks a week to keep an eye on who goes in and out of my door after midnight."

"Those Albanians aren't all that reliable."

Between midnight and four in the morning, the five floors of Cheltenham were soaped and scrubbed and polished by a small army of Albanian immigrants, women with head scarves and men like rugged gnomes. Few of them spoke any English. But by the time they submissively filed out at dawn, the imposing corridors gleamed like a hospital and you could safely eat off the blood-red carpets.

"This Albanian's reliable. She worked for the Albanian police force before she defected to the U.S. She picked Gleiner out of hundreds of attorneys from his photograph in the *Professional Directory.*"

"Do we fire him?"

Lamb raised an admonishing hand. "Not so fast. It's too late for that anyway. The damage is done. He'd just take more information over to the other side."

"Can we go for an injunction? Breach of confidentiality?"

"This deal is worth billions and billions to me. To us. You think I'm going to tie myself up in the court system over some associate nerd, while the whole Street gets a laugh at my expense?"

Beads of sweat were beginning to prickle over Hopper's upper lip. The thrill of sharing Ariel Lamb's confidence was only neutered by the gravity of the situation. If Ariel suspected David Gleiner of selling information, he, Hopper, would make it his business to keep the associate under strict surveillance. He would overload him with work, add to the already crippling burden of hours Gleiner carried. He would keep him chained to the desk. Gleiner would soon discover the consequences of monkeying in Ariel's affairs.

"I must be off," Lamb excused himself. "I'm giving a speech in the morning down at the International Monetary Fund. I think I'll make it an early night. Ah, Mel, you just on your way out?"

Samson, who was now carrying his scarlet Santa Claus hat under his arm, paused with Lamb. Hopper, nodding deferentially at the two tall, lean generals, withdrew.

"Nice party," said Lamb. "I'm glad you all raised that Brooks Brothers certificate to two hundred and seventy-five."

"We didn't want to be penny pinching. Fifteen bucks doesn't go so far these days."

Lamb flexed the monogrammed cuff of his wrist. "I don't know about that, Mel. See this Timex? You know how much I got that for?"

Samson arched his aquiline brows.

"A Nigerian was selling it for twelve on the corner of Broadway and Pine. I bargained him down to seven."

Samson, with a fleeting glance at his own Rolex, drew out a leatherlike credit card case from his pocket. "A present from my youngest daughter," he explained. "She got it up on Columbus Avenue. Nine fifty."

Lamb examined the case. "It's all a question of knowing where to get things."

"I'll try and find you one if you like, Ariel."

"That's very nice of you, Mel."

"Hell, it's Christmas, right? I like to get into the spirit of the thing. It was a good party this year anyhow." The two figures made their way together toward the exit. "By the way, Ariel, everything under control again with your little TBO?"

"Everything shaping up nicely, Mel. It's going to be a record year for the firm."

"Times are treacherous, my boy. We can't tread too carefully."

"Too true, Mel, too true. And you have a very, very happy holiday. And all the best to Barbara and the girls."

Lamb and Samson passed by Peter Courage on the stairs. He was returning for the third time to the postcard kiosk in search of

Gleiner. Perhaps Gleiner had been waylaid or had simply gone home to bed. Yet Courage was disturbed.

He paced back and forth, reading the T-shirts for the twentieth time. HAPPINESS IS A POSITIVE CASH FLOW . . . HE WHO HAS THE MOST WHEN HE DIES WINS . . . I LIKE OLD MONEY, YOUNG MEN, AND ME . . . He glanced at his watch. Soon it would be time to go to Cheltenham and wait for Kahn's inevitable call.

He must have been invisible behind a rack of giant teddy bears when Finnegan, Barrett, and Gloria staggered by. Finnegan, now only barely able to drag himself, had his arms around their necks as they propelled him through the lobby in search of a back exit.

"Where's Ariel Lamb?" he demanded. "I want to mess up his face."

"Shut up, Mick," said Tristan. "We'll get you home in a minute."

"I'm all right. Never been better. You look after the bimbo. Excuse me, I'm sorry, what did you say your name was? Miss, miss . . . anyway, doesn't matter. She's got good tits. Not a lot of good tits around Cheltenham these days."

"Shut up, Mick."

"You're a good friend, Tristan. So piss off, will you, and let me go look for Ariel. You look after Miss Gloria. She's a lusty wench. And horny as a cat, I'd imagine."

"I'm sorry, Gloria," said Tristan. "He's worse than usual this year. He's been under a lot of stress recently."

"It's no problem, Mr. Barrett. Anything I can do to help."

"You're a trooper. Just don't mention this to anyone, will you? Mick's in bad enough repute these days as it is."

"I wouldn't say a word, Mr. Barrett. You can count on me."

The bizarre trio passed by. Courage felt a twinge of compassion for Finnegan. Although he had never much cared for the man's insolence, he remembered how Finnegan had impressed him at odd moments. Finnegan, sober, had a rare command of language and argument, which could reduce his opposition to stammering. What had he done with his gifts?

"What happened to him?" Courage had once asked Gleiner.

"Cheltenham destroyed him somehow. He's their best performing seal and his tricks are getting slow. Twenty years ago he was a poor, bright street kid with a scholarship from St. Ambrose College in Davenport, Iowa. He married a rich woman, a zipper king's daughter, and she gave him champagne tastes. When she left him, on account of the drink I guess, all he had left was Cheltenham and his so-called brilliance."

"But he remarried."

"Lord knows how long that'll last."

Courage studied the T-shirts one last time. MY ATTORNEY CAN BEAT UP YOUR ATTORNEY . . . EXPENSIVE, BUT WORTH IT . . . It seemed pointless to wait for Gleiner any longer here. He had better face Kahn's last call before the trip to Buffalo. Gleiner's gossip would simply have to keep. Cold gossip generally fared better than the twenty-four-hour-old moo shu pork they lived on, he reflected as he climbed the hotel stairs. What was a tidbit of office scandal anyhow, when you had grown used to putting your whole life "on hold"?

SEVEN

*B*enedict Hamilton was waiting for Courage downstairs under the canopy of his apartment at Irving Place. It was exactly 5:15 A.M., Wednesday, and the deserted streets were still pitch black. Benedict waited under the beam of a street lamp, sprucely at attention, hair and shoes and briefcase all gleaming.

Courage, yawning, opened the cab door to let him in.

"Good morning," said Benedict brightly. He arranged the briefcase between them and smoothed down his suit. He smelled powerfully of aftershave.

Courage mumbled something unintelligible and held out the second section of the *Wall Street Journal.*

"No, thank you. I've already read it. There's a controversial review of the new Kandinsky exhibit. Also an article you should take a look at on the long-term dangers of securitization of debt."

The taxi turned onto the East River Drive and glided north, commanding the empty highway.

"Have you breakfasted yet?" Benedict asked.

"Maybe we'll get time to grab some coffee at the airport."

"I always start the day with a hearty one. Bacon and eggs and ham and biscuits. My family comes from North Carolina, you know. We've always been big breakfasters since my great-great-great-grandfather won the Battle of Lumpy Creek."

"What are you talking about?"

"Eighteen sixty-three. One of the little-known but significant Confederate victories. It was a Yankee rout."

Courage shouted at the driver, "I like your music. Will you turn the volume up?"

"Turn it up? Folks never asked me to turn it up before."

Out of the corner of his eye Courage saw Benedict reach into the briefcase, withdraw a manicure set, and snap the briefcase smartly shut. The deafening rock music drowned out both conversation and the scrape of filed nails.

They swung over the ramps toward the terminal. Wordlessly Courage handed Benedict his ticket.

"If we've got some time," said Benedict, "I think I'll stop off in the cafeteria and stoke up my energy."

While the younger associate sat down to a microwaved wreck of swampy eggs and bacon, Courage on an impulse decided to ring Michelle. He imagined her muscle-perfect body stretched across the bed, a Sleeping Beauty next to a phosphorescent designer telephone. He pictured her waking, stepping out of the shower, standing on her balcony high over 79th Street in her white terrycloth robe, to breathe in the cold, black morning.

The machine clicked. "This is Peterson. Please leave date, time, number, and message. It may take me a while to get back to you, as I am very, very busy, but eventually I will, if possible. You may speak now, after the tone."

Courage said, "It's Peter. It's Wednesday morning, quarter of seven. I'm at La Guardia on my way to Buffalo. There's no message. I was thinking of you, that's all. Are you out running? Or have you already left for work? I guess I'll call you when I get back to New York. Bye now."

Benedict was waiting for him punctually at the gate, leafing through a copy of some glossy French magazine with a picture of a château on the cover.

"You read that stuff?"

"Only when it pertains to my period. You see that Limoges

soap dish? I picked up a set of them last month in Baltimore, which were almost identical except for the shell motif."

"Let's go. The line's moving."

The airplane took off into an angry dawnless sky, lurching furiously before it planed. As they hit an air pocket and plunged several hundred feet, Benedict remarked, "Were you interested in discussing my comments on the Goldilox financials?"

"Shoot."

"First of all, we have here four years of income statements. In 1983 the company made a small profit of one hundred and forty-seven dollars. In 'eighty-three sales soared and their net income zoomed to sixty-two thousand. In 'eighty-four they're raking in approximately two hundred thou'. And then suddenly the following year they're back to nineteen thousand. I have a problem with the trend."

"Kahn explained all that to me. These guys are in a highly cyclical industry. Any small, nondiversified cosmetic company is dependent on what's fashionable. Until now, their only real product has been green, pink, and blue hair dye. In the early eighties they hit it lucky with the punk movement. There was a big demand in the youth market for funny-colored hair. By 'eighty-seven the whole fashion was getting passé, the market dwindled, and a couple of the majors moved in to capture whatever was left of it."

"I think we should alert the client that this is a company with no current viable product."

"We're lawyers, Benedict. That's not our problem. Kahn may be a tyrant, but he's no fool. He's staking everything on the success of this new rapid hair-growing formula."

The airplane eased its shuddering. Outside the window a winter sun bathed the cloudscape in pale light. Courage accepted a cup of coffee and a package of fruitcake from the stewardess.

"I don't know about you," said Benedict, disdaining the fruitcake, "but as a professional I have professional standards to maintain. I believe it's our obligation to warn the client of any perceivable business risks."

"It's not our job. He doesn't want to hear it from us. He's got MBA's to do that. We're just supposed to read the documents and make sure nothing's missing."

"I take a somewhat broader view of my professional responsibilities."

The aircraft lurched again, causing a hot cabriole of coffee to leap from Courage's cup onto his sleeve. "Look, Benedict, you've been assigned to me and your job is to help me get my work done. Lucky for you, I'm a pretty easygoing guy. A lot of Cheltenham senior associates would send you on the next plane back to New York. And give you a shitty report too. Got it?"

"I'll be delighted to return to New York if you find my work unsatisfactory."

"Cool it, man. I don't want to fight with you. I'm tired, I'm overworked. If I send you back to New York, you'll probably lose your job. I don't want to do that—to anyone."

"Cheltenham won't fire me. They wouldn't dare. I went to an Ivy League law school."

"You wanna bet? Wake up and smell the coffee. People are getting creamed all the time. They just don't admit it."

Benedict retreated haughtily. "I hope you find my work useful. If you would prefer not to hear my comments, I will keep them to myself."

"Do me a favor, okay? Here's the FDA application file. Just read it through and let me know if anything's weird."

The airplane plunged earthward in its descent toward the ice-fields of Buffalo. Courage leaned back and closed his eyes. He wondered if he could steal a few minutes in Buffalo, whether it was worth telephoning Gleiner during the day. There had been something about his friend's insistence at the Waldorf that still troubled him.

*   *   *

In the Pan Am VIP lounge at JFK, Gina di Angelo was sipping a glass of orange juice. Following Clancy's orders, she had just called in sick to her secretary. He insisted that someone might notice if they both took a long weekend of vacation time simultaneously. Maxwell, after settling her in a private corner with newspapers, had vanished next door to telephone his secretary and his wife.

He dialed his office first.

"Mr. Maxwell's line."

"It's me. Any calls this morning regarding Titanic Steamship?"

"Not yet, Mr. Maxwell."

"Okay. Anyone calls, tell them that I'm tied up the next couple of days and through the weekend at a seminar on Disputes Over the Three Mile Extent of Territorial Waters."

"Can you repeat that, Mr. Maxwell, slowly? I didn't catch it all."

"Never mind. Just say I'm at a seminar in San Diego."

"You want to leave me a hotel number where I can reach you?"

"I don't know yet where I'll be. Maybe the Marriott. Maybe the Sheraton. I'll catch up with you Monday. Just take messages."

Maxwell hung up and glanced across the room to where Gina sat next to the window. She was watching the planes taxi down the runway, while she smoked a furtive cigarette. Maxwell's glance swept over the other women in the VIP lounge, all middle-aged and stolid and grim. That caused him a gush of satisfaction. The light from the runway fell in a shaft across Gina's tight, narrow jeans, like an arrow. She belonged to him.

He slid his credit card back into the telephone. "Hello, dear."

"Where are you?" Eleanor's voice was still thick with sleep.

"At the airport. Is Oliver still there?" His nine-year-old son was his favorite.

"He's left for school."

"Don't forget, the HBO people are coming this afternoon."

"I'll let them in. You didn't leave me a phone number, Clancy."

"I'll call you. Probably tomorrow. If the cat's not better, I think you should take him to the vet."

"I hate those cats. You can take it when you get home."

"You agreed to have them."

"Only for the children. They scratch all my furniture and pee on the rug."

Maxwell smiled. He was content to endure the smell and hair and claw scratches as long as he was reassured that the two animals, Currency and Equity, were still ravaging Eleanor's house.

"I must run, dear. They're about to call my flight."

"Where did you say the thing was? Santa Barbara?"

"San Diego." Could he have possibly told her Santa Barbara?

"And don't eat shellfish. You know you always get a rash."

"I promise, dear."

Gina's face lit up as she saw him return. She hastily stubbed out the rest of her second cigarette and gazed at him with undisguised adoration. "Everything fine, Clancy?"

"Everything's just dandy. Not a care in the world. It's going to be a heck of a trip."

"I'm so happy we could do this."

"You'll love St. Martin. Nothing to do but sunbathe and make love and eat lobster."

"I'd love being anywhere alone with you for five days."

"You've never been to the islands, have you?"

She shook her head with a hint of shame, and thought of Cheryl, who had been to them all, as well as to Paris and London and Rome.

"Wait till you see the color of the ocean. There's nothing like it. And the flowers and the little birds."

The flight was called and they boarded the plane.

"We're flying first class, sweetheart?"

"Nothing but the best for you, gorgeous."

He had cashed in some of his frequent flier coupons to buy the tickets. Although Maxwell was a generous man by nature, he would not normally have been prepared to squander money traveling in luxury. He remembered the terrible battle that had ensued when Eleanor had once dared to upgrade them on a flight to San Francisco.

"But, Clancy," she had protested. "What does it matter? The client's paying for this anyway."

"There's no need to waste my client's money. That's how I keep clients. I give them the best service."

"They come back because you give good law. They don't give a damn about traveling expenses." The client was a prosperous cruise-and-hotel chain, with operations in twenty-four countries.

Leaving Eleanor to sit alone at the front of the airplane, he had strode down the aisle, past the formidable little curtain that divided them from cabin class, and insisted on spending the remaining four hours of the flight on his own among the economy passengers. When they met up at last at the baggage claim, Eleanor stared at him with pity and contempt.

"What are you trying to prove? You're always trying to prove something, aren't you?" She fished up her vanity case off the snaking belt. "You know, I used to like it the way you were always making a fuss about some principle or other. I don't anymore. We're getting too old for that."

He had stared back at Eleanor coldly, noticing with satisfaction the deepening lines around her mouth and throat, and the fringe of gray roots beginning to show at the hairline.

"Don't look so serious, sweetheart." Gina reached over the side arm of the seat and stroked the hair of his arm with her fingertip.

"Would you care for straight champagne or a mimosa?" asked the stewardess.

"What kind of champagne do you have?" Maxwell wanted to know.

"Let's see. We have either Mumm's Green Label or Perrier-Jouët." She looked at Gina curiously and then quickly back at Maxwell. Once again Maxwell enjoyed the flood of satisfaction. This stewardess who flew down to St. Martin perhaps five times a week had seen them all, the successful mature men who had used the façade of their achievement to purchase youth and beauty. She had his number, and Gina's, and he liked that.

"Would you care for caviar right away? Or will you wait until breakfast?"

"Right away."

When she brought them the plates with onion and shredded

egg and melba toast, Maxwell insisted on spreading the crackers for Gina and feeding her mouthful by mouthful. When he caught the stewardess turning her ancient eyes on them, the joy of ownership surged again.

"More champagne, gorgeous?"

Gina leaned back and held out her glass for him to fill. "I don't want to be drunk. I want to enjoy every second."

He leaned over and kissed her forehead to make her lashes flutter. She lay with her head on one side, basking in the morning light, as they flew smoothly south, into a turquoise sky.

"Can you pass me my tote bag, Clancy?"

"Sure. What do you want?"

"My book. I'm going to read a little."

He rummaged under her shawl and sunglasses and lipsticks to extract a battered paperback of *Anna Karenina.*

"This what you want?"

Later, when Maxwell got up to stretch his legs, he stopped to ask the stewardess for a bottle of club soda and whether the flight would be arriving on time.

"You'll be on the beach in an hour. I'll get the soda right away. Would your wife like something too?"

Maxwell tried to outstare her. It was useless. The eyes were wells of cynicism.

The plane gave a small start, and the stewardess caught his arm in mock fear of losing her balance. "Oh look, the captain's switched on the seat belt sign. We're on our way down." She winked at him. "I shouldn't do this, but if you return to your seat, I'll sneak you your soda anyhow."

Maxwell sat back again, leaning over Gina's body to drink in the vision of the lapis lazuli ocean approaching them every second. To the left he could make out the contours of the island's shore. The golden and pink coral sands beckoned.

Gina arched her back underneath him. Just as the stewardess returned with the soda, he leaned over Gina's lips to brush them with his own.

*　　*　　*

They arrived at a sleepy Buffalo airport. Even before you had inhaled a smack of the frigid air, you knew the city lay paralyzed by the cold.

"Let's get a cab," said Courage. "Jack Hagan should be in his office by now."

Hagan was the attorney who had been handling all the general corporate work for Goldilox, Inc. The "due diligence" task to be performed by Cheltenham consisted of examining all and any of the documentation in Hagan's files that pertained to the target company. While Hagan had already forwarded Goldilox's annual financial statements to Courage, allowing him to familiarize himself with the hair-product concern, the trip to Buffalo was intended to unearth the details of any outstanding contracts, commitments, loans, pending litigation, and FDA procedures. Courage had spoken with Jack Hagan a couple of times on the telephone. He found his slow-motion sentences and the nasal Buffalo whine somehow tranquilizing after an afternoon's frenzy at 57 Water Street.

They stepped through the terminal doors. Both men instantly pulled their coats tightly around themselves and Courage felt in his pocket for gloves. It was a raw, dry bitch of a cold day.

Courage, through clenched jaw and eyes, looked along the brown-and-gray street. "People actually live here," he said.

Benedict shuddered, fingering his cashmere scarf. "Maybe it's better in June."

"Don't you know the pattern? Clients always send us to Buffalo and Minneapolis in December. We get to go to Venezuela and Liberia in August."

The cabbie drove them between mountainous snowdrifts toward the center of the town. Courage had often traveled on Cheltenham business to a number of other "dead" cities: Beaumont, Texas; Emporia, Kansas; Akron, Ohio; Norman, Oklahoma...

and with a special shudder he always remembered Gary, Indiana. Once you arrived at those places, which suggested by the gray light of morning the ghost town of some nuclear disaster, the offices and interiors were all the same. The bankers were usually meat-and-potatoes types, outwardly cordial yet harboring a private suspicion of foreigners, out-of-towners, and particularly New Yorkers. The lawyers were focused, funneled, cautious people, accustomed to endless accumulations of paper. Cheltenham only dealt with the premiere firms in any of these godforsaken spots. And even those firms, as they grew larger and more sophisticated, had begun to catch some of the same waxy stamp as their Wall Street second cousins. It was like a gargantuan sea squid, Courage had once thought to himself as he sat sipping Jack Daniel's at the Fort Worth airport. Although Wall Street would inevitably remain the head of the beast, the inky mucus had now squeezed across the whole country, down the long tentacles, carrying in its flow the greed and toil that was meant to be making this country great.

The cab slid around the corners of the sad streets. The sidewalks were deserted. The driver ate a slice of yellow layer cake and turned on the radio. "Skies are brightening this morning in Buffalo. By noon we have the happy forecast for you that temperatures should hit nine or ten degrees. Makes a welcome change from last night's low of eighteen below. Well, folks, if winter's here, you now what can't be far behind..."

They appeared to have arrived in downtown Buffalo. Except for a handful of modern, commercial structures, most of the buildings still looked like warehouses. Jack Hagan's offices were located in a squat six-story house.

An obese girl in bluejeans greeted them at the door of Hagan's law office. "Jack'll be here any minute," explained his secretary-receptionist. "He called to say he got delayed shoveling out his driveway, but he'll be with you soon. Would you care for some coffee, or maybe a slice of pizza?"

She nodded toward a percolating coffee machine, next to which was propped a half-eaten pie of yesterday's pizza.

"No, thanks. We'll just sit down and wait for Jack." Courage took a seat on the knobbly tweed sofa, under a framed poster of the Eiffel Tower.

"I'd like coffee," said Benedict. "If it's no trouble."

The girl waddled over to the machine to pour him the brew in a mug that read, ATTORNEYS MAKE BETTER LOVERS.

"Gentlemen!" Like a grizzly bear in a padded snow jacket, Jack Hagan stampeded upon them. "I'm mighty sorry to keep you waiting. Hope you had a good flight and no trouble finding the place. Welcome to Buffalo." He held out a massive paw to Courage. "I'm glad to say you've brought some better weather with you today."

Courage took the hand. "I'm Peter. This is my associate Benedict Hamilton, who will be helping me out on this due diligence."

"Glad to meet you both," boomed Hagan. "I see we've been taking care of you, and you've got coffee. If you'll just follow me into my office, I'll get you set up with the files in no time."

Hagan's facilities consisted of the nook that stood for reception, one large room bursting with the usual stacks of paper, where Hagan worked, and a smaller room at the back, with a table, three chairs, a telephone, and a large unemptied ashtray.

"Will this be comfortable for you to do your reading?" he asked, motioning toward the straight-backed chairs. "I'm sorry the space is a little tight in here. Being a sole practitioner, I try to keep my overhead modest. Not what you people are used to, I bet."

"This is great," said Courage, wondering what Jack Hagan would make of the imitation fresco of Christ's Last Supper that greeted visitors to Cheltenham's fifty-first floor.

"I'll bring in the files," said Hagan.

"Do you mind if I call my office?" said Courage.

"No need to ask."

Courage called Gleiner at Cheltenham, reversing the charges. Gleiner's secretary took the call. "He's not in yet, Peter. He usually stops off at physiotherapy on Wednesday mornings. Can he get back to you?"

"Yeah. I'm in Buffalo. I'll give you the number."

"You're in Buffalo! I once knew a guy who had a honeymoon there. They're divorced now. You take care, Peter. They're expecting a snowstorm tonight all across the Northeast."

"That's great. Make my day."

Hagan returned with an armload of russet redwells. He spread them on the table.

"Cigarette, folks?"

Courage declined politely. Benedict sniffed disdainfully.

Hagan was unstringing the first redwell. "These are copies of their contracts with the manufacturers. Pretty straightforward, you'll find." He opened another redwell. "This is the original partnership agreement that I drew up for them. They each put in the same original fifty thousand in capital, they each get the same draw." Hagan suddenly looked at Courage sharply. "Hey, is that enterpreneur of yours really serious about buying these guys out?"

"He's interested."

"I sure hope he does. They're nice kids and they always pay their legal bills on time. It's a shame the way they've been squeezed out of the hair dye business."

Courage asked, "What's the status, Jack, on the FDA approval for the new product?"

"These folks in Washington, they sit on it. I guess you know they turned down our first application. They said they needed a wider test sample, before this hair-growing stuff should go on the market. Geez, they tested it on a batch of forty-five people. I'd have thought that'd be enough."

"Any bad side effects?"

"One woman said she got asthma attacks, but she'd always had them. Another said she got hemorrhoids. Who knows? One of them developed a brain tumor, but who says that's the product? You folks already have the financials, budgets, income statements, and so forth. Here's the file on pending litigation. Any questions about that, you can ask me."

"Fine," said Courage. "We'll roll up our shirtsleeves then and get moving."

"Anything you need, just give me a holler or ask my secretary. I've got a meeting now with a client who's buying a grocery store on Pumpkin Street. If you'll excuse me."

Still Hagan loitered in the doorway.

"You do a lot of real estate?" Courage asked.

"That's about the half of it. Otherwise, I fix people's wills, traffic violations, occasional divorces. Don't like them. I incorporate small businesses. Once in a while someone gets hit on Main Street by a stray baseball, and I'll take on a personal injury suit. It's a general practice."

"You like it?"

"Like it? Boys, I love it! I got nice clients, most of them pay their bills, I got this tidy office here, small but practical. I'm my own boss, out of here most nights by six, I do my best, and don't get a lot of complaints." He winked, brimming over with bonhomie. "No one'd call it a swanky practice like yours, but I wouldn't trade it for nothing."

"Right," said Courage as the thump of Hagan's footsteps finally receded. "Start taking a look through the pending litigation, Benedict. Any long comments, dictate them on the pocket recorder. I'd like to get home as soon as possible. I don't want to get caught tonight in that blizzard."

Benedict blinked mulishly. "If a job's worth doing, it's worth doing well."

*   *   *

Maxwell caressed Gina's bare shoulders as they bumped along the uneven road, past the shantytowns and naked children of the French section of St. Martin. The sky was delicious, a friendly breeze graced the warmth of noon, the cabdriver whistled and bobbed his head.

"You like it?" asked Maxwell as they put behind them the

tin-roofed huts and scratching chickens, to swing into the driveway of La Samana.

"Oh, Clancy, it's beautiful."

"Good afternoon, sir. Good afternoon, madame," said the concierge. "I hope you had a pleasant flight. Your name please?"

"Lamb," said Maxwell, and Gina shot him a glance of astonishment.

"One moment, please. Yes, we have your reservation here for Mr. and Mrs. Lamb. May I just take your credit card for an imprint, Mr. Lamb."

Maxwell did not hesitate. "I'd like to pay in cash."

"I'm sorry, but we do need the credit card."

"I don't have a credit card. However I'll give you an upfront deposit for five thousand dollars."

"You are planning to spend how long with us, Mr. Lamb? Five nights?"

"That's right. Until Sunday."

"Will you excuse me a minute? I have to check."

She left them alone in the cool, shady entrance. Gina searched Maxwell's face questioningly. "You could have used my name," she suggested.

"Too risky. Someone might check up someday. If you'd read as many discovery files in litigation as I have, you'd know that the key mistake is never to leave a paper trail behind."

"But Ariel Lamb," she repeated in bewilderment. "Did it have to be Ariel Lamb? Couldn't we have just been Smith or Schwarz or Sullivan?"

"Lamb's a fine name. It just came to mind while I was making the reservation."

The concierge returned and smiled ingratiatingly. "If you'll just let me have the cash, I'll make you out a receipt for it right away."

Gina's eyes widened as Maxwell pulled out his wallet from which he rhythmically counted fifty hundred-dollar notes.

"Lunch will be served on the terrace until two," explained the concierge. "You still have a few minutes to go down to your chalet first."

"Oh," said Gina. "We don't have time for a swim?"

The concierge smiled apologetically. Maxwell was disappointed too. Still buoyed up by the champagne from the airplane, he had been planning on some quick sex before eating. He interlocked his fingers in hers and squeezed them masterfully. "Never mind, gorgeous. Just wait till you see those lobsters."

Their chalet was simple but comfortable, with a tiled bathroom and a small window that overlooked a ribbon of jade sea. Gina changed out of her bluejeans into a Laura Ashley sundress, bought for her by Maxwell. She could almost pass for eighteen.

Maxwell studied her greedily while she brushed her hair. "You still hungry? We had all that caviar on the plane."

"A little," she admitted timidly. "Aren't you?"

"Hungry for you," he panted, diving for her mouth and forcing her back on the bed.

"Oh, Clancy, sweetheart, your Rolex is sticking into me." He had her slender arms pinned behind and underneath her.

"Forgive me, gorgeous." Suddenly the mist of the champagne had cleared and he felt a trail of sweat gathering at his neck.

They ate on the magical terrace overlooking the bay, where the minute yellow and crimson birds fluttered in and out of the vine-covered trellis, and emerald lizards whisked along the warm stone of the parapet. A waiter filled their glasses with an icy Montrachet and set down a garden of grilled lobster on the checkered tablecloth.

"We'll serve ourselves," Maxwell told him, reaching to fill Gina's plate with spoonfuls of seafood.

He raised his glass. "To you. To my secret princess."

"I'd rather not be secret."

"Be patient. Meanwhile—do you like it?"

"I've never been anywhere so beautiful." Or a tenth so expensive, she thought, not that the expense really excited her, only the treasure of a stolen weekend with Clancy.

Maxwell stared into the glittering bay, where the hill crooked its elbow to shelter the waters of the cove for the rich and powerful. "I just can't figure out," he said, his eyes drifting to the mid-distance, "why Bingham should want to buy the Titanic Steamship Company subsidiary."

"Which company, sweetheart?"

"Titanic's Great Lakes carrier. Transports coal and iron ore. Bingham, the CEO, has bought a major subsidiary for himself."

"He must think he's got a chance to make even more money."

Maxwell ladled another spoonful of lobster onto her plate, broke off a tranche of bread and placed it coaxingly between her teeth. "I love watching you eat. I want to fatten you up. The sub's run at a loss for years. Titanic wants to get it off their balance sheet. I don't understand why Bingham was prepared to take it. Your hair looks so lovely in the sunlight. Wait! Don't move! I always want to remember you that way."

"Remember me?" murmured Gina, opening her eyes wide. "But I'll be there, Clancy, won't I?"

He remembered the last time he had been to La Samana with Eleanor. They had eaten at the next table, or was it perhaps this one, the same gargantuan portions of grilled lobster. She had nagged him, reminding him of his allergies to shellfish, so to spite her, he had ordered a second serving. That evening he had sweated and burned, while his temperature soared, and an ache drilled through his brain, worse than any hangover. She had sat on the edge of the bed, dabbing at his face with a damp towel. Contemptuously.

He addressed Gina and the horizon. "Bingham knows the steel industry's shot. He must be counting on some form of government guarantee for his boats."

"Sweetheart, please relax. You aren't supposed to be thinking about this on vacation. Let's talk about us."

Maxwell ordered papaya and coffee. The midday sun was shifting now and cast a lasso of warmth around his shoulders. "I want that TBO to work, Gina. If it works, Ariel will be king of

Cheltenham. Now that I've pegged my future to him, I could be in bad trouble if Mel Samson wins."

She swallowed a bite of papaya and blew him a kiss through moist, juice-soaked lips. "Would it really affect you?"

"Whichever one survives, there's going to be a bloodbath. I'm betting on Ariel. I hope I'm right."

"Clancy?"

"Yes, my gorgeous."

"What's going to happen to me? At Cheltenham, I mean."

"Why, nothing. Why should it?"

"I mean, what about the 'nepotism rule'? That two lawyers can't be married."

He started and looked abruptly away from the coastline. "Don't worry about that. I'll find you a job somewhere else in a second. You can go into another Wall Street firm. Or I can get you a job in industry. One of my clients'll take you. For now, you just carry on. You're happy, aren't you?"

She arched back her neck, letting the sun kiss her throat. "I've never been so happy. Because of you. I know everything's going to work out all right."

"That's my girl."

An emerald lizard scuttled over the tablecloth and paused delicately at Gina's plate. They were two of a kind, thought Maxwell, exotic, trusting creatures. Gina's total trust sometimes made him nervous. He shifted his wineglass and the lizard pattered tremulously over the edge of the table and down the leg.

"If Titanic is sitting on a secret Title Eleven government guarantee, than Bingham's putting nothing at risk." His face gleamed with concentration. "Is the sun getting too strong for you? Do you want your hat?"

She studied the furrows in his forehead. The intensity of his logical thinking was so dense you could almost feel the heat of it. He pitched his whole soul into the struggle for clarity. Even at the apex of his lovemaking he held a part of his intellect aside, but that part was concentrated upfront when he grappled with the mysteries of some mechanism of admiralty law.

"Let's go swim."

He guided her from the terrace, between the tables of the remaining lunchers. He relished their appraisal that she was a little too old to be his daughter and a little too young to be his wife. Most of the women, in straw hats and caftans and cotton skirts, were about Eleanor's age. Gina roused their hostility and fear.

They passed the swimming pool, where the black pool boys flashed smiles of good-natured approval at Gina's legs, and turned down the path to their chalet. He swung around suddenly, catching her by the Laura Ashley sash, and pressed her back tightly against a palm tree.

"Oh, Clancy, someone'll see!"

"My name's not Clancy. It's Mr. Lamb. And I don't care who sees. I don't care, I don't care, I don't care!"

As he caught her lower lip between his teeth, out of the corner of his eye he noticed, like a déjà vu, a familiar balcony. It was familiar because it belonged to the chalet where he and Eleanor had stayed the first time they had traveled here, just after Oliver was born. That trip had been miraculously unspoiled. Eleanor had looked good. The birth had brought her a spell of contentment. Maxwell had eaten shellfish without ill effect, and drunk enough Montrachet each night to fall asleep peacefully tipsy. They had made love every afternoon before dinner, and even one evening on the beach under a tropical moon.

"Come on, gorgeous," he whispered now to Gina. "Let's go change before I lose all self-control."

"And disgrace Ariel Lamb's good name."

"Heaven forbid."

*   *   *

Goldilox's line of credit and its manufacturing contracts were straightforward. The contracts with the factory provided for delivery every thirty days of seven thousand bottles of hair dye, in pink, green, and blue shades. Goldilox must make payment within a further thirty days, or incur an interest penalty of 2 percent for every subsequent day's delay. Compounded.

Courage dictated the terms rapidly into his microphone while Benedict peered over the litigation files.

"Anyone hungry here?" Hagan's powerful baritone made them both jump.

"Can we order in sandwiches?" asked Courage.

"Better still, I could wheel you down the road and show you something of Buffalo."

Courage hesitated. "We don't want to stay out too long. I'm worried about that blizzard they've been predicting for this evening."

"You Big Apple folks are all wimps. We don't let a snow flurry get us down up here."

Hagan drove them to a seafood diner a few blocks away from his office. Inside it was dark, with anchors and harpoons strung up on the walls. A television set was loudly broadcasting an ice hockey game. Courage tried not to inhale the insistent stench of fish.

"I recommend you have the Maine lobster," said Hagan. "Folks come from miles around for that."

Benedict explained fastidiously, "Lobster makes me break out in hives."

"Shame. Then go for the fried clams."

When the waitress had taken their order, and brought Budweiser for Hagan and ice water for the Cheltenham team (there was no Perrier), Hagan cracked his knuckles and asked, "Any questions then about your due diligence?"

"You were right," said Courage. "Everything looks just fine."

"I've got a lot of questions," said Benedict. "About that litigation file."

"Most of that stuff's been settled. Bunch of frivolous claims," Hagan replied.

"No," insisted Benedict. "Not the claim of the first woman who turned blue. I wouldn't like to see you up against a jury on that one."

"What?!" gasped Courage. "Somebody turned blue?"

Hagan snorted disparagingly. "Sounds worse than it was. Some crazy lunatic, instead of putting the dye in her hair, went and swallowed half a bottle of it. Turned her blue all over."

"Permanently?"

"Well, so far. It was three years ago. It'll probably wear off, eventually."

"You mean she looks like a Martian?"

"Martians are green. Meant to be. The idiot woman was lucky she didn't die."

"Sounds like a serious product liability issue."

"What do they teach you boys down in New York? This is hair dye. It's not intended to be swallowed. If a consumer swallows half a tub of Ajax and suffers severe intestinal damage, are you telling me they can turn around and sue Colgate-Palmolive?"

"No, of course they can't," said Courage, but he repeated wonderingly, "She turned permanently blue."

"It's true she never actually settled, but that suit has been dormant for at least six months. I'll bet you they've packed it in. And now that we put a large warning label on the package, the other ones who swallowed later haven't got a prayer."

Courage put down his fork. "There were more?"

"Kooky thing about that. I never could make out why so many people should want to go out and eat hair dye. I figure it's because the principal consumers were these teenage girls and we know they're usually high on some substance or other."

Benedict treated them to a short exposé. "In 1985, after the first plaintiff went blue all over, Goldilox began to label both the bottles and outer packaging with a distinct warning, in one-sixth-inch lettering, that 'this product, if swallowed, may cause liver impairment, birth defects, and prolonged epidermal discoloration.' Despite the warning, two subsequent actions have been brought by discolored consumers. One of them, a twenty-four-year-old dental hygienist, is apparently bright green down to his fingernails—"

"There's your Martian," interrupted Hagan jovially.

"—and the other, last employed as a hat-check girl, has turned, inexplicably, mauve. Goldilox has suggested, in its reply to the complaint, that Plaintiff undoubtedly consumed a mixture of both their pink and blue dyes, however said Plaintiff has denied such allegation."

"It's immaterial," said Hagan. "Our case is watertight."

Courage mused. "I'm worried about the blue one. Before you put the warning on the label."

"Forget her. She was only a housewife anyway, so she can't even claim loss of earnings."

"Aha," interjected Benedict snappily. "But she's claiming interference with marital relations. Juries love that."

"They'll never buy it," Hagan roared. "She can have sex if she's blue. They can turn out the light. By the way, how's your lobster?"

"Marvelous," said Courage graciously. "Better than anything in New York."

Hagan beamed. "I knew it."

Courage insisted on picking up the check. "We'll charge it to Kahn," he promised.

Outside the weather had hit its peak of clemency, but the papery sky now threatened the arrival of the blizzard.

"I'd like to take one more look at the FDA applications," said Courage. "Then we'll shoot for catching a four o'clock plane."

"A Mr. Gleiner called from your office. He asked you to return the call as soon as possible," the large secretary announced as they returned to Hagan's small offices.

Courage dialed Gleiner's number swiftly. "David? You got a minute?"

Gleiner had picked up his own phone. The hollow echo on the line told Courage they were on the speaker. "Not really. I'm in here with Hopper. We're working on a new deferred-income plan. Looks like I'll be here until tomorrow morning. How's Buffalo? You enjoying yourself?"

"It's better than Gary, Indiana. But I'm not planning to come here for my honeymoon."

"Will you be back this evening?"

"God willing."

"You can catch me later, then. You know where to find me."

"Okay. Bye, David. Bye, Hopper."

The speaker phone picked up a savage snort, which passed for Hopper's response.

Although Hagan obligingly drove them to the airport, they missed the four o'clock flight. The next flights were fully booked until nine forty-five. With a shrug of resignation, Courage prepared himself for an extended evening of Benedict's company.

"It's been a big pleasure having you folks up here," said Hagan, gripping their hands. "I hope this deal goes through. I certainly look forward to working with you."

"We do too. You've been very helpful. Thanks for everything. And by the way," Courage added, "if you're ever downtown in Manhattan, don't hesitate to give me a call."

"It's pretty unlikely. I haven't been down in New York since 1983."

"You don't travel much."

"Oh, sure, we hop over the border to Toronto when we want some action. There's everything you'd need to find there."

When he clumped away, Courage and Benedict returned to the murky bar.

"Looks like we'll be back too late for your Fin de Siècle meeting. Sorry about that."

Benedict's face was a mask of duty. "The client comes first. We must always remember that, Peter."

*   *   *

Maxwell reached for the soap (a skimpy bar at the price they were paying), lost his balance, and plunged back deep into the tub, heaving a jet of water all over the bathroom floor. Gina, unperturbed, floated lithely on top of his body, like a mermaid remote from the cares of men.

"This tub's too small," grunted Maxwell, struggling to raise himself back on his elbows.

"I like it," said Gina. "It's perfect. It's all perfect."

Maxwell always took a bath with Gina after they had made love. He enjoyed watching her long limbs and tiny waist uncurl in the water, taking up so little space. It was like being alone in a tub, with his private fantasy suddenly made flesh. The crazy notion of ever doing the same with Eleanor, who was a grown-up, made him smile.

"We need some more hot water," said Gina. "I'll do it." Effortlessly she bent forward to adjust the tap.

Maxwell admitted that he had reached the age when men look better in hand-tailored suits than under the merciless glaze of clear water some time ago. It could have been worse, he reassured himself, with a fleeting glance down his stomach at muscles that were no longer firm. If his arms were too thin, and the skin sadly pale, a few hours of sun would soon put that right. Gina, on the other hand, truly came into her own as the Botticelli nymph when she nestled lightly between his legs.

"Stand up," he ordered. "I want to get out. It's time to go visit the beach."

She allowed him to dry her with the less than luxuriant towel, obediently holding out her arms and feet.

"All set?" he asked, scooping up his files on Titanic Steamship and the Bingham Stock Purchase Agreement. She was carrying her battered copy of *Anna Karenina*. They settled themselves in the sand, he under the shade of an umbrella, Gina in full sun, where she lay reading her novel spreadeagle as only the young dare.

"Maybe I should have brought some work with me too," she murmured. "My billing will be so low for the week."

"Don't worry about it, gorgeous. This is your treat. I'll figure out a couple of clients whose work you might theoretically have taken a look at. No one'll ever know."

"You'll charge them?" His nonchalance stunned her.

"They're big companies. They won't bleed to death. Are you still reading that Russian novel?"

A large man with a sun-pink paunch strode across the sand to Maxwell. "Pardon me, you got the time?"

Maxwell raised his reading glasses and peered at his watch with irritation.

"It's three thirty-five."

"Looks like this is a working vacation for you," said the intruder, undiscouraged by Maxwell's reserve.

"Looks like it."

"What's that you do, then? You're a banker, I'll bet."

"Not exactly."

"Don't tell me. I can usually guess. Let's see. You sure don't look like a college professor. Maybe some kind of politician?" He winked, with a glance at Gina, and scratched his chest.

Maxwell curtailed the inquisition. "I'm an attorney."

"Well, how about that. I guess I should have figured it out. Say, where do you practice?"

"New York."

"Oh boy, you must be a millionaire, then. I'm here for my twenty-fifth wedding anniversary, would you believe it? This place costs a bundle, but it's a big occasion." His gaze roved back to Gina. He held out a wide hand. "I'm a vet. My name's Chuck."

Maxwell winced. "My name's Ariel."

"How do you spell that?"

"A-R-I-E-L."

"Well, it's been very nice meeting you, Ariel. I hope we'll get a chance to talk some more. Say, maybe you'd care to come and join us for a drink before dinner one evening, you and"—he glanced at Gina—"your wife." Maxwell did not answer. "And by the way, you be careful of that sun. It's pretty strong, even at this hour. And don't work all the time, Counselor!"

Maxwell turned to Gina. "Shall we swim?"

Standing, she took his hand and led him toward the breaking

wavelets. As they reached the belt of wet sand where the sheet of ocean dribbled in fingers, he scooped her up and carried her triumphantly past knee depth. When he reached waist level, lowering her into the tepid jade sea, he kissed her hungrily in front of the whole audience on the beach, enflamed by the salt on her lips.

She swam a fast crawl, as he knew she would. Wishing he were younger, he struck out with a noisy, splashy breaststroke behind her. He could not keep up. A hundred yards out she turned around, treading water. "I love you!" she called, so clearly that even at the distance the group on the beach could hear the words wing through the still afternoon.

Before dinner he took her to the hotel boutique, where he insisted on buying three bikinis for her. His bill came to two hundred and eighty dollars.

"It's not exactly Century Twenty-One, is it?" said Gina, taken aback by the expense. Century Twenty-One, on Fulton Street, was the discount store where the attorneys sometimes crawled, after two sleepless weeks forced them to buy rather than launder whole new sets of underwear.

"Your name, sir?"

The saleswoman folded the bikinis in tissue paper and slipped them into a bag.

"Lamb."

"Could you spell that? And your room number? You'd like me to charge this to your hotel bill?"

"Yes. L-A-M-B. As in sheep."

"Like the animal."

"You got it!"

They returned to the chalet to change for dinner. This time Maxwell let Gina take a bath alone. Sunset was already upon them. Maxwell stared out of their porthole of a window at the crimson sky, in its tropical glory, which once again reminded him of his second trip here with Eleanor.

That time they had traveled with another couple, their long-standing friends Porter and Annie Madison. Porter, whom Clancy had known since Harvard, was now in charge of leveraged buyouts at Caroline Brothers and well placed to throw a few bones in Maxwell's direction.

While Eleanor and Annie Madison were changing for dinner, Clancy and Porter had met up for a drink by the swimming pool. Maxwell took a draft of his tequila and marveled at the sunset.

"About that hospital products concern we discussed," began Porter. "It looks like Management's going to take a stab at it."

"Ah," murmured Maxwell noncommittally, hoping hard that Cheltenham was to be hired to produce the paperwork.

"Should be some decent-size fees there," crooned Porter, staring fixedly at a parachutist who was just taking the plunge from a low-flying plane.

"I think I'll have another one of these," said Maxwell, shuffling the ice in his tall glass.

"Three of those and I'd be under the table."

"Practice. I wonder where the ladies are."

"I want to mention that to you," said Porter, shifting his attention from the parachutist to a water skier who skimmed the foam on the horizon. "It's about Annie's little job with Heritage Productions. I know she's just an assistant to the producer, but she's taking it all terribly seriously, and I'm encouraging her to have an interest of her own."

"As long as it doesn't interfere with the family," Maxwell agreed, "I think it's great."

"They're busy making some program at the moment about leading families in eighteenth-century Boston. Annie's all excited, thinks maybe they'll sell it to PBS."

"Splendid, Porter, splendid."

"The point is, she's really hoping Eleanor might let them do an interview on her clan. Just a couple of minutes, nothing fancy. They were such an important family, with their famous library, and being cousins of the Adamses and the Hamiltons and all that. It would give Annie a lot of clout with her company."

Maxwell looked away from the table. "I'm afraid it's out of the question. Eleanor absolutely hates that kind of exposure. When it comes to her family, she wouldn't dream of involving them in publicity."

"Hell, Clancy, this is only a dumb program. Some artsy cultural garbage no one's ever going to watch. Probably PBS won't even buy it. But it would make Annie happy."

"I told you, Eleanor likes to keep a low profile."

"I know, I know. That's why Annie hesitated to ask her directly. Look, if you'll just persuade her, I'll make damned sure Cheltenham gets the business for the buyout."

"It's really a matter between Annie and Eleanor," began Maxwell, wondering what Cyrus Sweet, as head of the Ethics Committee, would have made of it.

"We've known each other a long time, Clancy."

Maxwell drained his third tequila. "All right. She'll do it."

The sun was sinking fast now. Gina called out from the bathroom, "Sweetheart, would you bring my slip in here? It's on the top of my suitcase."

He found the scrap of silk and lace, which he vaguely recognized as one he had bought for her, and brought it into the bathroom. He admired her mottled body. "You got some suntan today."

"You too."

He went out, carefully closing the door, sat on the edge of the bed, and wrestled with a sudden attack of guilt.

He called the hotel operator and asked to be put through to New York.

"Hello?"

"Hi, Oliver. How was school?"

"Who's this?"

"Your father."

"Oh, hi, Dad. Where are you?"

"I'm busy working. Giving a speech in California."

"Will you bring me back a present?"

"Maybe, if you're good. What do you want?"

"A Nintendo."

"What's that?"

"For video games."

"I see. Well, maybe. How was your history test today?"

"I got all the answers but one. Who was the first person to sail around the world?"

"Vasco da Gama."

"Wrong! It was Magellan." Oliver's voice throbbed with triumph. He'll make a daunting litigator some day, thought Maxwell. "But I got that wrong on the test too," admitted his son, who clung to the truthfulness Maxwell had long since sacrificed.

"Is your mother there?"

"No. She went out."

"Where?"

"She went to see Mrs. Madison."

"Tell her I called. What's for dinner?"

"Broccoli." Oliver treated him to a theatrical retching noise that conveyed powerful contempt from two thousand miles.

"If you don't eat every mouthful you'll never get a—a what's it called?"

"How will you know? You're not here."

"I have ways of finding out." Maxwell ended his son's cross-examination as he heard Gina coming out of the bathroom.

"You look dazzling."

She fingered her cape. "You chose this color."

In the restaurant Maxwell ordered more Montrachet for Gina, while he switched to rum collinses. By his third drink he had decided that he might think about leaving Eleanor by the summer. Who would hesitate to give up a woman he detested for this exquisite creature, her long neck and arms resplendent in butterfly silk? He began the next rum collins and flirted with the idea of tampering with the brakes on Eleanor's Peugeot. At least there was good Cheltenham precedent. There had once been a partner at the firm, Humphrey Arbuthnot, a second cousin of the famous Horatio, who had been fatally shot by a deceived and irate wife. Cheltenham had, of course, taken on the wife's defense in the ensuing murder trial. The partnership knew that Humphrey Arbuthnot, in his grave, would have wished it so. To Maxwell's recollection, they had successfully raised a provocation defense and she had been acquitted. His thought train raced to Eleanor, with gun in hand, and then, even more petrifying, drawing up divorce petitions.

"Shall we have the grilled lobster again?" asked Gina. "It was the most delicious thing I've ever eaten."

"Whatever my gorgeous wants."

So they plowed into another platter of lobster and Maxwell promised Gina that every second spent away from her company was a lonely, squandered second in his life.

After dinner they danced until the effect of the rum collinses took its toll, coupled with the barbs of a headache reminiscent of a former evening.

"You're so flushed," Gina remarked once they were back in their room and as she patted after-sun cream over her throat.

"It's nothing. I probably spent too long on the beach." He lay on his back, eyes slitted, and feverishly watched her stroke the cream from her ankles to her thighs.

"Shall I get into bed with you?"

He wanted to say yes, of course, he wanted to stand, to hold her, to drag her hungrily into one of the narrow beds. But the sweat coated his neck and forehead, and his whole body felt paralyzed with the kindling temperature. She sat next to him, a naked Botticelli, and passed her hand over his sweat-soaked face.

"Clancy, sweetheart, what's wrong? You're feverish."

"It's nothing...don't worry...I'll be better soon...the lobster."

"Sweetheart, you're delirious. You're not making sense."

"Water. A glass of water..."

Then she was kneeling beside him, patting his forehead with a damp towel, as Eleanor had done once, and holding the glass of water for him to his lips. "You're going to be all right," she promised, cloaking her panic. "I'll call a doctor. There must be one here."

"No. No doctor."

"You need one, sweetheart. You aren't breathing right. And you're so hot."

"No!" Making a supreme effort, he raised himself on his elbow. "I'll be fine. It was the lobster. I'm allergic to shellfish."

"It's happened before?"

His unbridled brain romped and skidded in the shoals of delirium. Gina had been inexplicably annihilated, and where a moment ago she had knelt, scared, distant, useless, now there was Eleanor, dabbing at his lips with the towels and stroking his hand. "It happened last time...five years, six years...always that lobster...remember?"

"Sweetheart, don't talk. You'll just exhaust yourself."

"Annie Madison wants you to be on television."

"Who? What?"

"Porter'll give me their new leveraged-buyout business, if you'll rake up a few closet skeletons, Eleanor."

"Shh. Eleanor's not here."

"Who was Vasco da Gama?"

The long fingers kept stroking the back of his hand, stroking. "He sailed around the earth."

"Wrong. It was Magellan. You don't know anything. You've never understood, Eleanor."

Gina felt the raging body begin to subside into sleep. She went on stroking, soothing, mechanically now. Mechanical as the stubborn rhythm of the crashing surf outside.

"Just sleep," she begged.

He eased his hand from under hers, and rolled away onto his side. "I'm meeting Porter at breakfast tomorrow," he grunted. "I want that business."

When more regular breathing set in, she moved away, to step into the hand-brocaded kimono he had bought her one happier day, when she had admired it in a boutique window as they strolled past. The wavelets still rumbled incessantly on the beach. What had been a comforting, peace-giving murmur now became a ruthless, inescapable roar. She looked through the window, into the southern blackness, which offered no refuge. There was no-where to run to. In his bed Maxwell had begun to snore, an unhealthy rattle. Only the stars were clear, feverish and unnatu-rally bright through the still island air. She blinked at the Pleiades and Orion, the doomed hunter, and wondered what terrible crime she had committed to deserve this love.

✻   ✻   ✻

The airplane flew through icy skies toward New York. When they had taken off at ten in a light snow flurry, Courage's heart had soared as they lifted over the runway. Most of the passengers slumped quietly, drowsily, while Benedict leafed methodically through an article on the role of the spiral staircase in turn-of-the-century architecture. He had given up trying to explain its significance to Courage, from whom he received only a glazed stare.

Courage wondered whether he should call Kahn that night to report their findings, and decided that, risking his career, he would let it wait until morning. When he arrived home, he would disconnect his telephone, permit himself the rare luxury of a few uninterrupted hours of unconsciousness.

The Fokker 100 aircraft had climbed to its cruising altitude, and the captain had switched off the cabin lights. Suddenly Cour-age felt the immense pressure of the darkness, the obscurity of his own forgotten life in the plane, edging closer by miles through the night toward the river and bridges and Wall Street, spiritual center of the known universe.

Outside, somewhere beyond the window, the three stars of Orion's belt glittered, cold and mocking amongst the seven sisters of the Pleiades.

EIGHT_____

*C*ourage overslept.

When he arrived back at the forty-eighth floor at lunchtime on Thursday, he scuttled past the eighteenth-century reproductions of thoroughbred horses and cocker spaniels, hoping his lateness had not sparked off some new crisis in client relations.

Lorraine had abandoned her post in the secretarial pool, assuming he would not return until the afternoon. The usual stack of messages lay piled up on his chair, and his telephone blinked its red light that promised a further collection at the switchboard. There were the inevitable four calls from Kahn, one from Tristan Barrett, nothing from Michelle. An unexpected one from Cheryl Litvak read "Please call urgently, as soon as you get in."

When Cheryl answered, the echo told him he was on the speaker. "Oh, Peter, I'll have to get back to you. I'm on with a client who needs a new set of board resolutions."

"But, Cheryl, you said it was urgent."

"Yes, it is urgent. Very. I must talk with you. But this is urgent, too. The client can't enter into a contract without these resolutions. I'll call you back soon."

Courage called Gleiner's office, where there was no answer, so, steeling himself, he dialed Kahn and waited for the assault.

"Where the hell have you been?" The thunder of the accusation

160

filled the office and the telephone receiver jerked in Courage's hand.

"I was over at Salomon Brothers," lied Courage. Oversleeping was no excuse.

"Have you people lost all interest in your individual clients? You only care about servicing the investment banks? Maybe it's time I found a more conscientious firm to look after my needs. Do I buy this punk hair dye company or not?"

"There seems to be some ongoing litigation over dermatological contamination."

"You lawyers! Speak English, for Christ's sake."

"Some consumers swallowed the dye and it discolored their skin."

"Stupid schmucks. Can't they read the label? They swallowed?"

"One of them was a dental hygienist. He's gone green all over. He's suing for two million."

"Green? Two mil? Look Peter, don't confuse me with trivia. Just do what you're paid to do. Tell me: Does he have a chance?"

"I'm not sure. I want to evaluate it with our litigation people."

The buzz of an incoming call drowned out the torrent of invective. Courage switched lines.

"I can talk for a moment now," said Cheryl.

"But now I've got my client going apeshit."

"It's truly important, Peter. It's about David Gleiner."

"Just a minute. Don't go away. I'll be right there."

He changed lines again. Kahn was still ranting without interruption.

"I'll call you right back, sir. It's an emergency. Cheryl, you still there?"

"Yes. Did you just get here?"

"I had an eighteen-hour day yesterday. With Benedict Hamilton in Buffalo. I don't often oversleep."

"So you haven't heard the news? David collapsed last night. I mean this morning. About five A.M."

"Is he all right? Where is he?"

"Peter. Peter, he's dead."

"David is dead?"

"Cyrus Sweet told me. It was some kind of cardiac arrest."

Outside his window the clouds hung in a tranquil sky, in perfect equilibrium. Courage wondered if he were awake, if the effects of chronic exhaustion had finally caught up with him. He reached in his desk drawer for a half-eaten box of Crackerjacks. What he really needed was a cigarette. The sunlight pierced the river like a spear of steel.

"I wanted to tell you. I know he was your friend. I'm sorry, Peter. I really am."

"Why David?"

"Poor guy. I guess he was just so overworked it caught up with him. Oh shit, that's my phone again. I must take this call. I've got to get those board resolutions drafted so we can close on this."

"No, wait! Just a second. I have to ask you—"

She cut him off. Courage glanced wildly around his office, now washed by an iridescent rainbow of filtered sunlight. The rows of books on the shelf swam before him. *Commodities Law,* Prosser on torts, Williston on contracts, the 1933 Securities Act, stacks of bound volumes of completed deals, expensive black leather, the lettering tooled in gilt. Complexities and obscurities he had long since mastered, but what was the use, what was he to do now?

He called Tristan Barrett's number and spoke to Gloria.

"It's Peter Courage. Is he there?"

"He's in with Mel Samson. He said not to be interrupted."

"I have to speak with him. Right away."

"He's with Samson, Peter."

"I don't care if he's with Paul Volcker. I don't care if he's with God Almighty. Just get him."

"Peter, are you crazy?"

"Have you heard about David?"

"Yes. I'm awfully sorry. He was a nice fellow."

"He's dead, Gloria. Let me talk to Tristan."

She was firm. "It's no use. When you're dead you're dead. There's no way I'm interrupting a meeting with Mel Samson."

Courage buzzed Lorraine on the intercom.

"Get me a cigarette, Lorraine. Quickly. And call Gloria again and tell her I must talk to Tristan Barrett about David Gleiner."

"You eaten lunch, honey? You want me to get you something? A tuna sandwich maybe? Or a Coke?"

"Just get me Tristan."

She stepped into his office and left her pack of Salem Lights for him on his desk. "Poor David," she sighed. "Mercy on him." She closed the door discreetly behind her. Courage lit one and inhaled deeply. He pressed the key to the intercom.

"Yessir?"

"Have you got Tristan?"

"Not yet. But I have Mr. Kahn. Do you want to speak to him? He seems a little agitated."

"Tell him . . . tell him anything you like. I don't want to talk to anyone. No business calls. Take messages."

"Not even from Caroline Brothers?"

"Nothing."

Moments later Lorraine buzzed him back. "Mr. Barrett's gone out. With Mr. Samson. Gloria thinks they had a meeting at Davis Polk. Maybe you should talk to Mr. Finnegan. Gloria says he was the one who found him."

"Found who?"

"Your friend David Gleiner. Calm down, honey, okay? You aren't paying attention. It was Mr. Finnegan that found the body."

"Lorraine, do me a favor. Just leave the phone. Go downstairs and buy me a pack of Camels. And a beer."

"How about some tuna on a bagel? Or liverwurst? You like liverwurst."

"Thanks. No thanks. No food. No liverwurst. Just Camels and a beer. I'm going to see Finnegan. I'll be back in a while."

Courage went down to forty-seven, where the litigators strategized battles and campaigns surrounded by serenely smiling white-haired Gainesborough countesses with rosy-cheeked children. Fishman was riding in the elevator, scowling at a crumpled roll of telefax.

"Gary. Have you heard about David?"

"Gleiner, you mean? What a bummer. I've got a new problem come up on multistate commerce. Gleiner was the one who did all the original work. Who the hell am I going to get to do it now?"

Courage stared at Fishman, who went on flipping through the tangle of telefax. "He's dead."

"Yeah, I know. That's the problem. He really understood the taxation issues."

"Gary, he's dead!"

Fishman looked up, finally. The elevator doors opened. "Very sad. He was an unhealthy type of kid, but he had a good grasp of the multistate interpretation." He crumpled the telefax impatiently. "He's the perfect example of what I keep trying to persuade the partnership. We must provide gymnasium facilities for the associates. If Gleiner had been up there, working out regularly, maybe none of this would have happened."

Courage followed Fishman into the hall, past a painting of a duchess in lime-green satin. "What exactly did happen?"

"I don't know. What's the difference? The point is there's no other tax associate in this firm I can turn this matter over to without supervision."

Courage knocked perfunctorily on the door and burst into Finnegan's office. Finnegan, deep in a conference call on the speaker, paced up and down, dripping pepperoni from a hero sandwich in one hand. Startled by Courage, he placed a finger on his lips.

"We must talk," hissed Courage. "About David."

Finnegan gestured again for silence, glancing nervously toward the speaker machine, as if the instrument had a life of its own.

"We'll get more expert witnesses," he trumpeted. "We'll outgynecologize them. We'll bring in obstetricians from every hospital in the country."

A weary, battered voice bleated out of the speaker machine. "What do we do about these sex therapists, Mick?"

"Motion to dismiss. Sex therapists can't qualify as expert witnesses."

"Some of them are M.D.'s."

"We'll draft a motion to throw off any that aren't. I want gynecologists, gynecologists, gynecologists, nothing less. This one's a piece of pie, Harry. I'll bet you a hundred bucks we get a ruling by year end."

"Make it two hundred," came back Harry's voice. "Year end's pretty close and Vaginex is a pain in the ass."

Courage placed himself obstinately next to the desk. Finnegan, spreading his palms in a gesture of helplessness, waved at the squawk box.

"Now," begged Courage.

Finnegan shook his head resolutely and pointed to the door. Courage held his ground. "I have to talk to you, Mick," he announced loudly, enunciating into the speaker.

"Hey, Mick," said Harry, "with whom am I sharing this conversation?"

"Some associates just came in," explained Finnegan airily. Turning to Courage, he whispered, "I told you, I'm busy now. I'll call you when I free up."

"No!" shouted Courage, as the blood began racing in his temples. "My friend is dead. I have to talk."

Courage felt his breath coming quickly. He stepped closer to the gigantic oak desk that preserved a grandeur its owner had long since relinquished, and stared furiously at the cluster of china Toby mugs that functioned as paperweights. Finnegan's office, like his life, was an untidy one. The black-and-white photographs on the wall—no paintings—of somber, grateful CEO's and exotic legal adversaries from Tibet and Tokyo and Istanbul reminded the faithless that Mick Finnegan, in time past, had enjoyed in the glamor of a sexy, international practice. Somewhere perhaps his victories still had impact, as checks moved through clearinghouses in faraway territories, but here at Cheltenham he had been banished to his Elba of an office.

Surrounded by Finnegan's pitiful souvenirs, Courage suddenly blazed with anger. Pity turned to fury, all-encompassing and unchanneled. The physical sensation of it was almost exhilarating. Courage, who was calm and competent, usually brushed off provocation. Now it all surged up at once, rocketing through his body like a current, thrilling him with a short-lived burst of power.

He swung for the nearest of the grinning Toby mugs, with its sneering crimson lips, and hurled it violently at the speaker. The china clanged against the metal, setting off what must have been an unearthly screech in Harry's Midtown office. Finnegan stood transfixed on one leg, while Courage felt his own muscles quiver.

"Are you all right?" asked Harry. "There seems to have been some kind of an explosion."

Finnegan replied, with perfect self-control, "Sorry about that, old chap. We've been having electronic glitches all day here. The engineers keep testing up at the switchboard. Can I put you on hold for a moment?" He turned to Courage. "Pull yourself together, will you? What was that display all about?"

Courage, ashen, answered through his clenched jaw. "My friend David Gleiner died this morning. He was thirty-two years old. My secretary said that you were the person who discovered his body. Is that true?"

"Maybe it is. So what?"

"I just want to know what happened."

Finnegan stared at him hard. "Pity about your friend. It was very sad. I will talk to you about it. But not right now. I have to work."

Courage looked at the fragments of the Toby mug scattered about the blood-red rug. "How did he die?"

"He just...died. In his office." Finnegan slumped over suddenly at the titanic oak desk and burst into a flood of alcoholic tears. "It was horrible," sobbed the trial lawyer. "He was lying on the floor. His face was blue and twisted. I almost fell over him." His body shook with sobs. "I touched him and it was... horrible."

"Mick, stop it! Stop that!"

The sobs and howls redoubled. "They destroyed him, just like they've destroyed me. One day I'll be like that too, lying on the rug, at five in the morning..."

"Is that when you found him?" Finnegan gasped for air and nodded heavily. "What were you doing here at that time?"

He raised his head, eye sockets scarlet with tears, and stonily insisted, "Working."

Courage stared. Had Finnegan been attracted, like a moth, to a crack of light shining under the door, as he had lurched past the rows of dark cubicles?

The telephone sprang obtrusively to life. As it beeped relentlessly, Finnegan turned off the speaker and looked back at Courage. The weeping fit subsided under control. "It's no use talking to me today, Peter. I've got troubles of my own. You'd better go see Tristan. He can explain to you what happened."

Courage looked again from the shattered china to the twitching, self-pitying hulk of a man. He despaired of learning anything here. "All right, Mick. I'm sorry about your mug."

"Pax vobiscum."

Tristan was still out with Samson at Davis Polk. Gloria looked up from her paperback romance, holding the page of her book in place with a vermilion nail.

Courage fished out one of Lorraine's ridiculous Salem Lights. "You got an ashtray?"

Grudgingly Gloria dumped a pile of paperclips out of a dish. "You shouldn't smoke. You'll kill yourself."

"I'm upset about David."

"He's not the first associate who died since I've been here. There was that bankruptcy kid, what's his name, Chris..."

Courage remembered. "He went on vacation for the first time

in five years. Walks down to the beach, puts one toe in the water, and keels over dead. Gloria," he pleaded, "what exactly happened last night?"

"He died at his desk. From what I heard Mr. B. saying, it was probably a coronary."

"He was thirty-two."

"Yeah, well, if you stay up all night and never eat right, that's what happens."

"It doesn't make sense."

"I don't know, Peter, but when your number's up, your number's up. I guess it finally just like kind of hit him."

"What was Finnegan doing roaming around?"

"He keeps long hours sometimes."

"Was he drunk?"

"Maybe, a little."

A picture was taking shape. Finnegan, after an evening's carousing with Tristan or one of the younger unwitting associates, sometimes, rather than organize a limousine back to Connecticut, would return to the chaise longue in his office for a few hours' recuperation. Courage still shuddered when he remembered the evening that Finnegan had invited him drinking. Courage had been hardly a year at Cheltenham. They had kicked off with a few beers at The Captain's Ketch on Pine Street, moved along to St. Charlie's Bar and the Atrium Cocktail Lounge, and ended up picking up a Puerto Rican cook at the Edo Garden. Finnegan had insisted on taking everyone out to dinner at a Cajun restaurant in Chelsea, where he had become so noisy the manager had finally asked them all to leave. The restaurant warned them that the police would be called if Finnegan ever showed his face at the threshold again. Courage had suggested calling the car service to take Finnegan back to Greenwich, but Finnegan insisted on being dropped from a taxi back at Water Street on the doorstep of the teal-green slab, where unceremoniously he vomited long and loudly into the gutter.

The following morning Finnegan had been breezy and stubbornly unrepentant. He had only once subsequently suggested that they might "bend an elbow" together; that second time Courage had politely made excuses.

Before returning to his own desk, Courage took the elevator to the Tax Department on fifty. The usual climate of breathless quiet greeted him in the corridor, where the secretaries typed noiselessly on their word processors. It was a day like any other. The paintings of sixteenth-century European monarchs stonewalled intruders with their closely guarded secrets.

Gleiner's office door was closed. A sheet of putty-colored Cheltenham stationery was taped to the door, with the words "Please do not disturb" printed in block letters. Ignoring the warning, Courage entered.

Gleiner's office looked as it always had, filthy and chaotic. The window was still glazed with the grease of the nightly hamburgers eaten at the desk, the chairs, credenza, and file cabinet stacked with documents and random articles of clothing. A single sneaker stuck its toe from under the desk. The poster of Marilyn Monroe was propped against the wall, as it had leaned for many months. Gleiner had always been too busy to get around to hanging it.

Courage examined the top of the desk. Gleiner's precise handwriting covered several pages of a yellow legal pad with notes on the deferred-income plan he had been preparing. A number of black tax reports were piled beside the telephone. Under a grease-stained *New York Law Journal*, Courage found a plate on which last night's bolognese sauce still coagulated. Several Styrofoam cups, some of which held dregs of coffee, dotted the surface like patrols. There was no room for anything else but the usual Lucite deal souvenirs, a child's model of a saucer-shaped spaceship, and the framed photograph of Gleiner's parents.

Courage picked up the photograph and studied Mrs. Gleiner, a determined matron, with heavy lipstick and David's resolute eyes. His white-haired father looked less practical, even a little dreamy.

Gleiner had been the cherished, obedient son, who made every possible effort to be back at his parents' house in Brooklyn before sundown for dinner on Friday nights.

Courage had never asked the origin of the toy spaceship. He assumed it was some kind of talisman. Often lawyers kept bizarre toys or household objects in their offices, whether for sentimental reasons or because they had at some point put them down and then never found time to remove them.

The door sprang open. Ariel Lamb himself, followed by Hopper, strode in.

"Peter!" snapped Hopper. "Whatever are you doing here?"

"Gleiner was my friend."

"Can't you read? Didn't you see the sign on the door? The cops' orders."

Lamb, master of diplomacy, raised his hands in a conciliatory gesture. "It's a sad tragedy," he murmured, his voice pitched at a persuasive note of pathos, "but we must keep this office closed for a few days. The police may want to come back and take one more look. I'm sure you can understand, Peter."

"Why the police?"

"A mere formality. It's standard to report any unexpected death, particularly one involving a younger person."

"What did he die of, Ariel?"

Lamb stretched out an avuncular arm toward Courage's shoulders, in a calculated motion of masculine solidarity, then, changing his mind, withdrew it. "We're waiting to get the autopsy reports back from the pathologists. It seems to have been a heart attack. This has been a very sad day for all of us at Cheltenham. Unfortunately I never had the opportunity to get to know David Gleiner very well, but from everything I hear, he was a fine, conscientious lawyer, and quite promising in his work."

"He was a good person," said Courage.

"Oh, I'm sure he was that, too. It's always a special blow to us, Peter, when someone we know dies young and suddenly, but there's really nothing we can do except carry on with our work in the same tradition David Gleiner was so proud of."

Hopper had turned his back on them and was busy fiddling with the objects on the desk.

"What are you looking for?" asked Courage sharply, his rage now diverted toward Hopper. He knew it was an irrational diversion, but Ariel Lamb had that hypnotic effect on people. His rhetoric blandished the opposition, melted the foe.

"I need to take back these tax reports," muttered Hopper.

"Whatever for?" Peter snapped.

"There aren't any second copies in the library. We have to come up with an opinion by tomorrow."

"You're still finishing the project?"

"Of course. The client comes first."

"I'm sure it's what David would have wished," suggested Lamb placatingly.

There was no argument left. Defeated, Courage returned to his office, where he smoked the entire pack of Camels and gulped down the beer that Lorraine had brought him, returned Kahn's seven telephone calls, endured a brief conference with Benedict Hamilton, and made arrangements for the binding of the recently completed Caroline Bond Issue documents into leather volumes. He left Cheltenham early, before six. On his way home he stopped off in a dingy Irish bar, where he got so drunk he could hardly find his way back to his apartment. He had never got blind drunk by himself in a bar before. That night, though, he was certain he did not want to be with anyone from Cheltenham, or his other friends in the investment banks or law firms.

After his fourth double bourbon, he telephoned Ellis, the only outsider he could think of, from the bar.

"Peter, are you okay?"

"No, I'm not. I've very upset."

"What happened? Lost a client? Partner bawled you out? Didn't get your raise?"

"Is that what you think of me?" shouted Courage thickly, and hung up the telephone.

The following morning, nursing a hangover, he stopped in at Cheltenham for a short morning's work before heading uptown for Gleiner's funeral. The entire law firm had been circulated a brief memo, advising the particulars:

> We are deeply sorry to inform you of the death of David S. Gleiner, Class of 1980, Tax Department. We will all regret the loss of a valued colleague. Services to be held at Riverside Chapel, 76th Street and Amsterdam Avenue, today at twelve noon.

Courage was not surprised to find a scant turnout from Cheltenham represented at the memorial service. Cheryl Litvak arrived, in a navy-blue Chanel tweed, followed by a couple of earnest tax contemporaries of Gleiner whom Courage barely knew, and Cyrus Sweet, as sole representative of the partnership. Courage recognized Gleiner's parents from the photograph. His mother sat in the front row, chillingly still, any emotion masked by sunglasses with purple rhinestone frames. From time to time his father, the small man with the vague eyes, touched her arm.

After the service Courage declined Cyrus Sweet's offer of a ride back downtown to 57 Water Street. When the limousine had carried off the rest of the Cheltenham contingent, Courage hailed a taxi and asked to be taken to East 68th Street.

He found Ellis in his office at Hunter College, chewing a pen while he marked students' essays.

"I'm sorry about last night," said Courage. "I was drunk. Can I buy you lunch?"

"That's an offer I can't refuse. Can I have anything on the menu?"

"You bet. Even the shrimp."

They ate tandoori at Agra, where Courage knew they would find some quiet between the poignant twang of the sitar tape and the Shiva wall hangings of the god balanced as if forever on a dozen legs.

"Let's have extra raita," said his cousin. "So then, what's the problem?"

"One of the associates died yesterday morning."

"What happened?"

"It was a heart attack. He keeled over at his desk at five A.M."

"Ugh. Was he a good friend of yours?"

"He was a friend. I guess. I mean, by Cheltenham standards. We used to lunch together every week or so and gossip about the partners and firm politics and what was going on."

Courage realized that he had known Gleiner only in a professional capacity. He had hardly ever seen him, in five years, outside of Cheltenham. He had never even been to his apartment. Gleiner had visited him a couple of times at home, always for the express purpose of drafting something together or delivering work. Once Courage, who found himself with an extra ticket, had invited Gleiner to a Mets game, after which they had stopped off for a hamburger at Smith & Wollensky. Once also Courage had introduced him to a woman associate from Simpson Thatcher over a dinner in Chinatown. The date seemed to have been a success, although Gleiner had found himself too busy the next week to follow up on her.

"A little more than that. Maybe. David was kind of a lonely guy. I mean they all are down there, maybe he wasn't lonelier than anyone else. His life was super dreary. Billed eighty or ninety hours a week, never took a vacation, never had a girl-friend."

"He doesn't sound like your type, Peter."

"He was better then 'my type'! He had more substance than those white-bread Hamptons-condo-health-club preppy slime-balls I used to hang out with. David was a workaholic, but he was somehow solid at the center."

"Sad," said his cousin, spooning out chutney.

"I'll miss him. There's no one else down there I talk to much these days. But, in all honesty, if he'd jumped law firms, or gone to work for a company, I probably wouldn't have kept in touch with him either. Once you've left Cheltenham to work elsewhere, you're dead for all intents and purposes."

"What a place."

"It's more that I'm angry about his dying. He shouldn't have. They killed him—in a way."

Ellis leaned back, cupping his chin in his palm, and stared at Courage quizzically, as he was accustomed to doing when he wished to perplex some student with an unanswered dilemma of history. "Do you know how many young men were killed in World War One? The cream of Europe. All for nothing."

"That was a war. This is business. What we *do,* every day. It's supposed to be about living, not dying."

"I keep telling you, the way you people do it, it's not so different. You can come and audit my war class any time you like."

"I would, if I ever had the time."

Ellis shrugged. "Have you tried that tomato relish? It's got a real kick to it."

Courage waved away the food. He had hardly touched his own. "The rabbi's eulogy was pathetic. He talked a bit about how David was a kind, thoughtful person, which was true, and then he went on about ideals and striving for the best and never being satisfied with the second-rate. It was like a combination law-school transcript and the Cheltenham annual review. David was a tax attorney, for fuck's sake. What does that have to do with ideals?"

"I guess they meant he went to the best schools, and got the best grades, and got into the best firm."

"That was all they could say?"

"Peter, I'm sorry about your friend. But you can't bring him back. Nor can you change the system. You knew what you were getting into when you started. Those who live by the almighty dollar shall die by the almighty dollar."

"I like my job. It interests me and I'm good at it. I get a special satisfaction out of tracing a complex set of circumstances and facts down to a single, simple legal principle. It's the high-grade-puzzle part I enjoy. I'm what they call 'partnership material.'" Courage winced. "I don't hate the system. It's an impressive machine in a complicated world, and 'we people,' as you call us, deal with its cutting-edge complexities."

"So what's the problem?"

Courage sighed with exasperation and lit a Camel. He was not even sure himself anymore. "I don't know. All I know is, David should not have died."

"So he was a sick guy. He pushed himself over the edge and his body couldn't take the strain."

"They pushed him. They intimidated him. He was paranoid he'd lose his job."

Courage studied Lexington Avenue beneath them, where a beggar was harassing the passers-by. A Korean boy, wheeling a cart of lettuces, swerved to avoid a fat woman with a poodle, sending the vegetables bouncing into the gutter. A messenger on a bicycle swore and skidded onto the sidewalk. With a screech of brakes, traffic halted and burst into a caterwaul of horns.

"You're looking tired, Peter. You should take it easy for a while."

"I'm up to my eyeballs in work, but I'm taking Sunday off. No matter what."

"How about a vacation?"

"I'm sailing in March. In the Leeward Islands."

"You seeing anyone these days?"

"Yeah, I am. An investment banker at Caroline Brothers."

His cousin looked impressed. "Caroline Brothers! That's the new 'in' bank, right? I read a story about them in the *Times*. She must be pretty smart."

"She's very pretty."

"So spend some time with her this weekend."

"She's in Seattle. Anyway, I want to be alone."

"They're showing a Kurosawa festival at Cinema Village. You want to come along?"

Courage shook his head. "Thanks. But I'm not big on those Japanese art films. I'm going to stay in and watch the Giants game." Courage inched the check toward himself and fished for his Gold Card. "Don't worry about me. I'll be fine. Hey, how's that woman? The one with the pretty skin and the patchwork jacket?"

"What woman are you talking about?"

"You know, that one I met at your apartment. We had a little spat. She had those kooky ideas about economics. Eileen something? Hannah?"

Ellis suddenly remembered the incident. "Oh, you mean Helen Farmer."

"Yeah, yeah, that's right, Helen."

"I haven't seen her in a while. Hey, you wanna meet a cute ceramicist?"

"It wouldn't work," Courage declined hastily. "Your women are just too weird for me." He added up the tip. "There's something else. For two days before he died, David was urgently trying to tell me something."

"Like what?"

"Just firm gossip, I imagine. But something he thought pretty important."

"Don't let it get to you. It's always the little things you remember about people when they die."

"I woke up for a while at four this morning and I couldn't stop thinking about it."

"At four in the morning that kind of thing often assumes a crazy importance."

"You're right." Courage stubbed out his last cigarette and tore off his copy of the American Express receipt.

They parted on the street. His cousin thanked him for the lunch. "Don't forget, if you change your mind about Kurosawa," he added as he turned and scuttled north, back to the fatuity of a million corpses that had fallen in the muddy battlefields across France and Germany.

NINE

*C*heryl had been to Bigelow only twice before, when she had been interviewed along with her son. The school sent her a regular stream of correspondence, inviting her to parents' teas, class excursions, class concerts and art exhibits, graduations, Thanksgiving and Christmas assemblies, all of which found its way into her heap of unpaid bills and miscellaneous charity solicitations. A mass of printed invitations decked her home desk, all crested with the school logo of a steadfastly burning candle and the uplifting quotation from Marcus Aurelius.

Now she had arrived for her 5 P.M. appointment on Tuesday, and the receptionist directed her to Miss McKenzie's office on the third floor.

Miss McKenzie sat behind an array of bright geraniums, in a room of about the same size as Cheryl's office at Cheltenham. The walls were plastered with examples of student art: splotchy watercolors of forests and great setting suns, glitter and tinsel and tufts of cotton wool, tissue-paper cutouts and collages. At Cheltenham Cheryl had one framed lithograph on the white wall, a Rauschenberg that had cost her five thousand dollars.

Cheryl's gaze drifted from a painting of an elephant with a disproportionate trunk to Miss McKenzie's brown ankle-strap sandals, which were utterly inappropriate for December. The assistant headmistress was wearing a necklace of acorns and beads, presumably strung by some favorite student in art class.

"I wouldn't have asked you to come here today if we weren't deeply concerned about Bobby. You say you haven't noted anything unusual at home?"

Tread carefully now. Try to sound like a normal mother. Or suppose they've already talked to Bobby about his home, suppose he's told them how little he sees me. "Mostly he's good. He works hard. He does his homework. I limit the amount of TV he watches. I'm strict about that."

"Is he moody? Temperamental?"

Cheryl did not know. With her he was generally subdued, slightly formal. He might be quite different with Kim Phong. Annette the Swiss had complained about his temper tantrums, and she knew he had been churlish with the Russian. Cheryl left it to the au pairs to ration the amount of time Bobby was allowed to play with his beloved Nintendo, the bleeping, hooting videogame, which could absorb him for hours in "Double Dragon" or "Ikari Warriors." He used to turn nasty to the Russian when she interrupted his zapping.

Cheryl evaded the question. "You mentioned a further problem. After the fire alarm."

Miss McKenzie shuffled through a file. "Did Bobby by any chance mention to you that his class was constructing a model medieval village?"

At long last a question to which Cheryl knew the answer. "Yes, yes he did. He was quite excited about it, in fact."

Miss McKenzie frowned. "The children were all very proud of it. In fact we were planning to display it specially for the parents at the Christmas party lunch, which I'm sorry you weren't able to attend."

Cheryl shrugged apologetically.

"Which we couldn't do because your son got into the classroom alone during assembly and smashed the entire model to pieces."

"How do you know it was him?"

"One of the teachers caught him red-handed."

"Why should he do it?"

"Pique, it seems. He was annoyed because we couldn't use all his dead warriors. Some of them were just too... graphic. They upset the other children."

"Boys like blood and guts."

"Mrs. Litvak, I have a whole class to think of. I can't have the sensitive ones being terrorized."

"What exactly do you want me to do?" Cheryl recrossed her legs. Cheltenham paid her that robust salary to find the solutions to clients' complex problems. She thought of the hundreds of memoranda she had composed as a junior associate. Each memo was identically organized into four headings: The Facts, The Solution, The Analysis, and The Conclusion.

"You must talk to him again. Make him understand how his selfishness spoiled all his classmates' pleasure. He has to learn how to be part of a group, of a team."

While Cheryl was nodding obediently, she knew that she wanted her son to grow up ruthless; she wanted him to be a leader, not a follower. If all went well and she became one of the handful of Wall Street women partners, she would have achieved the pinnacle open to her ambition. Bobby, in his turn, as a man, could one day do even better. He could run an investment bank or a billion-dollar fund or a multinational conglomerate. Meanwhile, they must play their cards right. First things first; Bobby needed an education.

"I'll talk to him again. I promise."

Miss McKenzie stood up. "Bobby is clearly very intelligent, and I'm sure, with some effort and influence, he could turn out to be a credit to Bigelow and to you. Would you like to see our new science lab, Mrs. Litvak?"

She followed the assistant headmistress into the corridor, past the rows of classrooms, not unlike Cheltenham's hive of offices. She caught a glimpse of young heads bent over desks, scribbling onto yellow lined pads, as many of them would continue to scribble one day in the law-firm libraries. Proudly Miss McKenzie ushered her through the frosted glass door of their lab.

Cheryl feigned polite interest in the rows of vials and crystals and bunsen burners, the troughs planted with seedlings and the diagrams of the solar system.

A tangled-up coil in a mossy aquarium made her catch her breath. "What's that for?"

"It's quite harmless," Miss McKenzie assured her. "It's only a young common grass snake. And the tank is always kept sealed."

Cheryl turned away with a shudder to focus on a rodent skeleton.

"We've been able to renovate our old lab thanks to the generous donations of parents and alumni. I expect you were probably one of our foremost contributors."

Cheryl sat down abruptly at one of the long benches where the boys turned litmus paper blue and made flames glow in chemical wizardry. Suddenly she understood why Bigelow need no longer be an obstacle.

She pulled out a checkbook discreetly. "Actually, I've been so busy, I haven't had enough time to deal with my correspondence properly. I'd like to make a small contribution right now, if you wouldn't mind."

"I must say, that's very thoughtful and we always appreciate sponsorship. Make it out to the Parents' Association, please. Of course, you do know it's tax deductible."

Cheryl made out the check for a hefty sum. If she made partner it would not seem like quite such a chunk out of her salary later. With equal discretion Miss McKenzie's fingers slid it away, quietly noting the amount.

"We do so rely on support from our parents to maintain our facilities and standards of academic excellence. I'm sure we won't be having any more trouble with Bobby, you know. It's been a real pleasure having you visit us here today."

Cheryl nodded and obediently followed Miss McKenzie back

into the corridor. She tried not to flinch as they passed the convoluted coils of the sleeping baby serpent.

*   *   *

Courage checked his coat and joined the group, who were drinking champagne in a wood-paneled library decorated with shelves of leather-backed volumes, neatly arranged, like a doll's house, by color and size. Courage suspected the books had no text, that there were no pages behind the burnished spines. A crackling wood fire scented the air with pine.

Courage recognized the matronly woman with peacock eyeshadow who had occupied the telephone throughout their long night at the printer. As the senior Morgan Stanley representative, she assumed the role of hostess for the evening. Morgan, being underwriter to the bond issue, was responsible for compiling the guest list. They had invited about eighteen attorneys and bankers.

Courage took a glass of champagne from a silver tray and turned to deal with her.

"You're from Cheltenham, right?" she exclaimed, bearing down on him. "We met at the printer."

"It was a good deal." Courage lapsed into the automatic phrases, the formulas he had spoken fluently at so many other closing dinners. "I enjoyed working with everyone on it."

"They're a good team," she replied stoutly. "Have you been to Marie Yvonne's Cooking School before?"

"No, but I hear the food's out of this world."

"Let's hope so. We ordered a special case of 'sixty-seven Lafitte, which we expect you'll all enjoy."

Courage no longer cared much for closing dinners. As a beginning associate he had enjoyed them, not so much for a taste of New York's finest food, as for the aura of importance they bestowed. When the participants assembled for the first time after the backbreaking work of a deal, Courage thought of it as the closing of a chapter of history. When he was younger, he had considered that, by being on the team, he had been making history itself.

The shrimp from Milbank Tweed was talking to the virtuoso pig from Cleary Gottlieb. They were performing postmortems on the indenture. The shrimp wrinkled his forehead, to look thoughtful, while the pig merely grunted, swilled champagne, muttered inaudibly, and grunted again.

Courage found Michelle leaning gracefully against the fireplace, chatting with Brad Carpenter. "Hello, Peter. We were just talking about you." She extended her long, cool fingers. He glanced covertly at her cheek to check if his bruise was still there. If it was, she had covered it with makeup.

"Good things, I hope."

"Well, not about you personally. About Cheltenham actually. Are you involved with this exciting new TBO as they call it?"

"Maybe we shouldn't be discussing it tonight," interposed Brad Carpenter diplomatically. "It's highly confidential, and this group is a different team."

"Everyone on the Street knows the bare bones of what's in the wind," said Michelle.

Courage look piercingly at her. "Do they?"

She swept a strand of ashen hair self-consciously out of her eyes. Tonight she wore a military dove-gray suit, cut so starkly it demanded her perfect figure. She had evidently not had time to change between the skirmishes of the day and the refinements of Marie Yvonne's Cooking School.

"The bare bones, sure. That we're collateralizing our bonds with future tax payments. How we're managing that is the big secret." The china-doll blue eyes gazed back at him without a trace of intimacy.

Brad changed the subject. "Our nine-and-a-quarter-percent bonds were a fun deal. I enjoyed working with everyone on it."

"They were a good team," answered Courage.

Conversation faltered. Everyone picked up another glass of champagne. Brad tried once more. "You going away for Christmas, Peter?"

"I go up to my family in Litchfield," said Courage.

"We're thinking of buying a weekend house up there," said

Brad. "It's pretty in that part of Connecticut. And probably a good investment."

"Property's been appreciating."

"Who's that?" asked Michelle sharply.

Courage swung his head around to see who she was asking about. "That's my boss."

Ariel Lamb had just made one of his entrances. He stood tall, and very certain. While he did not immediately greet anyone in particular, the entire room changed in temperature.

"He's head of Corporate Finance," Courage explained. "Ergo, this was his deal. He brings them all in. This was mickey mouse. Four hundred million."

"Come on," protested Brad. "We worked hard on it. It was a good team."

"Oh, sure," agreed Courage mechanically. "I enjoyed working with all of you on it."

Lamb swung through the room, commanding everyone's attention, from the senior bankers down to the starry-eyed neophytes, the only ones who seemed to be enjoying the occasion, as Courage himself would have five years before.

Courage felt the arm clapped lightly over his shoulder. "Hi, Peter. Having fun?"

"It's been a good deal, Ariel."

"Splendid team. You all worked hard."

"Are you staying for dinner?"

"I wish I could." Lamb looked convincingly plaintive. "Unfortunately, I've got to run. I'm meeting with some new clients at the Parker Meridien."

Then the group was gliding into the private dining room adjacent to the library. Courage followed Michelle down a narrow flight of steps, taking care not to be separated from her.

The small dining room held four tables, where, to his dismay, he realized that places had been designated. In the brief confusion while the party scrambled for their seats, he managed to switch his placecard with that of a young Caroline banker who had been assigned to sit next to Michelle.

She frowned at his deft maneuver. "Is that wise, Peter?"

"Who cares? I came here to see you."

"Don't make ripples. Be professional."

As they sat, he reached under the tablecloth for her thigh. He felt the twitch of responding pressure.

The group had finally organized itself. Courage glanced around at the walls, covered in aubergine velvet. The Art Nouveau screens in each corner reminded him of an interior from one of those decadent European films so beloved by his cousin. Courage picked up the printed menu from his plate and read:

Caroline Brothers 9 1/4 % $400 Million Bonds
December 15

Smoked Eel Pâté à l'Ail
Iced Fennel Soup with Pistachios
Ceviche of Scallops au Framboise
Quail in Three Mustard Sauce with Oysters
Salade Indienne
Apricot and Tomato Sherbet
Petit Fours

Morgan Stanley was striking her knife against a wineglass for silence. "Ladies and gentlemen, on behalf of Morgan Stanley, it's my pleasure to see you here tonight. I'll keep this short. We've all put in some long hours. Speaking for myself, during the past two and a half weeks, I've only been outside twice in the daylight. After we closed last week, when I took a short walk along Fifty-second Street, I suddenly realized that the light was blinding me. Even through my sunglasses. I hadn't seen the sun for so long I felt like a bat or some night creature. And I asked myself, is this normal? Then I remembered a conversation I had a few weeks ago with one of our senior vice presidents. We agreed that when we finally get a chance to go away on vacation, we certainly enjoy it. But after a week or two we're always glad to get back to work. In all my time at Morgan, I've never really wanted a vacation to last a single day longer. And that's a little how I feel when a deal is over. After a couple of days, the only thing I can think of is getting on with the next one. I know you all feel the the same way, which is why I'm sharing this story with you. We do what we do because we know we're the best and we care about keeping it that way. It's been a splendid deal, you've been a great team, and I sincerely look forward to working with some of you again in the future on other new and exciting transactions. I hope you all enjoy our wines tonight, and Marie Yvonne's famous cuisine. So let's just try and relax now and have a good time for a couple of hours."

She sat down again, smiling grandly, as the waiters brought out the first course of eel pâté smoked with garlic. A round of polite, glacial applause acknowledged her address, accompanied by the chink of crystal as the invitees toasted one another.

Courage grazed his left knee against Michelle's, while on his right he shrank from the massive bulk of the virtuoso pig from Cleary. The pig, who took up as much space as Humpty Dumpty made his neighbors even more cramped by sticking out his stubby arms like wings, so that his elbows threatened their food. As the waiter set down the eel terrine in front of Michelle, her fine nostrils quivered an instant with revulsion.

The virtuoso pig was more direct. "What is this crap, anyway?" he demanded, spearing a slab with his fork.

"Just think of it as tuna fish," suggested the shrimp from Milbank, who was sitting on his right.

"I once ate jellyfish in Samoa," said Michelle. "None of the other tourists wanted to try it, but I thought, hell, it's only a fish, right? It's got to be low in calories."

But she left her plate untouched. Courage, who had become used to eating anything in his younger days when he sailed alone across the ocean, spread a mouthful on melba toast. The virtuoso pig stuck his knife into the pâté, scooped up a large chunk, and swallowed it directly off the blade, licking the silver with gusto.

"Not bad," he said. "Not as good as tuna fish, but I could learn to live with it."

"You take any time off last week after we closed?" Michelle asked the shrimp.

"Half a day. I'd promised Dorothy I'd take the baby to the pediatrician for vaccinations."

"Your first child?" asked Courage.

The shrimp nodded. "Ten months. It's been a rough autumn. Dorothy had a difficult pregnancy, and I felt kind of guilty because I was away in Cleveland on a deal when my son was born. Then he turned out to be a howler, so he was crying all night, and I got even less sleep than usual. Kids are great, but sometimes you've got to wonder if they're worth it."

The virtuoso pig had no interest in matters domestic. "You up for partnership next year?" he asked Courage, running his finger around the dish to collect any remaining dabs of eel.

"Not for two at least. How about you?"

"Sure, they'll vote me in by October, short of some gross miscarriage of justice. But I've been getting some other interesting job offers meanwhile."

Courage ran his hand under the hem of Michelle's gray uniform and up along her thigh. He felt the warmth through the nylon tights, especially when she squeezed her legs together.

"What kind of offers?" she asked the pig.

The plates were being cleared away and replaced with bowls of the iced fennel soup. Courage would not have minded drinking it so much, were it not for the unearthly bile green hue of the pistachios swimming in a slimy pool, surrounded by a halo of grated ice.

The virtuoso pig, to prove he could attack any edible concoction with the same ruthlessness with which he would force his client's position, struck noisily with his spoon, and replied, "One of them's a key IMF position for Africa."

"Legal?" asked Courage.

"Strategic. I want to get back to the economics field. I wrote my Ph.D. dissertation on Third World austerity."

"You're an economist too?" asked the shrimp, impressed.

The pig acknowledged his credentials with a noise that sounded as if he were gargling with the soup.

"Any particular countries?" said Michelle, covering Courage's hand with her own and edging it higher toward her crotch.

"The emphasis would be on Zaire and the Cameroons."

"It must be sort of painful," ventured the shrimp. "I mean, dealing with such poor places."

" 'Poor,' " sniffed the pig. "They're damned lucky they got their grubby hands on all our petrodollars in the seventies. Now it's time we saw some return in interest payments."

"How can you bleed a stone?" asked Courage.

"Ever heard of austerity programs?"

"But there's nothing left. What they need is schools and hospitals and agricultural aid."

"That's their line. Let me tell you—what's your name, Peter, right?—as long as they've got minerals and other resources, we can create a trickle of trade profit to service our debt. And when they've paid off some more of our principal, then maybe we'll think about building them some schools and hospitals."

Even the shrimp balked. "Surely that's not the IMF's attitude?" he protested.

"Maybe it's not the official line. But a good organization needs more than one viewpoint to give it efficacy. The IMF respects my abilities, and I intend to promote what I believe, as an economist, is in the best interest of the lender nations."

The ceviche of scallops, which followed the extraterrestrial tinted soup, was a visual pleasure to behold with its softly tinted raspberry sauce. Courage, who by now was becoming hungry and beginning to feel awash with wine, thankfully dug his fork in. He thought, I must try to stay sober. The alcohol, in combination with the pig's prodding elbows, was making him irritable. Sadly, the seafood coated with raspberry proved too exotic for him. In despair he laid back his fork.

"You don't like it?" said the pig. "I'll eat yours. The only trouble with these high-class closing dinners is they never give you enough food." Without waiting for an answer, he scooped up the ceviche in his pudgy, mottled hand, from Courage's plate. As he noticed that the shrimp had also surrendered the struggle with the ceviche, he helped himself to the remains from his right-hand neighbor too. "The problem," he explained to Courage, "is that the IMF, and the World Bank also, have been taking too lenient a stance during this entire decade. What we need now is a few hardheaded administrators to show these baboons that when we tell them to tighten their belts we mean business."

Not for the first time it occurred to Courage that anyone who tightened the pig's belt would risk a messy explosion. "Don't you ever feel a bit guilty," he suggested, although he perfectly knew the response, "about those starving, diseased, miserable people?"

"I've got a job to do. My duty is to preserve the lender's money, principal and interest, and in any way possible to make it grow. There's no room for sentimentality. You're a lawyer. You should understand that."

"I just design the mechanics for moving millions from one account to another." Courage was disliking this discussion more and more. "I don't actually take away food from starving children."

The pig smirked. "Bravo, your holiness. How'd you ever end up on Wall Street anyway? You ever thought about a career in teaching, or maybe with some not-for-profit group?"

Courage exhaled and checked himself from spoiling for a fight. Cheltenham training had gradually cauterized him, leaving him leperlike, with nothing but platitudes where nerve endings had once been functional. Tonight was unusual. The nerve endings, perhaps not quite destroyed, twitched again. In an effort to dispel his irritation, he slipped his hand under the elastic of Michelle's tights, and groped for the smooth, firm skin.

The shrimp was explaining to her the pitfalls of child rearing. "It's a lot of work. You'd be amazed. Even though he sleeps most of the night now, she's out there all day, taking him to the park and networking to get him into a good nursery school."

"School? Already?"

"You've got to start right away these days. The competition's a lot fiercer than it used to be. The minute they're born, you ought to start talking to everyone influential you know. Actually she started as soon as she found out she was pregnant."

"What did she do?"

"For instance, when she was three months pregnant, we gave a big cocktail party for all the string-pullers we figured would be helpful. Lucky we didn't leave it until too late in the pregnancy, 'cause it turned out she developed complications and had to have a caesarean."

The virtuoso pig was channeling his energies into the quail. He seemed to be crunching his way through it, bones and all, like a relentless garbage pulverizer. "Have you ever been to sub-Saharan Africa?" he asked Courage.

"Only to Monrovia. I once had to set up an offshore banking corporation there. The partner made some excuse so I had to stand in for him. Boy, was I glad to get back to JFK."

"Let me tell you—I'm sorry, I forgot your name again—Monrovia's like a luxury resort compared with some of my countries. If you had to work with these people, you'd soon stop thinking of them like Wharton graduates. It's easy to be Mr. Bountiful when you never get north of Fulton Street."

Brad Carpenter was standing to make another speech before dessert. Courage took advantage of the distraction to whisper to Michelle, "Do you want to try to slip out early?"

"Shh. That would look very bad. Someone might think we were seeing each other."

"Who cares? We are."

"It wasn't so bad last week when we were working on the same deal. What happens next time when we're on opposite sides?

"I'm sure it's been done before."

"Shh. I can't afford a smirch. I'm working on the big-time stuff now."

"I just want to talk to you, Michelle. Alone. Quietly."

Brad's flat voice droned through the room. "I have just one rather amusing anecdote I'd like to share with you. When we were pricing ten days ago, interest rates were kicking all over the place. Iran had blown up a couple of Gulf tankers, oil futures were zipping around like crazy, we all had a chill from the money supply figures on Friday, and it began to look like we might have to hold our horses. But then we figured, phooey, if we overshoot the market by a few basis points, there'll be some other catastrophe by Monday. It's been a bad week all around the world. And sure enough, over the weekend a chemical plant blows up on the Mongolian border, Chinese and Soviet troops skirmish, gold gets jitters, the Fed tightens, and would you believe it, we've hit the market with a bull's eye."

After cigars had been distributed, the invitees thankfully began weaving discreetly toward the telephones behind the gold screen, to make arrangements for their various limousines to collect them.

"Which way are you heading?" the shrimp asked Michelle.

She hesitated. Courage jabbed her anklebone hard with his heel, feeling the wince of her pain. The bruise wrought a magic that no tenderness seemed able to effect. Lowering her eyes, she murmured to the shrimp that she had to stop back at her office.

Then the party broke up quickly. Except for the Caroline Brothers people, Courage knew he might never see any of the others again. Once in the taxi with Michelle, on their way to 79th Street, he found he did not want to talk. So he kissed her instead, tasting the apricot sweetness of her mouth and skin, and he wished that Gleiner were not dead.

Once they arrived at Michelle's apartment, Courage took off his jacket. "I hate closing dinners," he said, stretching out wearily on the snow-white couch.

"You still hungry?"

"Starving. The only thing I could eat was about three mouthfuls of the quail. Before I choked on the bones. When we finally got to that tomato sherbet, I thought I was going to puke."

"Marie Yvonne's is meant to be some of the best nouvelle cuisine in the city. They got a rave write-up in the paper."

She brought out a ten-ounce jar of beluga from the refrigerator, with a bottle of expensive champagne.

Courage leaned back and closed his eyes. "You got any cereal?" he asked. "Like Corn Flakes or Rice Krispies?"

"I don't eat all that junk."

"How about cream cheese? Or peanut butter? Or—" He hesitated. "Or maybe even a can of macaroni?"

"Don't you like caviar?"

"Oh, sure," he answered listlessly and spread a thick lump.

"It's good to see you." She curled up beside him and raised her glass. "I thought of you in Seattle."

He touched her cheek lightly, where his hand had struck her. "I thought of you too. But it's been a bad week."

"It's always a bad week. What time do you have to be up in the morning?"

He shrugged. "Who cares?"

"I can probably sleep until seven-thirty." She glanced at the Cartier watch. "That gives us about an hour. Do you like games?"

"What?"

"You know. Like Scrabble and Trivial Pursuit and gin rummy."

"Not a lot. I haven't played anything in years." Once some attorneys from Shearman and Sterling had begun to teach him bridge, as they all sat waiting for two empty hours for a registration statement to come off the presses. He had never quite got the hang of it.

"I love games," she insisted.

"You're probably good at them. And you like to win."

"I always win."

He ran his hand under the jacket of the military uniform, which he slid off her shoulders. She was wearing a white silk shirt with pleats. He wanted to talk to her, about his life, about her life, about Gleiner, and he did not know how to start.

"You play Executive Monopoly?"

"What the hell is that?"

"It's like regular Monopoly, except with different names for the properties."

They spread out the board and apportioned the cash. After a couple of rolls of the dice, Courage licked some grains of caviar off his fingers, and said, "I'm sorry if I'm not a bundle of laughs tonight. A friend of mine died last week. I'm still getting over it."

She rolled the dice and moved her marker to Lower Broadway. "I'll buy that," she said. "Who was he?"

"Another attorney from Cheltenham."

"Gee, that's too bad. It's your turn. Aren't you going to move? What was it? Overwork?"

"Something like that."

"That's what they mostly die of, isn't it? We lost one of our associate V.P.'s last year. He just keeled over on Maiden Lane right in front of the Cardio-Fitness Center." She moved his marker for him. "You're on the Pan Am Heliport. Do you want to buy it or not?"

"No. I went to the funeral on Friday. Do you know, only one partner showed up."

"You should always buy utilities. They may be cheap but they bring in steady income. It's a good P/E ratio for Executive Monopoly. Oh, I get to collect two hundred dollars." She peeled it off avidly.

"If you died suddenly, would a lot of people from Caroline Brothers show up?"

"Who knows? Peter, do we really have to talk about this? You owe me seventy-five. Just concentrate on the game. You'll feel much better."

He rolled the dice mechanically and poured himself another glass of champagne. It was beginning to give him a headache, although he no longer cared. He wanted to be drunk, drunk enough to find some way to talk to her.

"Take off your skirt."

"Why?"

"I want to look at you."

She smiled and took off all her clothes, slowly stripping off her tights. The body was even more perfect than he had remembered. She turned onto her elbow and counted out more money. Then she rolled onto her stomach, sinking deeper into the fleecy rug, so he could admire the glorious curve of her back. He wondered how body and soul could dwell so far apart. Perhaps she had no soul, had pledged it long ago as the collateral for some bout of Executive Monopoly.

"Concentrate, Peter! You already own the Chicago Board of Options. You can't buy your own property."

"How much longer do we have to go on playing this?"

"Until I win. You just don't like losing."

"No! I've had enough." He stood up abruptly. "I'm going home. I'm tired. It's been a long day. And I'm bored."

The blue eyes looked up at him, appalled, from the floor where she crouched now. With an instinctive movement she drew a hand across her chest.

He picked up his coat from the back of the chair where he had thrown it. A quarter of one. He remembered her in the fashionably slashed jeans, standing beside him in the elevator at Cheltenham, wafting a cloud of sawdust scent. It had only been ten days ago, when he had wanted her with all the impulsiveness of youth. In almost no time she had mysteriously become the enemy, through no fault of her own. Even the delicate moon beauty did nothing for him.

He turned back abruptly to where she still crouched, paralyzed, speechless. "I'm sorry, Michelle. I'm having a rough time. We'll get together sometime again, when we've both got more time. Maybe we'll see a movie, or..." He moved toward the door.

His hand was already on the chain.

"Wait! Don't go yet!" Then she had her arms around his neck, urgent and imploring. "Please stay, just for a few minutes. I want to talk. I'm sorry about...the way I am."

He kissed her cheek and massaged the muscles in her neck. "Some other time."

"Tonight. I—I need to talk."

"Michelle, don't pressure me. You're always right, aren't you?

You always know best. I guess that's what makes you a star investment banker. You've got the right stuff, haven't you? But I don't need an investment banker tonight, that's not what I'm here for."

Now it was her turn to flare. "Don't bullshit me, Peter. You just don't like me. Maybe I'm not all that likable. I'm pretty and smart and incredibly good at what I do, but maybe I'm just not such a terrific person." Her voice dropped. "I'm in analysis," she ended inconsequentially, as if that condition somehow explained her shortcomings

"Don't worry. It's not you. My God, there are guys who would give their right arm to be up here with you in your apartment. You're a goddess, and you know it. You need someone incredibly smart and powerful. I'm not like that."

"My analyst says I'm too threatening for most men to cope with. I make them feel inadequate. She says that women like me always have a hard time. That it's lonely at the top. But"—her face looked thin and poignant in the light—"it's no goddamn way to live."

He did not hear her last words. His glance fell on the fleecy white rug, which struck some obscure chain of association in his memory. He knew it mattered and it was eluding him.

"Where did you get that rug?"

"I can't remember. My decorator found it. Probably some wholesale place. Why? You like it? You want one?"

He reached down to stroke the shaggy strands of white wool. It was soft, like the fur of an animal, a great white prize show dog or a stallion's mane. Why did the association seem suddenly so important? He half closed his eyes and studied the shape of the rug, wrestling with layers of memory to make the connection. It was an uneven oval, the contours reminded him of the continent of Australia.

"I'll call my decorator in the morning for you. When it comes to minimalism, the woman's a genius. She'll know."

"Let's get together when I'm feeling better," he suggested. "How about lunch on Thursday?"

"I can't do any lunches this week. We're working flat out on the Seattle deal."

"Thursday night? Dinner?"

"I see my analyst after work. It'll be too late."

"We could have a quick drink or something."

"No. I have to meet someone." Her face clouded. He sensed he had already trespassed beyond the threshold of her wounded pride. He wondered if it would be possible to make amends. He wondered if he cared.

"Never mind. I'll call you soon and we'll work something out."

At the door she kissed him lightly on the lips and slammed it swiftly behind her. He heard her sliding the chain back into place.

The elevator, like a sleek arrow, carried him away. His clothes still held a trace of the sawdust scent. The noise, from a canned choir, of "O Little Town of Bethlehem" drilled in his ears.

TEN

"Where's your highness been?" Lorraine accused Peter. "I had you paged ten times. Mr. Barrett's been looking for you all over."

"I needed some fresh air." He pulled out a gift-wrapped package. "This is for you, Lorraine. Merry Christmas."

She took the box enthusiastically. "God bless you, child. And a very merry Christmas to you too. Mind if I open it here?"

She ripped off the gold paper and, feigning surprise, pulled out a forty-dollar bottle of Poison, the same sultry perfume Courage had presented to her the past three Christmases. He had given her a large box of Poison soap last May for Secretary's Day.

"You're a smart boy. My favorite."

In illustration she wrenched open the bottle top and slathered a generous squirt behind her ears and somewhere mysteriously deep in her cleavage.

"Enjoy." He left her sniffing and dabbing, and closed his office door to call Tristan.

The partner picked up his own telephone. "Peter!" he exclaimed. "Wherever have you been? We've been trying to find you."

Courage could not rouse the energy to lie. "I sneaked out of the building for a few minutes. I've been glued to my desk here for a week. I absolutely had to do some Christmas shopping. I hadn't bought anything for anyone."

That kind of honesty always took them aback. "At five in the afternoon on a Wednesday?" gasped Tristan. "What's wrong with Sunday?"

"I was here all Sunday."

"Let's not quibble. I hope you've got no plans for tonight. Kahn's arriving any second."

"What's up?" Courage asked heavily, his mind already racing with his apologies to Michelle. Although the prospect did not ignite much enthusiasm (how swiftly the thrill and passion dies, he had thought, as he reluctantly accepted), he had agreed to go with her to a Royal Shakespeare Company benefit performance and then on to a four-hundred-dollar-a-plate gala dinner. Courage could take or leave his classical drama, and whether he in fact saw *The Taming of the Shrew* that evening was of negligible importance. The dinner, tickets courtesy of Caroline Brothers, would offer the opportunity to chat with some imported English Shakespearean actors, to whom Courage would have nothing to say and with whom he would share no common interest. He had not the energy to grapple with Michelle's relentlessness. The vision of apricots and moonshine was no longer enough. He had been quite surprised that she had asked him. He had promised, nevertheless, and to leave her dateless at the last second would add insult to injury after his recent rejection.

"Kahn wants a preliminary stock acquisition agreement drafted for Goldilox. He's leaving for Bismarck in the morning, and he needs to take something with him."

"Bismarck? Where's the hell's that?"

"It's the capital of North Dakota. Don't they teach you anything at Choate these days?"

"What's he doing there? Besides, we're nowhere near ready to make a serious Goldilox offer. We've got to assess the viability of those skin-discoloration cases."

"That's why we've got to talk to him tonight. He says the plaintiffs were schmucks to swallow, and he won't treat the pending litigation seriously."

Courage found the Hershey bar under his dictating machine, bit deeply, and called Michelle to make his excuses.

"It's Broadway and Forty-fourth," she said. "I'll meet you outside the box office at a quarter of eight."

"I'm really sorry. Something's come up here. I have to work again tonight."

"You tell me now?" she sighed. Then, drawing herself together, she remembered her own set of loyalties, as an investment banker, and swallowed the annoyance. "*Que sera, sera.* I guess it could happen to any of us."

"I am sorry. You know what it's like. Can you ask someone else?"

"At this hour? Anyhow, forget it. I'm used to getting stood up. Or standing up. It's practically a miracle in this city if two people can get some free time on the same evening."

Lorraine buzzed into the call. "Mind if I leave now, Peter? I've got Gloria on the other line for you. And by the way, thanks again for the Poison."

"You're welcome. I'll take the call." He told Michelle, "We'll get together one of these days. Really."

Gloria told him that Tristan and Kahn were waiting in Conference Room 4810. "Take a couple of Valium," she suggested. "Kahn's having one of his days."

Instead Courage finished the rest of the Hershey bar and sped along the forty-eighth-floor corridor.

In the conference room, a mushroom cloud of smoke from Tristan's pipe and Kahn's cigar already swirled around the crimson gladioli standing guard on the mahogany table. Kahn sprawled back heavily, threatening the two-hundred-year-old Chippendale chair with its ultimate destruction. Courage, whose usual encounters with Kahn were mercifully limited to the telephone, always forgot how tiny the tyrant actually was. Not more than five-foot-four, he estimated, and almost as wide. He had also forgotten the eyes in the egg head, which bored demoniacally through the haze of smoke.

"I want that draft delivered to La Guardia by seven-thirty tomorrow morning," rapped Kahn.

"We should be able to do that," promised Tristan mellifluously. Tristan was not the "we" whose duty was to draft through the night.

"I want," said Kahn, "to be ready to put the proposal on the table the day the FDA approval comes through."

Tristan puffed. "It could take a while. Those people in Washington move like snails, and Hagan's not exactly a dynamo."

"I don't want this company snatched out from under me," growled Kahn.

"I don't see a whole lot of danger of that," muttered Tristan. "So you really believe in this new product?"

"Believe! It's a revolution in the hair-care business! You see that?" Kahn tugged at the tufts of hair growing from the back of the bald egg head. "I've been trying it out myself. Twice a day, two tablespoons, first thing in the morning and last thing at night. I always believe in using the products of the companies I buy. That's why I never get a dog."

"So you think it works?" inquired Tristan politely.

"Works? It's a miracle formula. That hair's easily grown an inch in the last two weeks."

Tristan coughed dryly. "Can we get you some coffee or tea?" he offered.

"Never touch it. You got any spinach juice? Or beet juice maybe?"

Tristan turned helplessly to Courage, who explained deferentially, "I don't think they serve that in the cafeteria. I could get you orange juice if you like."

Kahn waved aside the offer with a beringed hand. Although he forgot the entrepreneur's miniature stature, Courage never had forgotten the flash of those jade scarabs and diamond-encrusted bands. "I only drink vegetables these days. Fruit screws up the digestion. Did you realize that? There's a free five thousand francs of medical advice for you from my doctor in Zurich."

"Most enlightening," said Tristan. "We do have some concerns we'd like to raise with you about the pending litigation against Goldilox."

"Blah, blah, blah!" shouted Kahn. "Don't I pay you people enough already in legal bills? You've got to invent me phony problems where there are none?"

Tristan, squirming at bay, raised his eyebrows at Courage.

"We feel it would be negligent," the associate dutifully took over, "not to alert you to the potential risk of the claims. Juries can be notoriously oversympathetic in favor of plaintiffs in product liability suits."

"You're telling me that when they put this green guy and this blue guy up there on the stand, they're going to award these putzes a million bucks for getting high on hair dye? Give me a break. You people here are getting a little overeager about dotting your i's and crossing your t's."

"We'd hate to see you get burned, sir."

"I'm a risk taker. It's my business. I got to be filthy rich by taking chances, and I plan to keep it that way. The day that FDA approval comes through, I want Goldilox, Inc., to be mine. I like the business and I see a synergy with Nutrexpress."

Nutrexpress, a fast-food franchise specializing in "organic" ingredients, was Kahn's favorite ongoing business. Its day-to-day labor-and-acquisition problems provided an endless source of headaches and legal fees for Tristan, Courage, and Cheltenham. Kahn had bought out the general partnership back in the days when Courage was just a starting associate and Nutrexpress operated a handful of take-out outlets in three states in the Southwest. In those debutante days, a limited range of gritty salads, peppered with wheatgerm and lecithin, were the only items available from the weird, orange, phallic-shaped huts that dotted the highways of Utah, New Mexico, and Arizona. The huts tapered outward at their roofs and were decorated with two bright green antennae. The concept, created by a once-fashionable San Francisco architect, had been intended to suggest the dimensions of a carrot. Back then, modest neon signs proclaimed, NUTREXPRESS, HOME OF HEALTHY HABITS—OVER ONE THOUSAND TONS OF VEGETABLES PROCESSED. Meanwhile, time and Kahn's boundless energy had metamorphosed the specialty franchise into a far-reaching empire. The carrot huts now speckled the roadsides of seventeen states. The menu included fried chicken, tacos, and chocolate sundaes, all manufactured with soybeans and other exclusively organic ingredients. The size of the neon placards had trebled and now read, OVER EIGHT HUNDRED THOUSAND TONS OF VEGETABLE-TYPE INGREDIENTS PROCESSED. (Vigilant consumer groups kept Kahn and Cheltenham under constant pressure to monitor the accuracy of the descriptive advertising.) Nutrexpress now did a brisk business of fifteen million after-tax profit, which had enabled Kahn to pursue his eclectic safari for new acquisitions.

"A synergy with Nutrexpress?" repeated Tristan in measured tones. "I don't quite follow the connection between organic food and a hair-growing stimulant."

Kahn's thin lips folded into a reptilian smile. Courage understood how that tight smile, and his surname of course, too, had earned the mogul a mythology of Tartar ancestry. Just so, Kublai and Genghis might have surveyed their armies encamped across the dusty steppes. In fact, as Tristan had once confided to Courage, Kahn carried not a drop of Tartar blood in his small, round frame. He was part Yugoslavian, part Albanian, part Hungarian. Yet the Tartar legend still clung. Although most of the time, Kahn successfully avoided any kind of press publicity, when the financial publications mentioned his corporate forages they rarely described him without the epithet "the Mongolian Marauder."

The thin smile stretched wide. "Easy. We'll cross-promote. Strike for the same demographic base. The population segment concerned with organic eating's gotta have an overlap with the one hepped up about natural hair growth."

"Natural," mumbled Courage. "I thought it was some mystery hormone."

Kahn chose to ignore this outburst of insubordination. "What's even better, we can heavily cross-advertise the carrot theme." To Tristan's raised eyebrows, he explained, "Surely every American mother has at some time maintained that eating carrots makes your hair grow longer."

It was quite impossible to imagine Kahn ever having had a mother. Tristan turned helplessly to Courage, who interposed, "I think you mean that eating carrots makes you see in the dark."

"Maybe, maybe," snapped Kahn impatiently. "That too. But also makes your hair grow long."

"As far as I recall," said Courage, "it's eating bread crusts that is meant to make your hair grow curly."

"There you go dotting i's again. That's why you people get stuck in this clerical backwater."

Courage would not have described Cheltenham, Arbuthnot & Crewe, one of the top ten law firms in the nation, as well as the oldest in the United States, as a backwater, but he and Tristan smiled humbly and shuffled their papers obsequiously.

Kahn leaned back heavily and the ancient Chippendale wood squeaked. "Don't go getting me wrong," he conceded magnanimously, "you're no worse than any of the other shyster law firms out there. Cheltenham's always given me reliable service—maybe not imaginative, but conscientious anyhow—and that's why I pay your astronomical bills." His Piaget watch, which was set for three time zones, suddenly gave out an unexpected alarm. The first eight chords of Beethoven's Fifth Symphony erupted sonorously from the small jeweled object on his wrist.

"The voice of fate," explained Kahn sententiously. "I must leave you gentlemen. I have at meeting at the Côte Basque with some people from Samurai Robinson."

Tristan cleared his throat. "You talking to them?"

"We've been kicking around a few notions for raising capital. I've been thinking of test marketing Nutrexpress in Australasia,

and some of their guys are sending signals. We're not in bed together yet though. You got connections there?"

Tristan's face took on his special withered look of lawyerly
discretion. "It's not a bank we've had any particularly close involvement with."

Kahn snorted. "Too bad. Anyhow I'll be on the seven forty-five
to Bismarck tomorrow. It's time Nutrexpress made an inroad into
the Dakota market." He wedged himself out of the Chippendale
chair, scraping the clawed feet back as he stood.

Tristan and Courage darted up swiftly.

"Let me tell you something, my friends." The little spitfire of
energy glowered up at the last scion of the old school of partnership. "A very successful businessman—never mind his name—
once said to me, 'If you can make a business killing in the
Dakotas, you can do it anywhere.' More people ought to remember that."

Tristan cleared his throat again. "I see."

"I want that stock acquisition draft messengered to American
Airlines by seven-thirty."

Courage held out his hand. Kahn's bejeweled fingers closed
around it. The palm was cool and damp. "I'll see it's there, sir."

Kahn strode out. There was just time for a spinach and mushroom juice cocktail before his next appointment.

*   *   *

Suzy Fishman puréed the spinach in the Cuisinart and added
the cod liver oil drop by drop to achieve a muddy consistency.
Tossing in a cup of chopped escarole, she tested the mixture with
a spoon.

The Fishmans, who both followed minutely regulated diets,
rarely ate out these days. Restaurant chefs and deceitful hostesses
might spike their food with polyunsaturates, dextrose, or nitrates.
Suzy, lean as licorice string in her black wool slacks, rested a
moment against the side counter. Her calf and inner thigh muscles

hurt when she stood too long. You would imagine, she thought, that working out three hours every day, the elasticized body would finally grow numb to the strains and excesses inflicted upon it. Yet she always seemed to hurt, although the pain brought satisfaction too. For she knew each day she was increasing, little by little, her aerobic stamina.

Gary had already changed out of his business suit into a black-and-white karate kimono and Japanese thong slippers. He looked smaller now, stripped of the insignia of his office uniform, and younger than his forty-four years, his beady brown eyes darting like a squirrel's. Suzy believed it was their diet that had not only stalled, but actually reversed the aging process in her husband. Gary Fishman—everyone said so—looked positively younger each year. He himself answered that it was a matter of attitude, as he simpered boyishly from under his ridiculously long eyelashes.

"You had a good day?" she inquired with ill-disguised indifference, fingering her heavy gold hoop earrings. It was unnecessary to ask. Gary was always positive and upbeat and all his days were good. That was, except when he became petulant with irritation at his fellow partners' misconstructions of the Internal Revenue Code. Then he would rant and kvetch, scraping the fiber off carrots and celery with his teeth, crunching sunflower seeds between his angry jaws like a bulldozer. Suzy, however, had learned to distract him from his tantrums. A reminder of his precocity (he was the youngest partner with so many points already), a flattering reference to the tautness of his diaphragm muscles, or, if his pique were serious, a quick frolic in the red satin garter belt was guaranteed to dispel the storm clouds.

"Ariel's promised Hopper another two points if the TBO deal goes through," he grumbled, sipping at his cabernet. Fishman always drank exactly two glasses of red wine each evening, one before dinner and one with his food. He had never, in his whole life, drunk one mouthful over that self-imposed limit; without his wine, nevertheless, he felt deprived of his day's deserved treat.

"How many will that give him?" asked Suzy absently, stirring the pot of linguini. With the other hand she felt for the knot at the nape of her neck, where her jet-black hair was tightly pulled into its shiny chigon.

"Nine. It's an outrage that he should have only three points less than I do, just for being Ariel's pet yes man. I'm the one who did all the work, closing up the tax evasion loopholes in Colombia and Equador."

She was not concentrating on his complaints, although somewhere at the back of her mind, she did not disagree that another few hundred thousand dollars would be refreshing. "If they don't increase your points, you can always move to another firm," she suggested. "Anyone on Wall Street would jump to get you."

She passed him a glass plate heaped with high-fiber linguini, and capped with a blob of the spinach mixture. He carried it dutifully out to the black lacquer dining table. Before she joined him he slipped a disc into the compact player, flooding the living-dining room with the Jupiter Symphony. For a year now, they had always played Mozart at meals. They also owned a Vivaldi and a Haydn disc, but those composers got infrequent airings. Fishman had become infatuated with Mozart. He had decided he must have it, every evening, with the same adamant regularity with which he drank his two glasses of cabernet sauvignon. The notes spilled with a naked wistfulness into the elaborate tomb where they dined.

Fishman had chosen the décor, which Suzy had implemented with the help of an army of designers. Twenty-eight stories high over East 87th Street, she had pasted a dark, sacklike fabric as wallpaper from floor to ceiling. The tables, the sideboards, and piano were all coordinated in black lacquer and splashed with a white tadpolelike motif. The furniture, which matched in black leather, squeaked and heaved when sat upon.

"What about the candles?" asked Suzy, emerging from the kitchen with her own plate. The Fishmans always dined by candlelight.

"Oh, sure." Gary jumped up like a child, rebuked but anxious to please. He lit the wax clusters planted in Lalique glass holders, with a Cartier lighter bought expressly for the purpose. No cigarettes were permitted to pass the threshold of the Fishman establishment.

"Where's Diane?" he asked, spearing his mountain of linguini.

"She's staying over with one of her friends from riding school."

Diane Fishman was their only child. She followed a schedule as precise as that of a prize racehorse. On Mondays and Wednesdays she took ballet lessons, on Tuesdays piano, and on Thursdays Intermediate French Conversation. Every other Friday she played the clarinet in a chamber music group. On Saturdays there was Hebrew School. Her only pleasure amidst all this hothouse nurture was the diversion of the riding lesson in Central Park on Sunday afternoons.

"I thought she had ballet tonight."

"She claims she's hurt her ankle. What's wrong with your linguini?"

"Nothing," he answered, hastily swallowing a mouthful and wondering what gave it that oily, fishy taste.

"That's right, eat it up. It's loaded with vitamins and minerals. Would you rather have broccoli pie?" she added.

"This is delicious," he replied humbly and tried to concentrate on the Mozart.

"Is the trip to South America still on for January? You'll get nothing but junk food down there, I guarantee. I'll pack you a lunchbox to take on the plane, and stock you up with granola bars, but that won't last long."

"I wish I didn't have to go," he whined.

"You must go," she admonished, tapping the lacquer tabletop with her obscenely overextended fingernails. "You've got Puerto Rico the week after," she added cajolingly.

"Yup, and Zurich the first week in February. What do you want as your present from Zurich?"

"Maybe a watch. I'll think about it. But no more of those stupid chocolates like last time. I ate them all at once and had to make myself throw up. I think I'll come with you to Hawaii in March."

"I'll be pretty busy with seminars."

"I'll shop."

Every evening, against the background cadences and trills of Mozart symphonies and concertos, the Fishmans discussed his future travel itineraries, which were preplanned about six months out. As an international tax expert, Gary had more opportunity to travel than many of the other Cheltenham specialists. Wherever he went in the world, he spent few seconds outside the offices of his clients or the hotel ballrooms where conferences were organized. Occasionally he might pass a quarter of an hour catching up on business news, fully dressed, by the edge of a swimming pool. In Switzerland he would see no mountains, except from the airplane as he landed; in Waikiki he would never set foot near the ocean. In all his years at Cheltenham, he had never visited a foreign museum, or the historic streets of a European capital, or even taken the time for a glimpse of a landscape. As he explained to Suzy and Diane, he was far too busy, during his travels, to indulge in ancillary excursions.

Suzy accompanied him occasionally. The trips represented an extended purchasing field. Otherwise she would send him off with a packed lunch of raw vegetables for the air trip out, and explicit instructions as to her requirements for a coming-home present.

She spooned another helping onto his plate. He began reluctantly to eat it. In matters of nutrition, and most other areas, she retained the whip hand.

"How about a chinchilla?"

"What?"

"From South America. I want a chinchilla."

"Chinchillas are pretty expensive."

"Aren't I worth it?"

"You sure Diane's out for the night?"

"I told you, she's sleeping over."

He reached across the table, plunging a hand into the turtleneck of her cashmere sweater, and excavated between her breasts.

"Careful. You'll stretch the wool."

"You really want a chinchilla?"

"I really need one."

"Okay. Get the stuff."

She dislodged his hand from beneath her sweater. Eagerly he watched her retreat to the bedroom closet.

When she returned he was lying stretched out on the low sofa, the string of the kimono loosened to show the dense hair on his chest, thick as a nest, where his gold neck chain rested. His eyes were closed under the long lashes.

"They're going to cut Finnegan's points again," he said. "Or fire him for sure this time."

She towered over him, swaying in the high-heeled cowboy boots. With one hand behind her back, she readjusted the slipping scarlet satin garter belt. Better. If only the wires of the half-cup matching brassiere did not cut so deeply into her flesh, leaving the ugly welts behind. Though he liked that, almost as much as his own submission. She recalled his throb of excitement the first time he had discovered the itching imprints.

"Why have you still only got twelve points?" she demanded, twisting the lash of her whip, like a wriggling snake, against his thigh.

He groaned joyfully. "Maybe I haven't been working hard enough."

She cracked it down across his legs, making a noise but not hard enough to cause real pain. "Why haven't you been working harder? You should have at least fifteen points by now."

"I'll have fifteen points soon. I swear I will."

This time she wielded it viciously, knowing as he squirmed that he had felt the sting. "Turn over. I want my chinchilla and twelve points isn't enough."

He rocked against the black leather with delight. "I'll make them give me more points. I'm one of the best tax attorneys on Wall Street. I promise."

"That's what you always say. Now prove it to me." She ground a sharp heel through the material of the kimono, into the small of his back.

"Oh, God," he implored her. "I'll show you how good I can be. Ariel couldn't pull off the TBO deal without me. The whole future of Cheltenham could depend on me. Oh yes, yes, yes! But I'll work even harder, I swear, I swear. Again, just once more! They'll see how well I know the Internal Revenue Code. Oh, God!"

Under the prancing tongue of the whip he collapsed in a convulsion of ecstasy. Suzy sighed and readjusted the garter belt where it had begun to slip again. In just another minute she could bring out the Tofutti dessert that was still waiting for them in the kitchen.

With the crash of the majestic conclusion, the Jupiter Symphony reached the chords of its finale.

*　　*　　*

Courage hunkered down with Kahn's contract. After several hours of juggling clauses, he had a rough preliminary draft out by eleven. As he cut and pasted a final section of boilerplate to be delivered up to Word Processing for typing, he enjoyed the relief of being able to seal off at least one chamber of his weary brain for the night. With some luck, the draft might be returned to him within a couple of hours, at which point he could yawn his way through it again, pruning the language and double-checking the stipulations.

Word Processing was hopping tonight. All twenty or so of the operators sat glued to their noiseless screens under the fluorescent glare of the factory light. Courage glanced across the sea of heads, divided by shoulder-high partitions, for a sympathetic face amidst the strange crew of dancers and painters and poets who eked out a living in the Wall Street night. One of the dancers, a blonde with turquoise streaks in her hair, smiled at him shyly, so he edged through the aisles to where she sat.

"Got any time tonight, Valeria?"

She put a finger to her lips. "Don't tell the controller. We're not supposed to give anyone priority time. But when I've finished working on this Maxwell job, I'll try and sneak yours in. Is it long?"

"About eighteen pages. But it's pretty legible."

Courage was one of the few attorneys who was popular in Word Processing. The nocturnal factory had a mind and heart-beat of its own. Those lawyers who had the time or sensitivity to notice might have registered the frisson of contempt, as they sauntered between the ranks of heads bowed with their own strange dignity. Courage's good-natured eyes and his easy man-ners helped keep the scorn at bay. They sometimes even invited him to their off-off Broadway plays, their gallery openings and recitals. He had never had the time or energy to show up, but perhaps one day, he thought vaguely, he might.

He returned to his office, wishing that Gleiner were around to help him pass the interminable middle hours of the night. Yet he was so immersed in redrafting the indemnification provision, at first he did not hear the soft knock on the open door. When the knock came again, he looked up sleepily and blinked.

The girl was wearing bluejeans and an oversized sweater, which was unraveling at the shoulder. He scanned her face briefly, trying to remember why he should remember her.

"Peter? Peter Courage?"

"Yeah."

"Can I come in?"

He waved her in. "You got my stock purchase agreement?"

She smiled with a kind of private amusement. Courage had never seen anyone in the halls of Cheltenham look so calm.

"Remember me? I'm Helen Farmer. We met at your cousin's party last year."

Surprised, Courage now gave her a second glance. Her dirty-blond hair fell in natural ringlets around a wide forehead. She gazed at him steadily with clear eyes.

"Whatever are *you* doing down here at one A.M.?"

She smiled again, without malice. "First time yet. I'm a proof-reader."

"Ah." He tried to recall that first encounter. "Aren't you some kind of student?"

"Yes and no. I'm writing an art history dissertation."

"I see," said Courage indifferently. Automatically his hand caressed his pencil where he had been caught in midsentence.

Goldilox agrees to indemnify the Purchaser for any and all liabilities, obligations, losses, damages, payments, costs, or expenses of any kind whatsoever that may be imposed on, incurred, or asserted against the Purchaser, as the result of any act or omission by Golidlox...

She hesitated. "I guess I'm interrupting. You're busy."

The phrases and adjectives he sculpted had never seemed so lifeless. "I'm waiting for an agreement to come out of Word Processing," he apologized.

"Ellis says you work pretty hard. That you're here most nights."

"We all are."

"You like it?"

Courage frowned, bewildered. "What do you mean?"

"Your work."

He stared again, into the clear eyes and at the shaggy, tousled hair, which made him think of an unmade bed. "It's my job."

The remote amusement quivered again. "You are busy. I'm sorry to disturb you." She turned to leave.

"No. Wait! I didn't mean to be rude. I just get tired. It's so late."

"You weren't rude." She already had one foot on the blood-colored carpet of the corridor.

"Please! Just a second. Tell me. What kind of art history do you do?" He sounded desperate, absurd. "I want to know."

"Japanese. The Muromachi period. Fifteenth and sixteenth century."

"Oh, those Muromachis," said Courage facetiously.

"I'm writing my dissertation on the nostalgia of the samurai warlords for a life of reclusion."

Courage made an effort to revive those chambers of his brain he had already shut down for the night. "If they were warlords, why did they want to be recluses?"

"Japan was a pretty crazy place in 1500. The samurai were all fighting among themselves and the monasteries had turned into big bureaucracies. Kind of like here." She cast a sweeping glance across his office, from the bookshelves lined with corporate and commodities references to the rows of redwells marking the floor like building bricks. "Both the monks and warriors felt a nostalgia for the simple life of the Zen scholar. They'd lost it themselves, so they encouraged it in their art."

"Like us," said Courage, thinking of the Last Supper fresco that stunned visitors to Cheltenham's fifty-first floor.

She stared at the pile of yachting magazines. "You still sail boats?"

"Not anymore. But I once sailed across the Atlantic."

"I know."

"My cousin told you?"

"That's why I decided to stop by."

So that was what intrigued her. He found himself wanting to explain it, wanting not to disappoint her. "When you're out there in mid-ocean, on a twenty-eight-foot boat, with no one else to help you, when you're fighting completely alone against the weather, it turns you inside out so you have to look into yourself. When you get back to the world of people, you never entirely forget that feeling."

Why was he telling her his one private memory, the secret recollection he had clung to during all the arid years at Cheltenham? Normally he never discussed those distant emotions with anyone. To talk about it risked bleeding it, bleaching it of its intimate magic. It was all he had left to remember from the days before life had become a routine of phone calls and drafting and obedience. Yet now he found himself fleshing out his single, simple memory in words for Helen Farmer.

"You speak Japanese?"

"Uh-huh." She added matter-of-factly, "Not fluently. I'd better be getting back to proofing now. I'm going cross-eyed over an indenture supplement for someone named Cheryl Litvak."

"Which conference room are you in?"

"4810. It's on this floor."

Courage nodded. "Maybe I'll stop by later, if I get a break."

Again, the calm smile. "I'll be there."

He stared after her in the glassy stupor that overtook him at this hour. She was not extraordinarily attractive, like Michelle with her glazed porcelain beauty, and he did not give a damn about samurai warlords and their obsession with Zen reclusion. But she had made him feel happy for a moment, detached as he had not felt since he had stood at the prow of *The Candle* watching the surface of the water. Her smile reminded him of someone, somewhere, too. He picked up a newly sharpened pencil and returned to the indemnification clause. Who was it he had seen who used to look at him that way?

> Goldilox shall indemnify, defend, and hold harmless the Purchaser from and against any taxes that may at any time be asserted against the Purchaser with respect to the transactions contemplated herein...

He wondered whether Michelle had gone out to the benefit dinner with the Shakespearian actors. He felt strangely glad to have spent the evening in his stuffy office, instead of being imprisoned next to her sawdust scent, subjected to hours of Elizabethan culture.

> Provided, however, that Goldilox shall not be liable for any amount resulting from the willful misfeasance, bad faith, or gross negligence of the Purchaser...

Courage moved a couple more commas around, and called Word Processing to see how his agreement was progressing. Another five minutes, they promised him. He took the elevator to the fifty-first floor.

He stopped by the reproduction in the hallway just outside the cafeteria. It was a picture of a woman, or an angel, or something, and she smiled with exactly the same certainty as Helen Farmer. She had the same wavy hair too, although Helen's was shaggier and not quite so long. He bent over to read the description on the gold plaque underneath. "Saint Anne: Leonardo da Vinci, 1452–1519."

Courage, who until tonight had never consciously noticed the picture, stared sleepily at the lips and eyes.

"So whose billable time are we taking advantage of this evening?" yelped the voice behind him.

Courage started. Hopper stood half hidden behind the eighteenth-century grandfather clock. The hands had long ago frozen at twenty after three. Hopper's red hair smoldered like neon in the dim pink emergency lighting.

"It's after two," answered Courage defensively, "and I'm not billing the time."

Hopper moved up beside him and Courage instinctively flinched. "Sure you are. And if you're not, you ought to be. Attorneys should bill every second they spend thinking about their clients' problems. Otherwise you're underbilling."

Rebellion exploded. "I wasn't thinking about my client actually. I was thinking about something personal."

"Personal!" echoed Hopper, with a note of disbelief. His metallic eyes drilled into the painting of Saint Anne. "What is it?"

"Da Vinci."

"Hmm. Well, I'm glad to see our corporate associates appreciating the efforts of our Interior Decoration Committee."

Courage shuddered. He tried to keep conversations with Hopper as short as possible. "I'd better get downstairs. I've got a document coming out of Word Processing."

"You want to tackle a bowl of Cheltenham's new guacamole late-night special? I'm told it's dynamite to get you through to dawn."

The invitation to guacamole was really an order. Courage dutifully followed him into the cafeteria.

"Not bad," remarked Hopper, skimming the surface with his tortilla chip. "Your name came up yesterday." Hopper leaned forward secretively. "Ariel mentioned your name as a possibility for the crack force TBO team."

"It's a big honor. But Tristan's got me loaded up as usual."

Hopper studied him dispassionately. "You're good at what you do, Peter. Tristan's dead wood. Or will be soon. The future of this firm's with Ariel and the TBO's the cutting edge. It's up to you what kind of future you see for yourself here."

Was Hopper overstating Tristan's slide from favor? Did his mentor no longer have the power even to save Courage, if it came to that? After five years' laborious apprenticeship under Tristan, must he now change sides and join Hopper's ranks of eager TBO flunkies? Better not appear too recalcitrant.

"Sure, I'd like to be on the TBO team. I've been kind of jumpy recently, since . . . since David died."

"David?"

Courage stared at him. "David Gleiner."

"Oh, yes. Gleiner. He was a conscientious worker, but he had no future here. Maybe it's just as well he never lived to find out the disappointment."

"There are other jobs in the world."

"Sure, he could have worked for some government agency or maybe"—Hopper's nostrils twitched in disdain—"gone in-house as associate counsel in some accounting firm. But that's no kind of life."

"It sure beats being dead."

Hopper looked unconvinced. "Anyhow, think about what I said. Put it this way, kid. Cheltenham's changing rapidly. You want to be with us when the guillotine starts creaking."

*   *   *

Finally the acquisition agreement was ready for Courage in Word Processing. He ran once over the draft, marked in a few cursory changes in red, and handed it back to the pool for corrections.

He went straight to Conference Room 4810.

She was proofing in a low voice, her head bent toward her proofing partner, a wasted creature dressed in rags and tatters several sizes too large. Courage used to wonder where the proof-readers, with their albino skin and spinal curvatures, came from. The voices oscillated in a monotonous cadence.

"I guess *you're* busy now."

She looked up. "Oh, hi. We've just got one more page. You want to wait?"

Courage sat down at the far end of the polished table, behind the fan of lilac gladioli. Yes, she was the painting from the fifty-first floor, if perhaps her lips were a shade fuller. She belonged to that alien world of scholars and freethinkers, who temporarily intrigued Courage at Ellis's Friday night dinner parties, and whose names he never remembered.

What had prompted her to look him up? Just because Ellis had once mentioned how he had once sailed *The Candle in the Wind* across the Atlantic?

The other proofreader gathered up the papers. "I'll take these down the hall." He scuttled away on shredded sneakers.

Courage pulled up a chair next to her. "Why are you doing this awful job?"

Her eyes widened. "To pay the rent."

"It's ridiculous. You have to sit up all night with these weird, lobotomized people. You're paid next to nothing. Why? Why?"

She did not take offense. "You want to talk, don't you?"

"Yes," he confessed. "I'd really like to talk. I don't know why, but I'd like to."

"Your cousin says you're a decent guy. A little hyper, but who wouldn't be?"

"Him. He thinks the law business is insanity. He's always comparing us with the armies in the trenches of the First World War."

She nodded. "You get a lot of casualties."

Courage stared, startled, at the wide forehead. "What are you talking about?"

She shrugged. "Burnouts. Nervous breakdowns. Depressions. Wasted lives. Even a few dead ones."

"Did my cousin tell you about that too? About the kid here who died?"

"Some woman who hemorrhaged?"

"Oh, that was last year. No, I meant a friend of mine a couple of weeks ago. . . . It doesn't matter."

He stood up. "It's almost morning. I'd better check my draft." He looked down at his watch again, and wished he could come up with one more excuse to see her. "You going to be here much later?" he asked.

"I think we're done for tonight. I'll look in on you if I'm back at Cheltenham again."

"When's that?" He tried not to sound too eager.

"It might be next week and it might be next year. It might be never. Who knows."

"Okay. It was nice seeing you again. Thanks for stopping by." He spun around and walked quickly out of the conference room.

He was only halfway to Word Processing when he changed his mind, turned, and retraced his steps straight back again. She was already zipping up her tote bag as he walked in. She wore an afghan coat with lamb's-wool cuffs, which looked about ten years old.

"Did you forget something?"

He took a breath. "Which way are you going? I thought maybe I could give you a ride home."

"Thanks anyhow, but the law firm pays for transportation if we work after midnight."

He took one final, deep breath. "Which way are you going?"

"Miles away. Up near Columbia."

"I'm on the Upper West Side. Can I give you a ride anyway?"

"It's late. Maybe some other evening."

"Just to talk. For a few more minutes."

"I have to get up in a couple of hours and take care of Chloe. My daughter."

"Can I call you at home? Sometime?"

"I mostly work nights."

"Maybe we could just have a cup of coffee. Between things."

She ripped a sheet off the putty-colored Cheltenham pad by the telephone and scribbled the number. "Early evening's best. When Chloe gets home from school. There's no answering machine."

"Thanks," said Courage and left the conference room once more.

The next version of Kahn's draft was waiting for him on his desk. He read it through indifferently. He knew it was a sloppy piece of work. Tristan was sure to pick it apart in the morning. He was dialing the Cheltenham messenger department to arrange for the drop at the airport in the morning, when the call came through on his other line.

"Courage," he mumbled wearily in the receiver.

"This is Helen Farmer."

"Helen!" His voice was alert now. "Are you still here?"

"I'm downstairs. My car'll be here in seven minutes. If you like, I'll drop you off."

"Don't go away. I'll be there." As he stuffed Kahn's draft back into the envelope, he noticed that they had misspelled "Cheltenham" on the last signature page. Although such a mistake could cost him his job—Courage had heard of senior associates being fired for less—there was no time left to stop now and rerun the page through the printer. Maybe Kahn would not notice. He left it off in the messenger depot and raced for the night elevator.

She was sitting in the car when he got downstairs. Breathlessly he slithered in beside her. "I'm really glad you called, Helen. Thanks. This may sound strange to you, but it's a relief just to talk to someone who has nothing to do with...that place."

"You mean your firm?"

"Not just Cheltenham. Any firm. The whole damn Street."

"Sure I do, Peter. I'm in a different one of these awful offices every night."

"Yes. But you don't subscribe to the religion."

"Religion is indeed the word."

"I just don't meet anyone outside of it. Except my cousin, from time to time. And my cleaning lady."

"You could if you wanted."

"Wrong. I've become such a yuppie. With no time and plenty of money."

"You won't think much of my apartment. You've probably never been in such a slum."

He shot her a covert glance in the dark. Was she inviting him to her apartment, then? They had already given the driver both addresses and were now about to turn east off the West Side Highway.

"I'd really like to see your slum. Just for a few minutes if that's okay. I promise I won't hang around and keep you up any later."

She leaned forward and told the driver. "We've changed our minds. Forget the drop on Columbus. Go straight on up Amsterdam to One hundred and eighth Street."

The driver shrugged.

"Charge it to the first number," interrupted Courage. He told Helen, "My client will pay. He's a crazy zillionaire."

"Okay," said Helen. She turned to Courage. "I've never taken anyone home before. I mean one of you people."

"We're human. And you needn't worry. We don't steal."

"There's nothing to steal. Except the kitchen table."

They pulled into a dark side street. Courage noticed the scrawl of grafitti across the walls on the ground floor and the windows, like gaping wounds, with no glass. Litter, wrappers, and an old bedspring were piled up outside the front door.

"Don't say you haven't been warned." They stepped onto the sidewalk. "It's six flights up and there's nothing to drink but Lapsang souchong."

"Lapsang souchong would be great."

The lock on the outside door had been smashed to pieces.

"You aren't afraid?" asked Courage as they passed rusty mailboxes in the hall.

"Only for my daughter. I don't care about the danger for myself. Nothing's ever happened to me."

Courage had to hold his breath on the vile-smelling stairs, which reeked of old garbage and boiled cooking and cats. She led the way.

"You know your neighbors?"

"There are crack dealers in that apartment on the fourth floor. A couple of students underneath. And a male prostitute opposite them."

"How long have you lived here?"

"About five years. It's a great bargain."

Courage shuddered as she jangled her keys in her door. "Come in. Don't fall over the skateboard."

She switched a light on and ushered him past an alcove kitchen into a small room lined with books. There was almost no room for furniture, except for a sofa, one armchair, and a narrow wooden table.

He waited for further directions. "Is this your study?"

She turned her head sharply, her eyes lighting up with private amusement. "No study. This is my bedroom and my living room."

"You sleep here?" He tried to sound casual.

She nodded toward the couch. "There's only one other room. It's about half the size. And that's Chloe's."

Courage sat down quickly on the armchair, trying to look at home. "How old is she?"

"Eleven. Would you like some tea?"

"If you're sure it's no trouble."

"I have lemon," she announced, as if it were an astonishing surprise he should stumble across such a luxury.

"No lemon," said Courage hastily.

"There's plenty."

While she filled the kettle in the kitchen next door, he stood up to examine her prints. He studied the black-and-white seascape over the table. The misty foreground was divided by islands of stark rocks, gnarled pines, and a soft hill of flowering trees. Tiny figures wound their way up mountain paths toward cottages nestled in the trees. Fishing boats dotted the horizon.

"It's a copy of an Eitoku screen," she said, bringing out cups and a cracked flea market teapot. She had sliced the lemon thinly on a plate. "One of the sixteenth-century masters. You see the progression of seasons, from winter to spring?"

"It's beautiful," said Courage, turning to the other print, which pictured a few rocks and bamboo shoots and a crane.

She poured the tea. "That's by Shobun. The rocks and branches symbolize the scholar, the intellect."

Courage pointed to the vertical row of characters in the upper corner. "Can you read that?"

"It's means, roughly, 'The poet and outcast is equally happy in snow or in spring.'"

"Is that you?"

She laughed. "Spring's better. They're predicting five inches of snow on Thursday."

"I hardly notice the weather anymore. Working at Cheltenham, you might as well be in Oklahoma City or Vladivostok or Bismarck."

Courage sat back again and sipped his tea. He noticed that she had given him the better cup. Hers was chipped at the rim.

"I have one real antique print," she told him. "But I can't show you tonight, because it's in Chloe's room. It's the only precious thing I have here. It was a present from her father."

She looked comfortable now, stretched out in her jeans across the short couch. Although some of her ease brushed off on him, Courage still felt starchy and intrusive in his office clothes. He wanted to know about her life, but he had no idea which were the forbidden questions.

"Are you divorced?"

"I was never married. We're still friends, sort of. He helps sometimes financially."

Suddenly Courage felt better, thinking again of the battered front door and the stinking stairs, and knowing that there was someone to look after this luminous, penniless woman.

"That's lucky." He settled deeper into the armchair.

"I take as little as I possibly can, and then only for Chloe. Absolutely nothing for myself." She raised her jaw with a fervid pride. She gave it away as she spoke, the secret of her personal martyrdom, which provided for her the same buttress as the ring of gold over which Courage's people fought like carrion vultures. Helen Farmer had taken some kind of private oath to its opposite.

"Why?" he asked simply.

"I guess because if I gave in on one thing, none of the rest would make sense either. It's not that I like living here, staring at the four walls of this broom closet every night, having to count every cent."

She was brave and crazy and strong and intelligent and also confused, all at the same time. He realized that her own life was just as mixed up as everyone else's, maybe even worse, but that she might understand his dilemmas, and what was more, he knew he wanted to tell her.

"When you were sailing your boat," she asked timidly, "did you ever hear the whales?"

"I never saw a whale. But often schools of dolphins followed *The Candle* for hours. They were the happiest spirits I ever saw."

She half closed her eyes. "I'd like to see that. Sometime. What was the most wonderful thing of all?"

Courage hesitated to tell her the truth. It sounded so trite, so foolish. "The sunsets," he finally admitted. "It's not like anywhere else. The whole sea comes alive."

The first glimmering of morning sneaked between the slats of the Oriental shades.

"I ought to leave," suggested Courage reluctantly. "I promised I wouldn't keep you."

She studied the tea leaves at the bottom of her cup. "There was something you wanted to talk to me about. Wasn't there?"

"Could I maybe have just one more cup of tea?"

She poured silently.

"It's about my friend David, the lawyer who died. He keeled over at Cheltenham with a heart attack in the middle of the night."

"How dreadful."

"We weren't that close. We used to have dinner together sometimes. It's to do with the way he died and the way everybody talks about it. They even started saying he was fortunate not to have had to live to see the day when he wouldn't make partner. He knew he wasn't on partnership track. He didn't want to be."

He saw that she was looking at him strangely, as if she were bewildered. What was it, anyhow, he was trying to say?

"He was thirty-two. He had his life ahead of him. And he threw it away, on that—that *factory*—for nothing. They sealed off his office for a few days. Then they cleaned it out. Any day now they'll stick some other tax associate in there."

"These guys don't waste space."

"I realize they can't make it into a museum. But nobody in that whole building really gave a shit, Helen. The day he was dead he was just another corpse, whose work assignments had to be re-routed."

She shook her shaggy head despairingly. "What do you expect? They're robots. You're right, of course. But what do you expect? They live and die by their billable hours. It's an army and the soldiers are expendable." She must have seen the hopelessness in his face, for she changed her tone. "You're tired, Peter. We both are. I need some sleep. I've got to be up again in a couple of hours to get my daughter's breakfast."

Courage stood defeatedly, and reached for his briefcase where it lay on the floor. Without answering her, he turned his back and stared again at the bamboo shoot that arched from the rocks. He had no right to keep her awake. He had promised not to stay long. Yet he felt his last hope slipping away. He turned around again. She did look tired in the harsh light. Her features were uneven and her face was naked, so different from the exquisite porcelain Michelle. But he needed this rebel scholar.

"David and I used to gossip together, mostly firm trivia. A couple of days before he died he tried to get hold of me. He wanted to tell me something, but I didn't pay much attention at the time. Then I got stuck on a shitty due diligence trip to Buffalo, so I never had a chance to talk to him. Since he died I've started wondering about it. Maybe he knew something important."

"How would he?"

"David was smart, in a quiet way. He kept his distance. Sometimes he saw things other people didn't pick up. He was a hardworking kid. He didn't keep kosher, but was religious in his own way. He came from a fairly poor family, who live out in Brooklyn. His father owns a delicatessen."

She nodded slowly. "Let's have one more pot of tea. I'll boil some fresh water."

This time he followed her to the kitchen stove. The gas rings were rusted over and the handle of the refrigerator was broken. Cut-out figures of jousting knights in armor were pasted across the cupboards. An avocado seed sprouted in a dish of water by the sink. Helen leaned with her back against the stove, her arms folded. The shoulder of her sweater unraveled another half inch. Courage looked quickly away from her skin to the refrigerator door.

"He worked hard, your friend?"

"He was a drudge, a real workhorse. He'd gone to City College and then Brooklyn Law School, so he always felt a little inadequate about ending up in a Wall Street sweatshop. You see, he didn't buy into the system, he wasn't dazzled by all the hoopla. So sometimes he saw things that passed the rest of us by."

"What kind of things?"

"He really grasped the politics and the balance of power. He had an uncanny intuition for what went on in those partnership meetings, behind the closed doors."

She glanced at her watch. "You think that's what he wanted to tell you about? That's what's been bothering you?" She sounded a trifle impatient.

Courage ran a cold hand through his hair. "No!" A flush of adrenaline rocked down his limbs and he was suddenly pleading for attention. "It wasn't just gossip. David knew something really important."

She turned her back to him, to pour the dregs of her teacup into the sink. When she finally faced him again, he knew he had ignited her attention.

She nodded slowly. "I believe you."

"It's not just curiosity. I feel I owe him something, to follow it through. It was the last gesture of his life. And God knows, he left so little behind him."

"I wonder...would he have told anyone else?" She narrowed her eyes, in weary concentration.

He watched her puzzled face. "I doubt it. We're a pretty paranoid bunch. We don't talk much to each other except about work or the weather or our summer vacations. I was David's only real friend."

She raised her head sharply as the bedroom door squeaked open. Chloe, dressed in a Star Wars nightshirt and clutching a scruffy E.T., stumbled sleepily into the room.

Helen jumped up. "What are you doing, sweetheart? Why aren't you in bed?"

"I heard a noise," said Chloe.

They had the same rug of blond hair, except that Helen's was darker, with age. "Go on back to bed. I'll wake you up when it's time for school."

Chloe blinked up at Courage drowsily. "Who are you?" She added with a touch of irony, "Santa Claus?"

"It's a friend," said Helen. "Not Santa. Santa doesn't wear a suit."

Chloe pattered back to the bedroom.

"I'll let myself out," said Courage hastily. "Can I see you again soon?"

"Call me after Christmas. I'd like that."

Courage, avoiding the skateboard in the hall, struggled with the triple locks and chains while Helen dislodged the broomstick wedged against the door. On the stairs he passed a derelict bearded man in a bomber jacket, who gave him a suspicious glance. He figured it was probably one of the downstairs crack dealers.

ELEVEN

Gina stood in front of her bathroom sink, peering into the cracked mirror, as she spread a layer of pale makeup over the bronze of her tan, and tried to disguise the evidence of her illicit island weekend. She was following Cheryl's advice.

"If you and Clancy both come back with obvious suntans," her worldly friend had warned, "it'll only add grist to the rumor mill."

So she stood in her higgledy-piggledy bathroom, where she never got around to throwing out the old tubes of makeup and toothpaste, and smoothed a blob of ivory foundation across her jawline. With the other hand she took mouthfuls from the carton of last night's cold moo goo gai pan, which was her breakfast.

Idly she listened to the morning news on the radio. Her mind was still back in St. Martin, with the emerald lizards and the brilliant birds and the tropical flowers trellised across the dining terrace in the morning sun. She clung to the memory. It helped to blot out the desolation of her barren apartment, which each morning she dreaded facing.

Gina often wondered how it was that certain people seemed doomed to live so inelegantly in New York, however much money they were making. Perhaps, she reflected, it was that she lacked the organization, the motivation. Every morning she awoke to the shame of her half-furnished apartment. Never being quite sure of a suitable replacement, she still kept the molting sofa, and the cracked floorboards seemed to draw up clumps of hair and dust however often she swept. Only the rug was beautiful. It was a Persian carpet, a sea of azure, flecked with golden arabesques and red sea anemones. The rug was the only object of value she had ever bought for herself. After she had paid off her student loans, she had spent twenty-five hundred dollars on it, the sum of all her savings.

When she returned home late at night, after the long hours at the firm, she would mechanically unfold cartons of Chinese food or open a can of tuna fish. She thought of Maxwell, always, remote in the brownstone on 83rd Street with Eleanor, and wondered if he would be able to give her a fleeting, secret phone call. She could of course never call him. She would kick the shoes off her aching feet, flex her tired ankles, and wonder how long she was doomed to live this way. Then her eye would fall on the rug, with its rich wash of color, and somehow the sight of the sumptuous carpet always restored her faith. Everything would work out in the end. Just be patient, he always promised, tracing with his fingertip the line of her neck and shoulders. She had learned patience too, just as she had learned all the elaborate systems of case citation. She had been living on faith and Chinese food a long time.

She took a last look at her unnaturally blanched face, swallowed a final mouthful of straw mushrooms, a swig of mouthwash, spat, and gathered the drafts of the letters to the Maritime Administration she had prepared the previous evening, before she had fallen asleep with the light still on. She threw her copy of the Ship Mortgage Act into her briefcase, locked the door, and headed along the dingy corridor into the brisk morning.

*   *   *

At 57 Water Street Benedict Hamilton stepped sprightly into the elevator beside her.

"Good morning, Gina."

"Hi, Benedict. How's work? How's your period?"

"I missed the Fin de Siècle meeting last night. They were showing *Gone With the Wind* on TV."

"Isn't that a little lowbrow for you?"

"Before my great-great-great-grandfather won the Battle of Lumpy Creek in 1863, the Hamilton planation looked a lot like Tara. Of course our family was much older, and our ancestry was pure Anglo-Saxon."

"Most of my family are still growing tomatoes in Naples."

The elevator doors peeled silently open. Straightening his tie pin, Benedict nodded smartly and stepped into the corridor.

Gina hurried to her office, where she read the annotations to the Ship Mortgage Act three times until the words ricocheted in her brain. For purposes of vessel ownership, Maxwell had explained to her, a corporation must be 75 percent comprised of United States citizens. But how could one possibly count up all those shareholders? And supposing there were layers of holding companies, what then? With the usual sense of impotence, of grappling with some simple problem with all the wrong tools, she dialed his private line. He did not answer. She read the text one last time, in mounting confusion, and set off to look for Cheryl.

Cheryl's secretary suggested Gina try the computer room. So she rode to the fifty-first floor, where she found Cheryl swathed in a sea of printouts, peering at the screen of Lexis, the computer used by attorneys to call up any published case. A half-eaten sandwich lay balanced on her lap.

Gina pulled up a chair. "Am I interrupting?"

"I need a break. I've already read two hundred and nine SEC 'no action' letters. We're trying to figure out whether, for purposes of registration, you create a separate security by stripping principal from interest payments."

Gina looked blank.

"It's a special project I'm working on for Ariel Lamb himself. I suspect it's to do with this new TBO they're all so steamed up about. He wouldn't say exactly. Just warned us several times that it was highly confidential." Cheryl studied Gina's makeup attentively. "You want to come with me to Bergdorf's on Saturday? I need a new Aquascutum raincoat. If I get some time off from these 'no action' letters, that is."

"I can't. I'm spending all weekend with Clancy. They always go skiing in Aspen over Christmas. Eleanor's taking the kids out to Colorado a few days ahead of time this year. So the house'll be empty."

Cheryl shook her head. "When's it going to be your turn to spend Christmas with him?"

Gina thought of home in Allentown: the incessant shouting, the television babble, the stench of garlic and frying, while her father got noisier and drunker every hour. But all she said was, "It's a whole weekend."

"It's time you spent more time with younger, single men. How about one of the Cheltenham associates?"

"Who? They're all such wimps."

"Peter Courage is cute."

"He's nice, but—I can't help it. I'm in love with Clancy."

"Has he given you your Christmas present yet?"

Gina shook her head. "I guess St. Martin..."

"Don't be dumb. That doesn't count. That's a trip. Trips don't count for Christmas and birthdays presents. Only things like jewelry or furniture."

Gina changed the subject. "He wants me to spend the weekend in the brownstone on Eighty-third Street."

"The man's a simpleton. This could be your big chance."

"How do you mean?"

"You can leave a trail of stuff behind. Nothing too obvious though. Maybe an earring, some hairs in the sink, dirty pieces of cotton balls. She could start divorce proceedings by New Year's."

Gina looked horrified. "I can't trick him into marrying me."

"You'll never get him any other way."

"He says next summer. As soon as Oliver's finished fifth grade..."

"Promises, promises. Cocktail party chatter. Oh my God, how

long have we been talking? Half an hour? I forgot to turn off Lexis. I've run up hundreds to the client."

"Who's the client?"

"Caroline Brothers. I guess they can afford it."

*　　　*　　　*

Gina had never yet crossed the threshold of the brownstone on 83rd Street. She had walked by the building many, many times, on both sides of the street, in the stark, metallic glare of winter and the spongy, leafy, sweltering summer, straining to make out the shadowy outlines of the furniture behind the black shutters. She knew now the cycle of Eleanor's window boxes; narcissus planted in April, followed by marigold and petunias and pansies, and finally swags of ivy late in the year.

She sometimes went miles out of her way to walk down 83rd Street. During the endless summer, while he took three-day weekends at the house in Massachusetts, or when she knew he was out of town on business, or even those evenings on which he had told her he was going out with Eleanor to the opera or to dinner at the Madisons, she would find some excuse to wander into the back streets of the Upper East Side.

It was a handsome brownstone, discreet but well tended. The rosy brickwork glowed demurely. The house had a distinguished veneer, an elegance beyond that of the neigboring brownstones. The stone steps were always swept, the door freshly painted in mint green, and the large bronze door-knocker polished.

She had developed a fascination with the whole family, whom she knew only through the photographs Maxwell had shown her. Eleanor she was sure she would have been able to recognize anywhere, that bony frame and the short, graying hair parted low on one side. One autumn evening she had seen Julia, the sixteen-year-old daughter, saunter along 83rd Street and spring up the stairs. She wore her green school uniform, green socks bunched around her ankles, and long brown hair caught back in a straggling ponytail. She was swinging a bag of schoolbooks to the beat of her Walkman in her ears. Gina, loitering in a doorway on the opposite street corner, wistfully watched her plunge into the familiar warmth of the house.

Maxwell called her late on Friday afternoon.

"Hard at work, gorgeous?"

"I finally understand the ninety-five percent U.S. citizen rule. If ninety-five percent of the shareholders have U.S. addresses, it can be inferred that seventy-five percent are U.S. citizens."

"Of course," he replied infuriatingly. "I could have told you that."

She resisted the impulse to tell him that, had he taken five minutes to explain the inference rule to her in two sentences that morning, she could have gotten some real work done. Instead all she asked was, "Did Eleanor leave?"

"On the twelve-twenty plane. All clear. I've got a great idea, my precious gorgeous."

"Shoot."

"Let's eat in tonight. We'll pick up some steaks on the way home, throw them on the grill, and spend a quiet evening. How's that? I'm going downstairs in about half an hour to get a cab. If you can sneak out discreetly, I'll pick you up on the corner opposite Fulton Street, by the Seaport."

"I'll be there." They were never seen leaving the building by the same elevator or, God forbid, getting into the same taxi or limousine.

Forty minutes later they were driving along the East River. The traffic was at its Friday night peak, as the armies of Manhattanites inched along in their cars to escape for the weekend. She sensed his nervousness. The cab smelled evil; the upholstery of the seat was split, spilling out its wads of stuffing. Both their heavy briefcases sat balanced on the seat between them.

"You're sure this is a good idea?" she asked.

"You don't mind, do you? Coming to the house?"

"It seems strange . . ."

They stopped off at the supermarket to buy steak.

"Do we need salad?" Gina asked.

"We've got plenty at home. Eleanor left me a lot of vegetables and some homemade applesauce. You like applesauce?"

Gina did not answer. Eating Eleanor's homemade applesauce seemed a terrible crime, almost as much a sin as sleeping in her bed.

Upon arriving at the brownstone, she stood aside so he could climb the steps first. As he slid the key into the lock of the mint-green door, a momentary panic overwhelmed her. She clutched at the railing to keep from stumbling.

Maxwell had not noticed. "Welcome," he announced brightly, and swung the door to admit her into the dark sanctuary.

Then the lights were on and she found herself in a hallway at the foot of the staircase, blinking at the tinsel and angels and glass bulbs of an enormous Christmas tree, which reached all the way to the high ceiling. Mountains of presents lay stacked underneath, grand, neatly wrapped boxes from Bloomingdale's and Saks, and shapeless, mysterious small ones. A bicycle, propped behind the tree, had been thinly disguised in brown paper.

"We always unwrap them when we get back from Aspen," explained Maxwell.

"It's a beautiful tree."

"Eleanor and the children like it. Most of the ornaments are antiques. They've been in her family for generations."

Gina timidly touched a painted wooden rocking horse that swung from its branch of fir, slowly, mocking.

"Give me the food. I'll show you the rest of the house."

She followed him downstairs to the kitchen, feeling her way cautiously past the dimly lit treads.

"Take care. The floor's uneven."

In the kitchen, with its huge wooden trestle table, you could imagine a family of six, eating pancakes, reading magazines, fighting. On the far wall hung a wide oil painting of some sunlit Mediterranean harbor, where sailboats bobbed in a sea of gloriously clear water, and flags of every color saluted the breeze.

"Where's that?"

"St. Tropez, Monte Carlo. I forget. We've had it a long time. Since our honeymoon."

He led her away from the gleaming copper saucepans and the faience glazed jugs and casseroles, and through the austere dining room, where she glimpsed an oil painting of Eleanor, posed some years back, in a salmon evening dress.

"How long ago?" she asked.

He looked at it reflexively and blindly, with the stare of someone whose eyes have become numbed from habit. "Fifteen years, maybe more."

Then she had been younger than Gina, the betrayed patrician whose pageboy of dark blond hair was now streaked with gray.

He led her into the yard, flicking on an outside switch that filled it with lurid stage moonlight. The rear façades of the buildings did their best to block out all but a corner of the sky. Somehow the yard guarded most faithfully the spirit of Eleanor, the chatelaine in far-off Aspen. She had filled the space with a bizarre collection of Florentine stone. Armless statues of cupids balanced on pedestals, chipped gargoyles grinned maliciously from the corners of the fence, and in the small fountain basin ice now gathered, fossilizing the skeletal autumn leaves. Ivy trailed over the back fence, winding its way along the broken columns and the chipped stone bench. A winter shrub, bristling with red berries, stood guard in the naked light.

"What's that?"

"It's got some long Latin name. Don't touch the berries. They're poisonous."

"It's freezing. Let's go in."

"Do you want to see the upstairs now, or shall we have a drink and watch the news?"

"Show me upstairs."

They climbed three flights, back past the Christmas tree, then the living room and library, and finally arrived at the children's bedrooms. The space reminded Gina of a dollhouse she had once coveted, but which had been much too expensive ever to own.

She had never before been inside a residential New York brownstone. The voyage backstage, beyond mere luxury and into the dimensions of time, of family years, filled her with awe and hopelessness. She supposed there must be other families who lived this way, behind the discreet façades of the neighboring streets. There must be children who grew up here, never fully imagining there was any alternative way to live, who could not have pictured the joyless streets, the spacelessness, the hideous furniture of Gina's childhood.

"This is Louise's bedroom."

Louise had the kind of dollhouse that Gina had long ago wanted. It was actually finer, being an antique, than anything Gina, in her childhood, would ever have seen. The tables and chairs were handmade, the curtains cut from wisps of faded brocade, even the miniature rugs dull with a sheen of old money. The dolls themselves had stiff cloth faces, not like real people at all.

Gina knew Clancy liked Louise the least. She sometimes even sensed his detachment from the two older children. Maxwell had chosen to pour out all the remaining wellspring of pride and adoration on Oliver. She had wondered, if it were not for Oliver, if he might have left them all sooner, the cozy unshakeable fortress on 83rd Street. She shivered involuntarily, crushed by the power of the house. Perhaps she had been wrong. Perhaps it was more than Oliver that held him.

"Our rooms are on the top floor."

She hesitated and gripped the banister, frozen on the balls of her feet.

He shrugged. "Come on," he ordered. She followed him obediently up the last flight.

He showed her his study first. She had a momentary sense of belonging. The bookshelves were lined with Gilmore & Black, Templeton on marine insurance, and Benedict's—the familiar admiralty titles she knew and read daily. A ream of Cheltenham stationery lay on the desk. Oliver's collages from school, lovingly framed, hung alongside the print of an eighteenth-century schooner.

He opened the bottom drawer of the desk with a small key from his key ring. Fumbling his way past the stacks of receipts and old check stubs, he drew out a folder of Cheltenham memoranda.

"Remember that?"

He handed it to her. "The Application of Equitable Remedies by the Admiralty Courts. From: Gina A. di Angelo."

"I wrote that!"

"It's the first memo you ever wrote for me. I always keep it here."

"Do you read it?" she asked, astonished, vaguely remembering the stilted sentences, the concepts half grasped and badly expressed, the errors in case citations.

"Sometimes," he said. "When I feel lonely for you."

It was time. "That's the bedroom," he muttered under his breath, pushing the door only half open. Then he stepped quickly downstairs. She had only a second to glimpse the patchwork quilt on the bed and the high-backed New England rocking chair. "I'll open some wine," he called out. "There's a good Bordeaux Cyrus Sweet gave us for Christmas."

Gave *us* for Christmas.

They sat downstairs in the kitchen. "We always do," Maxwell explained. "We only really use the upstairs when we have people over."

Gina volunteered to cook the steaks. Although it had seemed a simple enough task, she soon regretted suggesting it.

"Where do you keep the salt and pepper?" she asked. Maxwell, sipping his wine thoughtfully, sat buried in yesterday's *Wall Street Journal*. She supposed it must be a formality of his nightly routine, his glasses shoved way down on his nose, the paper held at arm's length, while Eleanor efficiently darted amongst her arsenal of gleaming copper pans.

He hardly looked up. "Try the first cupboard on the left."

There was nothing but cans of asparagus soup and spaghetti loops.

"Oh, that's Oliver's cupboard. It's all he eats. Try the next one."

Gina found a dazzling array of stacked china and assorted flower vases. With a mounting sense of panic, she edged her way across the floor, opening and shutting each cupboard hopelessly. "I just can't find them," she confessed.

He looked up blankly. "I don't know," he protested. "So forget it. We won't use any."

She chose a flat pan off the wall, although she hesitated to desecrate the lustrous surface that shone like a treasure of Mesopotamia, and managed to locate some butter in the refrigerator. Maxwell seemed totally engrossed in his newspaper. When the butter sizzled in the pan on the stove top, she added the steaks. The meat hissed violently, making him finally look up. "Smells great. I'm hungry. Oh, my heavens, that's her special pan. We musn't use that!"

Gina looked back helplessly. "I'm sorry...I didn't know."

"Goddamn it, we'll never get it clean. She uses some kind of special polish."

"Maybe that stain remover...Tristan's client...the crazy one."

"Come on, Gina, that's for fabrics. Anyhow, it didn't get the stain off my office rug." He and Gina had scrubbed and scrubbed one evening, with the small sample package Maxwell had filched off Tristan Barrett's desk, but to no avail. The electric-blue, black-hatched carpet was eternally defiled with a visible whitish smear.

"Where do you keep the steak knives and things?"

"Look in those drawers underneath. They must be somewhere around."

"You look, Clancy. Sweetheart, please. It's your kitchen."

With a tiny snort of irritation, he folded his newspaper with unnecessary care and banged around the drawers. "This is lunatic. She must have moved everything. They always used to be here."

"Don't you ever—I mean, set the table or anything?"

"Not usually. I think Louise and Oliver take turns. You know, half the time I'm not home for supper anyway. Oh, look what I found!" He triumphantly waved a bag of plastic picnic knives and forks.

She cut up the lettuce and tomatoes she found in the refrigerator and even discovered a suitable salad bowl with wooden serving spoons. Maxwell located some vinegar.

"How about the oil?" she suggested timidly.

"Ah, oil. Well, that's another problem."

In the end they threw away the salad, and smothered the overcooked, unseasoned steak with ketchup.

He opened another bottle of wine. "Maybe we should have gone out to eat," he mused, staring at the gristle on his plate.

"We still could."

"Better not. She might telephone, and I told her I'd be home. You want me to order in some Chinese food for you?"

"No. I'm fine." She ate Chinese food five nights a week already. "Who cares, sweetheart. Let's take the wine upstairs and go to bed."

He scowled at the bottle. "You want to drink in bed? You won't spill any, will you? You'll be careful? Gina, just one thing, you won't be cross with me, will you? You know I love you. Would you mind, just this once, not smoking upstairs? It gets into the curtains and bedspread. She has the most incredibly sensitive nose. You wouldn't believe what she can smell."

Gina remembered the princess and the pea, and the patrician bones of his wronged wife, and knew he was not exaggerating.

He took the wineglasses, she took the bottle and his newspaper, and they traipsed up the endless flights of stairs. The bedroom, now that she finally had a chance to see it, was chillingly austere. It was the only room in the house with which Eleanor appeared to have made no effort. The sole ornaments on the wooden dresser were a dish of dried flowers and an oval photograph of an old woman, some Eleanor ancestor. Gina sat down on the edge of the patchwork quilt and knew with certainty that this was a room that had never harbored passion.

He poured them more wine, taking excruciating pains not to let the bottle drip. She knew he was trying to get drunker to dispel the strain.

"The partnership finally voted today on Gary Fishman's gym," he told her.

"They're going to build it?"

"They voted him the money, contingent on the TBO deal going through."

"They're really worked up about that TBO. What if it doesn't work?"

"There'll be a bloodbath. We've hired too many slave associates. There'll be a lot of layoffs. For the first time in Cheltenham history."

"Partners too?"

"You bet. Ariel's ranks'll get thinned. And we'll all take a hit on our draws."

Gina unrolled her tights and loosened her skirt. When the telephone ultimately, startlingly yelped, it came as a release to the tensions, like an awaited death.

"Hello, dear... No, there's nothing wrong. I'm just a little tired... I've had a couple of glasses of wine, but no, I'm not drunk... Yes, I've eaten, I bought myself a steak... I had trouble finding the knives but I managed... I'm going to eat the applesauce tomorrow... The kids are fine?... Yes, I will remember to pick up your dry cleaning tomorrow... and drop off the Madisons' Christmas presents... No, I've no special plans for tomorrow night, probably just work here... That's very nice of the Madisons to ask me, but I'd really rather stay here by myself... Tell Oliver I miss him too... give my best to your sister... Have a good time... Don't break any bones... See you all soon... Good-night, dear."

He turned back to Gina, who had taken off the rest of her

clothes and buried herself under the covers. He pulled the pillow away from her head.

"Phew, that's over. I feel better now. I can relax."

He reached to turn out the light. He always left it on in her apartment.

"You like the house?" he asked, caressing her back.

"I's beautiful. It's so ... lived in."

"It's a big family. Even now that Michael's away with that rock group God knows where."

"Will you miss it, Clancy?"

"Miss what, gorgeous?"

"Living here. I mean, after all these years."

His hand froze on her inner thigh. After a long silence, he murmured, "Let's not think about all that."

"I'm sorry. I was just thinking, I guess Eleanor and the children would probably go on living here."

He answered in the voice she had heard him use with clients. "Eleanor will always live here. If she wants to."

She swallowed, trying to disperse the choking lump in her throat. She wished she were out of his bed, out of his house, even somewhere in the great universe out of his life, but she knew, for the thousandth time, that it did no good wishing, since there was no corner on earth she would want to be alive in without him. He kissed her.

"I'm sorry, gorgeous. I'm a bad lover tonight. I can't do it. I guess I'm tired."

"Shall we go back to my apartment?"

"It's not that! It's nothing to do with that. I'm just tired. And I'm a little concerned about Ariel Lamb."

"I don't mind. I'm glad just to be with you."

"Tomorrow will be better, I promise. Maybe I'll rape you in the morning."

"That would be great."

"Sleep well, gorgeous."

He soon fell into a wine-heavy coma, but she lay a long time miserable, trying to remember what life had been like before the walls had closed in on her. Everything she did now, everywhere she went, like a prisoner, she carried with her the cage of her obsession. Snatches of their remembered conversations and treasured repetitions of his small tendernesses superimposed all her other thoughts. She dwelled on him each night before she slept, and first thing as she awoke. Would she ever again be carefree, self-contained, somehow liberated?

The cat woke her early the next morning, the bundle of fur falling suddenly from a height onto her stomach. Sleepily she tried to edge it away without waking Maxwell.

"Have the children had breakfast yet?" he grunted.

Equity, a white Siamese with a stubborn disposition, bounded back into the hollow between Gina's ankles. Sitting up straight, she picked up the animal by its flexible middle and lowered it onto the floor.

Maxwell opened his eyes and asked, "What time is it?"

"Ten of nine."

"We've got to get you out of here! The burglar man's arriving any second."

"Will he come upstairs?"

"God knows. They have these wires that run underneath the rugs in every room. Come on, Gina, be a good girl and put your clothes on."

She swung one foot onto the cold wooden floor, feeling with the other for the scratch of the bathmat-size woven rug. She was still struggling with her underwear when the doorbell rang.

He grabbed his dressing gown breathlessly. "It's too late. You'll have to wait here now. Just don't come downstairs until I tell you."

A few minutes later, the entire house shuddered with a blare of what sounded like a hundred sirens. It went on and on and on. When the piercing wail finally subsided, she tiptoed in stockinged feet to the landing. She could hear their voices faintly downstairs.

She found Oliver's bedroom at the end of the hall behind the other children's rooms. It was the only room he had avoided showing her last night. The bookshelves housed a collection of handpainted Messerschmitts and Spitfires, a baseball mitt and Yankee paraphernalia, textbooks and atlases from school. A volleyball net was attached to one wall and a dartboard to the other. Eleanor kept everything tidy, the clothes in the drawers and closet neatly stacked and hung. He was going to be a reader, like his father, Gina thought. On the bedside table, a bookmark held his place in *Treasure Island*.

The anxiety gripped her again. She tried to breathe calmly, gasped for air, and ended by sitting down on the narrow bed while she struggled to compose her mind. Eleanor, she had decided, she would probably be able to fight. Even the imperious brownstone, with its legacy of childhoods witnessed, she might have tried to conquer. But as she sat among the Spitfires, she accepted with a thud of resignation that the spirit of the unknowing Oliver would somehow be the one that kept the Maxwell family intact long after Gina's time.

Did Clancy know? Had it dawned on him too, after the first flushes of passion had worn off? Had he said nothing to her, simply because he did not know any longer how to explain that he had made a terrible, unconscionable mistake? She knew how much it crazed him ever to be wrong.

The burglar alarm screeched again. She ran to the window. A body, falling from two stories, would probably only break a leg or a pelvis. If you ever wanted to end it all, you would do better jumping from the forty-seventh floor at Cheltenham. If you could find a way, that was, to smash the hermetically sealed windows.

"Whatever are you doing in here?"

She spun around. "Oh, Clancy. Have they finished?"

"All done. Come on, I'm taking you out to lunch."

First, however, there was Eleanor's dry cleaning to be collected. She waited for him outside the laundromat. Then there was the shopping bag of Christmas presents for the Madisons they needed to deliver along with the cat carrier containing Currency and Equity, which Maxwell wedged on the taxi floor. As they bounced over the potholes, the animals inside clawed furiously.

They lunched at the Pierre.

"Let's have a fairly decent bottle of wine. Anyway, I'm charging this to Aegean Lines."

"Can you do that?"

"I'll bill it as an office conference."

The maître d' took their orders. Gina recognized that he, too, belonged to the conspiracy of waiters and air stewardesses and sales assistants, all of whom smirked at her as if they knew she did not belong.

Over the rack of lamb, she took the plunge. "Clancy, my landlord's trying to evict me."

"Why didn't you tell me sooner?"

"It just happened. I mean, should I look for another apartment or should I stay and fight it?"

"We'll get you the best real-estate legal advice in Manhattan. You can have whomever you want from Cheltenham."

"Cheltenham's too hifalutin. They don't understand simple squabbles. David Gleiner—you know, that poor kid who died last week—got into some rent board battle. His landlord turned off the heat and hot water for a week. David had two Cheltenham partners and four associates working on his matter for eleven months and they couldn't do a damn thing. Finally he went to some guy in the Bronx, who charged him a hundred and fifty bucks and got the thing straightened out in a week."

"David Gleiner was a nobody. Who cared about his legal problems? You're different. You've got me."

"But is it worth all the hassle? I mean, if you and I are going to get an apartment together in the spring, I mean, what do you think?"

Maxwell stroked her cheek. "How's your lamb?"

"It's pretty good. I mean, aren't we?"

"Aren't we what, gorgeous?"

"Going to live together?"

"Gina, I'm too old for you. I feel guilty, screwing up your life like this."

"You never said that before."

"I've been thinking about it. You're so young and fresh, you just can't imagine what it feels like waking up in the morning when all your bones ache. Not being able to remember things. Just simple stuff, like the other day I was instructing some first-year associate, and I couldn't remember the name of the leading case on tortious interference to chattels."

"That happens to everyone. You have a photographic memory, almost. You remember millions of cases that you haven't even looked at since law school. You remember every newspaper article, and currency exchange rates, and all the capital cities of the world, and who's the president of every country, and the date of the burning of Joan of Arc, and the words of the third verse of 'The Star Spangled Banner,' and everything."

He laughed. "You give me too much credit."

She knew that was true. Sometimes, looking at the wine-flushed, sagging jaw, she suspected that sooner or later he must lose his edge. But even when the edge was dulled, when he lost the power of his maturity, even then she would still love him. It might be a different love from the frenzy that had made him her guru and her hero and her Vronsky all at once. Sometimes she wondered if, in the confusion of the early days at Cheltenham, she had been dazzled by Maxwell and the wonders of the law firm all at once. Perhaps, blinded by the awesome corridors, she had attributed undue brilliance to him. Then he would catch her again by surprise, impressing her with an obscure quote, or his lightning grasp of the mechanics of a prospectus with which she had wrestled all night.

"Maybe I should just move. Find another apartment."

He waved for the check. "Let's go buy your Christmas present."

"Where are we going?" she asked as he wheeled her down Fifth Avenue. The tourists were out en masse, surging with shopping bags four abreast down the sidewalk, while weary Santa Clauses rang bells on the street corners.

"Wait and see."

Her face lit up. "Oh, Clancy! Fred the Furrier!"

"I think it's time you had a nice warm coat."

Self-consciously Gina glanced down at the camel coat she had worn the past three New York winters. Cheryl, her upper lip curled in disdain, had scolded her for not replacing it with something more stylish. But Gina, although she felt the cold, had never seemed to have enough time to deal with such practicalities. It was easier to grab a scarf and wait until spring.

Fred the Furrier was doing a brisk holiday business. Career women, well-paid secretaries, and Mafia wives brushed though the racks, preened before the mirrors, and engaged in relentless dialectic with the salespeople. The coat-check girl, with the usual knowing smile that instantly took in the plot, superciliously removed Gina's camel coat.

"Why, Mr. Maxwell! What a pleasure to see you again. It is Mr. Maxwell, isn't it?"

The salesman turned the beam of his attention on Gina. "Remember me? My name's Patrick. I always remember you and Mr. Maxwell. We had such a difficult time getting that fox jacket to match the hat. But we managed in the end, didn't we?" He smiled winningly.

"You've certainly got a good memory," said Maxwell dryly.

"What was it, a couple of years ago? I always remember my favorite customers. And even before that, you bought that dramatic blond mink. It was a real poem. I hope it's being worn in good health, and enjoyed."

"I imagine it is." Maxwell produced a lawyerly cough and buried his discomfort in the examination of a dyed beaver. "I suggest we concern ourselves with the present."

Patrick bestowed a sly grin of complicity on Gina. "What will the lady be having in mind this time?" He rubbed the cotton of her shirtsleeve instinctively between his fingers. "Perhaps a coat more geared to evening wear?"

"Something simple," said Gina. "I've never had a fur coat before."

Patrick's smile froze in horror and the color drained out of his cheeks. "Oh, madame, forgive me, I thought it was you...the tawny fox..."

"Forget it," she said casually.

His cheeks went pink and then pale, and then pink again. "You understand, madame, I see so many people, and it was several years ago..."

Maxwell interrupted, holding up a Canadian squirrel off the rack. "Why don't you try this?"

"If madame will just step this way, behind the mirror," whimpered Patrick, muffling his embarrassment in the litany of his trade, "she'll have more privacy and a better view." He fussed around her, adjusting the sleeves and collar. "I think you might find those shoulders overwhelming. Trust me. But I do have somewhere just the coat that could suit you to perfection."

He reappeared with a dark mink. "A sonnet!" He beamed. As he bundled it around her, she caught a glimpse of the price tag hanging from the sleeve. Six thousand dollars. As if he sensed the tremulous change in her pulse, Patrick murmured, his mouth close to her ear, "It's a very good reduction."

"You like it?" asked Maxwell.

They ended up settling on the sonnet. Gina loved it and Maxwell told her several times in the taxi how it emphasized the line of her slender calves and made him want to bury his face under its pelts.

Over dinner in a local Italian dive, she asked, "So whom did you buy those other fur coats for? Eleanor?"

He looked startled. "Lord, no. Eleanor gets her own. She's got a fellow down on Seventh."

"So who?"

"I've always been honest with you, Gina, haven't I? I've told you that I've had previous affairs. Nothing ever, ever like this of course. They were just distractions."

"I understand all about that. But you bought them all fur coats?"

"Not all of them. Just a couple."

"You're a generous man."

"They weren't very nice fur coats. You look head and shoulders better in yours."

246

"You always go to Fred the Furrier?"

"They seem to have a good selection. There was never any problem before. That cretin. Why couldn't he have kept his mouth shut? Oh, Gina, I just wanted to get you something you'd like. And you do like it, don't you?"

"It's the loveliest thing I've ever had." Except maybe for my rug, she thought. But then, that had not been a present from Maxwell.

"Let's get the check," he said. "I think we need an early night. I've got to catch that frigging plane for Denver in the morning."

The temperature outside had dropped. She huddled in her new fur coat as Maxwell shuffled with his keys at the top of the steps.

"Will Eleanor call again tonight?" she asked once they were inside.

"Not yet. Let's sit down here quietly and have a couple of drinks. As soon as she phones we can go to bed."

"I just want some Perrier."

"How about some applesauce? It's pretty good, really. And one of us has got to eat it, or there'll be trouble when we all get back from Aspen."

"Throw it away."

He looked appalled. "We can't do that. I tell you, it's pretty scrumptious. She's got some secret recipe from her great-aunt Edith. Come on, we'll share it."

He found a couple of spoons and planted the bowl on the table between them. Still Gina held back, heeding the voices that whispered in her ear that to eat might bring down some terrible curse on the House of Maxwell. Insistently, he scooped up a spoonful and coaxed it between her lips.

They kept vigil all the rest of the evening at the kitchen table, waiting for the rescue of Eleanor's call. Maxwell suggested they could go upstairs and watch television. She shrugged.

"Will you be able to phone me from Colorado tomorrow?" she asked.

"I'll try, gorgeous. It may be tricky, though. You'll understand, won't you?"

"You mean I may not talk to you again till after Christmas?"

"I'll manage it somehow," he assured her grandly. "Even if I have to sneak out in the middle of the night, and tramp through a mile of snow, I'll find a way to call my gorgeous."

Eleanor's call, when it finally came, lasted less than a couple of minutes. When he hung up, he swung around brightly, as if he had achieved some stirring victory.

Sunday morning they had coffee downstairs in the kitchen, read the newspaper, and scoured Eleanor's copper sauté pan again. It had been soaking in detergent for thirty-six hours.

"All the food's come unstuck anyway," said Gina. "Now if we could just find some way to polish it up."

They settled on the metal polish that was intended for the great bronze knocker on the mint-green door.

Then she watched him pack, sitting upstairs on the edge of the patchwork quilt while he threw sweaters and pajamas and thermal underwear into his suitcase.

"I wish you were coming with me," he said, untangling a skein of socks.

Gina remembered La Samana, which had already receded into fuzzy outlines of a distant oasis. "Maybe next year."

In the corner of the case he tucked a small red Cartier box.

"What's that?"

"Just a trinket. A token Christmas present for her." He folded a wool muffler. "A salve to my conscience."

Without turning around, she felt the eyes of the framed Eleanor ancestor on the dressing table boring into her. "You feel guilty?"

He sat down deliberately beside her on the patchwork quilt and took both her hands. "Gina, every man's guilty in my situation. If anyone tells you otherwise, he's lying. I know it's hard for you being away from me over Christmas. But just remember this: It's much worse for me. All the time. I'm the one who has to come home to her every night, and sit pretending with the woman I don't love."

Gina thought of her own evenings in the squalid apartment, poring over Vaginex documents or wading through a chapter of Tolstoy. "I know it's awful for you. But it won't be long now, will it?"

What did happen, she wondered heavily, when was it he fell out of love with me?

"Let's just take each day one at a time."

She remembered with a pang the adolescent days of their affair, how he would knock on her office door with that urgent, lusty pounding she knew could only be his, how he would recklessly send her deliciously suggestive notes in unsealed envelopes through the interoffice mail. When was it last he had grabbed her, madly, uncontrollably, in the elevator between the forty-seventh and forty-ninth floor? Was this still the man who had once kissed her at 3 A.M. in Ariel Lamb's own office, squeezing her back up to the wall behind the credenza?

"Clancy, those other women. The ones you bought the fur coats for. Who were they?"

"They're ancient history. I hardly remember," he mumbled as he got up and resumed his packing.

She clawed at a loose strand of thread from Eleanor's patchwork. "Was it anyone from Cheltenham?"

"Mmm. Yes, there were a couple."

"A couple! You had two affairs with people at Cheltenham?"

"It's so unimportant. Anyhow, they've both left now." He smiled his creamy, cultured smile and she knew he was going to quote. "'Thou has committed fornication, but that was in another country, and besides, the wench is dead.' *The Jew of Malta.* Christopher Marlowe. Terrific playwright. Boy, those Elizabethans. Don't look so sad. I tell you, one of them's gone to another firm, not a very prestigious one either, and the other one's working for, let's see, oh yes, one of the Gulf and Western companies."

"They were both lawyers?" She could not hide her dismay.

"What do you think I am? I wouldn't sleep with just any old floozy."

"Did anyone at Cheltenham know about your . . . other girlfriends?"

"There's always the occasional rumor in a big law firm."

So that's what they're thinking, she realized, when they look at me that way. Three young women associates. Three fur coats.

"Were they pretty?"

"The Gulf and Western one was, kind of. But she as an airhead. The other one was very smart. Beautiful? I'd probably say no."

"You ever talk to them?"

"Oh, once in a blue moon. They call about a reference or something."

He zipped his suitcase closed with a flourish and sat again next to her on the bed. "They were just nice girls, but not important. And I've been a lonely man for a long time. I like female company. You know that. That doesn't mean that what you and I have is one iota less special."

"What time's your plane?"

He looked at his watch. "We'd better go."

He did not suggest she accompany him to La Guardia. In the past, when he left on business trips, she had always ridden with him in the taxi or limousine. They would sit, fingers intertwined, weaving though the traffic, while he made her rash and eloquent promises about their future. He would kiss her tenderly at the gate, and she would take a cab home alone, the words of the promises still singing in her ears.

He hailed a taxi on the corner of First Avenue. "Do you mind if I don't drop you off this time? I'm running a tad late for my flight."

She shook her head. "I'll get the next one."

He hugged her to him, cursorily. "Have a wonderful Christmas, my precious gorgeous. Don't eat too much turkey. And enjoy the coat and keep warm."

The cab door was slammed shut even before he had finished the sentence. He waved, mechanically, as the taxi drew away.

She dreaded returning to her apartment. She did not want to be alone, imprisoned with her despair, which kept growing, a malignancy out of control. So instead she took a taxi down to Cheltenham, grateful for the teal-green fortress, a twenty-four-hour refuge.

She worked in the library all afternoon. It was a relief to huddle with her cases and notes at a window niche, surrounded by several dozen associates, each isolated in a sphere of concentration. As she searched the card catalogue alongside Peter Courage, who was looking young and athletic in his faded Sunday blue-jeans, he said, formulaically, "You been here all weekend?"

"Not so long. And you?"

"Since this morning. I sure hope I'm getting out soon."

He looked so safe and normal in his Giants sweatshirt, for a moment she was tempted to detain him, to suggest they go for coffee and a chat. It would be a relief and a distraction just to sit with someone. But she resisted the impulse. Supposing she were to burst into tears, and then the whole Clancy weekend story might gush out. These days she could not rely on her self-control. Peter Courage seemed a friendly, decent person on the surface, but three years at Cheltenham had taught her that one could not be too cautious. Associates could rarely trust one another.

By six most of the lost souls had filtered out from the aisles. She worked on, in the lamplight, reading furiously, minutely cross-referencing even the most obscure details. She did not intend to charge the time to the client. It was enough to find solace in the well-thumbed soft pages of the cases, to extract the reassuring eloquence from the judges' opinions.

Later, in her apartment, after a half-eaten carton of moo shu pork, she stumbled into bed with *Anna Karenina*. Outside the December wind whipped up suddenly, banging against the drafty window. She got up to close it and shivered.

The mink coat hung in solitary state, not in the closet, but on a separate hook next to her mirror. She crushed the sleek sleeve against her cheek. Maxwell had stopped being crazy about her, and there was nothing in the world she could do. Would she ever know the moment it had happened? From now on the best she could hope for was excuses and protestation and watered-down fibs of devotion.

She slid the mink off the hook and wrapped it around her shoulders. Crawling into bed, she switched off the light and finally slept, caressed by the weight of the fur.

TWELVE

*T*ristan glanced around the marble foyer of the Downtown Athletic Club. The Christmas tree, brooding over a neat stack of wrapped gifts, glowed discreetly at the end of the room. A number of somber-suited men conversed quietly on the sofas and waited patiently by the wood-paneled pillars for their appointments. Inside the bar the pianist was playing "Night and Day." Finnegan waved at her. She had high teased hair and a red sequined cocktail dress with dangling red glass earrings.

They sat at the bar. "What'll it be, gentlemen?" asked the bartender, setting down pretzels and napkins. He glanced at Finnegan. "The usual?"

Finnegan's vibrant features took on his dangerous look. "We're drinking champagne, Larry. It's the Thursday before Christmas. Make it a bottle of Veuve Cliquot. That okay by you, T.B.?"

Tristan shrugged and reached for a handful of pretzels. "It's on you tonight, Mick."

The girl finished singing. Finnegan folded a ten-dollar bill in the glass on the piano. "How are you, m'dear?" he called. "All dressed up and ready to keep someone warm on this snowy night?"

"Thanks," she said, and smiled her toothy smile full of contempt. "We're quiet this evening. 'Cause of the snow, I guess."

"Keep an eye on me, mademoiselle. See I don't drink too much in this weather. I mustn't be too late," he explained to Tristan. "I had a long evening on Friday and Alice made a scene all weekend. I can't take it if she sulks all through Christmas too. A four-day weekend."

"How is Alice?"

"Not happy. She says it's nothing to do with the money problem, but I know if I were rich again, we'd be papering over a lot of our differences. Though I guess I'm hard to live with these days too. I'm depressed most of the time."

Tristan raised his champagne glass with irony. "To absent wives. At least you've got one. This is the first time I've been alone for the holidays."

"How about the kids?"

"They've decided to stay with Pam. She's gradually turned them against me. They've all conveniently forgotten that for twenty-five years I was the one who worked my tail off for them."

"They don't understand our pressures. Nobody does, unless they've been through it themselves. We all work like dogs, and all of us crack in our own way, sooner or later."

"All except Ariel Lamb."

"Ariel's not real. He's a wind-up doll. Some of us hit the bottle from time to time, like me. Some of us collapse in the hospital with exhaustion every three years like Mel Samson."

"And some of us," said Tristan, sipping thoughtfully, "look around and suddenly find after twenty-five years, our marriages are over. I miss Pam. I think of all the little things I could have done to make her happier, and now it's too late. She always wanted to take a trip to China. I wish I'd just taken off three weeks and done it. The worst part is, thinking of all those years she was so bored with me, and she never said a word."

"You were trying to make a living."

"I used Cheltenham as an excuse for not paying attention to her. It just never occurred to me that she could want any other kind of life. Our money, our house, our friends—I thought we

253

were lucky people. My head was buried in the sand, Mick. I put Cheltenham first, and now it's all I've got."

"If you'd like to come up to Greenwich, T.B., and spend Christmas day with Alice and me, we'd be delighted to have you."

"That's nice of you, Mick. But I think I'll just stay in town here and catch up on some paperwork. Kahn's gone off on one of his jags over these hair-dye people."

Finnegan waved to the bartender, who poured them more champagne.

"The past six months," said Tristan reflectively, "since I've been living alone, it's a comfort to know the firm's always there."

"You've been keeping some late nights, I know."

"I've nowhere else to go. Even when I'm just working alone at night, it's times like this I still get the feeling that the firm is our real family, and in a way, 57 Water Street is our real home."

Tristan had become something of a nightly regular, stalking the corridors of the forty-eighth floor often until well after midnight. Some people knew how lonely his broken marriage had left him. The ignorant ones put his work habits down to insecurity, a fear of insufficient billables. His face, although still a monument of breeding, looked tired all the time, and late at night he seemed to drag his hefty body.

"It's home for some," replied Finnegan plaintively, but without rancor. He had never been mean spirited. Even while he felt the rug being pulled out from under his crumbling career, he still managed to believe in Cheltenham, with a faith transcending the Lamb and Samson factional skirmishes. When Tristan and Finnegan looked back, Cheltenham still represented their whole youths to them, the struggles and pride and dedication of three decades of their lives. Although Ariel Lamb and his Corporate Finance army might snuff out their futures, even he, that upstart Caesar, could never take away the past professionalism they had served like holy orders.

Finnegan sighed. "Maybe I'm living in the past. The ax could fall at any time. Hopper's on the war path for my hide."

"Hopper! He's only been a partner a couple of years. And now so much power."

"He has Ariel's ear, which these days is enough. He reported that he caught me in the elevator reeking of liquor. It wasn't even true. All I'd had was a couple of glasses of wine and a couple of Irish coffees. Why does that virus hate me so much?"

Tristan answered slowly, "Hopper doesn't exactly hate you. He has no personal attitude. But he's mean and ambitious and ruthless. He sees you as an object of weakness in the Cheltenham fabric. Like an animal half gunned down. He needs a few victims to consolidate his power base. You're so easy to pick on."

"That's why he makes up rumors and defamatory lies about me, and casts aspersions on my professionalism in public. But at the same time, I find it hard to get scared of Hopper, with his carroty hair and that stupid grin."

"You're wrong, Mick. Beware the snake in the grass. He's as dangerous as that crackpot Fishman, who's got Ariel's protection and plenty of points, but is only playing with half a deck. Hopper's as powerful as Clancy and the senior people of our generation."

Finnegan took a pretzel and crushed it to powder between his fingers. "I missed the partnership lunch today. Were there any more jibes about my billables?"

Sooner or later, Tristan knew, Finnegan would get into irreparable trouble with the partnership. His billables were simply not adequate these days to compensate for his partnership draw, even at its reduced level of points. Besides, over the years Finnegan had rubbed too many people the wrong way with his flamboyant mannerisms, thereby destroying the foundations of support that might have backed him up through some lean years.

"There wasn't any discussion of partners' hours today," he reported. "Everyone was in a good mood, with Christmas, and also the record profits from last month. Looks like they want to can a couple of associates, though."

"Anyone we know or care for?"

"None of our boys. You ever come across a peculiar first year named Benedict Hamilton? Harvard."

"Isn't he something of a fruit?" Finnegan disliked homosexuality only second to his dislike of Hopper and Lamb.

"Seems that's part of the problem. Of course we at Cheltenham have never discriminated against any of our employees on the grounds of either sexual orientation or for reasons of political bias."

"Sure, that's the company line. But we don't need fruit. They detract from the sobriety of our practice."

"Here's to sobriety," interrupted Tristan, raising his glass for the final swig of champagne. "Shall we grab a bite to eat before we get too squiffy?"

"No. We'll crack one more bottle first. Hey, Larry, another one of the same. We don't like fruit, T.B. I certainly don't."

"Anyhow," said Tristan, who had listened to Finnegan's unequivocal opinions on "fruit" for almost two decades, "the point is that the kid has an impossible personality and no one wants to work with him because he's a pain in the butt."

"So? Since when did that ever impede anyone's career at Cheltenham?"

"That's part of it. He's been calling in sick a lot. He seems to be working an average of about four days a week."

"Probably gallivanting around with his pansy boyfriends."

"Whatever the reason, there's a rumor got started that he's got AIDS. You know what Cheltenham lunchroom gossip's like."

"AIDS!" squealed Finnegan. "We can't have that. The sooner he's out the better."

"Apparently that's what a majority of the partnership felt too."

It had been a bizarre partnership-meeting discussion, even by Cheltenham's standards of improbability. Hopper, with his usual nose for slaughter, had raised the issue.

"A rather serious report concerning one of our junior corporate associates has been recently circulating in the Cheltenham cafeteria," he'd said. " While we're not yet in a position to assess its veracity, there has been discussion in the firm that Benedict Hamilton may be suffering from the early stages of acquired immune deficiency syndrome."

"That's ridiculous," exclaimed Cyrus Sweet. "He's an attorney in a premiere Wall Street firm."

"There've been a handful of cases already in the major firms," said Clancy Maxwell.

Fishman became rapidly hysterical. "I propose that we have his office sealed off immediately, until we've established whether he's got it."

Clancy Maxwell enjoyed championing a liberal cause. "Don't be absurd, Gary. You can't catch AIDS from sharing a Xerox machine."

But Fishman, as obsessive about health as about the Internal Revenue Code, grew shriller. "How do you know? Maybe you can get it breathing the same air. And how about using the plates and forks in the cafeteria. And men's rooms!"

"I think we need have no fears for the standards of cleanliness in the Cheltenham cafeteria," said Ariel Lamb coldly.

"It's a serious concern for the Hiring Committee," mused Cyrus Sweet. His first thoughts flew to his favorite Cheltenham occupation, the recruitment of Ivy League graduates and the ever-increasing difficulties of attracting them. "First we have to gloss over the unpleasant incident of that man Gleiner's death, and then this. We'll be lucky if we attract any applicants next year from the better schools."

"I shouldn't be too concerned about that," interposed Ariel Lamb. "Now that we've developed the finest Corporate Finance Department in the country, any high-powered young lawyer would give his right arm to come to us, whatever our minor associate problems."

"'Minor'!" yelled Fishman. His face had turned the color of eggplant. "You call that minor?" Then he suddenly realized he was shrieking at his boss. He looked down at his plate of asparagus in confusion. The fifty-two heads present in the room turned in silence and amazement toward him. "What's the point of our building the gym," he muttered in embarrassment, "if we don't protect the clinical working conditions of our members and staff."

Mel Samson rapped on the table with his bony finger. "For whom has this associate been working?" he demanded.

Tristan spoke up. "He's been on one of my teams. Works under Peter Courage on some of my entrepreneurial matters. I understand that although he's fairly bright, he won't conform to our standards of discipline."

Ariel Lamb's soothing voice summed up the situation. "Would it be fair to conclude," he articulated, stressing the word *fair* in his special way, to remind the gathering of his commitment to all attributes of justice, "that this unfortunate young attorney has no particular contribution to make toward Cheltenham's future?"

Only Cyrus Sweet spoke up against the silence of assent. "Not necessarily," he reminded the Fuhrer. "Hamilton is a Harvard Law School graduate. Any Ivy League associates we attract play an important role in our future hiring success."

"Cyrus," purred the Fuhrer, "I give you my word, my personal guarantee, that by this time next year, you'll have at least a dozen acceptances from Harvard and Yale. After our TBO takes off, they'll be beating the doors down." The rhetoric mesmerized the room. Ariel Lamb had recently become given to making more and more time-specific promises. He must be immensely sure of himself, thought Tristan.

Now Mel Samson spoke up sharply, snatching the opportunity to reinforce his image as the man of action. "We agree he's got to go," he snapped. "So what's the deal and who's going to fire him?"

"Not fire!" protested Lamb. "Reach an amicable understanding."

"I forgot," rasped Samson. "No one ever gets fired from Cheltenham. So who's going to cream him?"

None of the partners relished directly wielding the ax, not even Hopper. It was one thing to make decisions in conclave, and another matter to deliver the deathblow, human to human.

"So how long does he get? The standard three months' warning?"

The notion of sharing contaminated office space with the alleged infection for a whole season drew a cry of outrage from Gary Fishman. "Three months!" he cried. "Let's just pay him off and send him on his way."

"We can't do that," Cyrus Sweet pointed out. "After all, we're only firing—uh, reassessing his future—on the basis of inadequate work. There's no cause to throw him out so suddenly."

"You don't call a terminal contagious infection a good cause?"

"Gentlemen," said Ariel. "May I remind you that this associate's medical condition has no bearing whatsoever on our decision regarding his termination. Except inasmuch as he may be unfit to perform the requisite work load."

For a brief moment the two leaders held a common front. Mel Samson added, "I'm sure you all realize that it would be extremely detrimental, and possibly subject us to litigation, if it should ever leave this room that Mr. Hamilton's disassociation with us has any medical basis. Our rationale is that his personality and performance does not dovetail with Cheltenham's expectations, therefore he would be advised to start looking for alternative employment at once. We'll give him references. Last paycheck in March."

When Tristan had finished recounting the meeting's business, Finnegan drained the end of their second bottle and remarked, "At least associates get three months' warning. When they can me it'll be twenty-four hours. Ready for the next bottle?"

Tristan looked anxiously to the bartender and back to Finnegan, whose eyes were beginning to glaze. A few drinks quickly took their toll on Mick these days. When they were younger men, and had gone out drinking on a Saturday night after an afternoon in the library, it had taken more than a couple of bottles to sweep him past the brink of sloppy drunkenness.

"I can't manage any more," Tristan protested, in an effort to decelerate Finnegan's pace. "Where shall we eat?"

"Christ Cella."

"Miles away. Somewhere closer." He did not want to drag the lumbering Finnegan across town.

"Le Cirque."

"Too far. And we've no reservation."

Finnegan pulled out a quarter. "Call them for us. We'll give them Ariel's name. They'll let us in."

"Come on, Mick," said Tristan firmly. "We're going to the Wall Street Club."

"I don't want to sit with a bunch of stuffed shirts. The ghouls in the graveyard."

"It's nearby. And they make a great T-bone." As they left, Finnegan tried to embrace the pianist. "Just one kiss for Christmas," he pleaded, swaying dizzily over her neck. "Pax vobiscum."

She continued hammering out "New York, New York." "I'm Jewish," she volleyed back. "You missed Chanukah. Good night, gentlemen."

Outside the soft, wet snow had started to accumulate. The partners took in deep breaths of air, sweeping the thick cigar smoke out of their lungs. The streets had emptied now, except for a lone beggar at the corner of Greenwich Street, who whined, "Can you spare some change so I can buy a sandwich?" Tristan pushed Finnegan relentlessly forward. The beggar insisted, "So I can buy a tuna fish sandwich." Tristan hustled Finnegan a few steps farther. "With mayonnaise!" called out the beggar to them in a dramatic crescendo. The suspended cry seemed to vibrate in the still air.

They took the elevator to the top of the building to the club where Tristan was a well-known member. Since Pam had left him and moved back to her mother's house in Boston, Tristan often ate a solitary dinner there before returning to 57 Water Street for the last watch of the evening's work.

He ushered Finnegan out of the elevator and through the austere lobby and bar, where the brown and gray upholstery provided a natural habitat for finance and masculinity. The small group of diners, all men, seemed to blend like chameleons into the camouflage of their environment. Tristan was heading for a table as far away from the group as possible, when Mel Samson's gravelly voice arrested them in their tracks.

"Good evening, Tristan, Mick," said Samson, staring out from his solitary table by the window. He was eating a bowl of chowder.

"What a pleasant surprise," lied Tristan. "May we join you?"

Finnegan swayed unevenly. Samson waved wordlessly toward the two empty seats across from him. He took another slow, deliberate mouthful of soup.

Finnegan crumpled loosely into a chair, while Samson merely glared at him with the hooded hawk's eyes.

"It's started snowing," reported Tristan unnecessarily, which left him feeling awkward. Samson continued to sip and stare with his indefatigable gaze. He had mastered the knack of destroying any opposition through silence. "You working late tonight?" Tristan mumbled.

"I had a meeting at Brown Brothers which ran on. I thought I'd stop for a bite before I called the car for Montclair. You should try some of this chowder."

Meanwhile Finnegan, who had caught the waiter's attention, was trying to order a martini.

"I see you boys have been out celebrating tonight," remarked Samson, beaming a lazer of reproof. He turned to the waiter in slow motion. "Cancel the martini. Make it a couple of glasses of ice water."

The waiter nodded automatically and showed no surprise. Samson had always, even when he was younger, treated the others like wayward children. In those days he had exhibited occasional outbursts of aggression, which now, as the senior statesman, he had long buried behind the hooded lids. Although Tristan was no longer actively afraid of Samson—he had known him for twenty-eight years, all told—he knew that as long as they both lived he would never feel at ease with him. Samson, in marked contrast to Ariel Lamb, made no effort to seduce the unwary into a state of submission. His was the pitiless steel-trap mind; his demands were absolute. Over the years, Tristan reflected, some of Samson's mannerisms had become their own parody: the gruff sentences, the economy of words, the chilling stare when silence was sufficient. But Tristan preferred Samson's austerity to his forced charm. It was only with clients, major clients, that Samson ever permitted a smile. The leer that pulled tight the fleshless lips was more disconcerting than the growl. Even worse, Tristan recalled from way back, was the grip of the bony handshake. Despite the fearsome smile and the merciless fingers, Samson had attracted and maintained a loyal client base. They respected his business acumen and his relentlessness. His Victorian chill was what was expected in a senior partner.

"You missed the partnership meeting today," he accused Finnegan.

"I had a meeting at the American Gynecological Institute. They originally endorsed Vaginex."

Samson nodded as if his mind were on other matters. Then, abruptly—it was another one of his tricks—he said, "It's time you got back to some quality litigation, Mick. All this pussy squabble is beneath a trial lawyer of your caliber."

Finnegan, who was still struggling for a lucid foothold in the conversation, gazed at him dumbly. Tristan wondered if Finnegan was still capable of serious litigation. At least the so-called "pussy squabble" helped keep him out of trouble.

Samson did not waste breath on chitchat. "Got any other matters, outside of Vaginex?"

Finnegan clawed inelegantly at a bread roll. "Dribs and drabs. The morsels they throw me. Last week Hopper came to me to ask me to help out with some research. Research! That's first-year associate work. I was doing research when that little punk was still in diapers."

"So, get an associate to do it."

"I don't have an associate anymore, now that Gina di Angelo's working full time for Clancy Maxwell."

"We've got over a hundred junior associates at Cheltenham. Find someone else."

"They all make excuses. They won't work for me. They know I'm washed up."

Samson motioned to the waiter. "Bring us three orders of chicken tetrazzini." He nodded toward Finnegan. "And a cup of coffee. Right away." It was typical that Samson, without consultation, should order their food for them.

Tristan changed the subject. "Kahn's still hell bent on buying Goldilox," he told Mel. "We think it's lunacy, considering the pending lawsuits for product liability."

Samson's lids drooped a fraction lower. "He's the client. As long as he pays our substantial fees, if he wants to lose his shirt, that's his business." Samson, as head of the General Corporate Department, retained ultimate responsibility for the client relationship with Kahn. Although Tristan had been looking after the Mongolian Marauder's legal muddles for years, Samson still had the last word.

"If he loses his shirt, maybe he won't be able to pay our bills."

"We've never drafted a document yet that doesn't provide for the settlement of legal fees first and foremost. He'd have to be selling knishes on Maiden Lane before he could get out of paying Cheltenham." Samson turned to Finnegan, exposing them to the dreaded leer. "You're screwing up your life, Mick. I don't like to see a good man go down. We all know you've been put out to pasture. All you need, though, is one smash hit, and the wheel could spin right back again."

Finnegan's eyes lurched wildly around the room, from the small group of somber figures at the far table to the window, where the edges of the skyscrapers blended into the night like a study in blacks and charcoals and indigos. "No one's sent me any respectable work in two years."

"Litigation's been slow. The Corporate Finance people have been making hay. Times are turning. I've got a new client for you."

"What?!"

"How would you like to take on a matter involving international transactions, conflict of laws, extradition procedures?"

Finnegan had always fancied himself as Cheltenham's "international" litigator, specializing, as he used to, in oil spills, toxic contamination, and industrial explosions. The disasters, which often took place in the poorer pockets of the world, had impelled him, in better days, to roam the five continents. Finnegan liked traveling. Long first-class trips on airplanes provided for the consumption of free-flowing champagne, while faraway hotel bars, with foreign clients, invited the occasion to "bend an elbow."

The prospect of real and glamorous work again sobered him suddenly, more effectively than the coffee or glasses of ice water.

"I'm listening," he replied, trying to control the excitement in his voice. His breath was coming faster. He could feel his pulse quicken. He took a deep lungful of air to steady himself. "Which countries are involved?"

"Latin America." The leer was wiped away to be replaced again by the deathmask. "It's a highly sensitive matter, Mick. And, I need hardly say, confidential. Are you sure I can count on your discretion?"

"My career may currently be in deep shit, but I am still a member of Cheltenham, Arbuthnot and Crewe."

Tristan was baffled. He knew that, whatever the quality of Finnegan's intentions, he would soon be telling his life story to bartenders, cooks, waitresses, and late-night drinkers all over town. He shuddered as Samson, like a spider, moved deliberately across the skeins of the web.

"You ever heard of the Valencia brothers?"

Finnegan reluctantly admitted to ignorance.

"They're a big farming family from outside Popayán in Colombia. They've been coffee plantation growers down there for generations, over a century. They also have agricultural interests in Peru, Equador, and Bolivia."

"Hmm. The name does ring a bell," bluffed Finnegan.

"I thought it might. You may not be quite up to date on their recent, uh, skirmish with the Colombian government."

"Remind me," encouraged Finnegan casually. He was starting to lose the thread of the discussion again.

"The government of President Vargas has now mobilized the Colombian army against the powerful Medellin cartel of cocaine traffickers. About six months ago, in an entirely unauthorized raid, government troops entered the Valencia brothers' property, where they allege they discovered twelve hundred kilos of recently harvested cocaine, in laundry bags, awaiting shipment. The brothers, José and Luis, took immediate refuge, first in the Bahamas and later in Miami. The Colombian government has now instigated extradition proceedings."

"They're drug dealers," gasped Tristan. "Gangsters. Cheltenham's never dealt with that kind of criminal practice."

Samson raised an imperious hand. "Alleged. We're talking about an old South American coffee-growing family, who may have been falsely implicated by corrupt local officials."

"Come on, Mel," said Finnegan skeptically. The onset of a hangover was making him defiant.

"Boys. The Valencias have never been convicted by a court of law in any jurisdiction. We are in no position to pronounce on their culpability. They do, however, control considerable resources and, I am pleased to tell you, have approached us at Cheltenham with a view to our representation in their extradition defense."

Finnegan shook his head. "It's a bummer. There's a slew of new extradition laws between the U.S. and Latin America with regard to drug-trafficking offenses. The August 1980 Agreement Relating to Cooperation to Curb Illegal Narcotics Traffic updates the original extradition treaties between the U.S. and Colombia, which were entered into in 1891 and in 1943."

"You're the best," growled Samson, impressed despite himself. "But I told you it was a sensitive and challenging matter. The spics need a defense counsel, if nothing else, to delay proceedings. I see no reason why we at Cheltenham should turn down such work."

"I see a lot of reasons," grunted Finnegan. "The guys are thugs. I litigate for multinational corporations. Besides, it's immoral."

Samson snarled. "Immoral? So that's what you call it these days? You're becoming sentimental, Mick, as well as pickled. I suppose you're also concerned about litigating toxic spills on behalf of careless corporations who've exterminated whole villages?"

"That's different. This has a sleazy ring to it. I'm already the laughingstock of Cheltenham. Now I'll be the butt of every sneer on Wall Street."

Samson was not accustomed to being argued with. He chewed a long mouthful of tetrazzini, resorting to his trump card of intimidation through silence.

Tristan, although pained to witness Finnegan's entrapment, recognized his own impotence. "Pardon me." He stood up. "I have to make a phone call. I'll be a couple of minutes." Huddled in the phone kiosk, with the change in his hand, he had realized there was no one for him to talk to. He no longer had a wife to call. Finnegan was his only real friend left at Cheltenham, and he was writhing in the dining room next door like an insect caught in a sticky web.

Why was it, he pondered, that Samson so urgently wanted to involve Finnegan in this shady drug-dealing proceeding? Finnegan was correct. The Valencias were an inappropriate client for a reputable Wall Street practice. Supposing Samson, by some bizarre twist, had taken a genuine interest in the plight of these South American thugs, why ever should he assign the work to a man who was likely to botch it? And why the emphasis on secrecy and discretion? At this stage Samson must want to disassociate himself. So why touch it at all?

Tristan looked through the glass doors of the kiosk into the sepia foyer—the entrance, as Finnegan would put it, to the graveyard. A pair of gaunt diners, with wire-rimmed glasses, strolled sedately out of the dining room.

Perhaps there was a compassionate side to Samson, long buried under the cultivated layers of ancient ice. Perhaps he had been touched by Finnegan's approaching Waterloo and genuinely wanted to pass him crumbs of work. Tristan dismissed the idea.

Colombia, Equador, Peru...those were the countries where the officers of Caroline Brothers were at this moment wrapping up the TBO deal at the highest levels of government. Cheltenham's prosperity and Ariel Lamb's future depended in part on the successful outcome of the negotiations. From Der Fuhrer's point of view, it was essential to preserve a climate of friendship with those South American officials. Yet here was Il Duce, encouraging Cheltenham to take on a sensitive client who was pitted directly against those governments. Spurring Finnegan to dive into the fray with utmost urgency.

Tristan smiled grimly to himself, as Samson's machinations began to take on a visible form. The old hawk had never been wilier. If the plan worked, and the South Americans realized in time that Cheltenham had taken an inextricable position against them, the whole delicate scaffold of the TBO structure could come clattering to earth. Finnegan, not Samson, would show up as the scapegoat. Open wounds always attract sharks first. Ariel's baby would be suffocated before birth, and Mel's seesaw would jerk upward again. It was no use warning Finnegan. Even if he figured it out for himself, there was nothing he could do without committing professional suicide in one shot. Whichever way he played it, Finnegan was on his way to the firing squad.

Finnegan and Samson were the last men left in the mausolean dining room. "So where are these spics hiding now?" Finnegan asked.

"The Messrs. Valencia are still in Miami. Can you catch an early plane down there tomorrow morning?"

"It's Christmas weekend coming. This can't wait?"

"You got any special plans for Christmas?"

Finnegan reflected for an instant on the four days of incubation in Greenwich with his frustrated wife, over whom he had lost all control. Four days of no Cheltenham, no camaraderie, no bustle and purring telephones, no alcohol. Miami was warm, and he could do what he liked when he got there. He was too experienced a trooper to believe that the murder of his Christmas vacation had any real significance.

"Yes, I have plans," he lied. "We're expecting a horde of Alice's family from out of town. But naturally firm business comes first."

"Good. So that's settled. You'll fly down and meet with the

brothers in the afternoon. They're staying on Seahorse Island, a couple of miles off the coast. You'll have to arrange a helicopter to get there. My secretary will give you all the details in the morning. I'll meet you at nine in your office to brief you. Now it's time you had an early night."

"Mel. Why do you want me to take on this slimy case?"

"I think you're the best man for the job. You're an expert at international negotiation. You need more work. Besides, everyone else is too busy."

"No, I mean why do you want Cheltenham messed up with these hoods?"

"Don't leap to conclusions. They're a big-shot family down there."

"They're drug racketeers. They should have some crooked Miami shyster lawyer representing them. They don't belong with the oldest and most respectable firm in the country."

"Times have changed," answered Samson wryly, "in case you hadn't noticed. We're all expanding our practices. It's competitive."

"It's one thing to cut back on the heavy-equipment leasing deals and branch out into the new financial instruments. It's a lot different to get mixed up in criminal narcotics charges."

Samson began to get impatient again. "I want you to do this case. All right? End of discussion."

Finnegan had once been a man of spirit. He countered Samson's steely glare with his own bloodshot, exhausted eyes and replied, "What if I refuse?"

"You can't refuse."

"It's the last straw. My career's fucked as it is. You want me to go lay my head on the block now?"

"You're talking drunk. You want a future at Cheltenham? You want me to go on protecting you?"

"I just want to get back and litigate real issues."

"Have it your own way. You want to go out into the world and hang up your shingle? We'll see how many prestigious matters come your way. You need this firm, Mick. I'm offering you your last chance to stay a part of it."

"If I get mixed up with these dago slimeballs, you guarantee me protection?"

"I guarantee you. As long as you keep in line. If you go all out on some drunken binge, I may not be able to cover you."

"How long will you give me protection?"

Samson knew, and Mick knew he knew, that Samson's guarantee was only as good as Il Duce's own standing. If Ariel Lamb won, no one would be around to look after Finnegan. That was the risk.

"I'll give you eighteen months. As long as you behave, and keep a low profile, and do the work I ask you."

After Finnegan's seventeen years in the partnership, Samson's offer was not an extravagant one. The bitter end, Finnegan realized, could be postponed only so briefly, and that at the cost of a whole reputation.

"And if I refuse?"

"You'll be fired in March, when the partner's yearly billing is reviewed. If Hopper hasn't already found some scandal to pin on you before that. If by some miracle they don't fire you in March, I will personally see to it that you're canned by summer."

Finnegan, who had glibly lectured partners, associates, and anyone prepared to listen on the ruthlessness of big-firm practice, was shocked. Despite his own political insignificance, he had made it clear ever since Der Fuhrer and Il Duce had declared war three years ago that his lot was thrown in as a faithful Samson supporter. He had always voted for Samson's proposals, from major matters, such as creating new partners, to trivia like the installation of additional duplicating equipment. It had all been useless. Samson had clearly ignored the feeble voice of support, until such moment as Finnegan's pathetic life served a viable purpose. Then the pathetic life became a bargaining chip.

Finnegan reconsidered for the nth time a future outside the monastic walls of 57 Water Street. The peat farm in County Clare no longer beckoned so romantically. He was too old to start again, and too dissipated. The physical comfort of Cheltenham had spoiled him, and the excitement of manipulating the megabucks had seduced him. Samson was right. He could no longer go out on his own and hang up a shingle somewhere on Lower Broadway. He might as well be driving a taxi or selling pajamas at Brooks Brothers.

Samson got up. "Sign for my dinner, will you, Mick? I'll reimburse you sometime. See you at nine tomorrow. You know, I envy you getting a good tan this weekend."

*T*he morning haze had lifted now, and the mountain sun glittered across the pillows of snow. Clancy Maxwell, inhaling great gulps of the thin, pure air, felt newly invigorated. There was nothing like a few days' escape in Colorado. Far beneath them tiny creatures snaked, slicing the slope. He put his hand on Eleanor's mitten. Their chairlift swayed like a swing on an antebellum porch.

"Look! There's Oliver!" She pointed with her ski pole toward a figure in a blue parka, ribboning beneath them. "I know he's improved a lot this winter. But I hope he won't do anything too dangerous."

Now there was the added pleasure, along with the joyous light and clean air, of watching his son's assured trail as he whisked away, leaving a balloon of powder in his wake.

"I'm sure he'll be fine." He enjoyed reassuring her. He spun an alliance with his nonchalant boy by defending him. He no longer even minded that his son had surpassed his own technique. A year ago the two of them had always skied together, getting up early while the rest of the family slept, to slip away on private adventures, discovering fresh trails and slopes, and to risk the morning ice before the glare had melted it into submission. Now Oliver, who had begun to ski too well for his father, preferred to compete with other boys, slashing downhill and jumping the gulleys, which made his mother blanch.

So while his son spread his wings, Clancy once again skied with Eleanor, whose neat, parallel rhythm restored his own sense of dash. He glanced at her profile as they swayed side by side in the chairlift. She was at her best here in the mountains. The woolen scarves covered some of the lines and the gray-streaked hair. He noticed once more the frame of the bones, as cool as a marble bust. He admired her for keeping up her skiing; somehow he suspected she would go on and on, perhaps another twenty years or more, undaunted by age and its ravages. They were all like that, in her family.

He smiled, remembering Eleanor's Aunt Deborah, who had once climbed on a motorcycle at the age of seventy-two. She had hurtled down a short stretch of road before she skidded on gravel, crashing the damn thing with a horrible screech. Clancy had opened his eyes a moment later to see the old woman step jauntily away from the heap of still quivering metal. She must have been shaken, but nothing on earth would have induced her to reveal it. Eleanor, who had neither glamour nor wit, carried the same invincibility. It was in her blood.

"There's the other one." Clancy gestured at the sixteen-year-old Julia, who flashed below them, escorted by one of the ski school instructors. Clancy noticed that she had taken off her hood, and let her long hair flow behind her like a banner. "You see who she's with again?"

"They're just skiing together." Eleanor tried to pacify him. "It's not exactly a date."

Clancy shook his head darkly. "I think she was out with him last night. She didn't get back until late."

"What's the harm? It's her vacation too. Let her have some fun."

"I don't like her hanging around with these working-class honchos. She's so young. And have you heard the way that kid speaks?"

Eleanor patted him with her mitten. "Don't be such a snob, dear. She'll never see him again after next week. She's just intrigued because he comes from the wrong side of the tracks."

What did Julia see in that hulking, brainless animal, with his twisted peasant mouth and his shag of banana blond hair, cut in thick bangs across his low forehead? Was it those primed muscles, or just the adolescent thrill of harvesting a little attention? Or was the kid exotic to his daughter, as Gina had once been to him?

Gina's Neapolitan earthiness no longer enchanted him. Her ignorance and lack of affectation, once so enticing, now irritated him. It was all very well taking some pleasure in the gentle sport of initiating her into the quirks of his social world, and studying her reactions. It was like the indulgence of snatching virginity. Although it had been fun to buy her a few trinkets—that coat had better be a final gesture, nevertheless—you could only enjoy the moment so many times. Her flushes of delight were growing repetitive.

The chairlift was approaching the wooden hut at the crest. Eleanor was busy coating her cheeks with the no-nonsense moisturizer she bought at the drugstore in giant urns and decanted slowly over the year. Clancy thought of the stream of petty details that had annoyed him recently. It was mostly Gina's lack of savoir faire. She had never learned, for instance, how to say thank you properly. She accepted his favors almost churlishly, as if she were afraid of betraying her origins by gushing. Her table manners he noticed too. The way she cut her meat or picked up her napkin was so precise, so studied, as if she were always nervous about scattering crumbs. However long he nurtured the relationship, he would never be able to teach her the casual ease that comes of self-assurance.

They reached the top and skidded away, leaving their empty chair to the pulleys. He held Eleanor's arm. As they slithered to the mouth of the trail, she leaned forward to adjust the clasp of her boot.

"I'll do that for you." He planted his pole beside her. As he bent to help her, he remembered an intimacy he had never felt with any of his slim-hipped mistresses, even in the tumult of their shrieks and passion.

He thought of the small red Cartier box that lay hidden among socks, the salve to his conscience. Although it had seemed expensive, now he wished he had forked out more. He hoped that she would like it. You never knew with Eleanor. Sometimes she appreciated costly gifts; at other times she winced slightly, as if the price made them vulgar.

*   *   *

Courage had been deliberating what to bring Helen and Chloe as a Christmas present. Since they were so poor, it seemed inappropriate to dump off the usual superfluous gestures: the basket of dried fruits, houseplants (they had no room), a cushion stuffed with rose petals. He considered tickets for a Broadway show or the *Nutcracker*, but decided Helen would be embarrassed by the price. Helen's intellect intimidated him; he had no idea how to choose a book that would interest her. Finally he decided to focus his efforts just on the child, and turned up with Boardroom Strategy, the latest best-selling board game, for Chloe.

He picked them up at the apartment on 108th Street. By the light of the crisp Sunday morning the streets looked even more derelict than at dawn when he had left on the previous occasion.

Chloe came to the door. "Hi, Peter." She greeted him with adult dignity. "Come on in. Did you have a nice Christmas?"

"Yeah, pretty good." He handed her the rectangular box, wrapped up in thin drugstore paper. She took it graciously. "For me?"

"I hope you like games."

"I like Go. I play with Mother." She untied the green cord with care and peeled the Scotch tape painstakingly away so as to preserve the paper. Courage felt a pang of guilt that he had not brought more. "Mother'll be right out," explained Chloe, who was busy folding the paper into a neat square.

She took a look at the box of the board game. Her face registered neither childlike disappointment nor feigned adult enthusiasm. She nodded seriously and thanked him politely. Courage knew that he had brought the wrong toy.

Solemnly she led him into her bedroom, past the jar of fir branches that served as their token Christmas tree. Chloe's room was lined with shelves of Helen's books on Oriental art and literature. Except for a couple of overloved stuffed dinosaurs on the bed and a mobile of jousting knights that dangled from the ceiling, there were none of the usual toys and games Courage would have expected from the children's rooms he remembered. He thought of his young nieces' bedrooms, with their video games and giant televisions and radio telephones.

"You like knights?"

"Do you know about King Arthur?" She had her mother's intellectual impatience.

"Well, vaguely. He pulled that sword out of the stone."

She fixed him with ardent eyes and lectured him. "King Arthur collected the strongest and bravest knights in England and made them all swear a special oath if they wanted to belong to his Round Table. It was a big table where they all sat and feasted on boar and goose and venison. If you wanted to belong, you had to promise to protect weak and innocent people and only use your strength to fight for honorable things. It worked for a while. The knights went around collecting more knights, and killing dragons and killing evil knights, and rescuing maidens the evil knights had locked up. But then it all went wrong. The knights began to do horrible, immoral things. It was the saddest thing you can imagine."

"Do you know what I do?" asked Courage. "I mean, for my work?"

"Mother told me. You're a lawyer. You work in a big office. Do you go to court and make speeches too?"

"No. I just write the papers up. In my office where I work there are three hundred lawyers, like me. Like those knights. But many years ago it was a lot smaller. In those days it was a special thing

275

to study law. People still remembered about the system of justice that was developed in England in the thirteenth century. You heard of the Magna Carta?"

"No."

"There was a wicked king called John, who had no respect for the laws or fairness or people's rights. The barons got together and forced him to sign a kind of constitution, agreeing that not even the Crown should be above the law. We've been following those principles ever since then, here in America too."

She nodded thoughtfully. He could not tell whether she was listening or just being polite. "You sailed across the Atlantic by yourself?" she asked suddenly. "Like Thor Heyerdahl on the *Kon-Tiki* raft?"

"It wasn't a raft. I had a small engine, which makes a big difference."

She studied him critically. "I'd like to do that. Will you take me next time? I'll be very good and do everything you say."

"I don't know if there'll be a next time." An image of Kahn's bejeweled pudgy fingers mercilessly eclipsed the vision of that endless horizon and the sunsets so bright you could touch them. "But if I go, okay, I'll let you know. Are you good at math?"

"Yuck, no, I hate it."

"You have to be good at it, so we can plot our course. You have to know how to steer by the stars, if we're out there all alone in the middle of the ocean."

"Do you know the names of the stars?" she asked, excited.

"You two ready?" Helen appeared from the adjacent bathroom, dressed in a fringed Greek shawl that had probably been fashionable in the early seventies. Her clear, naked face was not unattractive, although Courage could still not describe her as beautiful. She had heard him. "You know all the stars?" she repeated, in the same tone as Chloe, and Courage knew that he had finally—inadvertently—offered her something important.

"I know all the stars. In the Northern Hemisphere anyway."

"Where are we going for brunch, Chloe?" he asked. It was easier to seduce the child than the mother.

She looked at him coquettishly. "Do you like banana-cherry-chocolate splits?"

"Not more than four times a week."

"Have you ever been to Rumpelmayer's?"

Helen pulled Chloe to her, running her hand through her daughter's bed of hair. "Peter doesn't want to go to an ice-cream parlor, sweetheart. How about Chinese? We all like that. You can have spare ribs."

Courage protested. "Let's go to Rumpelmayer's. I like ice cream. Besides, that way we can walk through the park. You girls ready? But first, I've got to ask you one thing." He pointed at the scroll of Japanese characters that hung from the window, framed by a view of tenement houses scrawled with grafitti, drying laundry, and disgorging garbage cans. "What does it say?"

"It's a haiku by Oshima Ryota. Ask Chloe."

"She can read that?" Now he was impressed.

"Of course not. But she knows."

Chloe, without hesitation, recited:

> *Bad-tempered, I got back:*
> *Then, in the garden,*
> *The willow tree.*

They clattered down the vile-smelling stairs and out into the cold air. Courage, seeing a taxi cruise toward them, raised his arm. Helen pulled him back. "We'll take the bus down Broadway," she insisted. "It's quick."

"It'll take forever." Courage could not imagine squandering time sitting on a bus.

"We always take the bus," explained Chloe, gazing wistfully after the vanishing taxi.

"My treat," said Courage lightly, and scanned the street for another one.

Helen refused flatly. "We always take the bus."

Courage was still baffled by her obsession with her own poverty. It intrigued him to see her mental calculations dedicated to saving a dollar or two, such energies fostered by a woman who could read medieval Japanese poetry and discuss sixteenth-century Buddhism. In his own existence, real sums of money and daily transactions had lost their emotional importance. At his income level a few hundred dollars meant little more than small change. Ordinary money, along with adventure and nature and art, had lost its savor. He viewed it dispassionately as he drafted agreements for the hundreds of millions of other people's money. Yet Helen seemed to take such pride in her small calculations.

As the bus wobbled to a halt at a red light, Courage glanced at his watch. A woman who reeked of garlic and too much Chanel thrust her shopping bag in his face. A cab would have made a lot more sense. Courage, pinioned, inched his neck around. There were a couple of yuppies laden with boxes of electronic equipment, old women dressed meticulously in necklaces and patent-leather shoes, and a stoned-looking kid who shook his whole torso to the rhythm of his Walkman. Two freckled boys of about Chloe's age were carrying some sort of pet, perhaps a rabbit, in a wire-mesh box. So this was a Sunday morning crossing. Despite the bumps and smell and lack of space, Courage began gradually to take an interest in the life going on around him. It had been ages since he had even noticed the people around him. Everyone seemed to be going somewhere, somewhere connected to everyday life.

He remembered how one early morning, eight years ago, he had once dived silently from the bow of *The Candle* into the silky lagoon waters in St. Lucia. Across the surface of the water rose the mountains, lush with tropical vegetation. The sunlight brushed the waves in a shaft of oblique light. Bobbing up and down beside his boat, he felt himself connected to the exotic landscape like a minute hub at the center of a wheel. The boat and the surrounding water created the sense of connection, making him feel for once that he belonged completely in the scene. The landscape would still be there without him, long after he returned to the law library at Columbia, long after he had become a grown-up attorney, harassed and complacent, long after he was dead. Thank God, for a few minutes one morning he and his boat had been fixed at its nucleus.

Sitting on the Sunday morning bus, in such wildly different surroundings, he felt again the thrill of attachment.

At 86th Street they got off the bus and set out across the park, under the canopy of stark branches. A fresh powdering of snow had fallen since Christmas, frosting the stiff clods of earth and lining the craters of week-old snow. Chloe skipped a few feet ahead of them, circling and spinning in her red coat, which was already a size too small.

"She seems rather precocious for her age," said Courage.

Helen watched her daughter with pride and wistfulness. "Sometimes she has to take care of me, as well as me taking care of her. She knows it."

There were many questions Courage wanted to ask her then. He wondered whether Chloe missed having a father, whether Helen had ever thought of marrying or bringing a man into the house. He would have liked to ask whether they got lonely sometimes, the two of them in their isolated lives, or whether they had grown too used to their symbiotic existence, like thick bark embedded with a trailing vine. He wished he knew what Helen did with herself at night after the child went to bed in the adjacent room. Did she read and translate Japanese verse or did she leave the house on dates with sexy, bohemian brutes who indulged her fantasies as no white-bread attorney ever could? He slid his eyes toward her where her cloud of breath floated over the lamb's-wool collar. He wondered where that old coat had been, what she had been doing ten or fifteen years ago. He did not dare to ask about her private life, so he asked instead, "How long have you had that coat?"

She tugged at the tough, leathery material. "This? A couple of years, I think. I bought it from a peddler on Broome Street. You like it?"

"It suits you."

Their eyes met for a moment. She asked, curiously, "What was it like, law school?"

He remembered with a shudder the cavernous lecture halls, the institutional locker rooms, which smelled of sweat like those at Choate, the cramped students' lounge, which made him think of the subway. Except for a summer flirtation with a sexy librarian, it had been a joyless three years of training.

"Competition. Mortal combat for grades. A death struggle to get onto *Law Review.*"

"Was it interesting though?"

"It was fascinating." Courage drifted back to those classes where he had first discovered the principles of consideration, of hearsay, of estoppel, of seisin, or mens rea. The words themselves seemed invested with magic; as he became familiar with the concepts, for the first time in his youth he had felt some control of a chaotic world. His undergraduate courses in history and literature and elementary economics had never given him the same sense of uncluttered power. Particularly during his first year, law school had been like the dawning of a second adulthood.

Outside the school building at Columbia stood a statue by Lipschitz of the Greek hero Bellerophon, who fought on the winged horse Pegasus. When he was a student, Courage had always liked the emblem of going into battle against evil forces. Now the monsters had been replaced though, by mortgage-backed sercurities and TBO's.

"I liked reading cases," he told Helen. "The language is so polished. And there are plots."

"You still do that?"

"Almost never. That's for students. Real corporate law's a different ball of wax. It's like filling in credit card applications all day long. Life insurance, MasterCard, Macy's."

"I don't have any credit cards." She pulled her coat tighter against the wind. "How did you end up becoming a lawyer?"

"Family pressure. Peer pressure. Background. Education. Money. The late seventies. Responsibility. Growing up." He looked her straight in the eye and decided, for once, to tell the truth. "I wanted to be more like my father. I wanted him to approve of me."

"Does he now?"

Courage shook his head slowly. "It didn't change anything deep down. I might as well have gone on sailing *The Candle*. My older brother's still the blue-eyed boy."

"It's always the way," Helen assured him. "You can't live for other people. It boomerangs on you."

"You did that too?"

She avoided the question. "What's your father like?"

"He's a real Yankee. Believes in hard-earned money and the Protestant work ethic. Early to bed and early to rise. He's president of a large insurance company in Farmington, which my great-grandfather started actually." He swallowed and took a breath. "How did it boomerang on you?"

"Chloe's father," she said finally, "is a thoroughly decent, honest, gentle person. But I just couldn't give up my life to live with him. He has no horizons. No sense of adventure. Not the tiniest little bit."

"Maybe...sort of...dull?" Courage asked hesitantly. She had touched on his secret fear, the tiny shame he did not talk about to anyone. He suspected that he himself had grown dull, as the pursuit of his career demanded, and he put behind the romance of adventure. He sacrificed it for conformity, which earned him high marks most of the time. Only Helen Farmer seemed unimpressed by his somber credentials. She had come to look for him in the middle of the night because she had heard he was a sailor. Not because he earned a senior associate salary, or was partnership material, or had been to all the right schools, where he would probably in turn send his own children one day. She had poked her head of tousled hair around the door of his office just because his cousin had mentioned to her the story of *The Candle in the Wind*. The night he had first met Michelle Peterson at the printer, his erstwhile goddess had made him feel paltry and insignificant, a minor character in the Wall Street parade, with no spoils of war but his *Law Review* article on river pollution control. Helen had cared about something else. She had sensed the independent, adventuring soul that lay in long hibernation beneath the conventional trappings. Her recognition exhilarated him.

"Yes. Dull. Not dumb. Just dull. And also kind and good. It's not easy to leave a kind person. It's easier leaving a rat."

To leave for what, Courage wondered. A solitary life in a garret slum, with a couple of Japanese prints and a fatherless little girl? "What does he do?" he asked.

"He teaches high school. Baltimore. Where I come from. Biology."

"Married?"

"Eventually. He's happy now. And he deserves it."

But are you, Courage burned to ask. Do you harbor some recipe for contentment in your poverty-stricken life, have you located a quiet center, or are you, too, still watching for that adventure you missed before? Is it adventure enough to be able to fathom the obscure nuances of sixteenth-century haikus? Or have you found the excitement with someone else, whom you will not mention? Does he climb the moldy stairs late at night, when Chloe has gone to bed, and knock on your door?

Despite the cold weather, the park was alive, as always, with runners. As the men and women pounded past them, their faces set in grim determination, Courage remembered his running "date," which had led to Michelle's bedroom. Although he had not spoken with her recently, he felt no guilt or obligation. He assumed he might sleep with her sooner or later again, that is, if their schedules could mesh when he called her at the last second. Now that he understood the bruises she craved, it had uncomplicated the barriers of sex. He supposed he had not called her because after the days devoted to Kahn and Tristan, he found himself too tired to listen to her self-serving chatter.

"Did you ever discover what your friend David was trying to tell you?" asked Helen. They crossed the bicycle path at 72nd Street and veered east.

"No. It's like he never existed. It's been a pretty quiet week, on the whole, with people away in the islands or skiing. Even the whole TBO biz has calmed down momentarily."

"The what?"

Courage explained to her in the most lucid terms he could muster, the mechanics of an asset-backed security and the application to Ariel Lamb's wonderous TBO. He was impressed by her swift grasp of the mechanism. Arrogance had stolen up on him along with his peers. It was irreconcilable with the myth that they were the crème de la crème to accept that people who were not employed in the highest echelons of the legal and banking professions had the same intelligence and comprehension. Encountering Helen's sureness of mind was both a comfort and a rebuke.

Chloe still trotted ahead, leading them east toward Fifth Avenue.

"Was David working on the sacred TBO before he died?" asked Helen.

"He was doing some preliminary tax research. He told me he thought the whole thing had been overblown, that in the end the deal wouldn't work. And yet, he just may have been wrong. The whole Corporate Finance Group is staking its future on it—" He broke off in mid-sentence, staring into the middle of Fifth Avenue.

Helen tugged at his arm. "What is it, Peter? A ghost?"

A woman was walking three terriers, a dachshund, and a dalmation across the street. Helen followed his stare.

"The dog," said Courage. "That's what her white rug reminded me of."

"What are you talking about?"

He frowned, trying to piece together his own recollections. "I had a sort of date with a girl named Michelle Peterson from Caroline Brothers. She had this fleecy white rug in her living room, shaped like the continent of Australia, and every time I looked at it I knew it reminded me of something vital, but I couldn't make the connection. I've just figured it out. I was with Michelle another time, we were running right here in the park, and I saw a woman just over there"—he pointed toward the elongated can-opy of 888 Fifth—"walking a Great Pyrenees."

For an instant he sensed a trace of annoyance. "Who is this Michelle, anyway? Why is she important?"

Courage was tempted to tell her the whole truth. Until now he had been scrupulously honest to the last detail. He needed this woman badly, as a listener; there was no room to start with fabrications and half lies. Why not admit the liaison, which every day seemed less significant anyhow?

Helen's fearless eyes glistened, whipped by the gusting wind. It was hard to imagine trespassing the boundaries of friendship that were beginning to take shape between them...and yet, it was possible, in some circumstance, at a certain time, she might take a more exclusive hold on his life. Just for the sake of hedging his options, he rewrote a little history in describing Michelle's role.

"Michelle's nothing. Just a girl I met a couple of times on a deal. I hardly knew her. What mattered was seeing the dog." Quickly, Courage took Helen through Gleiner's report of his emergency visit to the gastroenterologist, where he had caught a glimpse of Ariel Lamb's mistress. "That's what's been at the back of my mind since he died," said Courage. "At the time it just seemed like a funny story, but looking back..."

"I don't get it. So your senior partner has an affair. It's not the first time on Wall Street."

"You don't know Ariel. He's like a toy soldier. Totally into control. It's too weird to imagine him letting go of that power even for a second to get involved with some bimbo."

"Maybe she's not a bimbo."

"That's not the point. Ariel cares too much about his position. I can't see him risking a personal involvement against it."

"So maybe David made a mistake. From what you say, he was feeling pretty nauseous that night."

"No. He checked with his doctor. Her name's Betty Law and she really does live there." He told her the story of the mysterious package from Lamb addressed to Ms. Law. "What he wouldn't have expected was that David would by chance notice that particular address on the package. I mean, normally, who would notice or care? It was just coincidence that David happened to have one of his many doctors in that very building."

Helen called out to Chloe, "Come here, sweetheart! We're crossing the street." Courage looked questioning. "Don't you want to take a look?" Helen suggested blandly.

It was a Fifth Avenue palazzo, with a modern façade and a deeply recessed canopy leading into a baroque palm-decorated lobby. From across the street they could see that the ceilings were high and the windows wide, to admit the costly light and air of Central Park. In a couple of windows Courage made out the shapes of gigantic abstract canvases. What looked to Helen like a Rodin bronze figure was displayed on a windowsill on the third floor.

The names of the ground-floor doctors' offices were stenciled on a slatted door between two terra-cotta urns of white poinsettias.

ERIC GOLDFARB, M.D.

ARTHUR DELIPIZZA, CHIROPRACTOR

ELEANOR HEMINGWAY, D.D.S.

"I wish we could get upstairs and take a real look at this Betty Law," said Helen.

"No way. This is a rich, rich people's building. The security'll be incredible." Courage nodded in the direction of the doorman in a gold-braided uniform, who was busy helping an elderly millionairess into a waiting limousine. The car slid away as the doorman turned stiffly back.

"Leave it to my daughter. She's going to break in for us."

Courage protested, incredulous. "You can't do that! She's only a kid. She might get in trouble. It's not fair."

"She'll be fine. She's cool when she needs to be. And she likes excitement." They caught up with the lively figure in the tight, cherry-colored coat. "This way, sweetheart," said Helen, taking her firmly by the hand and steering her away from number 888.

"Where are we going?" Chloe tugged away petulantly. "You promised we were going to Rumpelmayer's."

"We still are. But first I've got a dangerous assignment for you."

Chloe looked resolute. "What is it?"

"It's a special spying mission. Peter and I need to find out about a lady who lives in that building over there. We want you to slip in past the doorman, go to her apartment, and ring the doorbell."

"Mother, it won't work. First of all, how do I find out which one her apartment is? And then if she answers the doorbell, what do I say?"

"When you get in the elevator, just tell the elevator man you want to go to 'Law.' He'll take you to the floor and tell you which door."

Courage looked at the dreamy scholar with growing awe. "But Chloe's right," he pointed out. "What's she to say when Betty Law answers the doorbell?"

Helen thought briefly. "She'll say she's looking for a birthday party. We'll get her a balloon from that balloon cart over there. By the time they figure out she's made a mistake and gone to the wrong address, she can get a good look at Betty Law and the apartment, and see what's there."

Courage hesitated again. "I'm still not sure it's right. I don't think you should ask a child to do that."

Chloe told him, coldly, "This isn't my first dangerous assignment."

Helen ran a hand through the tousled hair. "She's practicing to be a spy when she grows up."

"Yeah, well, since there aren't any knights left, and they wouldn't take girls anyway, there's not a lot else I can do."

They bought a silver moon-shaped balloon with HAPPY BIRTH-DAY scrawled across it in pink letters.

"We're going to wait for you over there on Madison," Helen instructed her. "We'll be having a Coke in that coffee shop. Okay? You're to come straight back here when you finish." Helen promised Courage, "She won't screw up. She's street smart. Don't worry. No one will ever suspect her."

Two Cokes and a slice of cheesecake later, Chloe returned, still bearing the balloon triumphantly, like King Arthur's sword Excalibur.

Helen jumped up from the table, forgetting for once to haggle with Courage over her share of the small change. She ran to the door as soon as she saw the cherry-colored coat, and hugged her daughter. "Did you get in?"

"Sure."

"What happened?"

Chloe looked suspiciously at her mother. "Are we going to Rumpelmayer's right now or what?"

" 'Course we are," said Helen. "That was the deal."

They set off along Madison while Chloe explained. "I had to wait a couple of minutes till the doorman wasn't looking. They brought out an old man in a wheelchair and he got busy helping him through the door. So I walked straight into the lobby. I told the elevator man, 'I want to go to the Law apartment.' He said, 'Sure thing, kiddo. That's Six B.' So we went up."

"She answered the door?" Helen squeezed Chloe's waist.

"No. I didn't see her. The gardener answered the door."

"The gardener!"

"Yeah, he was Japanese. Like in that movie we saw last week."

Chloe's education, in addition to medieval legend and Japanese art, had been rich in foreign art cinema and film noir. Although she would have died before allowing a television into the house, Helen haunted the downtown and West Side revival movie houses with her daughter.

"You sure he was a gardener?"

"He was wearing a kind of tunic, like a short bathrobe, with a green frog embroidered on the sash. We were in a hall with black marble tiles and little flower beds, planted with azaleas and miniature pine trees. And big rocks like sponges with holes in them. And a little fountain. I could tell he'd been digging flowers 'cause he was holding a spade and there was some earth on his tunic."

"That doesn't mean he was a gardener."

"He was. I know he was. I said I was looking for the birthday party, so he left me alone for a couple of minutes. I looked in the next room. There was a big Japanese pot, full of pink and white roses. This high." She gestured to her shoulder. "There were maybe a hundred roses in it. I started counting them while I was waiting for the gardener to come back, but I only got to thirty-two."

"You'll make a great professional one day," praised Courage. "So what did the gardener say?"

" 'Somebody make mistake. No party here.' "

"You never got a look at her?"

"I heard a voice. I listened hard, but it wasn't easy to tell what they were saying. Whatever it was, it didn't sound like English. But it might have been the TV or something in the background. Then the dog ran out. An enormous white one, as big as I am. I wish we could get a dog, Mother. I'd take care of him, honestly. He started jumping up on me, which I didn't mind, but the gardener pulled him down. The dog got a hold of the gardener's tunic and started pulling it off. It was weird. He had a tattoo on his arm, of a frog. Mother, would you mind if I got a tattoo?"

"We'll talk about that some other time."

"Anyhow, he was very nice and gave me some candy as he let me out."

"Where is it?" asked Helen sharply.

She faced her mother squarely. "I ate it."

"That was not smart. You know good spies don't eat strange people's candy. It could have opium in it or a truth serum!"

"It looked pretty safe to me."

"Anyway," said Courage, "you did a fine job. You still hungry?" She nodded avidly. "As a token of my appreciation for your splendid work, I'd like to invite you to a second, additional brunch at Rumpelmayer's at a date to be agreed on some time in the next two weeks."

Chloe giggled. "Is that a real promise?"

Helen demurred. "I've got proofing jobs at Citicorp and Credit Lyonnais next week. Don't go making deals behind my back."

Courage grinned. "This is a date between Chloe and me. If you'd like to join us, that would be okay, but we can manage without you. Right?"

Chloe nodded vigorously.

And he had already decided he really wanted to see Helen again, soon. He truly liked her. He liked her impulsive, zany spirit. He liked the wisdom shared between mother and daughter. He wondered whether Chloe's vision was a grown-up one, or whether Helen herself had retained some instinct of childhood's fluid horizons. Somewhere their shared fantasy met and touched, like a cat's cradle taut between ten fingers. And he liked, immensely, Helen's perceptions, which had nothing to do with winning games and scoring points. She was just a relief to be with.

As he held open the door of Rumpelmayer's for the two of them, he noticed something else. He liked the way her unmade bed of hair curled over the lamb's-wool collar down her neck.

✳   ✳   ✳

The telephone rang through into the barn where Margaret Lamb had her "studio." She stood ten feet away from her latest opus. After a decade of working her way through various phases of minimalism, she had finally located her pictorial expression in the more retro influence of gestural abstraction. She had dispensed with brushes forever; her arm muscles, trimmed by years on tennis courts, now hurled the liquid colors at her voluminous canvases from a distance of about ten feet. The exercise both physically and emotionally exhausted her by the end of the day. But she was quite certain she had found her real voice. It no longer troubled her so much that she had not yet found any critical acclaim or purchasers, other than Cheltenham, Arbuthnot & Crewe. Once a year, in March, she exhibited in Soho. The expense of renting the gallery space was no object. Ariel had always been generous about that. It was, after all, her principal extravagance. Since, at the age of forty-two, she had made the decision to devote herself entirely to her art, she had had few other outside interests or expenses.

The ringing telephone interrupted her reverie, as she loitered, mesmerized by her own creation. The tumbler of Dewar's leaped in her hand, the ice cubes clinking against the glass. She liked to be slightly drunk while she worked. It unleashed her inhibitions. Pushing the escaped strands of hair out of her face with paint-stained fingers, she reached for the telephone.

"I'm at Magnolia Road," said Ariel. "I'll be there in fifteen minutes."

"I'm working," replied Margaret vaguely. "What time is it?"

"Almost ten. Are you in the barn?"

"Yes." She slurred her words. The scotch took some of the edge off them. "It's been very productive. I've almost finished *Homage to Whispers in the Grass.*"

She hung up and took another long, satisfied look at the black-and-yellow patterns of dripping paint, which had struck the canvas violently and arbitrarily, creating their own order in a chaotic universe, as indelibly and mysteriously random as constellations of stars. Finishing the glass, she reached absentmindedly for the bottle, tilted it, and changed her mind. She needed a few serious words with Ariel tonight.

She had not expected him back so early. Most evenings during the week he stayed in Manhattan, dining with his more important clients or drumming up business with new ones.

Margaret was not unhappy with the schedule. As a younger wife, and mother of three, she had dissipated her twenties and thirties chauffeuring children and cooking dinners. Never again. When the youngest daughter had turned sixteen, Margaret had roasted her last leg of lamb with mashed potatoes and Brussels sprouts. Thereafter she had never done more than reheat a glazed cornish hen from the local gourmet shop for herself and Ariel on the rare nights when he came home early from Cheltenham.

She liked her quiet, solitary evenings in the barn. They had converted the old red farm building, installing heat and water and electricity. She felt comfortable there, surrounded by her own canvases hung from the high walls, and the phosphorescent spirals of kinetic sculpture (an earlier phase) that dangled and swayed from the beams. She spent as little time as possible in their nearby sixteen-room house. She had grown to regard the libraries and studies and bedrooms and dens as a luxurious jail. The slipcovers and curtains grew faded from sunlight, the rugs collected stains, and the sticky dust gathered beneath the beds, where the cleaning ladies, unsupervised, ignored it.

It was a good marriage. In her own way, she had taken the only possible revenge on her husband for his egocentricity. His indifference could not touch her in her barn, with her scotch bottle and mammoth canvases. As for him, he no longer wanted a wife, but he needed one for the sake of appearances in his career. Somebody else might have interfered, made demands, got in the way. Margaret simply drank a little, grew deeper wrinkles, and stopped bothering to dye her iron-gray hair. She left him alone.

The great barn door swung open on its creaking hinges. Ariel, looking like a tailor's dummy in his exquisitely fitted suit, stepped into the chaos of empty paint tins and bundles of linseed-oil soaked rags. Margaret, who was beginning to look like a witch with the strands of gray hair poking into her eyes, peered at him from the dimly lit corner where she was waiting.

She rose from her half-crouched position and came slowly toward him. "How's Cheltenham?"

"Intriguing." He moved aside to examine courteously the new painting. He never knew how he was meant to comment. But Ariel, master of diplomacy, had learned from years of client contact the potency of the earnest inspection. He risked an observation. "This is good, Margaret."

She nodded matter-of-factly. "I know. I want to talk to you." She changed her mind and poured a couple of fingers of scotch. If she started slowly sipping now, it should carry her just through the conversation.

"I have to make a couple of phone calls. Can it wait till later?"

"No. It won't take long."

He shrugged. He made no effort to dominate her. Even a show of mastery would disrupt the supreme indifference. He had long ago used up all the energy reserved in this life for Margaret.

"The children think you're having an affair."

"That's ridiculous." He spoke sharply.

"I know." She took a secret look at her new picture and approved. "I don't think you are. Maybe I'm wrong. But they think you're seeing some woman in New York."

"I'm not."

"They've been spying on you since they've been here for Christmas vacation. Listening in on your phone calls and reading your bank statements."

She enjoyed the rare opportunity of seeing him react. "My children have been doing that?"

"They resent you. You've always been so distant. You never paid them any attention."

Ariel was tempted to retort, "Neither did you." But he bit the words back quickly. This was no time for quibbling. He needed to get to the truth, and immediately, before the scotch made her too fuzzy.

"What did they tell you?" he asked.

The Lamb children had grown up a fearless clan, toughened and sharpened by years of parental neglect. They had all inherited their father's genes for intelligence and their mother's for her primitive gift of survival. All three children were reserved, aloof, talented. None of them had ever shown much compassion for other people. They had seen no examples at home.

"They say there's some woman you've been calling in the middle of the night." She looked up triumphantly, gloating in her imperturbability.

Ariel frowned. What exactly did Margaret know, and how much was sheer conjecture on her part? He had lost touch with her so long ago, he could no longer differentiate a real accusation from her mocking banter. Her confrontation was like those hideous neon sculptures she used to make, with spheres bobbing up and down, glowing with artificial light. While you stared at them, you could not figure out where the real source of light began.

"It's nothing. Just business." He moved closer to his wife, taking care not to step in the sticky black and yellow puddles of coagulating paint. He tried to inject a note of sincerity into his words, which came out flat. It was so much easier to woo the investment banks. "Margaret. I'm not having an affair."

"Maybe you are," she answered coolly. "Maybe you aren't. But I wish you'd talk to the kids. I don't want to have to listen to them about it." She stole another glance at her new work. "It upsets my equilibrium. It interferes with my creative process."

"I know," said Ariel soothingly, his voice as smooth as a hot toddy of brandy, lemon, and honey. "I know, I know," he would have murmured to the managers of First Boston and Salomon as they voiced their concerns for the uncertainties of a volatile market.

"I really don't care," repeated Margaret, growing insistent on Dewar's, "if you are. I never thought it was in your nature, but men start behaving strangely when they reach your age. And I guess I wouldn't that much blame you," she added, remembering it must have been at least a year since he had touched her body. She did not miss it. Sex with Ariel had never been more than a clinical, gymnastic exercise. The only real passion she had ever found, first with a yoga instructor and later with the local liquor store proprietor, she had conserved minutely in her heart, and tried sometimes to give expression to in her paintings.

He looked at her firmly, almost kindly, through his tortoiseshell glasses. "It's just not true, Margaret."

"Okay. We won't discuss it anymore. I've finished work for tonight. I'll come back with you to the house."

She slipped off the old paint-spattered Brooks Brothers shirt she wore as a smock. It had been one of his. She hung it with ritualistic care on its rusty nail hook. He turned out the lights for her.

"Be careful of the ice out here," he warned.

They walked side by side along the trail of paving stones that led to the sprawling house. She wobbled precariously on the treacherous ground and lurched at his arm for support. He guided her, standing straight and unflinching as a rock, like the steel infrastructure of a downtown skyscraper.

Always strong, always politic. "I do so like your picture," he repeated.

She smiled to herself, into the dark. Her husband, for all his earthly power, knew nothing whatsoever about art. She knew she would probably paint on in Montclair until the end, unrecognized, undiscovered. Her talent, she told herself, might never find a receptive audience. That happened to many artists. It was such a difficult field. But she smiled again in her secure knowledge. Whatever Ariel thought about her work, whether he liked it or whether he was contemptuous, it did not matter one bit.

*   *   *

Eleanor Maxwell poked her head around the door of Oliver's bedroom in the chalet.

"It's long past bedtime for this young man," she announced. "He has to be up for ski school tomorrow morning."

"Oh, please, Mom. Just a couple more minutes. Look, Dad's about to go bankrupt."

Her son pointed to the heap of paper money amassed on his own side of the Executive Monopoly board. Clancy had no remaining assets, just a scribbled notepad of IOU's to his son.

"It's almost eleven," said Eleanor sternly. "You'll be tired all day tomorrow."

"Just a couple more minutes," intervened Clancy. "I think we're almost done. It's not often we get a chance to play together."

Oliver sensed his advantage and pitched into the negotiation. "Dad's hardly ever home in the evenings in New York. You said so yourself, Mom."

Before she could answer, he deftly rolled the dice and moved his marker, a silver limousine, three blocks down the board. "I've landed on Broad Street. I'm buying another hotel. Your turn, Dad."

Clancy, whose marker was the push-button telephone, moved into the Frankfurt Stock Exchange. Oliver counted out two hundred dollars and handed them over to him.

"Now you can pay me back," he told him flatly, "for your mortgage on the Chicago Merc."

Clancy caught his wife's eye as he handed the money across. "It's almost over," he promised. "And the kid's right. I get so little chance to see him."

"I'm going to bed," she said. "Tomorrow's our last day's skiing."

"So how does it feel, trouncing your poor father?" asked Clancy as he passed Go and landed at the World Trade Center. "I think I've had it this time."

"You're well and truly busted, Dad. Sorry about that. But this is business. Nice guys finish last."

"I know that. And when the heat's too much, you just gotta stay out of the kitchen."

He left Oliver picking up the stacks of money, and climbed up the stairs to their pine-gabled bedroom.

He had been getting on better with Eleanor recently. Of course his marriage would never recapture the flavor of vitality that Gina had brought him in gasps, but a marriage, after all, was a long-term, extended matter, while a romance, however heady, could not be expected to sustain its momentum. Gina's doggish devotion was becoming infuriating. That, and, once you scratched the surface, the complete vacuum of breeding. Was Gina beginning to accept the inevitability of the approaching end? Watching her, though, hurrying along the corridor of the forty-seventh floor, he could not be sure of anything. Perhaps he had never known her at all.

Eleanor was brushing her hair with the silver brush her great-great-grandmother had used over a century ago in Salem, Massachusetts. He extricated the brush gently from her fingers.

"Come to bed. I've missed you."

FOURTEEN

*T*he church hall reeked of an unidentifiable odor, a queer mixture of chalk, boiled vegetables, and religion. Mick Finnegan sniffed and glanced around at the empty stage, the piano, the long scrolls that hung down on either side, reminding the gathering of their pledged commandments and exhorting them to trust in God.

Finnegan, who had abandoned the Catholic religion at the age of seventeen, still had a confused attitude toward churches. The stale smells reminded him of his brutal, uncomplicated street-kid days before he had gone on scholarship to St. Ambrose College to become a flawed genius.

Another half hour to go. He tried to redirect his attention to the speaker, to get his mind off the mirage of vodka martinis and chateaubriand.

"I'm here to tell you this," rumbled the speaker, "I couldn't get a grip on my life until I admitted that I was born with a disease, that I had always had it, and I always would until I stopped drinking, came to A.A. meetings, and put my faith in God."

Finnegan knew he was not destined to find salvation. He did not believe in God and he disliked all forms of organized religion. A.A. was a nondenominational faith, but Finnegan had no creed left to share with group believers. They were a well-meaning bunch, he reflected, but all in all they were just another club. He had had enough of clubs. He had belonged, and glittered even, in the only club that would ever mean anything to him, and now he had been ostracized.

He had only agreed to attend the local A.A. meetings as a last bargaining chip to delay the inevitable collapse of his marriage. He had known four days ago on Friday, when he slunk through the church door, that the experiment would not succeed. They insisted to him that he was "in denial," merely putting off the ultimate recognition of his alcoholism. Maybe he was. All he knew was that, stripped of the income, the professional glory, and the luminescence of stardom, he had no interest in making a humble comeback into the ranks of the world's infantry.

A young man in a pink shirt, who might have been a broker or a bookkeeper, raised his hand. "My name's Phil and I'm an alcoholic," he announced.

"Hi, Phil," chanted the chorus.

Phil directed his confession to the speaker. "I want to thank you for your description of your drinking habits, which exactly pattern my own. I always liked the romance of drinking. I wanted to be an exciting, glamorous person and I couldn't find that quality anywhere in my real life. I wanted to be a hero..."

Finnegan closed his eyes. Eight years ago, when he was still riding high, it had seemed he could have almost any woman in the world he wanted to be his wife. Alice was the one he had chosen. She was both soft and strong at the same time, like no other woman he had ever met.

She had been a psychiatric ward nurse when they had first married. She was sympathetic, young, and squeaky clean. What a joy to find an opposite to his first wife, a spoiled princess. Alice, on the other hand, delighted to play audience and give adulation to his stardom. He felt more comfortable with her too. She came from an upbringing closer to his own. Her father owned a grocery store. She had never been to college.

He knew she was upset the night he had returned from Samson, reeling out of the limousine at midnight and smelling of liquor. The next morning, when he told her how he had been cornered into taking on the Valencia cocaine farmers as clients, she looked at him over the bowl of raisin bran as if he were still in an alcoholic stupor.

"They're drug dealers," she protested. "They're the worst kind of criminal."

"I know that. But they're entitled to legal counsel like everyone else. And if I don't do it, I'll be fired for sure by March."

"I hate it," she murmured. She frowned so miserably that he realized that behind her clean, sweet face lay a capacity for disgust he had not suspected.

The discussion took its inevitable course. "I know you could do something else," she pleaded. "That terrible place you work in has just destroyed you. You're brainwashed. It's like some kind of cult. I know you'd be happier if you'd get back with normal people."

Dryly he reminded her that they were not ready to forego the Cheltenham dollars, even at the level of reduced partnership points. "Anyway, there's nothing else I could do. I'm middle-aged. I've been a eunuch in the golden palace too long."

"Sure there is. You could teach, maybe. Or do community law service. Or even work for the government."

Finnegan looked through the French windows of the breakfast alcove, down the lawn toward the empty basin of the swimming pool where he still swam fifty laps each morning in summer. His pool was his final refuge where he could be compulsive and violent.

Alice claimed she was not concerned about the money; he wished he believed her wholeheartedly.

He had left for Miami that morning, according to Samson's instructions, and remained through Christmas on Seahorse Island with the Valencia thug brothers. So Alice had been abandoned once again for the holidays. Although he telephoned every evening to tell her he was deep in litigation strategy, he knew she was skeptical. And she was right. He spent most of the time sitting in a wicker chair at the back of the house, canopied by a tangle of weeds and creepers, staring at the surface of a shallow swimming pool, where a slick of oil floated like a water lily. He talked to the Valencia brothers, a long stream of unintelligible rhetoric woven around the subject of extradition and narcotics laws. He balanced a chipped china mug of tequila in one hand, while he puffed José Valencia's Cuban cigars with the other.

He had no illusions. He had not been sent out to dispense legal advice. The Valencias did not understand what he was talking about, nor did they seem particularly concerned. Finnegan was there, puffing and sipping and inhaling the sticky, swampy air because he was the pawn in the major offensive. Operation TBO.

He shuffled uncomfortably in the metal chair and recrossed his legs. Would this infernal A.A. meeting never end? Another man was holding forth, bewailing the disorder of his life, the unpaid bills, the debts. Compulsively Finnegan raised his hand. He was still playing the lead, whether he was arguing before the Supreme Court of the United States or the local Greenwich A.A. meeting. The heads turned toward him.

Biting his lip, he muttered, "My name is Michael and I'm an alcoholic."

"Hi, Michael."

For a moment he fell silent, paralyzed by the futility. Then it all spilled out in a torrent.

"I only came here tonight because my wife said she would leave me this time if I didn't give it a try. I'm here to please her, not to get cured."

There were nods and grunts from various corners of the room, as if they had all heard the same story before now.

"Maybe I'll behave a little better if I stop drinking, but it won't solve my real problems. I'm a trial lawyer. My career's crashed. I used to be a big shot in my business, with an outstanding reputation. I sacrificed my whole life to my company, my law firm, because I believed it was the most important place on earth. Now I've been disgraced, rebuked, maybe I'll even lose my job. All I want is another chance, to perform some quality work, to show them what I can do. I was the best. I've still got the talent."

"Michael," said the young salesman in the pink shirt, "all of us sitting here tonight have had problems holding down jobs. The only way to solve that is to stop drinking. Then when you get your next job you'll actually be able to deal with it."

Finnegan lost himself in a rage of self-pity. "There won't be another job! I wasn't just some middle-management nonentity, I was at the pinnacle of the business world. Do you realize what that means?"

"All sorts of people make comebacks," someone urged soothingly. "Just stop drinking and come to meetings every day. You'll be amazed to see how it works. I guarantee you."

Finnegan's pulse pounded at his temples. "Goddamn it!" he roared, filling the whole stale, echoing, stinking hall with his bellow. "I could cross-examine any one of you people into the ground after twelve martinis. I'd still be the best. There's nothing wrong with my professionalism. It was filthy, fucking politics." He sensed the ripple of embarrassment quivering through the hall. He sat back down on his metal chair, suddenly shamefaced. Whatever had provoked him to create such a spectacle?

"Michael," insisted the man in the pink shirt, "you've just got to trust in God and the help of all of us here. In time, it'll work. You'll see."

Finnegan nodded. He half lowered his eyelids, as the meeting wound to a close, and concentrated on the discussion he'd be having the next morning with the general counsel of Vaginex.

*   *   *

Gina was resorting her Vaginex files, and organizing the exhibits of the distorted vulvas, in preparation for their pending settlement. As she dumped a stack of redwells on her desk, the butterfly ashtray that Maxwell had bought her at the street fair fell off the edge and shattered.

She had been breaking and losing things more often than usual. An earring rolled away in the gutter, she left her American Express card behind at Barnes & Noble (and later left the Jane Austen she had bought in a taxi), she managed to lose her old address book, in which scrawled street numbers preserved a final link with Allentown and college days at Temple.

She looked at the broken ashtray mournfully for a moment and burst into tears. She slumped over the files and wept for that ancient September day, when she had been happy; she wept for love's decay, for the pewter-gray skies of Allentown, which she hated, for her parents and brothers, who made her ashamed, and with a fresh gust of sobs she cried out her eyes for the earring that had skipped away in the gutter and vanished.

Gina's family cried noisily when things went wrong. When life was festive, when the men won a few bucks at the track, or a child was born or baptized, they hugged and danced, or even cried. But to cry about a broken ashtray made no sense.

She did not hear Cheryl's knock. She raised her tear-blotched face, relieved to see it was not Maxwell or Finnegan.

"Can I borrow your notes on trespass to chattel? I've got a client—" She broke off as she registered Gina's sniffling. "What's wrong? What's happened?"

"I'm sorry." Gina found a half Kleenex in her top drawer under the clutter. She pointed helplessly at the chunk of ashtray while she scrambled for words. "I was carrying that stack of redwells and, and—" Another tidal wave of tears made her gulp for air.

Cheryl hated nothing as much as finding herself a witness to tears. Other people's SOS's for help limelighted all her own corners of inadequacy. She knew theoretically how you were meant to respond. You were supposed to offer physical, immediate comfort: a pat on the shoulder, a supportive embrace, a hand softly stroking the hair. She could not bring herself to do it.

She clung to the threshold of the office. "Can I do anything? You want some water?"

Gina continued to sob and point futilely at the ashtray pieces. Cheryl ventured a few steps inside and picked up the largest of the fragments.

Bewildered, Cheryl interlocked the jagged edges. "We can fix this."

"I'm fine now." Gina swallowed. "Really." She noticed Cheryl's mink. "You're on your way home. Already?"

Cheryl glanced at her watch. "I promised Kim Phong I'd try and make it by ten. Peggy Ann has an earache again. I somehow got the doctor to make a housecall. You know what a miracle that is in Manhattan. I felt dreadful when I couldn't be there myself this evening..."

She sighed. Gina was not the only one with problems.

"How's Peggy Ann? Is she okay?"

"He's put her on erythromycin. Children have such delicate eardrums. If you don't catch infections quickly, they can lose their hearing permanently." She moved closer to the desk. "You got those notes?"

"Somewhere." Gina's notes were all in a jumble. She kept resolving to sort them out. She patted her eyes again with the Kleenex.

"Gina. You really are upset. The notes don't matter. They can wait until tomorrow. What is it? Work?"

The answer surprised Cheryl. "Can I ride home with you? I won't stay long. I know you have to look after Peggy Ann."

She was taken aback. Gina had not been to her apartment for many months. "You see, I don't want to go home alone, not yet. And I don't want to stay here any longer tonight either."

"That's okay." Cheryl tried to sound natural. "Get your coat, then. My limo's waiting downstairs."

"How's Bobby?" Gina asked as the car turned onto the FDR Drive. She began to feel guilty about imposing on Cheryl's morsel of time.

"Remember how last month I wrote Miss McKenzie a check for..." She glanced at their driver and left the exact sum unspoken. "A check to buy one last indulgence for my son's bad behavior? I figured my contribution to the science lab would keep them off my back at least until after the Cheltenham new-partnership vote. Now it looks like I may have to get my checkbook out again. I can't afford this."

"Another check?"

"It's beyond a joke. Bobby let a snake out in the middle of a geography quiz."

"Where did he get a snake?"

"It came from the very science lab that I have helped to finance." The "fucking science lab" was the precise phrase in her brain. "It was only a grass snake, completely harmless, but it found its way to the teacher's desk and coiled up under the globe. The poor teacher saw it, went into shock, and they had to call an ambulance to take her out of school."

"What a nightmare!"

"You got it. I did try to explain to him about consequences, about cause and effect, and how even what seems like a prank can turn into a major disaster. It's not easy explaining to a kid the principles of 'proximate cause.' I mean, we spent a couple of weeks in law school on it. Remember *Palsgraff* v. *L.I.R.R.*?"

Gina half closed her eyes. "Proximate cause: that which in a natural and continuous sequence unbroken by an efficient intervening cause produces injury without which the result would not have occurred. What happened to the geography teacher?"

"She recovered. Luckily. She's in her sixties, due for retirement soon."

"Was it really a prank?"

"No." Cheryl looked away, out at the grim expanse of river, where on the far shore a few lights blinked. "He thought he was going to fail the quiz." The fucking quiz. "He doesn't like geography."

"They won't expel him, will they?"

"Not quite yet. They're still sending me handwritten thank-you notes for my last check." The notes were penned in italic script by Felicia McKenzie's superior, the principal of the Bigelow School. The pale blue ink matched the letterhead logo. "But my credit's wearing thin. They're going to need another check, and I still can't decide how big to make it."

Kim Phong opened the door for them. She was wearing a red kimono with black squiggles.

"That's pretty," said Cheryl. "Could you bring us a bottle of

Nuits St. Georges from the kitchen? And maybe a plate of those great little eggroll things you make? Any calls? How's Peggy Ann?"

"She's sleeping now. The doctor gave her some codeine and started the antibiotic. He said to call later tonight, if her temperature's still high."

"You go take care of her," Gina begged Cheryl. "I'll wait for you here."

"Would you mind coming in with me?"

The child lay on her side breathing peacefully next to a pink bear. Cheryl ran the back of her hand over Peggy Ann's forehead. "I think the temperature's down. Would you feel too? What do I do, Gina? Do I call the doctor back or not tonight? I have to make interpretive decisions on five-hundred-million-dollar issues. But kids are different. I never know. We'll leave her for now. Come. I want to show you my new Chanel jacket."

Cheryl had two walk-in closets in her bedroom, each one about the size of Gina's kitchen. Clothes hung along three walls; shoes and bags and belts, all color coded, stood guard in ranks on the shelves overhead. As Cheryl flipped briskly through the clothes hangers, the silk and taffeta rustled, conjuring up a medley of expensive perfumes.

Gina touched a cream-colored fabric with navy braid trim. "I've never seen you in this."

"It's a Givenchy. An old maternity dress. I don't know why I keep it."

But Cheryl did know. She had worn that dress almost every day at Cheltenham when she was a second-year associate, pregnant with Peggy Ann. It remained as a trophy of her victory over the malicious whispers and dubious stares. The lawyers hardly believed that a second year in a Wall Street firm would have the audacity and shortsightedness to encumber a beginning career with a birth. Four or five years down the road, that would be understandable, once the woman in question had already been irrevocably edged off the partnership track. Assuming at that stage she had found her niche in one of the less demanding practice areas, such as copyright or health care, then it might be acceptable, if inadvisable, that she should let up on her billings for a few months. But a second year, who was expected to put in unlimited grueling hours and no excuses, if you please—what was the point of throwing away a career before you had even started? Cheryl nevertheless stayed up all night at the printer, boarded airplanes on a few minutes' notice to Tacoma and Atlanta and Oklahoma City, and billed the requisite hours up to the eighth month. Just before the birth her blood pressure had shot up alarmingly. Yet mother and child had pulled through, and now, eight years later, some of those same men who had scanned her with scorn or malice would soon be voting for her partnership. Although the details of the Cheltenham voting procedure were a well-preserved secret, she had discovered one of the questions they must answer on the ballot. That question was, "Is he one of us?" Eight years later, she knew she had indeed convinced some partners that she was one of them.

She handed the Chanel jacket to Gina. "Try it on."

Gina obeyed. The mirror showed her that the shoulders were overly padded for her narrow frame. She had the feeling that she was trespassing in borrowed clothes. She slid it off quickly.

Kim Phong knocked. "Shall I bring the wine in the living room or the study?"

"Bring it in here." Cheryl explained to Gina, "I want to show you my new candlesticks." She pointed to where they stood on the dressing table, softly burnished bronze decorated with teardrops of colored glass. "Eighteenth century. I bought them last July when I was in Rome for a couple of days. You haven't been in my apartment for a long time, have you? We could light them right now. You have a match?"

Gina pulled out her lighter and lit tremulously the wicks of the rust-colored tapers. "I wish I could go to Rome."

"You will, you will. Thank you very much, Kim. Just put the tray down next to the Lichtenstein. That's right, the picture. We'll pour our own wine."

"Next year, maybe I'll go to Italy," said Gina.

"Take your vacation there this summer. It's only seven hours away."

Gina did not know how to explain that it was no longer merely a matter of finances, that she simply never seemed able to get her life in order. She glanced around the bedroom, always immaculate and tasteful, like a photograph from *House and Garden*. Cheryl was by nature orderly. Gina had been raised in a world that took no account of future planning. You shopped for food and clothes in small quantities. When you had money in your pocket you spent it. Your pay envelope arrived once a week, so you lived from Friday to Friday.

She asked, "Would you ever go with me to Italy?"

"Maybe. But I can't make any plans till after the partnership vote."

Then Gina wished she had not mentioned it. After the partnership vote Cheryl would be a different person too. She and Gina would still be friends, in the lukewarm context of a Cheltenham friendship, yet would it be seemly for Cheryl, as a junior partner, to travel with a fourth-year associate?

"You'll get it," promised Gina. "I know you'll get the vote."

"Who cares? If I don't I'll do something fun for a change. Maybe I'll open a Wall Street boutique. To sell designer clothes to professional women. We need one." That was sheer bravado. Cheryl had become accustomed to letting fall nonchalant responses, as a smokescreen to hide her anxiety. If she did not make partner, she did not know what she would do. During the past couple of years she had not allowed herself the indulgence of even considering an alternative plan of action. Of course there would always be a job for her. One of the banks or accounting firms would hire her as general counsel. They would pay her handsomely, she would be allowed to go home, without paranoia, at five-thirty or six at night. But there would be no glory.

"After all the work you've put in..." Gina tried to reassure her. "Plus you're so damned good. You'll get the vote."

"Who knows? I still can't figure out whether Ariel's on my side or not."

"Maybe you should seduce him." Gina giggled. She felt suddenly better, for the first time in days.

"You think I haven't thought of it? I wish I knew how to. He's so cool, it's impossible to imagine him making a move. Of course, that's his attraction."

Gina sensed a minute tremor in Cheryl's voice. So Ariel Lamb, of all people, was her secret heartthrob. Cheryl must like the power and inaccessibility. It explained some of her own aloofness, and her reluctance to take a more general interest in men. "Anyway," said Gina, "you're better off with the fantasy. He'd probably be a terrible letdown in bed. In, out, and wipe it."

Cheryl looked mildly shocked, not so much at the description as the profanity of its application to Ariel. "We'll never know," she replied firmly. "But sometimes I wish Cyrus Sweet were more powerful. I could have had him in a second."

"He's not unattractive for a man of his age. There've always been stories about his flirtations too."

"I bet he's good. He's got that calm self-confidence."

Gina reflected. "I thought it came from his good breeding."

"It all goes together."

Gina nodded. She recognized Cheryl's superior expertise in these matters. "How about Fishman?" she suggested. "Maybe you could buy his vote with a roll in the hay."

"Fishman! Fishman? He never learned how to do it. He jerks off at night over the Internal Revenue Code."

"Initiate him."

"Forget it. I'll bet that hypochondriac wears three layers of condoms even with his wife. Like winter underwear."

"There's always Hopper."

"Great, if your idea of a good time is dressing up as Ariel Lamb and letting him lick your feet." Cheryl refilled Gina's glass. "At least you're feeling better. Now. What was all that about? Work? Or that pompous Clancy Maxwell?"

Gina's mood swiftly clouded again. "How do other women

keep men interested? What do I do, Cheryl, when every single day, I feel him sliding a little farther away?"

"You're asking me? Me? I'm the world's failure in that department."

"You left your ex-husband. He didn't leave you."

"He wasn't strong enough for me. He dragged me down. He resented me. I never found a man, at least one who was available, who was strong enough to measure up to me."

"Clancy isn't all that strong. He's never had to fight for anything, except maybe intellectually. For him, war is words."

"I know love is blind and all that," said Cheryl. "Still, I'll never understand what you see in him. He's such a pompous ass."

Yes, Clancy was pompous, but Cheryl, who had grown up in the spruce lawns of suburbia, would never understand the obsession. She had not been where Gina had been.

When Gina spent time with Clancy, she felt as far away as the moon from the dreary streets of her childhood. In one sense Clancy was a pure creature. He had never seen those rickety clapboard houses where the paint clung in moldy patches. He had not smelled the constant stench of burning rubber and sulfur in Allentown.

Whatever Clancy was, he had never been contaminated by that. He had only picturebook knowledge of Gina's unending loop of inferno highway, bordered by fast-food outlets selling sweet, sweet doughnuts and hot dogs, drive-ins and loveless motels, and the car dealers at every corner, a reminder that steel was still king. She could never forget the vandalized placards, erect like primitive totem poles: lighting companies, welding companies, refrigerator parts, furniture companies, bottling plants.

In Allentown the di Angelos were just another family of poor wops, second-generation failures. For all their ethnic sentimentality, Gina's parents had no real interest in Naples. The families had struggled to get to America, where gray Allentown was their promised land. They dreamed of marbleized Formica, Gothic mansions and swimming pools, Las Vegas and Frank Sinatra, and weddings and funerals, with catered football sandwiches. Within the small Italian ghetto in Allentown, they took some comfort from the other families who had not been successful and were ever hopeful that thanks to some deal, some family connection, some turn of events, things might improve.

Gina's father Felipe had worked for many years in a barber shop until he had finally been able to start his own. Business was generally bad, you could only charge two bucks in a neighborhood that poor, but the important thing, he believed, was that he had his regulars, who came back and talked year after year of memories and pipe dreams. The regulars made Felipe di Angelo feel important.

Gina's mother supported Felipe like an ancient cypress. Their wife-mother culture demanded it and as soon as Gina was old enough to be useful, she was expected to help her mother in the kitchen, where the neighboring women clucked over the neighborhood sluts.

There had almost never been time left in the day for herself, and still worse, virtually no privacy. You could hear the noise of the radio or the television or Felipe's booming voice in every corner of the frame house, as if the walls were cardboard. An hour's escape to read a book was the ultimate luxury. A few years later, when she got her scholarship to Temple University, it was the peace and privacy Gina most relished.

For many of the other kids, college was simply a rite of passage, a refreshing opportunity for freedom, getting stoned, drinking, and sex. Classes represented an extension of what had been drudgery in high school. To Gina it was all a labor of love. She got A's without much trouble.

Gina found three main cliques dominated the campus in her freshman year. There were the rich suburbanites, who drove Pontiac Grand Prixes and Cutlass Supremes, kept phones and TV's in their dorms, wore designer jeans and competed more ruthlessly over their wardrobes than their grades. Then there were the cool middle-class rebels, dropping acid, barefoot, sweeping floor-length peasant skirts along the sidewalks, and traveling on weekends to Grateful Dead concerts. Finally, there were the lowlifes, a ragged mixture of poor ethnic street kids like Gina, some inner-city blacks, some Irish, a number of Poles. The boys dressed and talked tough and affected to disdain their middle-class peers.

Gina could have fit right in with the lowlifes, hung out with them in their noisy bars, and dated the studs, in their lumberjack shirts and nylon windbreakers. She could speak their language and she understood their mixed-up values. But she preferred to live in isolation and longingly observe the suburbanites, who would have nothing to do with her.

In her fourth year, as a last-ditch effort to acquire the kind of education she needed to escape the Allentown stigma, she started carrying on with her Renaissance History professor. He was forty-seven. He smoked a pipe. He had a carrot-red beard and a bald spot, like a friar, on top of his head. He was married to a social worker, had three children, and it was his idea that Gina should try for law school.

The affair lasted exactly six months. On their free afternoons, when neither had classes, he used to drive her out of town into the country and pull the car off the road into a muddy ditch, where they would neck. Gina lost her virginity on the leatherette back seat, wedged between the baby harness and some camping equipment that belonged to the teenage sons.

"Take the LSAT's, the law board exams," he suggested. "You've nothing to lose."

"I ought to get a job. I've got no money."

"There are student loans." His beard tickled her thigh.

In the end, that history professor gave her as good an education as all her courses in Milton and Petrarch, not in sensuality, but in how to talk like a middle-class grown-up. They talked about Solzhenitsyn and Watergate, petrodollars and famine in Africa. He corrected her grammatical mistakes and cleaned up her blue-collar pronunciation. He instructed her what clothes not to wear, although he was too cheap, as she later recalled, to replace them.

She remembered his lessons with a dash of gratitude. It had been hard to like him as a person, particularly when he was humping her squeezed up against the baby harness, but she had needed him badly at the time. After years of isolation and the humbling rejection by the suburban brat pack, Gina's confidence was slipping. Her carrot-haired professor put the pieces back together, taught her a few tricks, and sent her off to take the law boards. She herself had been most astonished by her high scores.

Those scores had swept her through three years of law school, from which she had graduated summa cum laude and managed to make research editor on the *Law Review*. Then dizzily on to three years of Cheltenham, the oldest firm in the country, and now to a high-rise over the East River, where she sat on the edge of the bed sipping Nuits St. Georges from a Baccarat glass by eighteenth-century candlelight.

"What's that?"

It sounded like a scratch at the door. Cheryl got up and opened it. "Bobby! What are you doing up so late?"

He hesitantly stepped in, a small figure in an alligator dressing gown, the hood with its long row of teeth hanging down behind.

"I woke up. Kim Phong said you were home."

"You shouldn't disturb Kim Phong so late, Bobby. Unless you're sick or something. It's her time off. Remember Gina?"

He nodded. "Are you finished with those duck things? Can I have the rest?" He turned to Gina with a burst of enthusiasm. "Kim makes the best food. It's as good as a Chinese takeout. She even knows how to make stew out of snakes. She's not afraid of snakes. They eat them in her country all the time, she says."

Cheryl sighed. "Don't you think we've had enough about snakes recently?" She tweaked the alligator hood. "Come on, back to bed."

Ignoring her, he turned to his new audience. "You like jokes?"

"If they're good ones," said Gina.

"What do elephants have that no other animal has?"

"Dunno."

Bobby skipped away to the door, and turning dramatically, announced as he made his exit, "Baby elephants."

Gina stood up. "I must go home and let you sleep. I'll get a cab downstairs. Thanks for the wine."

After she had walked Gina to the door, and taken one final look at her daughter, Cheryl was still not ready to slide between the Ralph Lauren sheets. She sat for a long time at the dressing table, playing with the collection of lipsticks, drawing pink and red dabs and bows, blotting, and drawing again. It sometimes helped her relax. She let the candles burn on, hissing softly as the globules of rust wax dribbled down to the glass surface.

It had not escaped her, Gina's awe, as she discreetly peeked around the apartment, her open wonderment at a pair of candle-sticks that had cost eleven hundred dollars. Gina's open naïveté over the small luxuries of New York professional life constantly astonished Cheryl, who had spent her childhood in the maple- and sycamore-lined streets of an Indiana suburb. Cheryl had always lived in comfort. As an undergraduate she had taken a suitcase full of nineteen cashmere sweaters to Mount Holyoke. There she learned that a lot of sweaters are no proof of culture and sophistication. Cheryl had worked hard since her first years in the East to surround herself with what she hoped were the trappings of real class. It was easy enough to fool Gina, by drop-ping blasé remarks. She wondered if she convinced some of the members of the older school, the Tristan Barretts and Cyrus Sweets. Or perhaps they never noticed, perhaps they had never been paying attention. Maybe all they cared about was her wealth of billable hours.

Several years ago at a Cheltenham cocktail party, Cyrus Sweet had remarked to her over a frozen daiquiri, "New York cuts everybody down to size." He said it in his gentle, Kentucky drawl, smiling his patrician smile, with no suggestion of malice. It still haunted her, just what he meant by that. Was it no more than a philosophical observation, or was he subtly hinting that they still saw her as an outsider, a rich middle-American suburbanite, and that they would tick the box marked "no" when they got to the question "Is he one of us?"

I tried to do everything right, she reflected. I've worked my ass off for nine frigging years, through Saturdays and Sundays and nights and Christmases and New Years. I've brought up two children alone, with almost no help from my family and none at all from the failed advertising executive I married. For nine years I've coordinated the colors of my accessories every day, beige and navy and burgundy, and no one has ever seen me lose my temper. I'm thirty-eight years old. I found some white hairs last week and the skin on my neck is beginning to creep. Will I soon start looking old, before I've had any real fun at all? I guess the trips to Paris and Monte Carlo and London were fun. I've seen all the Andrew Lloyd Webber musicals and I've eaten truffles Perigord at the Tour d'Argent. God, I'm not asking you for fun, it's probably too late anyhow, but give me the one thing I want, give me the vote. I've earned it, give me a break, give me a fucking break.

The mask in the mirror smiled back sweetly, cool as a cucumber, clean as a whistle, tough as nails.

She took one last look and blew out the candles.

FIFTEEN_____

*G*ary Fishman, clutching his lunchbox containing zucchini sandwiches and live-culture yogurt, boarded the first-class cabin of Avianca Airlines and flew down for the whirlwind tour of Colombia, Bolivia, and Paraguay. It was a grueling, frustrating trip. Shunted between dusty, bureaucratic offices, overbearing dignitaries, and Third World airports, he had no spare moments to buy Suzy's chinchilla. Returning Sunday night, he cringed at the anticipation of her ire; he looked forward heartily, however, after a week of empanadas and feijoadas, to his first Nutrexpress chocolate chip sundae. He made the cab take a detour from JFK to find the orange phallic-shaped hut in Queens.

Little did he know. Scandal had erupted on Friday, getting Nutrexpress a mention in all the national press. Kahn, caught at the apogee of his wealth and influence, had received the first driblets of the disastrous news by telex at the Hotel Okura, where he was again pacing the carpets. A couple of hours later he was aloft over the Pacific, headed back to New York and refuge at Cheltenham.

Courage, sitting across from him at the conference table on Thursday, almost missed the former paroxysms of rage. Kahn did not adapt well to the role of the beaten man. He still rocked back heavily in the same Chippendale chair he had nearly split apart a few weeks before, he still puffed clouds of cigar smoke. Only the gladioli were now peach and no longer scarlet. The Mongolian Marauder, however, seemed to have shrunk and shriveled overnight, or somewhere over the North Pacific.

"There's no need for premature panic," reassured Tristan. "We'll get our Litigation Department onto this immediately. We're all going to keep cool." Courage spotted Tristan's underlying queasiness at the prospect of losing their best-paying entrepreneurial client to bankruptcy. "How about a V8 Juice?" Tristan suggested.

"Make it a double bourbon," answered Kahn. "No ice."

It was up to Courage to call through to Catering to arrange the refreshments.

"Now," said Tristan. "Let's get this straight. In their class action complaint, the consumer groups allege that Nutrexpress franchises in various states, while falsely claiming to use only organic ingredients, have in fact been serving fried chicken, tacos, and chocolate sundaes processed...ah...the usual way."

"It's cheaper," grunted Kahn, puffing smoke.

"That may well be," interrupted Tristan hastily. "But that's an issue for the plaintiffs, and not for you, to raise. Nutrexpress now conducts business in forty-eight franchises in seventeen states. I think we should stress that you are not in a position to monitor the ingredients of every kitchen at all times."

"Look, fellas." Kahn munched at the cigar. "I'm gonna come clean with you, 'cause in the long run it'll save me time and money on my legal bills. And God Almighty only knows how I'll be able to pay legal bills once it really starts hitting the fan." Tristan, at the mention of the emotive subject, looked quickly away. Kahn continued, "I knew from day one my tacos and sundaes and all that crap were exactly what the other fast-food manufacturers were marketing across the nation: crap. My food was no more organic than what they give you at Burger King or Pizza Hut or Taco Bell. Difference was, mine tasted a lot worse. 'Cause we used the lowest grade ingredients. Cheaper, get it? But the public still went on buying my crap, even though it tasted so fucking awful, since they figured it's got to taste awful if it's made with organic ingredients. Okay, you're my attorneys. I gotta be straight with you. It was a scam. But man, was it a beautiful scam."

Kahn, even in defeat, was fascinating. "How did you keep it so long under wraps?" Courage burned to know. "Surely the wholesalers could have leaked the truth anytime."

"Oh, we bought a little organic crap along with the horsemeat and pigs' trotters. And we import our chocolate from South America. They're not going to squeal on us from down there. Specially as it's reject shavings they can't export elsewhere."

"My God," breathed Tristan. "How about the books?"

"We cooked 'em." Kahn sounded almost cheerful for a moment. "It's easy, once you know how." He suddenly sobered again and twitched. Over the Pacific somewhere, he had also developed a nervous tic. "Fellas, give it to me straight. Will I be doing time?"

"Let's just take this step by step," Tristan urged. Courage knew he was thinking about the legal bills.

At that moment the page came through for Courage. Tristan nodded him permission to take the call from the telephone in the private alcove next to the door.

"I have Miss Farmer on the line from a phone booth," purred Lorraine's milky voice. "You want to take it?"

"Put her through. But then no more calls from anyone else. We've got an emergency here. Just take messages."

"I'm downtown," said Helen. "I've got a proofing job this afternoon at Samurai Robinson. You want to stop off for a sandwich with me if I finish up in time?"

He held his mouth close to the receiver. When he spoke softly, Tristan and Kahn could not hear him. "Wish I could. We've got a mammoth crisis on here."

"They've got some big project in the mill at Samurai. They've gone outside and hired an army of proofreaders and emergency word processors. I'm about to go upstairs. I thought I'd call you first. Any idea how long you'll be?"

Courage hesitated. He really wanted to see her. They had eaten at the Hunan Balcony on Sunday night, chaperoned as usual by Chloe. He had talked to her about the TBO and the pressures of being chosen for the crack team to work on it. He had explained to her how the other associates envied him for being selected, and yet how, perversely, he was still resisting the honor. It just seemed like more work.

It was dawning on him that he wanted Helen, although for what, and how, and why, he was still unsure. It was beginning to make him nervous. It was not such a bad sensation, that quickened pulse, but he did not want her to suspect. Maybe later, he had thought, when all this was somewhere behind them ... if that ever happened ... she had a small scar above her lip and her fingernails were ragged. Yet she smiled like the da Vinci on the fifty-first floor as she crumbled a fortune cookie.

"There's no telling at this end. You'll have to call me back in a couple of hours. Have me paged."

"Will do. I hope it's not late. Samurai's the pits. They're a bunch of arrogant superswine. Think they run the world."

"They kind of do."

"They've got very plush offices. Even better than yours."

"Enjoy the scenery. Call me later."

Courage returned to the conference table, where Tristan was trying to calm their volatile client by suggesting strategy. "We'll get the litigation boys onto this in the morning. Our best man, Mick Finnegan, is unfortunately in Miami today. In the meantime, I think we should concentrate on rebutting their argument that you've been using 'inorganic' substances. I mean, what does 'organic' mean anyhow? Who the hell knows?"

Kahn's serpent eyes gleamed with a trace of their former brimstone. "I like it," he said. "I like it."

"Our main goal should be to contain this story in the national press. Maybe make an early deal with the other side."

"It's a consumer group. I know those putzes. They won't deal. Besides, deals are expensive."

"Life is expensive. If this story gets much more big publicity, your business is liable to collapse, regardless of the outcome of the litigation."

Kahn leaned across the table and tugged at Tristan's sleeve. The scarab ring flashed unexpectedly, mighty again. "We're gonna fight this, okay? You guys got guts? I've been a good client, right? I treated you good. I always paid my bills on time. Now it's my turn. I need all the spunk that's in you. We're going to shove hot lead and sodium nitrate right up their tushes till they wish they'd never messed with us. Right?"

He leaned back heavily in his chair, panting slightly from the exertion of his battle address. With a sickening screech, the eighteenth-century Chippendale mahogany finally split asunder.

*   *   *

Half a dozen blocks away, on the corner of Pearl Street and Maiden Lane, Gary Fishman sprinted through the lobby of the Cardio-Fitness Center, where he liked to put in an honest forty minutes several afternoons a week. Nodding cheerfully at the trim receptionist, he plucked a beaming red apple from the bowl on the desk, a symbol, like a happy still-life, of a streamlined, goal-oriented self-betterment. He hurried to the locker room to change into shorts and a T-shirt. Boy, was it good to be back, after the gut-bouncing cab rides through the diesel-stinking streets of those Latin capitals.

The exercise area was almost deserted on this January late afternoon. A couple of souls, one immersed in *Barron's*, pedaled determinedly on the bicycles. Fishman glanced up at the television monitor, softly tuned to the financial news, with the ticker tape ribboning along its lower edge. Making his way past the fronds of foliage, Fishman began his cardiovascular warm-up at the rowing machine, alongside a solitary figure in a sweaty T-shirt. The lonely rower turned its red head. It was Hopper.

"Hey, Gary."

"Hey, Hopper. Quiet day?"

The enzymes of rivalry were speeding already, even before he had clambered up onto the saddle of his rowing machine. God-damn Hopper and his seven points. Fishman would show him whose cardiovascular system was in better shape.

"Fairly routine," grunted Hopper, not to be outdone. "Been up since five A.M. Had a breakfast meeting at the SEC in Washington at nine-thirty this morning. Got back in time for lunch at Caroline for some TBO fine tuning."

Fishman pumped harder at the oars, sneaking a glance at Hopper's monitor. Fishman knew he was going to enjoy this fitness competition. "I guess you've been putting a lot of hours into that TBO."

"We all have. It's the quality of the deal structure that matters." He spat the words out like machine-gun fire.

"Sure, sure. But keep a few spare baskets for your eggs. Just in case. That's the comfort of my tax practice. I'll always have plenty of international clients, no matter what happens with the TBO."

Hopper pumped harder. "The TBO's the biggest animal we've ever caught. Your whole tax department couldn't touch that kind of money."

"The animal's still out there."

Hopper's biceps were beginning to tire. "I'm thinking of the future of the firm. Though I can understand why you might underrate the deal. It's not like you've got a lot to gain. The tax work's basically ancillary. I'm moving on to the treadmill now."

Fishman rowed a few more strokes before he moved over to join Hopper at the next phase of their exercise program.

Hopper looked up, panting. "What's all this doom and gloom about the TBO? Didn't they treat you well down there last week?"

"They treated me okay. Though I nearly choked on the food. But there's something in the wind. They're stonewalling us. They aren't in love with our deal anymore."

Hopper missed a beat on his treadmill. "You serious, Gary? You think it's to do with that narcotics bullshit?"

"Might be. They just aren't in bed with us anymore."

"You coming to the Cheltenham party next week at the Guggenheim?"

"Depends how much work I've got."

"Ariel wants to make the announcement about the TBO at the party. Keep that under your hat, will you?" Hopper smirked, the proud possessor of the most intimate information.

"He can't. There's still no deal."

"They're going to telex him. Maybe even tonight. A letter of intent."

"I've just got back from these guys. I'll believe that telex when I see it."

"How much you wanna bet?"

Each point valued roughly a hundred thousand dollars. Before tax. "You vote me another point in April at the compensation meeting."

"Done. And if you're wrong, I want your vote for another point."

Hopper's naturally ruddy, freckled face now glowed like a ripe plum, under the sheath of sweat. His breath came in shorter gasps.

"You should go easy," warned Fishman. "You've gotta build up stamina gradually, if you aren't used to working out. Got any history of hypertension in your family?"

Hopper gritted his teeth. It was not mere physical strain. "My father died of a heart attack. One big coronary. Not so long ago."

"Gee. That's rough. I'm sorry."

"Don't be. He screwed up my life and my mother's. The woman's a saint."

Fishman remembered vaguely that Hopper still lived with his mother. He had even brought her to firm functions once or twice. She was a squat, intimidating old Gorgon, with rapidly blinking eyes like Hopper's, and the same formaldehyde skin. She presided in a corner, somber in a black silk dress, greedily stuffing lobster claws into her mouth while her mechanized eyes minutely followed the path of her son.

"It's time you got married," said Fishman smugly. "Before people start wondering."

Although Hopper remained the last young bachelor among the partnership, his bachelorhood was oddly accepted. It was unthinkable to imagine him living with a wife, or with anyone actually, except his weird Medusa of a mother. No one suspected him of homosexuality; it was difficult to suspect him of any sexuality at all.

Hopper, leaving the anguish of the treadmill, moved on to the pulleys. "I don't need a wife, Gary. For the time being I want to concentrate fully on my work."

"All work and no play," reminded Fishman, who was probably one of the dullest people south of Fulton Street. "You got any outside interests, Hopper? You like to travel? You like to read?"

"I read a lot on entomology, when I get the time. Which is not much, when I'm billing twenty-nine hundred hours a year. I've got my collection too."

"I'm going to jump rope now." Fishman picked up the jump rope and snaked it lovingly before he started to skip. It reminded him of the delicious things Suzy had done to him before the South American trip. Since he had returned empty-handed, without the chinchilla, the scarlet underwear and the delectable horsewhip had been withheld. "Your collection?"

"My mother and I collect butterflies. You should come over to Brooklyn Heights and have dinner with us sometime. Our apartment's a real museum."

"I didn't know you did that."

"Since I was a kid. We've got cases and cases of them on every wall." He let go of the pulleys to spread his fingers. "The wings are so beautiful. Soft like velvet, colors you can't imagine, emeralds and crimson and huge purple-blue spots."

Fishman shuddered as he bounced over the rope. He had always been squeamish about insects. It was lucky he lived in Manhattan. He could not even handle a moth or a spider in the bathtub. Suzy was not crazy about them either, but somebody had to get out the Kleenex and squash.

Hopper leaned his head back, exhausted. The red fuzz of hair was now caked with sweat. "You know those Tiffany lamps in my office?"

Fishman grunted. They were the only note of decoration in Hopper's sparse hermitage.

"They were a gift from my mother when I graduated. I like them 'cause they remind me of butterflies' wings."

Hopper was weird, no doubt about it. Fishman had never before held such a long conversation alone with him, unrelated to legal matters. Nor had most other people. Once was enough, however, he thought, as he finished off his exercise program with a few minutes' stationary jogging on the rolling belt. "You catch them yourself? The butterflies?"

"Sure. That's the fun part. It's like surgery, once you get used to sticking the pin in. My father could never understand that. He said it was barbaric. He didn't understand beautiful things."

"I'm heading for the shower."

Under the gush of the water, Fishman called out to Hopper, after checking that they were quite alone. His reedy voice collected timber from the echoing walls. "What would you do, Hopper, if the TBO didn't make it? Would you stick with Ariel anyhow?"

The answer, rich in acoustics, came back like a fanfare of trumpets. "Ariel's one of the few true geniuses left in the practice today. We've got a number of competent lawyers around, but no one else with real vision, real insight, like Ariel. The man has a mind like a robot. He's unerring in his predictions. Sometimes it's almost like he has a sixth sense. I've learned most of what I know from him. I'm very lucky I got to Cheltenham at just the right moment in history."

"He wasn't always such a big shot. He only hit paydirt when this corporate finance stuff got hot and sexy."

"Ariel could have done anything. He'd have made a great trial lawyer too, if he'd gone in that direction. But he chose the most abstract, intellectual field. It's his nature."

"I know you're his biggest fan. But let me tell you, the guy doesn't know shit about the Internal Revenue Code."

"That's why we keep you here, Gary, to advise him. Ariel needs support people to look after the details. His mind's on the broader picture."

"'Support people'!" Fishman snorted contemptuously and scrubbed with deodorant soap. Who did that upstart Hopper think he was, with his kinky collections and his lousy seven points?

That fanatic devotion to Lamb was somehow unsettling too. It was as if the little pipsqueak needed a father figure—any psychiatrist could have told you that. Still and all, he knew his securities practice inside out, and it was a mean feat to catch him out on the '34 Act.

Fishman scooped up another shiny apple as he passed the reception desk, and tossed it cheerfully like a tennis ball before he bit. He was looking forward to his Mozart and his Cabernet tonight.

*　　　*　　　*

Courage was relieved when Tristan finally sent him downstairs to Wall Street to buy a couple of hot dogs with sauerkraut for Kahn. The attorneys were making every effort to cater to their flailing client's least whim, partly on the condemned-man's-hearty-breakfast theory and partly in the hope that he might miraculously pull through and still come up with the legal fees. They had offered to import for him any delicacy he could name from any restaurant on the island. But the bourbon had gone rapidly to his head after so many years' abstinence on vegetable juice, as recommended by the doctor in Zurich. It was all systems go. He wanted a hot dog, straight off the street, and nothing else would substitute.

Courage winced as the old woman handed him the food, noticing the filthy strips of cloth bound around her fingers. He decided to stick with the box of Crackerjacks in his desk. Kahn could probably take on any bacteria and annihilate it, even those of this grimy creature in her head scarf. Courage gave her his winning, youthful smile as he handed over the change. She took the money like a sleepwalker. She did not smile back.

"There was a message for you," said Tristan, spreading Kahn's snack out on the conference table. "You can call back now if you want, while we eat."

"Give me five minutes?"

He slipped into Benedict Hamilton's office next door, which had been abandoned for the night, and used his phone. Benedict always left his office shipshape: legal pads and files and casebooks all perpendicular, the sharpened pencils like spears, erect in the mug. There was not a curve in the room except for the row of antique inkwells adorning the shelf.

"You still busy?" Helen asked.

"Worse and worse. It looks like our best client's going down the tubes. It's really flipped him out. He's gone through a kind of personality change, like the Moonies took part of him away. What catastrophe does to people! But you know, for the first time ever, I'm almost beginning to like him a tiny bit."

"I've hardly had a thing to do since I called you last. I had to proof a few pages of definitions to a servicing agreement. There was something about it that caught my eye, so I made a copy when they weren't looking. Have you a minute? Can I read it to you?"

"Literally one minute. Shoot."

"Here goes. 'Bond: Any one of the certificates executed by the Trust and authenticated by the Trustee... Trust: The trust created by this agreement, the estate of which consists of the Receivables and all moneys thereunder, blah, blah... Single Bond: A certificate evidencing Fractional Undivided Interest in the amount of one thousand dollars...'"

Courage interrupted. "It's just the standard list of definitions for any asset-backed agreement. The receivables are deposited in a trust, and the trustee pays out to the bondholders over a time period in monthly installments. It's nothing out of the ordinary."

"Get this. 'Receivable: A government-guaranteed obligation, representing the revenues due and owing from citizens of that government over the time period set out in Annex A.'"

"My God." Courage whistled. "It's taxes."

"Now put this in your pipe and smoke it. 'Seller: The duly elected governments of blank, blank, and blank, as represented by authorized officials of said jurisdiction.'"

"What do you mean, 'blank'?"

"It's just not filled in."

"Shit, they've gone ahead and done a TBO!"

"That's what I was wondering."

"You've got to see some more of the agreements."

"I'll do what I can, but everyone seems to have forgotten about me. They left me sitting in their lobby. It's very quaint, all built like a Japanese garden, with shrubs and rocks."

"Samurai Robinson's got a lot of money to throw around on interior decoration."

"No kidding. But there's a nice authentic touch to it. They've got a Buddha that looks like Tokugawa period to me."

"You should know. You're the expert."

"And a little pond with real water lilies floating in it. And carp! They must have brought all the stuff right over from Japan. I'm sitting here reading Matsuo Basho in the very kind of garden it was written in."

"Call me again in a couple of hours. I've got to get back to my lunatic."

Helen settled down in the brocaded dragon upholstery, which softened the angles of the antique wooden bench. Even the lighting of this enchanted reception area, calculated to soothe the souls of the fiercest money warriors, was designed to simulate a misty twilight, a uniquely Japanese hour. Chrysanthemums clustered at the base of an arc of bamboo. Dwarf juniper and cherry trees clung to the soft formations of archaic rock. The subtle fluid motion of the stream water lulled her, just as it had seduced many a CEO between the meetings of a frenetic schedule. She turned back to her page:

> *Summer grasses—*
> *All that remains*
> *Of soldiers' visions.*

Courage, the weary foot soldier, trooped back to Kahn's conference room, where the odor of hot dog hung in the air. The street food, or maybe the bourbon, seemed to have resuscitated Kahn with a fresh tide of vigor. He leaned forward, slightly more cautiously. The wrecked Chippendale chair had been discreetly removed to one side.

"The whole knack of my business," he told them, "is to create opportunities out of kooky situations where no one else sees they exist."

"First of all," reminded Tristan, "let's try to salvage what we can from your Nutrexpress empire. Maybe there'll be time for new deals later." He did not sound optimistic.

"Wrong," countered Kahn. The wood of the replacement Chippendale creaked. "Now's the time to strike. When no one expects it."

"Strike what?"

He brought the tips of his fingers together in a gesture of cunning. "Before this tornado blew up I was back in Tokyo again, for another round of discussions with Misuki."

"I thought you'd given up on them," said Courage.

"I never give up. On anything. Now, no one said anything about buying their lousy semen-stain-removing technology. We all agree it's an overrated product. But let's flip the thing on its backside." He made a rapid motion like a magician pulling a rabbit out of a hat. "If I can't buy from them, I figure I'll sell to them instead."

"Sell them what?"

"Goldilox, Inc."

"Goldilox! That can of worms? How about the outstanding litigation? And we still haven't cleared the FDA approval."

"Fuck the FDA. It's got no significance in Japan. As for the lawsuits, there are ways of dealing with that."

"Name one."

"We insulate the liability with a dummy holding company. Something that's got no assets to protect."

"It won't work," Courage explained. "The courts look right through that kind of shell holding company. It's called 'piercing the veil.'"

Kahn grew impatient. "I know, I know. I haven't been talking with you people for fifteen years for nothing. The billions of bucks I've paid you have at least bought me a little legal education. I explained all that to Misuki."

"End of story?"

"Not on your ass. They decided they want me to be the holding company."

Tristan raised his hand. "It wouldn't be a valid risk for you. As we've already discussed, a successful outcome of those blue and green plaintiff suits could wipe you right out."

"That's what I figured. So I went back to my hotel, took a steam bath, got myself a shiatsu massage, and went to sleep, reckoning something would come to me, sooner or later."

What had come, sooner, was the telex announcing Kahn's impending cataclysm.

"I think we've covered most of the ground we usefully can tonight," broke in Tristan. It was not characteristic of him to suppress a client in midflow of billable time. But Tristan's sciatica was pinching. He needed a quiet evening at home.

"Wait! Don't you want to hear the deal? Three days ago I was in no position to buy up Goldilox for Misuki. I had too much to lose. The beauty is, now that I've lost everything anyway, I can!"

Tristan and Courage stared at him. Kahn never ceased to astonish.

"I'm sick of the fast-food business anyhow. It demands supervision of management; as you people know, I don't like to do that. I'm a planning man, I'm a creative type. This is what we do. We form an offshore corporation, which is me. Misuki pays the company a robust sum for my services. Nobody'll ever trace it. We do it nice and neat. Meanwhile Nutrexpress, which is a bag of shit anyway, buys Goldilox. Nutrexpress goes belly up. The consumer groups clean up on us, our business goes to hell, we run at a loss awhile, maybe we go into bankruptcy in the end. We're a rag of a company, but we're still holding Goldilox."

"Where does Misuki come out in all this?"

"We've covered the risk for them. Maybe we're unlucky and we never get FDA approval for the U.S. Maybe we lose all the lawsuits. Maybe no one wants long hair anyhow. So it's a dog and Misuki's lost nothing. But maybe we hit the jackpot, and start creaming it in. Then Nutrexpress sells Goldilox right over to Misuki at an immensely advantageous price."

"I'll give it some thought," Tristan promised. Courage could feel the familiar headache dawning, which always followed shortly in the wake of Kahn's grandiose scams. Yet you had to give it to him. He had the makings of a military genius, ready for a surprise ambush at the very crest of battle.

Courage heard himself paged again. With a shrug of apology he moved to the side table to answer the call.

"Peter, where are you?" Helen's voice sounded feverish.

"In conference still. Is it urgent?"

"You bet. I've got to see you. Right now."

"We're packing up soon. Can't it wait?"

"No way. I'll meet you outside the building."

"I can't. Maybe in a half hour."

"No! Right now. Downstairs."

"I'll call you back."

"Peter," she beseeched him, and there was an authority in her tone she had never used before. "I've got to see you right now. If you screw me around on this, I'll never help you again. I'll never see you again. It's that important!"

Awkwardly excusing himself from Kahn, and muttering something about a personal crisis, he grabbed his overcoat and took the elevator down. She was waiting in the lobby, nervously pacing between the marble columns. In one hand she was clutching two yellow irises, which bewildered him.

"Let's walk toward the Seaport," she said. "We can pick up a cab over there."

"Where are we going?"

"Uptown."

"Will you kindly fill me in? I walked out on a major meeting just now with a guy who's deep in it. This had better be important."

"I've got some idea what your friend David was trying to tell you, the day before he died."

Courage stopped in his tracks. "So what exactly happened after you went back to reading Banjo in the shade of the whispering pines?"

She told him.

Nothing at all happened, for a while. The place became eerily quiet. From time to time, investment bankers with deep frown lines would wander through, clutching food cartons. Sometimes they waited by the telephone for answering calls from their homeward-bound limousines. It was the regular evening atmosphere, the twilight hour of the changing guard, before the place should spring back to nightlife.

Helen went on reading poetry, soothed by the violet shadows and the gurgle of the stream. A nervous associate with a sweat-stained shirt brought her another short document to proof. It was some kind of chart, broken down by regions; it extended back three years in time and five years into the future. The numbers, worked out to the final cent, were in millions of dollars. She found another proofreader, also idle, in a nearby conference room. She interrupted him from the sonnet he was busy composing on the back of a custodian agreement, and together they plowed through the table. A nine was substituted for a three and a missing zero inserted. After they were finished, she returned to the sanctuary of japonica, azaleas, and wisteria.

While she was again admiring the stripped, gnarled bark of the miniature white pines and the pomegranate bonsais, twisted around the rocks like ancient trees clinging to life on a windy cliffside, the Japanese gardener came in.

He was about five foot two, with a round body and a melon-shaped face capped with a graying fringe of hair. He wore baggy cotton overalls and a padded jacket, and carried a couple of crates of flowering crab apple. He set his precious cargo down a few feet away from her by the edge of the artificial stream, where the vermilion lacquered bridge arched over the water. Squatting down, he bent to dig a hole in the soil.

"Did you plant this beautiful garden?" she asked him in Japanese.

His melon face lit up with surprise and delight. He stood up, bowed, and thanked her for the compliment. In Japanese.

They were obliged to exchange the ritual formalities. Afterward he asked where she had learned to speak the language, so she explained—haltingly, as her spoken Japanese was neither idiomatic nor completely grammatical—that she was a student of fifteenth-century samurai art and also a lover of gardens.

His name, he told her, was Yutaka Yamamoto. His family had been a long line of gardeners. His father had tended the famous Ryoanji temple in Kyoto, where the ancient rocks, reminiscent of waterfalls and tortoises, cranes and ravines, sprang from a sea-bed of gravel. His great-great-uncle had pruned the shining maples and mountain ash in the Sento Imperial Palace Garden. Yutaka, a second-generation American, lived in Bull's Head, Staten Island, where he dreamed of one day being able to cultivate his own outdoor garden in the old tradition.

"But this is so lovely here," insisted Helen.

Yutaka replied that he considered this bizarre lobby a travesty. A true garden, he explained to her reverently, must borrow its personality from the surrounding nature, be it rhododendron forest or distant mountain contours or reflecting lake. It was in such a tradition that his ancestors had always worked, celebrating the astonishment of nature alongside the changing seasons. A garden should be equally rich in snow as in spring. It saddened him to have to come here three times a week, with his cuttings of dog-wood and magenta-colored apricot blossoms, to nurture his plants imprisoned so far from the sky.

"Do you work in other gardens too?" she asked.

He worked on Tuesdays in the grounds of a certain Mr. McCray in Locust Valley and on Friday afternoons on a tea garden in Pelham that belonged to the president of Happy Ocean Swimwear, Inc. During the rest of the week he worked for a Japanese lady here in Manhattan, an unusual woman, very rich and very lonely. He spoke of her with an awe, even dread, that went beyond the deference of service.

"I like that one," said Helen, pointing to a five-needle pine, its roots exposed starkly above the surrounding moss, like a crumpled, pale skeleton.

"Ah, that tree," said Yutaka, and she could tell he valued it more preciously than a child, "is over three hundred years old." He showed her a spray of trailing forsythia. "That one is almost four hundred. Very valuable."

They looked at each other solemnly.

He described to her his life work: the mysterious technique of pruning back the roots, which causes the branches to grow stunted and dwarfed, the laws of ample sunshine, of giving the plants just enough water to dampen the soil, and above all the importance of raising the bonsai on a high ledge. "More beautiful for the eye to see," explained Yutaka, "and closer to the wind. It's the wind which cripples the trees high up on the mountains and gives them their magical shapes."

When she asked Yutaka if he ever thought of returning to Japan, he grew self-conscious as he reminded her that he was an American and Staten Island was his home. His ambition was straightforward. He only wanted to make enough money to be able to create his ideal garden. It did not seem to ruffle him that Staten Island offered no snow-capped mountains or flowering cherry groves for inspiration. He only asked for sky and wind and rain and something green to work with.

He finished transplanting the crab apples deep in the moss at the foot of the bridge. After packing up his crates and tools, he stood square again, ready to set off, like the toiling figure on a woodcut, endlessly hurrying toward his rice paddy.

"It was a pleasure talking with you," said Helen.

He bowed again, lower. "It was my pleasure. Would you do me the honor of taking this with you?" He leaned over a clump of white and yellow irises.

"Don't pick them," she protested. "They're so pretty right there."

"Just take two. Put them in a vase with a single leaf."

As he bent with his knife to cut the stalks, she noticed the tattoo on his arm.

"The frog tattoo," repeated Courage, screwing up his forehead in a frenzy of concentration. Helen leaned forward to the cab-driver and told him to take the 63rd Street exit off the East River Drive.

"The frog!" exclaimed Courage. "Isn't that what Chloe said about the man in Betty Law's apartment?"

"You get it? Yutaka works for Betty Law. She's the lonely, rich Japanese woman he was telling me about."

Courage stared at her. "Yutaka works for her and also goes three days a week to look after the reception area at Samurai Robinson. Ariel Lamb goes to visit Betty Law late at night after work and at least once even sends her a package of documents by messenger."

The cab crossed Second Avenue, heading west along 63rd Street. "And your law firm," Helen added, "pins all its hopes on cleaning up with this TBO stuff, which Samurai Robinson seems to be doing too."

Courage reached instinctively for her arm in his mounting excitement. "It's the gardener! It's Yutaka! He's the one who's carrying our secret TBO drafts over to Samurai."

"It's crazy but it works. There's no other traceable connection between Lamb and Samurai. As long as he's careful, he can even have private meetings with Ms. Law, whoever she really is. The worst that can happen is someone might suspect he's getting a little action on the side."

"Like David suspected. Like what he told me before he died."

"Maybe David didn't know about Yutaka. But he did suspect Betty Law and Ariel Lamb were in some kind of cahoots." The beam of a street lamp bathed her face for a moment. Helen told the driver to turn up Madison.

"Where are we going?" asked Courage.

"To 888 Fifth. We've got to find this woman."

"How can we get in to see her? The place is a fortress."

"She has to walk her dog, right? The Great Pyrenees. She must walk it once at night before she goes to bed."

"What'll we say to her anyway?"

"Maybe nothing. But we've got to see her."

They got the cabbie to let them out a few hundred yards away from the crenelated canopy of Betty Law's apartment building. The weather had turned colder again, and Courage noticed Helen shiver in her outmoded lamb's-wool coat. He hated it, that she should be cold in her ragged clothes, especially on his behalf.

"We can't wait all night here," said Courage. "You'll freeze to death."

"I'll be okay."

"Take my scarf." Before she could protest, he took it off and wound it very carefully, in three loops, around her neck. It was the first time he had ever touched her skin. The cloud of her breath wafted between them in the cold air. She, too, had recognized the moment. The irises quivered faintly in her hand.

He could hear her shivering again in the cold beside him. He wanted to reach out for her, to pull her next to him, if only to give her warmth.

"Don't wait any longer," he begged. "This could go on for hours. You'll just get sick, in this weather."

"You want to stay alone?"

"Yeah." He preferred it that way. He was no longer sure why he was waiting, or what would happen if he finally found Betty Law. He no longer even knew exactly why he had become involved in this intricate web, which seemed to lead to nowhere. Gleiner was dead and no one could bring him back. Lamb had maneuvered so agilely, leaving no loose threads to trap himself. But why? he kept asking himself. Lamb had scaled the utmost pinnacle of a Wall Street legal career. Why should he, of all people, now self-destruct?

She nodded. "I'll go. Call me as soon as anything happens."

"Here. Take the cab fare."

"No. I'll take the bus across town."

She set off resolutely, as by now he knew she would, striding into the wind, which whipped through the tangle of her hair, still holding the irises high, like a scepter. Watching the spirited figure until she vanished beyond the traffic lights, Courage wished again there were some way he could lure her into his world, or even some bridge by which he could slip into hers. Yet their planes seemed so far apart.

Just after midnight Betty Law finally emerged from beneath the long canopy, wrapped in the lynx coat, tugged along by the oversized dog. She nodded at the doorman and spoke some words to him Courage could not catch. This time, as she stepped out into the gutter, Courage sprinted forward to plant himself directly before her face.

He blinked at the bell of gleaming Oriental hair, and the dash of green in the scarf around her throat. As she narrowed her eyes in the wind, still tugging at the animal, he realized what it was that Gleiner had understood. Ms. Betty Law could not conceivably have been Ariel Lamb's mistress. Or anyone else's, probably.

Her face had been disfigured in some accident, a car crash perhaps. While the jaw had been raggedly reconstructed, all the features were grotesquely out of line. Bluish-purple scar trails ran across her forehead and cheeks. Even the eyes, which might have been her only remaining attraction, shifted with a vicious intelligence that made him quick to look away. Ms. Law, insulated behind her money and solitude, was Ariel's consort in fraud.

SIXTEEN

Samson, after a solitary chicken tetrazzini at the Wall Street Club, returned Thursday night through the packed slush to 57 Water Street and knocked on the door of Clancy Maxwell's office. Gina, her shoes kicked in abandon somewhere under Maxwell's desk, sat cross-legged on the electric-blue rug, surrounded by a mountain of contracts of affreightment. They were preparing to litigate a breach of contract on the part of *The North Sea Goddess,* which had been docking at unauthorized ports. Maxwell, also in socks, lay stretched out on the sofa.

"You busy?" inquired Samson sardonically, with a curt nod at the blushing Gina.

"Yes, we are," replied Maxwell, nonplussed. "You wanted to talk?"

Gina, now on her knees, was searching wildly for her shoes.

"I don't want to interrupt anything."

She had found the shoes at last and was edging toward the door. "I'll see you later," she blurted out and hurried away.

"It's one thing," said Samson, brazenly seating himself behind Maxwell's desk, "to be menopausal. It's something else to get sloppy. If you've gotta shtup the help, Clancy, can't you do it a little more discreetly?"

"I don't know what you're talking about."

"Gimme a break. The whole fucking firm knows."

Maxwell had known Samson a long time. He went to the point. "What do you want, Mel?"

"I want you to stop supporting that TBO."

"The TBO's a big money maker. Maybe the future of the firm. Why should I?"

"Because," answered Samson with his acid smile, "I would rather have you on my side than against me. And if I don't have you on my side, Miss di Angelo's going to lose her job."

"On what grounds?"

"Lewd cohabitation with a member of the firm. Getting laid all over the office."

"What kind of grounds is that? Even if it were true?"

"We don't encourage intraoffice liaisons. Of course our official reason will be inadequate work. That she bills too high for too little output."

"That's disgusting. And you've no proof of anything."

"Oh, no?" Samson drew out a yellow interoffice envelope. "I told you, Clancy, you've gone mushy. At your level of experience, I'd expect you to know better." He handed Maxwell the note, scribbled on a sheet of Cheltenham stationery. Maxwell glanced fleetingly down at his brief description of what he imagined doing to Gina in the library, in the elevator, in Ariel Lamb's office, and on the couch at the fifty-first-floor reception.

"It's not dated," remarked Maxwell feebly.

"Erotic correspondence does not require the same elements of specificity as do negotiable instruments. This will be quite enough for the Management Committee, I assure you. Unless of course we decide to present it at a general partnership meeting."

"You'd do that?"

"Maybe. I can make a fool of you, even if I can't fire you. But I can fire your little cutie. And I will, unless you back me up on the TBO."

Maxwell turned away from Samson. His eye fell on the silver-framed photograph of Eleanor leaning against the summer house. She was holding a basket of freshly cut roses.

"What do you say, Clancy? Not only do we kick her out, but we'll see she leaves with crappy references. She won't get another decent job on Wall Street."

"We always give okay references." Maxwell glanced at the whitish stain he had never succeeded in removing from his rug since the night he had first seduced her.

"Not this time," Samson assured him. "So how about it? Are you going to save the cutie's ass?"

"No. Fuck the cutie's ass. I'm going with the TBO. And fuck you too, Mel."

It was worth the sacrifice of Gina, if only to relish the expression of surprise and capitulation on Samson's face before he stalked to the office door. Samson was not accustomed to his machinations backfiring. Before he walked out, he said, "I guess I didn't expect that, Clancy. Maybe you're a tougher piece of work than I gave you credit for."

The following day Gina received a phone call that the formidable Duce was waiting for her in his office. Surprised, with no inkling of what was to happen, she hurried along to the corner office, where the lean furniture was chrome and all the tables and credenzas glass. He was standing with his back to the wall when she entered, in front of his one large painting of black horses galloping against a red sky.

She saw that he was on his speaker phone, hurtling a string of interrogation across the room. He paid her no attention and did not motion for her to sit. She glanced a couple of times, nervously, toward the couch, but did not dare to make herself too comfortable. He kept her standing for twenty minutes.

"How are you?" he barked to her as his conference call finally wrapped up. It was perhaps the third time they had ever spoken since she had joined the firm.

"Fine. Thanks."

"Good. You've got to start working faster. Your work's too slow."

This was the accusation she had dreaded for three years. One day, she had always known, it was to be leveled at her.

"Has someone complained?" she asked. Her voice quavered.

"Uh-huh. We can't carry your billing rate, unless you speed up."

She blinked at him anxiously. Perhaps that meant she need only double the hours she put in and then halve the billed time. She would have to ask Clancy to help her pad her bills.

"You get one month's probation," said Samson. "That's it. If you can't show us some quality performance by then, you and Cheltenham are parting company, my dear."

"You mean I'd lose my job?"

"You got it. And by the way, if they ask any of our attorneys for references, we'll be compelled to tell them the truth. And don't try using Maxwell's name as your reference. We'll tell them about him too."

She gasped. She had never in her darkest nightmares expected so abrupt a beheading. It was true her work had always been slow, but it was reliable, conscientious. No one had ever called it incompetent. Besides, Samson must know that Clancy would protect her. Why should he go into battle with her lover over a few expensive time bills?

She wanted to ask again, to make sure she had heard right. She opened her mouth. No words came out.

"It's no use running to Clancy. He won't bail you out, my dear. When you do speak to him, however, as I have no doubt you will, you can give him a brief message from me. Just tell him that next time he sells a girlfriend upriver to the South Americans, make sure he does it for some stable currency."

"I—I don't understand."

"He'll understand. You may go now."

Dizzily she stepped into the corridor and dived for the nearest bathroom. She leaned heavily over the cool porcelain of the sink. Next to her one of the women associates, who had been up all night, was brushing her teeth. Gina took a couple of deep breaths, which hurt her lungs, and ran a jet of cold water.

"You okay?" asked the associate, spitting toothpaste. "You on a deal too?"

Half nodding, Gina buried her face under the stream of icy water.

"That's it," said the girl sympathetically. "That helps. Last week I had two all-nighters back to back. Jesus, I was hallucinating by the end. The whole team was walking around like zombies. We had one guy stepped in front of a bus and nearly got his head sawed off..."

Gina did not understand why she had been singled out. Before she had fallen in love with Clancy she had cared about her job at Cheltenham more than anything else in her life. More than literature, more than her family, more than her friends. She had invested every particle of her intellect and energy in it, and then some more besides. She had met Clancy and then she had loved him, loved him even more than her career. She could even bear to lose the career now, to have it snatched viciously away from her, if only he still cared. That was the real trouble. He was losing interest, every day more flagrantly. Each night she lay awake, sometimes still wrapped in her fur coat, racking her brains to figure out why. Was it something she had said or done? Had she herself changed unknowingly since the days he had first met her? Had he just suddenly come to his senses, and snapped out of the romantic daydream in which they had been living for two years?

"I've got some Dexamil if you really need it," offered the associate, who was now busy reapplying blusher and mascara. "I hate doing speed but sometimes you have to when you've got client responsibilities. It helps when you haven't even got time to take a shower." Cheltenham had recently installed showers, as a concession to all-night work hours.

Gina shook her head, straightened up, and walked, like a tightrope aerialist, in an unbroken line to Maxwell's office. She entered without knocking. He was busy talking to Hopper, and hardly turned.

"I can't talk now," he told her curtly. "I'll call you later."

"It's important."

"So's this. We're trying to build a fleet of airplanes, and our equity lender's just defaulted on its monthly payments."

339

"I'll stop back later," said Hopper. "I have to talk to Ariel anyhow."

The moment Hopper closed the door, she swayed toward him and collapsed against his chest. He held her for a minute, then gently eased her away at arm's length.

"What's wrong, gorgeous? You got the curse?"

If she had not loved him so much, she would have wanted to kill him. "I'm about to lose my job. I just saw Samson."

"Now, don't cry, there's a good girl. It's only a job. We'll find you something else. Something with better hours."

"Clancy, you knew this was about to happen, and you didn't tell me. I know you knew. Samson said something about selling me upriver."

"There, there. You want a Kleenex? That's better? I didn't know, gorgeous baby doll, I promise. Samson came to see me last night and we got into a squabble. I never believed he'd do this."

"Can't you do anything?"

"It wouldn't help in the long run, Gina. Even if I did manage to save your job this time, you'd always be sitting on a time bomb. You'll be better off in another firm. Or how about going in-house in a company?"

What he really meant, which she and he both realized as he said the words, was that the time had come for him to want her as far away as possible from 57 Water Street.

"I don't want to go in-house. I've given up my life for three years to Cheltenham. I wouldn't mind leaving for a real reason— like we used to talk about, if we had gotten married—but it's not fair that they should use me as political cannon fodder."

"Nothing's fair, gorgeous. Least of all on Wall Street." His tone was patronizing. "It's not like school here. Just because you work hard and study, you don't automatically get to graduate on to the next grade. It's high-stakes poker. Anyone who doesn't realize that'll get burned badly sooner or later."

He steered her by the elbow toward Eleanor's couch, where they had made love so many more times than she could possibly remember: late at night, on Sunday afternoons, and even occasionally during the day when Maxwell's secretary was out of the office and the gust of desire had flared and ripped through their bodies.

"That's better," he said, coaxing her down on the cushions. "You got some Valium? Or how about a little sip of cognac to calm you down?"

Gina had recently started taking Valium almost every night in order to sleep, and more and more often during the day when she felt her throat stiffen and the walls closing in around her. Maxwell knew. He sent her to his tame pharmacist on 67th Street, who dispensed the tranquilizer without prescription. As the pharmacist handed the vial over the counter, she tried to ignore his lecherous wink. He knew who was paying for this beaten woman.

She sat straight on the couch, where Clancy had once caressed her slender form from every conceivable angle. The tears evaporated. Dry-eyed and bewildered, she searched his face questioningly, as if for the first time. The horrible awareness formed in her brain; she tried to beat it back down; it re-formed, and screamed out, I've simply become an embarrassment to him. He wants me to be pacified, to be out of his office, to be out of his life, to be far from here.

"That's better," he repeated, taking a seat across from her in the armchair, and shuffling restlessly through a *North Sea Goddess* file. If anyone came in now and took one look at Gina's ghostlike face, even the most hardboiled, unimaginative Cheltenhamite would know some drama was afoot. "We'll start working on your résumé," he promised. "Not tonight, 'cause I've got to go out to some frigging dinner with the Madisons, but early next week for sure. I'll help you, don't worry. I don't mean to brag, but I write very good résumés."

"You won't save my job?"

Goddamn it, thought Maxwell, why won't she focus her eyes? The unfixed stare, like a wall painting from Pompeii, was starting to give him the creeps.

"You don't understand the problem. Mel's trying to use you to blackmail me. He wants me to give up Ariel and the TBO in return for saving your career. I can't allow myself to be the victim of that kind of extortion. You see that, surely."

"What about my career?"

"Your career'll be fine. You're just a junior associate now. You have scads of opportunities. We'll find you something. My career is at a pivotal point. The TBO's a gamble, we all know, but it could turn out to be the biggest cash cow on Wall Street. You wouldn't want me to sign all that away, would you?"

The words of her reply rang as flat as the Pompeiian eyes. "You used to promise you'd protect me, Clancy. Where's your loyalty now?"

He started lecturing her again. How he loved to assume his didactic stance. She heard his words clearly, although in her mind's eye she could only see the visual picture of one of her English literature professors from Temple University, striding and strutting before a lecture room of sophomores and reciting:

> *When lovely woman stoops to folly,*
> *And finds too late that men betray,*
> *What charm can soothe her melancholy?*
> *What art can wash her guilt away?*

Gina had always despised that professor for his pompous strut, as he picked up his feet like the claws of a sea gull, even though he could recite all the great sonnets and quatrains of the English language written since the time of Christopher Marlowe. Yet as soon as he began to pace and puff, his treasury of knowledge lost its luster.

"Loyalty," said Maxwell, warming to his theme, "is a complicated concept, dear child. One day, when you're a little older, I'm confident you'll understand what I'm talking about. For now, you'll just have to believe what I'm telling you. It operates on multiple levels, it's never simple and one-sided. Of course I have a loyalty to you and you know that I always will. I also have a loyalty to this law firm, where I've worked most of my adult life, and a personal loyalty to the practice itself. I naturally have a loyalty to my family. Whether or not I like it, I must continue to provide for them. And sometimes I have to take the course that will best enable me to do that."

"Sure," she answered in a voice that seemed to come from someone else. He had worked himself up into a pitch of articulation. He was enjoying his own rhetoric. She had never felt so clearly that she knew him, every fiber of him. This confrontation was offering him a longed-for opportunity to cut the knot. Swiftly and surgically. He was hardly disguising his relief. Without this ugly little scene of reproach, they might have been compelled to bump along, another month, another season, while Maxwell's lukewarm interest turned gelatinous. He would have had to exhaust his energies lying both to Gina and Eleanor. The repudiation of Gina, although it created a brief sour taste, short-circuited all that manipulation. Besides, he warmed to confrontation.

He glanced at his watch. "Time to get back to earning our livings. Give me a call before you leave the office tonight. We can go over those interrogatories."

She had less than a moment remaining to take in a final look at all her memories. The bookshelves lined with first editions, which had impressed her during her Cheltenham infancy, and which she had later learned he never opened; the cut-glass decanter, defiantly exposed on the ledge; the silver-framed photograph of Eleanor, who had won after all, leaning against the porch, nursing a basket of flowers; the whitish stain on the rug, which used to make her smile gleefully, and now only reminded her of the indelible stain on her soul.

She knew him. She had truly known him. She had reached as close to the bone marrow as was possible with another human being. She understood his ambition, his ambivalence, his frustrations. She had seen him make a fool of himself in a thousand fatuous situations. She had long suspected the depths of his disloyalty, and God knows, she had seen him lie often enough, without even so hating the lying. His file-cabinet retention of obscure legal cases no longer cut much weight with her, any more than did the literary knowledge of the professor who used to strut. She knew his all-consuming vanity and understood how he had used her to feed that vanity. The terrible, unspeakable truth was that, despite all his limitations, she still loved him.

She had always loved him, from the day he had interviewed her and she had sat, innocently swinging her slender ankles, her feet in the open summer sandals. The raging love had obsessed her every time destiny had thrown him in her path, in the elevators or cafeteria or library. When he finally took her, his prize victim, marked out for him and long due, she had become intoxicated with a sweet, burning, stifling delirium she had never before suspected existed.

It had been impossible to disbelieve him when he sketched out his fantasies for their future life together. Cheryl's skepticism had seemed so laughable. Then gradually even Cheltenham's palatial corridors had lost their hold on her. She had broken faith with the vows of ambition. She only wanted to work there because he was working there one floor upstairs.

"I have to leave early this evening." She stood and straightened her hair.

> *The only art her guilt to cover,*
> *To hide her shame from every eye . . .*

"No problem. Take the rest of the afternoon off if you like. We can do the interrogatories tomorrow or the day after."

Gina stayed late at Cheltenham on Sunday night, to avoid the desolation of her ramshackle apartment. Most of the hours she huddled in her own office, staring at cases without taking in their content, unable to bill the time, unable to go to the library upstairs for fear of running into him. She had several times heard it said that in moments of anguish, Cheltenham was always there, to provide a refuge. It hardly seemed a refuge for her, especially since Mel Samson's threats. Anyhow, life without Clancy merited no efforts.

Every time she heard a knock at her closed office door she both hoped and dreaded it would be Clancy.

"Come in."

Mick Finnegan sashayed through the door. He was wearing his maniacal, geared-up-for-battle look.

He picked up the second volume of *Anna Karenina,* which lay splayed across the desk in front of her. "You reading this? You got time for reading? You got no assignments you're working on?"

She knew he meant no harm. It was his idea of communication.

"I've finished it. I was just rereading something."

"Good book," he announced dogmatically, returning it to her. "I need your help, Gina. Tonight. None of the other associates wants to work for me. I can't understand why. I treat them well. But they all make excuses."

"I'll do it, sure." She was grateful to pick up some billable time from a new source. Most of the other partners had stopped using her months ago, since it had been tacitly acknowledged that she worked for Maxwell, as his personal associate-disciple. Now she shrank from calling Clancy to get more assignments.

"You will? Great." He pulled up the chair across from her and planted his feet on her desk. She lit another cigarette and stubbed it out. The ashtray was already overflowing with butt ends. "It may be a long night here," he warned her. "I need this work done urgently, by tomorrow morning. It may be tricky."

"I'll do it. More Vaginex?"

"Not this time. This is more exciting. International narcotics." Swiftly he explained to her the fuzzy outlines of the Valencia brothers' saga and their cocaine garden in the midst of the rolling coffee plantation. "This is the issue. The U.S. and the Colombian government have several extradition treaties, which have been recently updated to include crimes of narcotics trafficking. As in any extradition proceeding, a U.S. judge—here, the 'asylum' country—must consider five elements: the existence of a treaty between the U.S. and Colombia, the existence of pending charges or an indictment in Colombia, the establishment of the accused's correct identity, the recognition of the crime as punishable in the U.S., and finally, the sufficiency of evidence that the accused may be guilty. This last component is our only straw of hope. It is not the function of the proceeding judge to determine guilt, but rather to assess competent legal evidence, which may be of a lesser quality than required for a trial on merits."

"I followed the Demanjuk proceedings," said Gina. She still cared sentimentally about an idealized notion of justice that her peers had put well behind them. She had followed avidly the extensive reports of the hearings involving the deported Nazi criminal.

"Then you will be aware," proclaimed Finnegan sonorously, "that we must contemplate whether the evidence is sufficient to cause a person of ordinary prudence and caution to entertain reasonable belief in the accused's guilt. We shall maintain that in the case of the Valencias all evidence procured by the Colombians was both illegally obtained and inconclusive."

"You said they found three thousand pounds of cocaine."

"That's their story. We shall suggest that the evidence is likely to be a fabrication, planted as a trap to implicate politically sensitive opponents."

"That much cocaine?"

"Never mind the quantity. Those spics have coke to spare, they're up to their ears in it. The point is, we must show that the Valencia brothers have been running a viable coffee-growing export business for many years, from which they derive substantial profits, and would therefore in no way be induced to traffic in illegal contraband on the side."

Gina reflected a moment, digesting the plan of attack. "How about political exiles? Aren't they entitled to asylum, as an exception to the extradition laws?"

Finnegan warmed to the subject. "Ah-ha. Do not imagine, my dear girl, that I have not considered every chink in the arsenal. Alas, it is a necessity that the crime *itself* be political in nature, in which category narcotics dealing does not fall. No, our only resort is to undermine the sufficiency of the evidence."

He heaved up an overstuffed redwell, bursting with scraps of flimsy paper. "These are some of the records of their coffee business for the past five years. I want you to sift through them, put them in some kind of order, and make an outline to prove that the business is profitable."

"But these are all in Spanish." She rifled through a few sheets of smudged, illegible scrawl.

"You speak Italian, don't you?"

"A little."

"Okay, so it's almost the same thing. We don't need a hundred percent accuracy. Just a showing of healthy business procedures."

She shuffled wildly through more papers. There were some charts and numbers and slips that looked like invoices. Her panic mounted. "I don't think I can do this. Not by morning, definitely. This is a total jumble."

"Sure you can. You're a good little associate, Gina. Once you get your teeth into it you'll be fine. Don't go letting me down now, after you've agreed." He registered the blind despair in her face. "Come on. I'll be around myself till midnight. I'll buy you a drink if you finish early."

"I'll be here all night, Mick." The last thing she wanted was to drink with Finnegan. He leaned over and grunted, "The work'll do you good, maybe. You've got to snap out of all this. I've got a kind of idea what's been going on lately in your life. I don't want to pry or interfere. I just want to say one thing, as a friend. You were my associate before you started working for him. I always liked you, and if I'd been in any position of influence, I'd have tried to help you in your career. You're a good worker and one day you'll be a fine lawyer. Just forget him. He's not worth it."

Gina turned her face away so he should not see her expression, and pretended to light a cigarette. Silently she acknowledged the gesture. Finnegan, systematically bent on destroying his own life, genuinely wanted to help other people.

After he left her office she dumped the entire contents of the redwell on the desktop and halfheartedly went about trying to glean some sense out of it. After all the years of wallowing through mountains of documentary evidence, this was the most confounding she had ever faced. She could make no sense out of the Valencias' system of bookkeeping, if indeed there was one at all. There was no chronology either; most of the papers were undated. Half resigned, half despairing, she abandoned the ordeal to stop for a break in the cafeteria.

Cheryl Litvak balanced her tray on the counter, waiting for her order of surf and turf.

"What's wrong?" she asked. "Tired?"

Gina shrugged. "More Clancy troubles."

"Clancy's a worm," said Cheryl cheerfully. "He's scum, he's a creep, he's a barking dog. Forget him. You can do so much better."

Cheryl took away her surf and turf, while Gina carried off a slice of pot roast, tough as leather, which yielded only to the sharpest knife edge.

Back on the forty-seventh floor, she pored over the Valencia records again, while the plate of pot roast congealed in front of her. She found a Spanish business dictionary and managed to translate a few of the headings. She isolated what looked like statements of income and expenses. Painfully, she began to copy out a table of annual profits, which she knew was really pure conjecture.

An hour later she left her desk, piled high with the Valencias' unfathomable records and the untouched pot roast, to take a walk down by the Seaport. The night was unusually mild for January. Somewhere on the other side of the towering buildings of Water Street hung a full moon. She picked her way over the boardwalk of Pier 17, which led toward the river. The Seaport was deserted. Although many women would have hesitated to walk there so late alone, she was beyond caring. When she reached the railing she paused, blinking away from the glare of the high moon, into the opaque water. She wondered if Clancy suffered any remorse at all for having discarded her. Probably not. There had been her two predecessors, after all, also the recipients of fur coats, and she was certain he had shed no tears over them. He probably considered the coat a sufficient buyout in itself. She shivered.

Once more she returned to Finnegan's infuriating task. Just as she devised another system for constructing a phony profit analysis, weariness swooped down. She called Finnegan. He was still, as he had promised, in his office.

"I need a couple of hours' nap," she pleaded. "Is it okay if I take the file home and work on it there?"

"Absolutely no way. That original file musn't leave these premises. It's our sole copy. Make a duplicate if you must, but for heaven's sake make sure you get through it by tomorrow A.M."

She padded away, clutching the stack, to the Xerox room down the hall. Clearly she was not going to be able to produce what he demanded by tomorrow. She knew that the outlines she had drawn up were next to useless, just an excuse not to show up empty-handed. She wondered what the point was of going on with this at all, of even making the effort to take home the copies. All she could think was how welcome it would be never to have to come back to Vaginex, or *The North Sea Goddess*, or Finnegan's Valencias.

She squared off an armful of the paper and set the machine to collate. She pressed the starting key. She waited for the monstrous duplicator to burst into its usual hum. Instead all the warning lights flashed scarlet, directing her to instructions that uselessly suggested she should check an operating manual.

It was truly the Xerox machine that did it. She might have survived the shame and fury instilled by Mel Samson, she might have overcome the searing heartache of Clancy's rejection, if the Xerox machine had only spun into its monotonous click. She stared at it for a moment, considering whether there was any point in struggling with instructions that explained the workings of its intestines.

She wiped the pot roast gravy off the knife edge before she took it with her into the shower.

*　　　*　　　*

Clancy Maxwell met Mel Samson early the following morning in the waiting room outside the intensive care unit at the Beekman Downtown Hospital.

"How did you know?" asked Maxwell, draping his coat over the radiator. There was only one narrow bench to sit on and nowhere else to put it.

"I got into the office early. The news has spread around already. The Management Committee's holding a special meeting this afternoon to decide what steps to take. Obviously we can't fire her now. We'll have to try to find a way of paying her off. If she pulls through, that is."

"Is it that bad?"

Samson shrugged and lowered his fleshy lids. "Who knows? We haven't seen her yet. By the way, I told them I was her uncle. If you want to see her, you'll have to say you're a relative. They won't let anyone but family into intensive care."

"What if the real family shows up? Do they know?"

"One bridge at a time. I just want to see what kind of state she's in. Christ, Maxwell, why did the idiot broad have to go carving up her wrists over all this? It's only a job, right?"

Maxwell flinched, but he did not argue. The waiting room was no place to get into a spat with Samson. Besides, he, too, could not entirely repress his irritation with Gina.

"Mick Finnegan called me late last night. It was very awkward, with my wife standing right there by the phone. Mick just said she'd tried to kill herself and they'd taken her to the Beekman Downtown. He wanted me to come straight over here, but obviously I couldn't do that. I mean, that would have been the end of my family life."

Samson's lips extended into the ghoulish leer. "You going to stick it out at home, then?"

"Not for Eleanor. It's my son. You know how it is."

The other man nodded.

"Where did she do it?" asked Maxwell.

"*Psycho* style. The women's shower on forty-nine. One of the Albanian cleaning women found her on the floor and ran out shrieking her head off. Collided head on with Finnegan. Why the hell did she have to do it at Cheltenham? We've already had enough trouble this year with that tax associate kid, what's his name."

A nurse, passing by, stopped to ask the men for whom they were waiting.

"Miss di Angelo," said Samson. "I'm her uncle."

The nurse looked inquiringly at Maxwell. "I'm her brother-in-law," he blurted out.

"She's doing pretty well. She's in stable condition. You'll be able to come in and see her in a few minutes. But only stay a short while. She's still very weak."

When she had moved on, Samson told Maxwell wryly, "You and I, brother, we could be in deep shit. Emergencies make strange bedfellows."

Maxwell preferred not to dwell on the far-reaching consequences of Gina's act of desperation. "Why are you here anyhow, Mel? What are you going to tell her?"

"That we're all wishing her well at Cheltenham, that we're really just a family, specially at times like this, etcetera, that she's always got a home with us."

"In other words, that she's not getting canned after all."

"I'll make that perfectly clear."

The lawyers eyed the narrow bench. There was no room for them both to sit, side by side. Samson, hands in his coat pockets, paced restlessly. "You're a good shipping lawyer, Clancy," he said finally. "But you're a fool anyway. You should have struck a deal with me. The TBO's up shit creek now. The South American governments are mighty pissed that Cheltenham's defending those narcotics brothers. Why didn't you play it my way? We might have avoided this fiasco."

Maxwell refused to be intimidated. "You're a cold fish, Mel. Always have been. You killed her. Just the way you fucked over Mick Finnegan. Maybe even Ariel too in the end."

"Don't be dramatic. I didn't kill her. She's still alive. She's just a hysterical kid. Maybe you should have shown a little foresight before you started humping her all over the firm."

The same nurse came back. Samson, who could never forget that the value of any day on earth was measured by billable hours, called out, "Hey, excuse me, when are we going to be allowed in there?"

"You can go in now," said the nurse. "But you have to wear surgical gloves and gowns. And don't stay too long. She needs rest."

Maxwell, embarrassed, asked, "How is she? I mean, will she be okay?"

"Oh, yes," answered the nurse, looking surprised at the question. "She's young and strong. Luckily she was found early. She said she'd never tried anything like that before. Something must have made that kid pretty unhappy."

The partners avoided looking at each other as they wrapped the yellow paper gowns around themselves and put on the surgical gloves. They entered the intensive care ward. The place had a restrained professional bustle about it, not unlike Cheltenham in midafternoon. The heart and respiratory monitors of the patients clicked and beeped softly like the endless purr of the law firm's telephones.

Gina looked tired, but still herself. Except for the bandages around her wrists and the intravenous drip, she might have been any Cheltenham associate resting, exhausted after an all-nighter at the printer. Samson and Maxwell, flapping in their canary-yellow gowns, stood like two angels of death on either side of the bed.

"How ya doin', kid?" asked Samson cheerfully.

She rolled her eyes in surprise toward him and shrugged her shoulders in a small gesture of impotence.

"That was a real dumb thing to do," he went on jovially. "You're never going to be that dumb again, I'm sure."

She swiveled her head toward Maxwell, on the other side, and reached with the tips of her bandaged fingers for his hand. In wretched embarrassment he glanced first at his own hand in its rubber glove, and then at hers. Avoiding Samson's eye, he touched the fingertips fleetingly and withdrew.

"What's a smart kid like you doing such an asshole thing for?" Samson growled. "Jesus, we didn't train you for this. We need you in our Admiralty Department. We can't afford to lose a solid, dependable associate like you."

She did not turn again, but raised an inquiring eyebrow at Maxwell. He flushed. What could he possibly say?

"Everything's going to be okay," he finally muttered. "Everyone at Cheltenham sends you their best."

"Now listen, kid," interrupted Samson, who was anxious to get to his ten-thirty appointment with the president of a gold bullion trading company. "I don't know what prompted you to this ill-advised action, and that's your business. But I do just want to clear up one misunderstanding, in case there was any ambiguity. Cheltenham's your family, for as long as you want us, and even thereafter we'll always be there as your friends and colleagues. You've got a home with us. It's way too early to make promises of course, but there's a chance in another two or three years we might consider you as partnership material. So, no more foolishness, dear Miss di Angelo. You just hurry and get back on your feet and we look forward to seeing you in the office."

With an explanatory nod toward the clock, Samson raised a hand, Indian-chief style, at Maxwell, and hurried out.

After stepping into his waiting limousine outside the hospital, he cleared his throat and unfolded the business section of the morning paper. He had to read the leading article twice to make sure he had grasped its content.

A queer mixture of horror and elation coursed through him as he read.

NEW "TAX BACKED OBLIGATION" BROUGHT TO STREET BY SAMURAI ROBINSON

New York, January 12: Samurai Robinson, the industry giant that commands a $2.6 billion capital base, has just filed its initial offering for the latest variety of debt obligation to join the alphabet soup: the so-called "TBO."

"At first we thought it might be one of those one-shot things," says Toshiji Hiroko, a Samurai Robinson managing director, "but now we think we'll be churning out series of them into the next decade."

Samurai is serving as sole manager of the public offering...

*T*he Cheltenham winter party at the Guggenheim Museum was one of the most well-attended in the calendar of firm social events. Its popularity had nothing to do with the paintings, or even the rare opportunity for the lawyers to nourish their eyes on surroundings other than the blood-red corridors and the downtown skyline. It was an attorneys-only party—which meant paralegals and other support staff were excluded—but one of the few functions of the season at which guests were permitted. A number of the wives liked the notion and encouraged their overworked husbands to bring them along. Moreover, by the middle of January, Christmas seemed a distant memory. The Street soldiered on through blizzards and dirty slush and a spate of new deals, after the frenzy of year-end closings. Everyone was glad by Friday evening to get their hands on a drink.

Finnegan arrived at the museum promptly, at six-thirty, when only a handful of lawyers and their guests stood around the open bar, a table arranged on the ground floor of the hollow atrium, seven stories below the skylit dome. He ordered a double vodka martini and glanced about for a convivial face. He was in excellent spirits, for the first time in many months, no question about it. His Irish ancestry, or so he maintained, had left a deep-rooted sense of superstition in him. When your luck was well and truly out, there was no struggling against the grain; when it finally turned the corner, however, it was oysters and roses as far as the eye could see, and there was no holding a good man back. Sometime during the early hours of yesterday morning, Finnegan's guardian angel had suddenly decided to pay attention again, reviving his flailing career with a dramatic turn of events in Colombia. Tonight he was celebrating his good fortune.

"You're looking particularly winsome tonight, m'dear," he greeted Gina di Angelo, who, to everyone's surprise, had not only put in a full day's work so soon out of the hospital, but insisted on making this appearance to prove she was still alive, and actually flourishing. Illness, if anything, had improved her looks. It added to her pale and interesting quality, emphasized by the austere lines of her charcoal suit.

"I'm feeling better," said Gina. "I'm looking forward to going down to Miami on Monday. You were so right about the Valencia case, Mick. It's turned out to be my most fascinating since I joined Cheltenham."

Finnegan smiled privately into his clinking ice. On the contrary, he could not have been more wrong about the Valencia matter. The recent developments had astonished him more than anyone else.

"We're going to get a lot of mileage out of this," he promised her. "You and I both."

"It's a real opportunity. Being in a Wall Street firm, and for once working on something that makes you feel worthwhile."

"It deserves another drink. Let me get you a refill."

They had become unexpectedly the saviors of the hour when a further series of narcotics arrests in Colombia had shed a new light on the brothers' positions. The United States Drug Enforcement Administration and the Justice Department had reevaluated the evidence, and concluded that perhaps the Valencia brothers had been wrongly accused after all. Their coffee business was indeed, as they maintained, an established and profitable one. It now transpired that a long-standing vendetta with the local authorities might have resulted in their becoming the innocent plants of three thousand pounds of narcotics. The cocaine, ready for shipment, had most likely been transferred from the plantation of a nearby tobacco farmer. While the Colombians, embarrassed at losing face, continued to press for extradition, the official American stance had shifted to one of political protection. The State Department became obligated to step into the fray, in order to appease the South Americans, whose continued cooperation was required in the joint efforts of the two nations to combat international trafficking. Meanwhile, however, the media got wind of the bare details, and scrambled to paint the brothers as refugees, victims of persecution. Justice, therefore, must be seen to be done.

Finnegan had his own personal ideas about José and Luis, who had struck him as thugs on first meeting and continued to do so. But he kept those ideas to himself. If the national media and the government chose to go into battle on behalf of his dubious clients, who was he to reject surprise glory?

"I had a job offer today," Gina told him. "From a major San Francisco firm. To work for a year in the New York office, and then the following two years in Paris. They'll match my Cheltenham salary and give me an extra year's credit toward partnership."

"Nice. A lot of kids would give an arm and a leg. But you're not going to take it, are you?" He sounded only a trifle worried.

"I would have taken it a few weeks ago," she admitted as they strolled up the winding ramp where the paintings hung alongside. "It's a peach of a job. But since the Valencia matter picked up, it totally changes things. I know I'll never find anything so thrilling in another firm."

Finnegan smiled surreptitiously at the Cézanne portrait of a crafty, shifty-eyed peasant who grinned at the world with a guile the attorney understood. Gina di Angelo was truly a sweet kid, brimming with worthy intentions and prepared to work like a dog, but she really had no idea. With her idealistic longings, she had espoused the cause of the brothers as a symbol of political freedom; Finnegan had to restrain himself from dropping hints

357

that old José and Luis might equally turn out to be just as slippery as their tobacco farmer neighbor.

"You seem to be getting on pretty well with José," he teased her.

So far Gina and José had only spoken on the telephone in a mixture of pidgin English and Gina's pidgin Italo-Spanish. She was obviously looking forward to meeting him in person next week in Florida. José's telephone voice was gentle and rather plaintive. When Gina blushed at Finnegan's suggestion, he realized he had hit a true note. Such a nice kid, he thought, but really no taste whatsoever in men.

She pretended to be studying a Gauguin. "It's tragic, thinking of what those men have been through. And coming from one of the old, aristocratic families of the region too."

Finnegan thought of José's liquid eyes and heavy brows, and wondered whether Gina might be swept away when she met the gangster face to face. If she could put up with the rancid cigar smoke... Both brothers were on the short side, which some women objected to. Clancy Maxwell was a short man, though, and that had not put her off.

"You're a loyal wench, Gina. You made the right decision about that job offer. Especially since the news on the TBO, we're ripe at last for our moment in the sun."

"I could hardly believe it, Mick, when they told me. After all this fuss, will Cheltenham just give up?"

"Looks like we haven't much choice. Samurai Robinson's scooped it."

"How could it have happened? Do you think there's a connection with the Valencias?"

"Unlikely. It's obvious that Samurai had the deal pretty carefully structured and in place well before I took on the drug boys. The South Americans must have been playing Samurai against us all along."

"What will happen to our Corporate Finance Department? It's a big setback for them."

"Good. It's time the litigators had their chance again. The pendulum swings, my dear. And that's not all that swings. Our beloved Fuhrer, A. Lamb himself, may be swinging from the rafters after all he promised us."

"I guess he must be very disappointed."

"Very."

Gina pointed to a Van Gogh, painted from the asylum only a year before the artist killed himself. The swirling mountains of St. Remy seemed to suck down the unnaturally blue sky, like a vicious whirlpool. "That's how I felt, inside, the night I flipped. But I'm better now. Really. Thanks again, Mick, for getting me on the Valencia case."

"*De nada*. That's enough art for me. It gives one a mighty thirst. Let's go downstairs to the bar."

On their way back downstairs, Finnegan and Gina passed Hopper staring intently at a small Maillol bronze of a woman examining a crab; she squatted almost like a frog, legs splayed wide apart, with one palm upturned. Behind him stood his mother, in her ceremonial black, her eyes trained on her son with the same absorption as the statuette's on the crab.

"Good evening, Brother Hopper."

Hopper scowled at the rumpled, jovial litigator. Before this unthinkable TBO debacle, he would have merely nodded curtly at him or even pretended not to hear. But now Finnegan's star peeped suddenly over the horizon, while Hopper's own, inextricably bound with Ariel's fortunes, had plunged into descent.

"Hi, Peter," said Gina as Courage scurried past them.

"Gina! You're looking terrific. Have you seen Ariel anywhere?"

"Is our Fuhrer attending this occasion, then?" Finnegan put in.

"His secretary said he would be. He's been away from Cheltenham most of the week."

"Can one blame him?" asked Finnegan with mock feeling. "Of course his predecessor took to the bunker in the final days, but our Brother Ariel is made of sterner stuff."

Courage looked at him sharply. "Is it *so* bad for Cheltenham, then?"

"The crash of the *Hindenberg* can hardly compare with the

crash of the TBO. The only adequate analogy that comes to mind is 1929. Sure, it's bad for him, young fellow. Our beloved Fuhrer promised the partnership of Cheltenham, Arbuthnnot and Crewe that the TBO would put the chicken in our pots for years to come, and now Samurai's stolen it from Caroline."

"Did you see the story in the *Times?*"

"Today's story?" asked Finnegan. "Or yesterday's, or Monday's?" He turned to Gina. "See you at the bar. My glass is empty. Pax vobiscum."

Courage pointed toward Cheryl Litvak, who was just out of earshot. "She looks like she's held together with Scotch tape these days," he told Gina. "How does she do it, billing ninety hours a week and then making the cameo appearance at these parties?"

"She has to. She mustn't offend anyone. It's the eleventh hour before the vote."

The woman in the beige Kimberly knit who was talking to Cheryl Litvak shifted away from the Manet. Her shoulder-length hair was parted on one side and caught up in a tortoiseshell barrette, the kind only children or very aristocratic East Coast women wear. Her low-heeled crocodile shoes showed up Cheryl's cerise sandals as just a trifle loud. With seemingly effortless courtesy, she invested her entire attention on Cheryl, who looked strained and forced, as she labored to carry her own side of the dialogue with exquisite correctness. The woman was so dedicated in her attention that she did not see Gina staring at her. Had she noticed her, she would not have realized why she was being scrutinized. Eleanor Maxwell moved gently aside from Cheryl as a throng of real-estate associates swept by them.

Gina's heart pounded painfully, and she looked down at her wrist to make sure her glass was still steady in her hand. She had never stood close to the enemy. Time modulated as she utilized every microsecond to study the object of so much misery and yearning and curiosity.

Eleanor, with an encouraging smile, turned to her and said,

"Hello, I'm Eleanor Maxwell. What kind of law do you practice?"

Gina took a couple of steps closer, hypnotized by the possibilities of the encounter. Eleanor's face close up was not menacing at all, with its pencil-thin lines etched benevolently around the eyes and mouth, and the cheeks ruddy from gardening. She wore no makeup at all except some crookedly applied lipstick.

"I do litigation. I used to do shipping before."

"Ah. My husband does admiralty. You might have worked with him. Clancy Maxwell."

How would a woman like Eleanor Maxwell react if she found out that her husband had been betraying her all along, undermining the stability of her proud house? Would the revelation crumple that elegant carriage, like the columns of a Doric temple brought shuddering to earth by a landmine?

"Yes, I used to work with him sometimes. More recently I've been dealing with extradition treaties."

"That sounds very interesting. Do you get much opportunity to travel?"

Or did Eleanor already suspect Clancy's infidelities, perhaps the whole history of them, and had she resolved on a blank façade of composure? Was it her nature to shore up rifts seamlessly, to veil over all improprieties?

"I haven't traveled much yet. I'm going to Florida next week."

"Palm Beach is nice this time of year. Of course I prefer New England myself, even in the winter. I'm a real Yankee, you see." Eleanor laughed, almost apologetically.

Supposing I were to tell her right now, supposing I were to look her in the eye and say, "I've been sleeping with Clancy for two years. Once we did it in your bed."

"We have a summer house up in Massachusetts near the Cape," Eleanor went on. "That's the place I love best."

What would you do if I told you I used to want to kill you, but instead I just tried to kill myself? That a week ago I was lying in the Beekman Downtown, with an intravenous tube in my arm, and that Clancy was standing by my bed, nervously spouting all the usual platitudes? Would you feel pity or fury?

"I saw the photo of the house," answered Gina. "In Clancy's office. You have a beautiful garden."

If I were to tell you all that, would you make a scene, right here and now at the Guggenheim? Would you scream, would you slap me, would you tremble or burst into tears?

"I adore flowers. I work on the garden myself all summer. Sometimes Julia—that's my eldest daughter—helps me a bit, but most of the time she's busy with her own things. Up until recently she was horse-mad, and now she's boy-mad. Were you crazy about horses too when you were a girl?"

The question slipped out naturally, as if Eleanor could not imagine any child who had not been brought up learning to ride.

"No," said Gina. "I liked to read."

I can end the melodrama right now, I can break the whole vicious cycle. I can have my revenge on Clancy, for all his lies and manipulations, for his indifference, for having battered me so badly I lost the will to live. I don't want to hurt her. But only by hurting her can I ambush him.

"Do you enjoy gardening yourself?" asked Eleanor.

"I only have a small apartment here in Manhattan. There's no balcony or anything. Actually there isn't even much furniture."

Eleanor asked earnestly, "Do you have a sunny exposure? Which direction does your apartment face?"

"Southeast. Yes, I get sun in the mornings."

Do it. Say it. Cut her down right now, in front of all these people. Show them, just for once, that they can't trifle with my life, that they can't treat me like an expendable slut.

"I have something important to tell you." Gina steadied her voice. For a surreal moment, the two women looked at each other openly, the one washed out, the other still full blooded. Gina wondered, in their suspended instant, "Does she know, does she know?" and at that moment she knew that even if Eleanor had avoided the sordid details of this dead affair, she already knew enough. Retribution passed over.

"What you need," Eleanor insisted firmly, "is a window box. I have quite a few here in the city, and you can't imagine what a lovely splash of color they make. In fact, this year I'll have plenty of extra narcissus bulbs left over. They have the most divine scent, you'll see. I'll send some down to the office with Clancy for you."

"That's so kind. But you really don't have to do that."

"I want to. It would give me real pleasure to think of you growing my lovely narcissus in your apartment."

Gina turned slowly away from her and pretended to wave at Peter Courage. From the corner of his eye, Courage caught sight of Clancy Maxwell, seemingly intent on a painting by Picasso.

When would Ariel arrive? All Peter's efforts to find him at Cheltenham, both yesterday and today, had been fruitless. Or would he altogether avoid the museum party, which had originally been planned for the announcement of the TBO victory? Yet it made no sense. Ariel was the only lawyer at Cheltenham who had known all along that there would be no triumphal announcement. He must have something up his sleeve.

Even before he heard the familiar silvery voice he caught a whiff of sawdust scent behind him. Michelle Petersen stood framed by the crowd of waltzing figures in the *Moulin de la Galette*, who swayed luridly under the gas lamps of Paris in 1900.

"What are you doing here?"

She laughed, and he wondered in amazement how he had ever found that laughter so enticing. "I was invited. All the corporate finance people from Caroline got invitations. Tonight was supposed to be the big unveiling here. Remember? Do you have a date?"

"No, I'm alone. I'm sorry I haven't called you. It's just been crazy. You know what it's like." She acknowledged his excuse with a shrug. "So who else is here from Caroline?"

"No one I've seen yet. I guess they're all holed up, licking their wounds. The TBO disaster was a big blow to us. I thought Brad Carpenter was going to have a seizure when he heard."

"Has anyone figured out how it happened?"

"It's unbelievable. And what beats me is, how the hell did Samurai come up with the pool figures for the future tax receivables? We had associates at Caroline working on them for weeks, and those bastards down the street have produced almost the mirror image of ours."

She rattled on in Wall Street jargon, a diatribe of abuse, as if she wanted to avoid any personal discussion. He frowned and nodded absently, looking over her shoulder all the time for a glimpse of Ariel. Somehow, against the competition of all these paintings that had withstood the tests of time, Michelle's doll-blue eyes and her moonshine hair seemed to lose their radiance. She had always been just that, of course, a china doll, with a wardrobe crammed with designer clothing. It made him wish once again he had Helen here with him tonight. He had not seen her since Wednesday, when she had left him keeping vigil in the cold for Betty Law. He had called her immediately after the encounter, from a phone booth on the street, then later from his apartment.

Keyed up as he had been, already he felt the sense of anticlimax creeping over him then. Helen had been keenly interested in his report, yet he sensed her slipping away from him at the same time, as if she had played her part and it was time to go home. He found himself helpless. As long as he continued to live in the snug fortress of Cheltenham, or any of the sister firms, it was clear his life and hers could have no common threshold.

Michelle was still prattling on about new deals, old gossip, and smart restaurants.

"Excuse me," Peter interrupted. "I see someone I must speak to. The kid thinks I got him canned, but it had nothing to do with me."

"Sure, Peter." Michelle nodded her porcelain head and glided away to the adjoining gallery where Clancy Maxwell, still brooding over the unauthorized docking of *The North Sea Goddess* at the ports of Bremen and Cherbourg, was meandering around the Mondrians.

Benedict Hamilton, his feet planted firmly and his hands in his pockets, earnestly confronted the Modigliani painting of the girl in the yellow sweater.

Peter went up to him and said, "I'm really sorry about what happened, Benedict. I didn't trash you in my associate report. I know you think I did, but I didn't."

Courage, remembering the agony of his own first two years at the firm, always tried to find something positive to report about the junior associates who worked for him. Life was just too short to take it out on the neophytes. Those early years were too much like the life of an airplane pilot: hours of boredom punctuated by moments of sheer terror. In Benedict's case, although his charity challenged his imagination, he had still managed to scrape together a description of the junior's enthusiasm for legal practice and his pride in his thoroughness. He did not mention that Benedict had proved the most obnoxious, insubordinate, and opinionated first year he had ever been forced to supervise.

Benedict went into a spasm of blinking and for a moment Courage dreaded he might be about to burst into tears. He pulled himself together though, and replied coolly, "Forget it. Whatever you may have said, I know perfectly well what's going on here. They just don't like faggots."

"Don't leap to conclusions. Maybe you put the wrong people's backs up."

"It's true, I'm candid. I say what I think. Less-educated people often do feel uncomfortable around me. Shall we get a drink? But you know as well as I do, it's my sexual orientation they really objected to."

They walked along the ramp back to the bar. "I guess you're looking for another job," said Courage. He added, guiltily, "If you need any help, I'd be glad to give it."

"Thank you. But I doubt it'll be necessary. They've given me three months. Cyrus Sweet—whom I don't trust, incidentally—promised that every partner from Cheltenham would give me first-rate references. With my Ivy League education and credentials, I should be able to walk into any Wall Street firm I choose."

"Is that what you want to do? What are you drinking?"

"Rum and Coke. Maybe. I'm thinking of going into investment banking."

"For the money?"

"Naturally. With my social background and education, and the kind of hours they expect us to put in at the law firms, seventy or eighty grand just isn't enough."

"You're still only a first year."

"I have, unfortunately, champagne tastes. Always have. The best fin de siècle furniture doesn't come for a song. And you should see what I have to pay for mirrors."

The woman with her back to them was dressed in a denim skirt and emerald-green running shoes. The wisps of her brown-and-gray-streaked hair were caught up at the back in a gaudy sequined clip. She stood as still as a statue, her whole attention focused on a canvas of one monochrome wash of blue.

Courage nudged Benedict. "Look at Margaret, Ariel's wife."

Benedict shuddered. "What a dreadful woman. She thinks she's an artist, you know. Have you seen those vile mobiles of hers they hung up in the Lexis room? You'd think, considering the working conditions they inflict on us, they wouldn't have to subject us to the indulgences of the senior partner's wife."

"Excuse me," said Courage, sidestepping Benedict's whine, "Mrs. Lamb?"

She turned her head slowly and looked at Courage vacantly, as if he might have been a museum guard. An overpowering billow of Dewar's wafted on her breath.

"I'm Peter Courage. Corporate associate. We've met once or twice before."

She made no effort to pretend to recollect. "Have you seen this painting? If you stand just here, at this angle, you get the whole impact."

"I was wondering if you knew where Ariel might be."

"He was upstairs before. With the Kandinskys. He was talking to that man Fishwit."

"Fishman?"

She lurched a step, reaching for Courage's arm to steady herself. Her grip was stony. "Do you work in the Lexis room? Have you seen the ceiling sculptures? What do you think of them? They're mine, actually. What do the other young lawyers think?"

"We all appreciate them, Mrs. Lamb. It's refreshing to have something so...different to look at while we're working. Will you forgive me, I have to find Ariel."

As he hurried back up the ramp, circling higher and higher toward the skylight, he heard Benedict still straggling behind him. He must shake him off, somehow. That was the trouble with trying to be kind. You always ended up with double grief for your effort. That was what Gleiner used to say. Although Gleiner had still gone on offering shy help to the other associates, and being overly generous with his time.

"I've always considered Kandinsky an overrated painter," prattled Benedict, trotting resolutely at Courage's heels. "In my opinion he got too much credit for establishing the principles of modern abstraction. After the early twenties his work lost its initial bite."

They found Ariel at last, next to a wall of said Kandinskys, alone in the gallery with Zuleika Elizabeth Sweet. By now most of the attorneys, having put in their five minutes' cultural duty in the galleries, had returned in congregation to the bar downstairs.

Zuleika Sweet never forgot a face. "Why, Benedict Hamilton," she drawled charmingly. "It is Benedict, isn't it? How's work? And how's your Fin de Siècle Society?"

He told her. In minute detail. Nodding and smiling encouragingly, she edged toward the back of the gallery. Benedict followed her like a limpet. Courage stood alone in the corner of the empty room with Ariel.

Lamb straightened the cuffs of his pinstripe. "How's Kahn? Any more press on Nutrexpress?"

Courage found a new, older voice. "I know what you did about the TBO."

Lamb answered, as if in another language, "You like Kandinsky?"

"I've met Betty Law."

"Ah, Betty. Interesting woman. She collects things. Art and rare Japanese trees."

"You know her."

"Of course I know her. She bought a couple of Margaret's paintings. You see, my wife's had a slow time breaking into the commercial art world. It was—how shall I say—a welcome sale."

"How do you know her?" Courage spoke calmly. Anyone overhearing might have missed the trace of irony.

Ariel Lamb did not give an inch. He answered smoothly, just as if he were making conversation at the most banal of closing dinners. With an ingratiating cocktail smile, he murmured, "I met Betty years ago. She used to be a shiatsu masseuse, ran a pretty successful business, going out on call to the major hotels in the city. All perfectly legitimate, I'm sure, not what you're thinking. She even had some kind of diploma in physiotherapy. She was a very attractive woman in those days, Betty. She had that flawless Oriental skin."

"That's how you met her?"

"I'd been working flat out, finalizing the proofs on my *History of Regulation in the Thrift Industry*. I slipped a disc and started getting back problems. One of our clients recommended her."

"You had back problems?" The notion of Ariel on the massage table defied imagination.

"Oh, I'm fine now. I worked them through. Poor Betty. I guess I must have felt sorry for her. That's why I helped her with her lawsuit. It seemed halfway like pro bono work."

"What lawsuit?"

"The poor girl got involved in a sad accident. She was working in one of the major hotels—I shan't mention which, since it subsequently became a Cheltenham client—when a crystal chandelier from the ceiling came loose and dropped on her head. It was a clear case of occupier's negligence. I got her a settlement for three quarters of a million. Not that," he added hastily, "I would normally get involved in personal-injury claims. As I say, it was kind of a pro bono thing. I believe all lawyers should put some time into nonbillable matters. It's a shame we can't encourage it at Cheltenham."

"So that's what she lived on afterward?" Courage thought of the grandiose Fifth Avenue palazzo and the lynx coat. Three quarters of a million would never have taken her very far.

"Good heavens, Peter. I'm not familiar with the state of Betty's finances. But I figure it helped. She couldn't go on doing shiatsu looking like that. The clients like them to be pretty, you know. Have you seen my wife anywhere? We should be getting back to Montclair soon."

"There's time. I'd like to tell you about some research I did yesterday on Lexis."

"I'm sure it's most interesting, but do you think it could wait until Monday? How about stopping by my office just before lunch."

"It can't wait. Happy Ocean Swimwear, Inc."

Lamb looked blank. "Is that a client of ours?"

"Not of ours, no. Yesterday I ran a Lexis search on them in the *Times* and *Journal* files. Just going back a couple of years. They were bought out last June. The bidding became a real horse race. No one expected the stock to go above seventeen but it went for thirty-five."

"Lucky guys."

"Not just lucky. Gordon McCray."

"The fund manager?"

"His portfolio outperformed the Dow by nine hundred percent. Nobody does that well. Unless they've got Yutaka Yamamoto pruning their azalea bushes for them."

Ariel's eyes slithered around the room. It was still deserted.

"Sorry, Peter. Doesn't ring a bell. Never heard of him."

"Let's not prolong this." Courage suddenly realized for the first time that at six feet, he was exactly Ariel's height. "I know you're anxious to get back to Montclair. Yutaka, Betty Law's gardener, is the go-between. You give Betty Law information. She passes it to Yutaka. He sells it to the purchasers, whom you and Betty never meet."

Now the major cards were coming down. First the royal flush and later the aces. Still Ariel smiled tightly and did not miss a beat. "I think perhaps we might carry this discussion on in a less obtrusive place."

"They're all downstairs. Getting shitfaced at the bar. This is just between you and me and those splashy paintings, whatever they are."

Lamb leaned elegantly over toward the plaque and read, " 'Vasily Kandinsky, 1866 to 1944.' I kinda like this one," he commented.

The painting looked like a patch of black sky, surrounding a collection of multicolored moons. Cobalt and lilac and a couple the color of strawberry ice cream. Some of the moons intersected; others floated free. Some moons had pupils, like monstrous eyes; some were speckled with small black spots that made Courage think of contaminated fruit. All hung, a shameless carnival of color, in a sea of immeasurable depth, against inky, fuzzy pools of black.

"I like it too. You're all in there." He pointed at the lilac moon. "You and Betty Law and Yutaka." He motioned to a red spot. "There's Samurai Robinson. And somewhere down here"—he gestured to the opposite corner—"you've got Happy Ocean and McCray the fund manager and a whole other bunch. No one's connected and everyone's connected."

"Why did you get involved, Peter? Are you so ambitious, then?" Lamb looked at the painting. "You want to play out there too?"

"No. Why? I want to know why. You run the Cheltenham Corporate Finance Group. Yet you deliberately smuggled the technology of our best financial instrument ever out to a rival investment bank. Why?"

Lamb ignored the question. A lifetime of negotiation had left him a master at thrust and parry. "Why do you care, Peter? You want money? Clout?"

"I'm just angry."

Lamb nodded back again at the moons. "I wouldn't take it too seriously, kid. We aren't in law school anymore, you know. They don't teach you the rules that make the big money move."

"Hmm."

Courage began to wish he had planned his confrontation better. It was not going as he wanted. Lamb just stood there, imperturbable as usual, as if they were discussing some obtuse SEC examiner's time-wasting comments on a registration statement. Courage had hoped at least to gain some advantage from the shock value of his accusations. Yet Lamb just nodded vaguely and took the remarks in stride as though Courage were already an accepted participant in the constellation of moons.

"What do you want, Peter?" Was Lamb growing nervous underneath the cool?

"I—I want to straighten this out."

"Come now, let's not go overboard. You must want something. Otherwise we would not have anything to discuss."

"What if I blow your story? What if I expose the TBO? If I tell them who gave the billion-dollar deal away?"

"Are you threatening me?" Lamb was frankly mocking now. "To whom are you going to squeal, pray tell? To Mel Samson? To the Management Committee? To the Interior Decoration Committee?"

Lamb was right. Unraveling the tangled truth was too complex, would take too long. No one would give him the attention, not even Samson, Lamb's archrival.

"What are you offering? The TBO's bust. You're no longer even running the firm."

"Ah-ha," said Lamb icily. "Now perhaps we're getting somewhere."

"How about Hopper, your devoted slave? Was he in on this, too?"

"I'll give you Hopper. His number's up anyway. Can we be friends then?"

"You'll *give* me Hopper?"

"He's already been reported to the Bar Association. He should be hearing from them in a week or two. Like all sleepy institutions, they move slowly."

"Reported for what?"

"Practicing for ten years without a license."

"Hopper's unlicensed? How do you know? What'll happen to him?"

"One question at a time. The Bar Association takes a dim view of partners at Wall Street firms, or anywhere, who hold themselves out as bona fide attorneys when they have never in fact passed a bar examination in any state."

"He never passed the bar? How could he have got through Cheltenham? No one ever found out? They never asked questions?"

"I did."

"But Hopper! He's so erudite."

"The bar's a silly exam. Lots of people fail first round. So they take it again. Which Hopper did. And failed twice."

"How do you know?"

"I checked the records. Ten-minute phone call."

"He didn't take it a third time?"

"He's arrogant. He doesn't like failing tests. He did conscientious work for me as a junior associate, so I let him know that provided he continued to perform, I'd guarantee him a secure future at Cheltenham."

"He knew you knew?"

Lamb smiled vaguely. He was not going to fall for that one. "There were no discussions."

"And nobody else ever checked?"

"They never do. A couple of times we really got egg on our face when it turned out one of our employees never even got through law school. That's the beauty of working for a premiere firm, Peter, my boy. We're all so *noblesse oblige* and above that kind of thing, that no one would doubt an attorney's word. *Honi soit qui mal y pense*. And, in theory, gentlemen don't read each other's mail."

"What's going to happen to him?"

"Obviously they can't disbar him, since he was never admitted in the first place. There will, however, be a sizable outcry, within our quaint circle. It will no longer be possible for him to continue as a member of the firm."

"So Hopper can't practice law anymore?"

"No way. It's almost a pity. He was the most knowledgeable of them all. His grasp of the 'Thirty-Four Act was quite prodigious."

"What else can he do?"

"Not much, I'd think. He's an odd bird. Not equipped for an environment outside our sanctuary."

"And you've turned him in?"

"Come now, Peter. Pay attention. All I told you was it would shortly come to the Association's attention."

"But he was so loyal to you. A real storm trooper."

"Make up your mind, kid, what you want. A moment ago it was his ass. Well, it's yours, on a platter. He's gone." Lamb pursed his lips and flicked his fingers in a dismissive gesture.

An eye for an eye. A tooth for a tooth. A promising career for a life.

"Now that we seem to have settled a troubling score," said Lamb, "you'll have to forgive me, but I really must get downstairs. They'll be closing the bar soon. And I do need an early night in Montclair." He started to move along the wall of Kandinskys. "But before we wrap this up I'd like to mention one final proposal. You interest me, Peter. I need hard workers and also men of character around me. I'd like to take you with me."

"Take me where?"

"To Samurai Robinson, of course. Where do you think? The Holy Sepulchre?"

"Oh." Suddenly it was all clear.

"I'm making the announcement on Monday or Tuesday. I'll be heading up their Euromarket division."

"How can you do that? Especially after they've walked off with the TBO? It's a fiduciary breach."

"Euromarkets have nothing whatsoever to do with Latin American asset-backed obligations," Lamb gently reminded him.

"I guess you'll be getting pretty well compensated for that."

"About twice as much as at Cheltenham. Plus bonuses. I'll manage to live quite comfortably, I reckon."

So there was a parachute after all. No wonder Ariel Lamb could discuss his treachery so calmly with Courage. He had created the TBO along with Caroline Brothers and managed to bluff Cheltenham for months, knowing all the time he would sell it for double elsewhere. The answer was so simple if you just plugged the formula in: double the money plus bonus. That had been Lamb's incentive all along for juggling, and letting slip, so many lives.

"I can probably arrange roughly the same scale of compensation increase for you too," said Lamb. "How much are you making now? You should come out about three hundred percent ahead in a good year. At the beginning. It could escalate quickly after that."

"Why do you want me?"

"I need an attorney to work with closely. My own position will be much broader based. As head of Euromarkets, it will be my responsibility to develop and supervise all European and Europe-syndicated offerings, both debt and equity. It could become the key job at Samurai, since they've already got such a tight hold on the Far East. I want someone I can rely on. I need superb legal skills, but I also need character. You're a go-getter. You have the fighter instinct. This is a right-hand job and I can't afford a wimp. Let's discuss it over lunch."

Lamb had turned the tables neatly. Now it was Courage's moment to reel. Lamb was offering him an extraordinary opportunity, the type of position a few years back he would have been unable to visualize and hardly dreamed existed. No one could quibble over the money. Close to half a million in a good year, and he was still only thirty-four. Maybe this was the prize he had sweated for all these years, renouncing sleep and social life without question, lured by the golden ring.

Supposing he were to accept. He had no illusions about the longevity of the situation. Either he himself or the job or even possibly Samurai Robinson would probably burn out in a few years' time. They were like supernova, those jobs: huge stars at the edge of the galaxy, which spurted and flared up in a dazzling combustion of hydrogen, only to collapse deep and dark within themselves, leaving a black pocket in the universe.

Not that it mattered. A few years earning that kind of money, with access to the personalities at the nucleus, and he could clean up comfortably for some time to come. He could probably retire before he was forty, to a luxuriantly padded future, or if he chose otherwise, move on to a still higher rank and learn to juggle real power.

The stress and renunciation the work demanded would be no worse than what he had learned to endure at Cheltenham. But if he declined, how could he carry on here as a senior associate, an anonymous foot soldier, kowtowing to every partner's whim, a life of deference to Tristan, to Mel Samson, to Gary Fishman?

"As I suggested earlier," remarked Lamb, moving toward the exit, "why don't you stop by my office just before lunch on Monday? We can iron out the details then. I'm sure I need not add that this arrangement, for the time being, is a matter of strictest confidentiality."

Courage tried to imagine how such a vault would change the fabric of his life, how that kind of money would affect him. The image of Helen Farmer flitted by. Would he still visit her late at night, in the tenement on 108th Street, to drink tea with shreds of lemon? Would she disapprove of his second wedlock to even more serious money, or would she treat the transition with the indifference of a foreigner from another country? Courage still had not figured out why he hankered for that aloof, eccentric woman, with whom he had really nothing in common except a longing for adventure. Yet he sensed if he could only make the ninety-degree turn, or one of a hundred and eighty if that were required, perhaps he might, later, be able to work it out. He thought of all the things he would enjoy buying for her, which would be easily accessible with his new wealth: real art, trips to the Orient, jewelry. Of course she would never accept any of it, and they would just go on squabbling over who should pick up the checks in Chinese restaurants, and Helen would refuse to take taxis.

He could live with that. Yet if he lost Helen altogether, if she passed out of his life in disgust, he would be sorry. Although she was still a ghost, while Cheltenham and Ariel Lamb were real, it was all mixed up at the moment. One day Cheltenham might no longer matter, and then he might be ready for her.

Gleiner had been real. He was dead, but he was still in the cast. What would he have said if they had been able to stroll down to the Liberty Café for one of those blackened crayfish sandwiches, to discuss Ariel's offer? Maybe "Go for it," just as he had always reminded Courage that there was no shame in being partnership material.

If he went for it and went along with Ariel, joining the constellation of lurid moons, he, too, would have blood on his hands.

That was Ariel's cunning. Lamb was too smart to try to conquer the infidels; instead he converted them. If Courage fell for the bait, he would lose the right even to his twinges of malaise. A lot of thoughts would have to be blocked and buried forever. The rite of passage would be over, the initiation complete. Then he would have to take his place in the fraternity, sharing their collective guilt and immorality, as well as the spoils of war.

Worse, he would be stepping right into Hopper's shoes. Lamb had manipulated and supported Hopper, wielding the shameful bar secret over him, and Hopper had served him with the loyalty of the insane. Then, when it was time for Hopper to go, Lamb had stamped him out like an ant. Once Courage stepped into the configuration of overlapping moons, he, too, would become beholden. To begin with, Lamb would probably use his power discreetly. Make no unconscionable demands. Then one day, when he needed something...

"See you Monday," said Lamb, leaving the gallery.

"Wait! Just a minute. There's nothing to talk about on Monday. Thanks and no thanks."

"Are you crazy? Or just dumb? Sleep on it. You realize what I'm offering. You'd rather go plodding on at Cheltenham?"

"You'll have to find someone else. I'm the wrong stuff."

Lamb did not get it. He mistook it that Courage was simply stalling to negotiate better terms. "We haven't got time to barter, Peter," he snapped.

Benedict Hamilton stepped out from behind a partition of Miros.

"I'll do it," he said. "I'll take the job."

They froze. Benedict, most extraordinary deus ex machina, straightened his glasses and smoothed his cuffs.

"You were here all along?" asked Courage finally.

"The better Kandinskys are at the back."

"Who are you?" asked Lamb.

"My name's Hamilton. I'm a first-year corporate associate. The one that got fired for being a faggot, remember?"

If Lamb remembered anything about it, he did not let on. He shook his head wonderingly. "You're telling me you've been fired? And you want to come and work for me now?"

"I heard the whole conversation," said Benedict flatly. "I think I've got a good idea of what the job entails."

Ariel Lamb was beaten at last. He was in Benedict's unlikely power. "Okay," said Lamb. "Be in my office on Monday. Noon sharp."

"I'm always punctual," said Benedict.

The first thing they teach you in law school, Courage still remembered, the first class on the first day, is that being a lawyer has nothing to do with justice. Your job is blind: to make out the best possible case for your client. There is a kind of aesthetic in that, you realize gradually, as you mature in your profession. Because real justice, like perfect love or wisdom, does not exist on this earth. There are occasional times, however, when you do get what you deserve. You make your bed and you lie in it.

If justice could be complete, Ariel Lamb would have merited a volley of punishments. But here was a start. Courage beamed: Ariel Lamb and Benedict Hamilton.

EIGHTEEN

*I*t was early April, one of those seductive Manhattan days flush with the promise of spring. The journey to work, whether by car or cab or subway, was a heady pleasure after the almost unendurable rigors of yet another winter. Even the dourest female attorneys and secretaries had managed to find some splash of color to add to their work clothes that morning. For the first time since sunlight had gone underground, as if forever, in November, the Cheltenham cafeteria was a wasteland at lunchtime as everyone headed for the Seaport.

The grace of promised spring even touched the recesses of Mel Samson's soul. No one had ever been privileged to glimpse what really went on in his formidable psyche, but had anyone snatched a look in this morning, he would have discovered an old melody humming between Samson's flapping ears.

Tchaikovsky's *Waltz of the Sugar Plum Fairy* swelled in his eardrums as he stalked down Broad Street on his way to the offices of Samurai Robinson. From the outside, you could never have guessed. The hawk still wore the expression of an old Wall Street warrior musing on the ramifications of a clause.

He could not beat down the sense of exhilaration, brought on partly by the weather, and partly by the excitement of his meeting with Ariel. He had no idea why he should so anticipate seeing his ancient enemy face to face.

The official reason for this first meeting since Ariel's departure two months earlier, Samson suspected, was a kind of excuse they both contrived. Although by tradition Cheltenham had never counted Samurai in its roster of clients, Lamb was throwing the firm the crumb of a $300 million subordinated debenture. A standard Eurodeal, nothing flashy. Cheltenham would easily pick up half a million in legal fees out of the transaction, which, while not a bill to be sniffed at, was not exactly a justification for fireworks either.

Why had he done it? For the mere sport of showing off to Samson, a victory parade of his new power and money and trappings? That seemed insufficient reason. Ariel had been in the big league too long to indulge in that sort of petty vanity. On a deeper level, Samson concluded, they had begun to miss each other. They had hardly spoken at all at Cheltenham during the past three years, divided by their unrelenting rivalry, yet they had nevertheless worked together under one roof for twenty-eight years. As Ariel had crept up in the ranks, they had developed a mutual recognition of ego. There was no one else on their level to match them, in craft or authority. Above all, because they were born to fight, they had relished their own last vicious struggle. Neither man had a loving nature.

Samson passed through the exotic garden of Samurai Robinson's twenty-fifth-floor reception. Like most of his fellow members from Cheltenham, this was one of the few investment banks he had never visited. He took in the scarlet lacquered bridge and the swill of water tumbling over the black oval stones. Samurai Robinson, he noted, had a lot of money to spend.

The receptionist, an ivory-skinned Japanese girl in a real kimono, buzzed up to Ariel Lamb's office and promised Samson a secretary would be down shortly. He took a seat on the carved bench and watched the gardener at work, shoveling fresh earth around the roots of a twisted pine tree.

The secretary appeared, ushered him into the corridors and up a flight of internal stairs to Ariel's new office.

Its dimensions were breathtaking, even by Wall Street standards; it was as large as a garage, the vast space magnified by white and gray fabrics and a mirror along three walls, which created the sense of a high-tech Versailles. Ariel had never been much of one for visual taste, but whether or not you liked his new décor, it worked. He rose from his desk and crossed the room to greet Samson. The two men shook hands.

"Nice," said Samson.

"Big."

"You could put your old office into this four times."

"By the way, what's happened to my old office?"

Samson had prepared several little surprises. "Finnegan's got it."

"How in hell . . . ?"

"Mick's become quite a star again these days. Ever since those Valencia brothers got taken up as heroes of political freedom. Naturally Cheltenham shuns too obvious publicity, but the kind of press Finnegan's defense has attracted was exactly what we needed. We've added several dozen substantial clients."

"Is he still drinking?"

"Only on Sundays. As far as I can tell. We voted him back four points already. He's due for another four in July if his momentum keeps up."

Samson recognized the blotch of colors that hung over the sofa as one of Margaret Lamb's. "I see you finally found a suitable wall to hang this."

Lamb shrugged. He was indifferent to all but the symbolic importance of his surroundings. A Rembrandt or a panel of grafitti —it had no effect on the ebb and flow of interest rates.

Samson turned to the other picture above the desk. "Is that hers too? It's not bad."

"No, that's a valuable one. Painter called Kandinsky. I got it off a German collector for a couple of million. There's one a lot like it in the Guggenheim."

Samson glanced again at the pattern of lurid, overlapping moons, glowing out of a dark background. A couple of million. Collectibles, he reflected, were becoming a good buy in today's low-inflation climate.

Ariel motioned him to the serpentine sofa. "So you think Cheltenham's still equipped to take on this Eurodeal. I hear that since I left, the Corporate Finance Group has been devastated."

"They're still kicking. We had a few defections, but we've got the staff left. We'd overhired anyhow on the strength of your promised TBO."

Lamb ignored the barb. "That's going well here. Of course I'm in no way involved from the Euromarket side. We keep to the principles of the Chinese Wall."

"Of course. I saw your tombstone in the *Journal* for the offering." It had secretly jolted Samson, the morning he opened his newspaper to the framed box advertisement for the TBO participations, always referred to in the financial community by its somewhat macabre nickname.

"It was fully subscribed. Now it's mainly a matter, they tell me, of monitoring and servicing the pool of tax receivables."

"That," said Samson, "was always the catch." There was no need for them to mention the recent wave of threatened defaults from the Latin American debtor nations. Austerity measures, currency devaluations, and IMF reschedulings threatened any day to send first a ripple, then a tidal wave headlong into that pool of uncollected taxes. The TBO, most impressive and most fragile of superstructures, was in constant danger of collapse. Such a collapse, which would precipitate a default on the payments to the bondholders, could send Samurai Robinson into a tailspin. Then where would Ariel Lamb be, with his office of mirrors, and what would happen to the exotic bonsai garden in reception?

"Anyhow," said Ariel, who preferred not to dwell on the perils of his position, "now that Hopper's left too, which partner would take responsibility for our Eurodeal?"

"I'll find someone to oversee it. You know these deals are cookie cutter. Any of the senior associates can cope. Any news of Hopper?"

"I took him out to breakfast once," said Ariel. "He seemed to be surviving the blow pretty well."

"It got ugly the day the report from the Bar Association came in. We had to call a team of paramedics to sedate him."

Samson's lip curled as he remembered the scent of Hopper panting and gasping at his desk chair. With a horrific lunge he had grabbed two of his Tiffany lamps and shattered them against the wall. Then he had collapsed writhing on the rug, a broken wreck. "They gave him oxygen, which made him light-headed. He started babbling about butterflies and chloroform."

Lamb did not respond. "I understand he's gone into the butterfly business."

"That's a new one."

"He told me he's got a part-time job at the Museum of Natural History. Meanwhile he's doing a masters in entomology."

"Bugs and shit?"

"Roaches and all. But he tells me the butterflies are his thing."

"Well, he's out of the securities practice. He'll never work as a lawyer again."

"It's rather sad, really," mused Ariel, more philosophic than grieved. "He was the finest of them all. Especially when it came to the 'Thirty-Four Act."

"Dumb schmuck. Trying to get through life without the bar."

With a sharp rap on the door, Benedict Hamilton stepped in. He barely acknowledged Samson. Interrupting blithely, he told Lamb, "I have to leave early this afternoon. It's the Fin de Siècle Society spring cotillion."

"I need you tonight. The Kingdom of Sweden wants to raise another five hundred million. We have to meet with the government delegation."

"Not tonight," snapped Benedict. "I can't come. I'm on the cotillion organizing committee."

"We'll discuss it," said Ariel weakly.

"A number of well-regarded fin de siècle collectors are expecting to see me tonight. It's my period, you know." With a brisk nod at Samson, he strutted out.

Samson shook his head in amazement. "Who's that?"

"He used to work for us. For you. We—you fired him. So now he's here."

"Oh, yeah. I recall. The faggot. What the fuck's he doing here?"

"I hired him."

"So I see. You like him?"

"No. I hate him. But he's here."

"So why do you put up with him? Throw him out."

"Hmm. Shall we eat?" asked Ariel. "I reserved us one of our executive dining rooms upstairs."

"Y'know, it's such a glorious day, I'd rather take a stroll downstairs. I was sitting on airplanes all yesterday and I've got a long afternoon of meetings ahead. Would you mind?"

"No problem. I'll cancel the dining room."

The streets were full of jubilant office workers, strolling with carefree steps, faces upturned to the caress of spring sun. They blinked like miners returning to the daylight after hours below earth. The street vendors were doing a brisk sale in kebabs, falafel, tacos, spring rolls, and even the first sign of ice cream.

"Did you hear?" asked Samson. "Cyrus Sweet is actually retiring next month."

"Cyrus! He's not old. And his practice was bearing up, all in all."

"He says he's going back to Kentucky to breed horses. You know what I bet? He'll get bored down there. A year or two and he'll be back again in legal practice. I bet you twenty bucks."

"Done. You may be right, though. He's a soldier, Cyrus."

"You hungry?"

"Kind of."

"You want to stop for a hot dog?"

"Let's go down Wall. They've got the best ones."

They turned off from Exchange Place, where a peddler was

selling discount bunches of daffodils. He stood at the center of his yellow flowers, which surrounded him like a pyre.

"We voted in Cheryl Litvak," said Samson.

"I guess if you've gotta take some woman, she'll do as well as any. She sure worked her ass off for nine years."

"She'll be working twice as hard for the next eight. These kids don't realize how hard it is to keep up as a junior member these days. The strain of both logging hours and seeking out work."

"We breed the myth into them. Like all the other bullshit we sell them. In truth it's hard, unglamorous, unsexy drudgery."

"Yes. But somewhere, at the end..."

"The golden ring."

They stopped by the old Ukrainian woman's cart, where she scowled at her customers as she ladled out sauerkraut. She had unwrapped the pieces of cloth from her fingers and packed away the blanket she used as a winter shawl. The dress she wore, pale blue and dotted with daisies, she had recently bought off a street rack. It was still almost clean.

"A couple of hot dogs," ordered Samson. "Mine with just mustard."

"Onion for me," said Lamb, reaching in his pocket for change.

"No, no, let me," protested Samson, waving the money away. "My treat."

"No, I insist. You were my lunch guest anyhow."

"Next time."

Lamb managed to whip out a five-dollar bill. "It's on me. Final."

Samson relented. "Okay. But watch it. Brazil's behind in interest payments."

The old woman in the head scarf counted back the change for Lamb. She passed them their lunches, wrapped up in paper napkins. Spring had touched her too. At last she granted him a toothless smile.

"Thank you," said Lamb politely. He turned to Samson. "So which associates would you put on the Eurodeal? Peter Courage, I presume."

"He's gone."

"He left Cheltenham? Where for? Morgan Stanley, First Boston, Salomon?"

"Guess again. It took us all by surprise, I've got to admit. Everyone knew he was partnership material, hardworking, well-liked. Jesus, even a WASP. We tried to dissuade him, of course. Offered to put him on partnership track a year early. Virtually promised him the damn thing."

"He got a better offer."

"*Au contraire.* He freaked. Went down to the Bahamas to work for some little office that incorporates offshores. Like clerical stuff, almost."

"Courage? Amazing. You know, I thought for a minute that kid had real potential. One of the best. You never can tell how they'll turn out, right? But why the Bahamas?"

"He likes to sail. Apparently he just sold everything here, took off and bought himself a boat. Wacko. He calls Tristan once in a blue moon. They always had a pretty good relationship."

*　　　*　　　*

As Ariel Lamb and Mel Samson gradually faded like a yellowing photograph, Peter Courage found he was still thinking about Helen Farmer, when he lay reading on the deck of the new boat, or strolled down the beach at night. He stepped through the cool sand, under the rich and real darkness. Only a hint of starlight lit the froth of the surf, but now he knew so well the shapes of the trees, the orange and vermilion flowers, it was as if they waited for him, alive behind the night. He smelled the breath of salt and the musk of vegetation, and learned the ultimate luxury of thinking nothing at all.

Sometimes he wondered if Helen remembered him. They had spent so little time together in New York.

Before he had left the city, he had timidly suggested to her that she might bring Chloe down to the islands to see the ocean and the boat.

She had gently refused. "You need some space alone, Peter. To cool out. There's no rush. Call me when you're back in town. There's all the time in the world."

One evening in March, when the scented island air was perfectly still, he boldly scribbled on the back of a postcard:

> You were right. It did take time. But now, every day feels like a grand beginning.
>
> I found this haiku by Issa. Maybe you already know it—

> *How red this moon is!*
> *And who owns it,*
> *Children?*

> I miss you. With warmest regards, Peter.

When she pulled it from her rusty mailbox, she smiled for a long time. So he had found the poem by the frail eighteenth-century rebel-poet, who understood that the moon, that great big toy, belongs to all and to no one.

A few days later, she sent him her own translation of another classic.

> *Mikagirishi furusatono sakura sakinikeri.*

> *Back in my home,*
> *Which I left behind,*
> *The cherry trees are in bloom.*

_____Acknowledgments

A great many people helped me in many different ways during the writing of this novel. I am grateful to all of them, particularly my editor, Jane von Mehren, Christine Wallace, Sylvia Westerman, Barry Nathan, and most especially my father, William Drucker.